Aurius

Catherine Fitzsimmons

To Logan & Emo
Thanks for your support!
Catherine Fitzsimmons

Brain Lag Publishing
Ontario, Canada

This is a work of fiction. All of the characters, events, and organizations portrayed in this novel are either products of the author's imagination or are used fictitiously.

Brain Lag Publishing
Ontario, Canada
http://brainlagpublishing.wordpress.com/

Library and Archives Canada Cataloguing in Publication

Fitzsimmons, Catherine, 1981-
Aurius / Catherine Fitzsimmons.

ISBN 978-0-9866493-0-1

I. Title.

PS3606.I887A87 2010 813'.6 C2010-906231-0

Cover artwork by Catherine Fitzsimmons

This book uses Black Chancery, Medieval Dingbats, WWDesigns, and BudNull typefaces, courtesy of dafont.com and grsites.com.

Acknowledgements

Aurius was a labor of love from start to finish. It surprised me in numerous ways, and I think now that it was just waiting to be written. As with many novels, that part was a mostly solitary experience, but also as with many others, there was still a number of people who helped it along its way.

Thanks first and foremost go to the Office of Letters and Light, the good people behind National Novel Writing Month (nanowrimo.org), without whom this may never have been written (or at least taken a lot longer). Thanks to the ladies at Tim Hortons on Iroquois Shore Road in Oakville, Ontario, who kept me company every morning before work as I scribbled words out in a notebook during that first plunge into NaNoWiMo. Ryan Harron and Lizy Miceli, for being alpha readers and taking the 50,000-word plunge with me in November 2007, and for being a wealth of information and my biggest fan, respectively. Michalina Ratajczak for her comments on the back cover blurb. Janna Fong for her input on the cover image. Heather Milne for her comments on the typesetting. And to everyone who gave me other comments or encouraged me along the way—Lindsey Wagner, Sarah Petrulis, Andre Podolsky, Stephanie Haas—thanks. You helped me more than you know.

And of course, Ryan, who was there with me every step of the way, encouraged me, gave me honest opinions, let me disappear into the computer room for hours, who is everything I could have asked for and more, from the bottom of my heart, thank you.

Air

JUST A FEW more stitches and... there.

Jacob Marshall stepped back to admire his handiwork. A proud grin spread on his face. It had taken him months, but he had finally finished his re-creation of the tunic of Garrett, the hero of the video game *Legend of Aurius*. It was beautiful, the crimson cloth perfectly fitted to his body with the gold scrollwork painstakingly hand-embroidered around the edges. It was the hallmark of his sewing ability, the best he could possibly make, and possibly ever could.

A voice called up from downstairs, "Jake, your friends are here!"

"Coming," he replied. He didn't bother to correct her. If his mother knew he had never met the people waiting outside for him and knew them only as text and images on an internet message forum, she would pitch a fit, and maybe refuse to let him go.

Carefully folding the tunic in his arms, Jacob strolled out of the work room into the upstairs hallway. His duffel bag lay beside the staircase, packed and open. He glanced briefly at his bedroom door at the end of the hallway, closed to mark his departure. He smiled at the large poster plastered to the door portraying the main characters of *Legend of Aurius*. He never tired of looking at that poster.

Setting the tunic delicately inside the duffel bag, he zipped it shut and jogged down the stairs. He brushed his shaggy hair out of his eyes, for once glad of its dull brown hue.

As he jumped onto the floor of the downstairs hallway, his mother leaned into the dining room through the kitchen doorway and called out to him, "Call me every night, okay?"

"Yes, mom." He barely suppressed a roll of his eyes. He was only going to be gone two nights. It wasn't as if he hadn't done it before. Nothing was going to happen that weekend. Except, he thought with an eager chuckle, perhaps a prize for his work, and the recognition that came with it.

Jacob's mother's voice continued as he approached the front door. "Be sure to eat healthy meals while you're there."

"Alright," he replied, now trying harder to keep the sarcasm out of his voice. He wasn't a kid, he knew how to eat well. There wouldn't be much time for food, anyway. He had nearly reached the front door.

"Have fun, honey. I love you."

"Bye," Jacob called back, though the word might have been swallowed by the front door closing behind him.

Smiling at the dark grey sedan parked against the curb on the street, Jacob strode down the walkway, the long plastic tube attached to his duffel bag slapping his back with his pace. He glanced at the people in and around the car as he approached it. A woman with shoulder-length dirty blonde hair peppered with highlights stood on the far side of the car, waving enthusiastically at him. Another young woman, already in costume with a patterned purple Japanese *kimono* robe, waved from the front passenger seat, long black hair spilling over the seat. The male driver, brown-haired and wearing glasses and a red polo shirt, raised a hand with an amused smile. Sitting sideways on the back seat, legs dangling out the open door facing Jacob, was a third young woman, covered in rainbow striped clothes and bangles with bright pink hair pulled up into pigtails.

Jacob waved back at the motley group, feeling his excitement rise with each step. They were all older than him, he knew, most of them attending college in town. The girl in the *kimono* was even skipping one of her summer classes for this. Jacob scoffed inwardly at the disdain his mother would show if she knew he was stepping into a car with people he only knew from the internet. It didn't matter that he had never met these people. He already knew them.

The trunk popped open as he neared the car. Jacob veered toward it. The blonde woman stepped around to help him wedge his bag in with all the others filling the trunk, but Jacob hesitated, clutching his bag possessively.

"Don't worry," she assured him. "We've done this lots of times, even with glass in the trunk. Everything'll be fine." Jacob gave her an unconvincing smile as he reluctantly relinquished the duffel bag. He looked straight at her for the first time. She was almost his height, not unattractive, but slightly overweight and wearing an uninteresting cream-colored blouse and brown skirt. He stopped the thought short, reminding himself of his own flabby stomach dressed in a plain T-shirt and blue jeans.

Besides, he thought, *it doesn't matter what she looks like now. In costume, she's someone else entirely. Just like me.*

The woman held out her hand. "My name's…"

"Let's," Jacob cut in, silencing her with an apologetic smile, "hold off the introductions 'til we're out of sight, okay? I don't want my mom to realize I've never met you." Her look of surprise faded with a knowing smile and a nod. Closing the trunk on Jacob's bag, she moved around to the passenger side. Jacob slipped into the car behind the driver next to the brightly colored girl, who he realized was about his age, and that he didn't know her.

"Hi," she stated before he could say anything. She began to reach her hand up. "I'm…" The blonde woman cut her off, her index finger raised.

"No introductions 'til we're around the block." At the looks of confusion in the car, the blonde woman added, "And out of parent disapproval range." The others nodded understandingly and the driver started the car. Jacob smiled, realizing he was truly among friends, people who understood the hobbies that no one else did, and the measures it took to continue them. The driver, the only other male in the group, had almost given up costuming entirely because of his father's disapproval. Jacob knew the driver's father thought he was going camping that weekend.

"Thanks." Jacob glanced back at his house rising behind the magnolia tree that shaded the front yard. His mother, watching from a window where she pulled back the curtain, waved as she caught his gaze. He waved back as the car rolled forward and began driving down the street.

The pink-haired girl's head twisted around to watch the house as it faded into the distance, becoming slowly obstructed by trees and other houses. "Okay, that's far enough! I'm…"

"I'm Karen," the blonde woman cut across, reaching her hand across the seat to Jacob. Raising his right arm awkwardly over the pink-haired girl, he took Karen's hand and shook it. "Or SilentAngel on the message forum," she added, "and this is my cousin, Jasmine."

Pink pigtails swaying as she turned, Jasmine beamed at him. "I've never been to a Japanese *anime* convention before. I'm really excited." Jacob smiled in response. It would be helpful having her around, as she could help them carry things their costumes wouldn't be able to hold.

"Are you in our room, then?" Jacob asked, concerned that their shared hotel room was already going to house more people than there were sleeping spaces.

"Actually, I live in town. I have a friend who lives near the convention center, I'll be staying with him." She flashed him a wide smile. "This is going to be so fun!" Jacob grinned, her exuberance infectious.

Twisting around in her seat, the *kimono*-clad girl reached her hand back. "I'm Emily, a.k.a. PaintedGrasshopper." Jacob nodded as he shook her hand.

"And I'm, obviously, Eric," the driver called back. "But I answer to ChaosKnight, too." Emily and Jasmine chuckled.

"Nice to meet you," Jacob answered. "I'm, well, I guess you know I'm Jake, or Garrett203."

"So, what's this big, ultra-secret costume you've been working on?"

Emily asked, her curtain of black hair swaying over her shoulder as she turned to glance at him again.

"Not until tomorrow," Jacob responded, fighting to keep an idiotic grin off his face. He couldn't wait to show it off.

"Aw, come on," Emily chided.

"Pretty please?" Jasmine asked.

"Just give us a hint," Karen piped in.

"Come on, we're giving you a ride," Eric added. Jacob's eagerness to display the costume only escalated with the chorus of voices ringing through the car over the Japanese pop music playing through the stereo.

Finally, Jacob stated, "Well, okay." The girls cheered and Jasmine clapped at their victory, though Jacob was just as excited to show it as they were to see it. Reaching into his jeans pocket, he pulled out the finishing touch of the costume, the piece to which he was too attached to let out of reach even for a moment. He held up Garrett's famous amber teardrop pendant, set in steel shaped into a rounded triangle two inches across, etched with runes around the stone.

The girls' chorus of pleads and cheers immediately deepened to oohs and ahhs as they gazed at the pendant.

"I should've guessed." Emily smiled. "Garrett from *Aurius*. I was wondering when you were going to make a costume of him."

"What is it?" Eric asked, trying to glance over his shoulder. "I want to see!"

"It's Garrett's pendant from *Legend of Aurius*," Emily answered.

"Did you make that?" Jasmine asked.

"Yep," Jacob stated proudly as he pocketed the pendant. "A guy at my stepdad's auto shop does this sort of thing as a hobby and he showed me how to make it. It took a few tries, but he knows a lot about metalworking. The really hard part was finding a piece of amber that was good enough for it. I can't tell you how many rock bins I dug through, and Adam still had to drill it a bit to get it the right shape." Jacob's construction of the pendant was crude, but he was immensely pleased with the results of his work. No one else had a pendant like his.

"That's cool," Karen remarked. "I can't wait to see the rest of the costume." *Neither can I,* Jacob thought with a wide smile.

"This is going to be great!" Jasmine exclaimed, bouncing slightly in the center of the back seat of the car in her excitement.

Jacob settled back in his seat as he watched the suburbs pass by outside the window. *Yes, it is,* he thought. A full weekend at the biggest *anime* convention in the area, no mother or stepfather to nag at him, no girlfriend to worry about, no school, no college plans, and the first showing of his crowning achievement, an accomplishment that would finally give him the recognition he had always wanted.

It's going to be a great weekend, he thought with a smile.

The early afternoon sun glared into Jacob's eyes as they drove down the highway. They had left later than Jacob had wanted, arriving just as the convention was opening Friday evening. He would have preferred to arrive some time earlier, so he wouldn't miss a minute of convention events while they checked in to their hotel room and got settled in, but he wouldn't complain. The drive took nearly two hours, but if he had to take a train or bus, it would have taken him closer to six. He supposed he could have asked his mother if he could borrow her car, if he knew how to drive. He quickly banished that thought from his mind. He vowed that he wasn't going to worry about such things this weekend.

Finally, they exited the highway and turned toward the convention center. A smile spread on Jacob's face as they approached the large building.

"That's where the convention's taking place?" Jasmine exclaimed. "It's huge!"

Karen smiled, amused. "I told you this was the biggest convention in the area."

The convention center was as large as a warehouse, but with the inviting architecture of a huge restaurant. Crowds of convention-goers already swarmed around the building, but Jacob knew there would be three times as many people the next morning. People in costume were scattered throughout the throng, their vibrant and eccentric outfits and outrageous hairstyles standing out starkly against all the people wearing ordinary clothes. Normally, Jacob would have brought two or three costumes so he could wear a different one each day of the convention, but Garrett's outfit had taken up all of his free time. Besides, he had put so much work into it that he wanted the whole weekend to show it off.

"There's our hotel," Emily stated, pointing at a building rising behind the convention center as they passed by the bustling entrance. Eric turned the car into the parking lot outside the hotel.

"So, tell me more about these workshops," Jasmine asked Karen as they pulled into a parking space. Jacob heard Karen answer as he stepped out of the car.

"Well, at a big convention like this, there's workshops for pretty much any aspect of *anime* or Japanese life or video games. Writing, drawing, character designs, voice acting..."

"Cool!" Jasmine stated. "I'd love to make a *manga* comic some day."

As Jacob pulled his duffel bag out of the trunk, lying on top of everyone else's things, Eric pointed at the black plastic tube attached to it. "What's that?"

Jacob shouldered the bag with a grin. "You'll see." The trunk slowly emptied until Jasmine pulled out her backpack, a battered beige pack covered in designs written in white-out with keychains and bangles dangling off every available surface.

Laden with their luggage, they crossed the parking lot into the hotel lobby, Jasmine and Karen chattering away all the while. Emily, moving with practiced fluidness in her *kimono* and wooden sandals while carrying a garment bag and pulling a rolling blue suitcase along behind her, glided discreetly over toward Jacob.

Leaning close so the others wouldn't hear, she asked, "So, what happened with Tina?" A bitter frown crossed Jacob's face.

"She didn't want to come." He didn't want to think about Christina at all this weekend. Thoughts of the argument they'd had the last time he spoke with her still angered him, and all the things he'd said and wished he'd said raced through his mind. He had been planning for this convention for months, how could he abandon months of work and preparation just because she wanted to do something different? True, it was their first anniversary, but it was at this very convention last year that they'd met. She could have enjoyed herself, and he could have bought something special for her, if she'd only agreed to come, but she was too stubborn to do that. Then she'd had the nerve to say he was too wrapped up in his costuming, that it was an obsession.

Reaching slender fingers out from the handle of her suitcase, Emily touched his arm. "She has a point, you know. You should spend some time with her next week." Jacob glanced at her, but said nothing. He respected her opinions, and on the message forum, she was often a voice of reason or helpful source of feminine insight, but she didn't understand that he needed these conventions to escape a harsh and meaningless life. Costuming was the only thing that made him special, the only way he could be somebody important.

Jasmine turned around abruptly as they entered the hotel lobby and asked him, "Hey, are you going to the rave tonight?"

"I don't really dance," he replied hesitantly, and again he thought of Tina. He would have gone to the dance party at the convention with her if she had asked him. Instead, they would both be spending the weekend alone. He shook his head, trying to clear it of the depressing thoughts. He could worry about Tina when he got home.

"What's up?" Jasmine asked, cocking her head inquisitively at him shaking his.

"Nothing."

The hotel lobby was crowded and rang with other convention-goers, but after several minutes, they checked in, receiving spare key cards for everyone but Jasmine, and rode the elevator up to the fifth floor to their room. Jacob concentrated on how much he intended to enjoy the weekend as sleeping arrangements were decided.

As Jacob deposited his duffel bag at the end of the couch where he would be sleeping, Karen asked him, "Hey, Jake, how're the college applications going?"

"Oh, good," he lied quickly. "I'm working on a few right now."

"That's good." Karen smiled, though he caught a disappointed glance from Emily over the blonde woman's shoulder. Jacob frowned at his bag, wishing Emily, or PaintedGrasshopper as he knew her, wouldn't act so much like his own mother sometimes.

The evening passed too slowly for his taste. He was itching to show off his new costume, but he had promised he wouldn't unveil it until Saturday morning. Still, it was a restful evening, which Jacob appreciated, as he knew he would be constantly busy and almost entirely on his feet from early in the morning to late at night the next day, with only a few hours' less respite on Sunday.

Finally, morning came, and Jacob awoke to find Emily and Karen already up and preparing for the day. He had planned on an early start, but they had more elaborate costumes than he did and it took them longer still to manage complex hairstyles and apply make-up. Eric had risen and Jasmine had arrived by the time it was Jacob's turn to use the sole bathroom in the suite. *All the better*, he thought as he slipped into the bathroom amidst Jasmine's fawning praise of Emily and Karen's costumes. *More people to see it first.*

Hurriedly, he slid out of the sole shirt and pair of jeans he had brought. Fumbling slightly in his excitement, he pulled on Garrett's light brown pants and shirt. Over those he added the tunic, as well as the medieval leather gloves and boots. Finally, he strapped on Garrett's double sword belt, clipped the amber pendant around his neck, and tied his patterned red, black, and gold headband, the culmination of several hours of work alone, around his forehead. He then stood straight to appraise his appearance in the mirror. It was perfect, he thought. He could not have made the outfit better and his own likeness to the hero of *Legend of Aurius* was closer than he could have hoped. Not even his own flaws could bring down his elation, his skin too pale from spending so much time inside, the too rounded jaw, the freckles that still pocked his cheeks below his eyes. He had tried on the homemade outfit before, but three differences made his heart swell with pride and excitement this time. Now, the outfit was fully complete, his hair had grown out into Garrett's distinctive, casually lanky length, and this time, the convention waited just a few hundred yards behind him, the masses ready to see his ultimate achievement.

Taking in a deep breath to try to wipe the idiotic grin off his face, Jacob opened the door and stepped out of the bathroom. Emily, Karen, Jasmine, and Eric paused their conversation to glance at him. Jasmine 'oohed' her admiration.

"Very nice," Karen remarked.

"Well done," Emily added. "You must've really worked a long time on that."

Eric simply nodded in approval and, Jacob thought, a little wistfulness. Jacob drank in the praise, but all too soon, they resumed the conversation they had been engaged in.

"So, what about lunch?" Jasmine asked.

Jacob hid his disappointment at being turned aside so quickly by clearing his throat.

"Actually," he stated, "it's not finished yet. Can you hand me that?" Eric turned around with a curious look, grabbed the black plastic tube, and passed it over the girls' heads to Jacob. Taking it gently, Jacob unscrewed the top and upended the tube. The others looked over curiously. A sword in scabbard slid out of the tube into his waiting hand, fitted with a buckle to attach to the sword belt. The rendition was about as crude as the pendant, but it was unmistakable. As he clipped the sword to his belt, the others uttered even more impressed sounds.

"That's amazing! It looks just like Garrett's sword!" Jasmine exclaimed. Jacob beamed, though the weight of the sword was awkward against his hip. *It doesn't matter,* he thought, *I can't be Garrett without it.* He realized then that the double-wrapped sword belt, which he had ordered from a medieval reenactment supply store online, balanced the weight of the sword across his body as it had been advertised to do. He shifted his weight from foot to foot, testing the way it felt hanging next to him.

"Are you sure they'll let you take that in to the convention?" Emily asked worriedly, eyeing the sword.

"It's just a prop." Jacob slid the sword out of its scabbard and showed it to the group. The blade was a flat slab of steel an eighth of an inch thick, and though the tip tapered into a point, it was rounded off so that it couldn't cut. Emily frowned, but said nothing more.

"Did you make that, too?" Karen asked.

"Well, Adam did," Jacob admitted, then quickly added, "the guy from my stepdad's shop. He said it would take too long to teach me how to do something like this, so I paid him to make it for me. I bought the sheath separately, though."

The others nodded, then continued discussing their plans for the day. Jacob felt disappointed again and glanced at the detailed embroidery he had sewn around the hems of the sleeves, hours upon hours of careful work looking between a paused screen on the game and the tunic to get every stitch exactly where it should be. He straightened with a deep breath. Thousands of people were going to be at the convention today and tomorrow. He had plenty of time to show off all his hard work on the costume.

Karen lifted the extended frilly end of her Gothic, Victorian-style sleeve to glance at her watch. "I have to run the Japanese fashion panel from 3:00 to 4:00, so shall we meet back here to get ready for the costume masquerade contest at 4:30?" The others uttered their assent and Jacob nodded.

"Well, then, everybody ready?" Emily asked with a smile. Her elaborate dress rustled as she spread her arms questioningly. Jacob sifted through the group in the narrow space beside the second bed to the couch, where he dropped his jeans and T-shirt. Reaching into the pocket of his blue jeans, he removed his wallet, a battered shred of brown leather, and rearranging his sword belt and the tails of his tunic, he slipped it into the pocket he had sewn into the light brown trousers of his costume. He was glad he'd had the foresight to do that. It would have been awkward and only inviting trouble if he'd had to carry around his wallet or just his bank card to buy anything he wanted from the dealers' hall.

All chattering amongst themselves, the motley group left the hotel room. Karen was dressed in her frilly and lacy black and white dress, layered with petticoats and stockings. Emily wore her bizarre asymmetrical dress of a character from a Japanese *anime* cartoon, spattered with strange cuts and patterns. Jasmine wore a frayed punk outfit of various colors, baubles and bangles hanging by the dozen around her neck, arms, ankles, and ears. Eric was unadorned in a grey T-shirt, blue jeans, and a black flannel overshirt. Finally, Jacob wore the garb of Garrett, the hero of *Legend of Aurius*. They made their way down the hall towards the elevators, receiving a few strange or approving gazes from other visitors to the hotel.

Squeezing into an elevator, Emily's awkwardly protruding outfit causing uncomfortable repositioning, they rode down to the lobby, which teemed with convention-goers.

"Whew!" Karen exclaimed, her voice rising to be heard over the crowd. "It's going to be busy."

Carefully, they sifted through the throng toward the entrance of the hotel. Jacob felt caged in and uneasy with the crowd pressing him in. It didn't take long before someone stopped him to ask to take a picture of his costume. A smile spread on his face from the attention and the comments called through the crowd.

"Hey, cool Garrett!"

"Awesome!"

"How long did it take?"

"Even the sword!"

Jacob smiled as he answered the barrage of questions directed at him and the others, but found himself suddenly uncomfortable when they asked who he was and more about him. He glanced longingly toward the exit, but it was still far away.

"Pictures outside, please!" came Jasmine's voice. She grabbed his sleeve. "Come on!" Gratefully, he allowed her to pull him through the crowd in Karen's wake. When the older cousin stopped for another photo, Jasmine pulled him past her and on through the front doors of the hotel.

"Thanks," Jacob stated with a smile after he caught his breath in the still busy, but open air outside the hotel.

Jasmine smiled back. "No problem." Jacob glanced at the door of the hotel, but nobody had followed him. He realized he had only been stopped for photographs once inside, but the crowd had been maddening.

"Good thing we registered last night," Eric's voice came from off to the side. When Jacob looked to him, Eric nodded toward the convention center. Jacob glanced across the hotel parking lot at the convention center. The entrance teemed with people, packed together twice as tightly as inside the hotel in a line that stretched around the block.

Karen stepped out of the hotel. "Sorry about that. Sounds like they might want to commission me for an outfit."

"Shall we go?" Jasmine asked. Everyone nodded, and with that, they began crossing the parking lot towards the convention center. Jacob looked at the line waiting to register for the convention. It seemed every third person in line was in costume. He saw characters from video games, from Japanese *anime* cartoons and *manga* comics, American comics, television shows, and movies, mascot characters depicted in full body suits or creative outfits with only a few accessories portraying the character, the same costume on more than one person in line more than once, some people dressed in traditional Japanese or other Asian garb, and even a few people decked in elaborate cardboard costumes of robots or machines from various sources. Jacob smiled at the wildly dressed throng. These were people who understood the way he felt. People who respected the rich characters and compelling stories in television, movies, and video games. People who related to the characters in them, who grew attached to them and felt for them through their adventures. People who longed for a different reality, whether simpler or more complex, a more dramatic and engaging reality than the one they had to live in. Here, Jacob thought, among these people, he could be Garrett. He could be someone everybody knew, someone special, someone worthwhile.

His smile widened as his eyes passed over a group of people in line dressed up as other characters from *Legend of Aurius*. They were talking excitedly and pointing to him. One of them, dressed as Serina, the healer and lead female character from the game, waved wildly at him, holding up a camera in her other hand.

Turning to the group that had brought him to the convention, he stated, "I'll see you guys this afternoon."

"Bye!" Jasmine exclaimed with an excited wave.

"Four-thirty," Emily reminded him with a smile.

"Have fun," Karen added, voluminous knee-length skirts swaying as she walked. Eric simply nodded at him. Turning, Jacob veered toward the *Legend of Aurius* group in the line.

"Wow!" stated the girl dressed up as Serina as he drew near. "Your costume is amazing!" Her costume was mostly accurate, but with the vinyl-like material reflecting the sunlight, he thought it looked too fake. He was glad he had decided to use regular cotton cloth for his costume. Hers also lacked the detail around the edges like Garrett's costume, and her hair, while mostly right, didn't have the volume and graceful flow that the original character's hair did. Still, it made him happy just to see someone dressed as her, and to hear the group's remarks on his costume.

"That is insane!" Jacob turned toward the deeper words to find another Garrett among the group, though his tunic and headband were plain, the shade of the shirt was wrong, and he had no pendant or sword. He was, however, taller and better built than Jacob, and perhaps older as well, and Jacob couldn't help but feel inadequate, even with the better costume.

"Did you do all that by hand?" asked someone else. Jacob turned to find another girl dressed as the tough, physically powerful character Kalista. He tried to focus on the fact that her outfit was the best made of them all, rather than the fact that he hadn't liked the character in the game. With an admiring expression very unlike the character, however, she rubbed her thumb over the embroidery on his sleeve.

"Yeah," Jacob answered with a proud smile.

"That's amazing!"

"Can we get a picture?" the Serina-girl asked.

"Sure," Jacob answered. "Should I get out my sword?" Gesturing to the hilt hanging at his side, the costumed group turned their heads to face it.

"Oh, my god, you have the sword, too!" the Serina-girl exclaimed. "Yeah, get the sword, too!"

As he drew the fake sword from the scabbard, the Kalista-girl asked incredulously, "Did you make that, too?"

"A friend did," Jacob answered, realizing that as much as he appreciated Adam's work on the sword, it would be much easier that weekend to save the lengthy explanation. The Serina-girl turned on her digital camera and the Kalista-girl pulled another out of a canvas bag hanging over her shoulder. Stepping back a few paces, Jacob struck a pose mimicking an official character design image of Garrett, holding up his prop sword. He watched tiny red lights flash on their cameras, but held his pose as cameras of a few other people in line blinked at him. The Serina-girl lowered her camera, gazing briefly at the display screen before glancing back at him.

"Thanks!" She wrapped the camera's strap around her wrist. "We'll see you around, okay?" Jacob nodded, but before he could walk away, she called out, "Oh! What's your name?"

"Jake."

"I'm Melanie," she answered with a smile. "This is Dana and Max." They shook his hand each in turn.

"Your Garrett's awesome, man," Max stated. Jacob only smiled, then turned and approached the entrance for people who had already registered for the convention. He had been hoping, selfishly he realized, that Max would say Jacob's costume was better than his. Flashing his badge at the security guard beside the entrance, he stepped inside into a world where reality no longer mattered.

The convention hall was immense, with tens of thousands of square feet of exhibitors and dealers' booths and various rooms where panels were held all through the day. The booths were crowded with all manner of merchandise from hundreds of series, tables filled with toys, knickknacks, books, CDs, DVDs, games, clothing, decorations, Japanese food, snacks, and drinks, and other things Jacob couldn't even identify. The hall roared with the simultaneous conversations of thousands of visitors swarming between booths, lining up in front of autograph tables, and chatting amongst themselves. The size of the convention was mind-boggling, but Jacob was unsurprised, as this was his third year visiting the convention.

Inside, though many people looked at him, only a few more than usual asked him if they could take a photograph. He was somewhat disappointed that he wasn't getting more notice for his costume, but the impressed and admiring looks he received made him feel proud. For once, he was being noticed, and people respected him for the work he put into his costume. He was eagerly looking forward to the costume contest that afternoon. Though he saw his share of more polished or professionally-made costumes as he wandered through the dealers' hall, none of them seemed to have quite the level of detail as his did, with the embroidered hems and headband, the handmade pendant and sword. And none of the exceptional costumes he ran across were from *Legend of Aurius*. He knew he had to win at least some prize at the contest.

The thought kept a smile on his face all day as he strolled through the exhibitors' hall and attended various panels.

It's going to be a great weekend, he thought.

2

BETWEEN THE PANELS, photo shoots, and hours spent perusing the dealers' hall, it was 3:30 before Jacob could take a break. He inhaled deeply as he stepped out of the hall into the sunlight. The area just outside of the convention center still bustled with people, but the air didn't feel so cramped. Pausing a moment to stretch sore muscles, he walked around to the side of the huge convention center. Most of the building was surrounded by city streets and traffic, but the eastern side of the hall faced a span of forest with paths winding through it. Following one path, he walked into the forest, trees around him stripped by an abnormally hot summer. He passed by a few groups of people from the convention having lunch in the sparse woods. A pair of joggers rushed past him in the opposite direction, staring peculiarly at him as they went.

Veering off the trail, he followed an almost invisible path to the edge of a hill leading about twenty feet down to a small ravine. Jacob smiled as he slid carefully down the leaf-strewn decline. A group of people dressed up as characters from the game *Wizard Moon* had brought him here earlier that day to take pictures of him for a costuming website they ran. It was a perfect location. With the hill rising in a semicircle around the small ravine and a large, flat boulder positioned next to an old, leaning oak tree nestled in the center of the semicircle, it looked just like the opening scene of *Legend of Aurius*. He had been shocked when he first saw it. The likeness wasn't perfect, but the similarity was uncanny.

Now, it provided him a nice, quiet place to rest for a few minutes. As he reached the floor of the ravine, voices off to the side drew his attention. Glancing across the ravine that stretched away toward the highway before rising up to meet it, he found a group of people some paces away, dressed in all black Gothic outfits, riddled with chains, buckles, and belts. Two of them glanced over at him briefly, but soon, they all ignored him. They were live-action role-players, people who dressed up and acted like their characters in scenarios a designated game master would dictate, like a director of an unscripted, improvised movie. Turning away from them, Jacob settled in on the boulder, leaning back against the tree, and gazed up at the sky through the jagged branches cutting through the air. It was nice, he thought, being able to see nothing but nature in the middle of a city sometimes.

Closing his eyes, he let his body relax. He thought about the morning and early afternoon that had passed and a smile spread on his face. He had again met Melanie, the girl dressed up as Serina, and had posed for some more photographs for her.

He had already found various things he wanted to buy from the dealers' hall. He didn't have much money to spare, but he had seen some action figures he had been seeking for a while, which were on sale, and a new cloth wall scroll of *Legend of Aurius*. He was also hoping to stock up on some of his favorite Japanese snack treats, and he wanted to get a new printed T-shirt. If he bought all of it, however, it wouldn't leave him much money for food for the rest of the weekend. The question was deciding which items he wanted most.

Suddenly, a voice called out from a distance, "Garrett!"

Jacob frowned, keeping his eyes closed. He had relished the attention he received from all the people admiring his costume, but he was tired, and what he really wanted was a few minutes to rest quietly.

The voice persisted. "Garrett, come on! The priestess is waiting!"

Jacob opened his eyes curiously. It was, word for word, the opening line of *Legend of Aurius*. He glanced forward at the one speaking to him. His eyes widened and his heart skipped a beat. Standing before him with an impatient look on his face was a perfect rendition of a guard of Merakis, the first town in *Aurius*. In fact, the hairstyle and features exactly matched the soldier that roused Garrett at the beginning of the game. It was the most accurate character depiction he had ever seen, especially for such an insignificant character. Jacob blinked in confusion.

"Come on! We must get back to Merakis!" With that, the man who looked so much like a soldier of the town turned and began walking back the way he had come.

Jacob glanced at the forest around him, wondering briefly if he was hallucinating. He knew he couldn't be dreaming, as everything was far too vivid for that. He couldn't see any other people anywhere around. *Did I fall asleep?* he wondered. And why was everything suddenly so quiet? He could no longer hear the shuffling sounds and distant murmurs of the live-action role-players, and even the traffic on the streets only a few hundred feet away seemed to have died down. The silence was oppressing, and he was suddenly overcome with a desperate need to return to the convention.

Several paces ahead now, the guard stopped and turned to look at him.

"Hurry up!" The insistence in the guard's voice caused Jacob to scramble to his feet and run after the man, though his confusion only mounted.

He looked around in all directions as he walked hesitantly behind the guard. There were no signs of any other people anywhere in sight. The only noises to permeate the silence were their own footsteps across the leaf-strewn ground. Nothing looked any different than it had a moment earlier, but why did everything suddenly seem so foreign, so not right? Who was this man, and why was he saying everything the guard from the opening of *Aurius* did? Was he dreaming, somehow? Was this a cruel joke being played on him?

The thought made him stop in his tracks.

A moment later, the guard stopped, glancing back at him. "Come on! You'll be late for the ceremony!" Jacob uneasily continued following the man. No, it couldn't be a trick. The people at school who enjoyed picking on him weren't smart enough to pull off something like this, and if they wanted to laugh at him wearing a costume of a video game character, they could have done that back at the boulder. Besides, the guard was clearly at least thirty years old.

For several minutes, Jacob walked behind the guard through the forest, the edges of the ravine eventually falling and flattening out beside him. *Just,* he thought, *like in* Aurius. There was no sign of the highway anywhere around.

As they passed a bend in the forest, Jacob stopped, gasping. The town of Merakis lay before him. Even though the game had showed this scene from above, he clearly recognized the buildings ahead. Houses, shops, a pub, an inn, and rising above the thatched-roof buildings in the distance, the church where the game began. He could scarcely believe his own eyes.

Are they making a movie of Legend of Aurius, *and did they mistake me for the star?* He knew the thought was absurd as soon as it crossed his mind. He didn't see any cameras or crew around, and when he had come in off the highway, he would have seen something. He couldn't dare to hope that what he desperately believed had happened was true.

"Come on!" the guard snapped, interrupting his thoughts, and grabbing his arm, he pulled Jacob at a quicker pace down the cobbled street.

Jacob's eyes roved around the town as the guard led him through it, still baffled at his surroundings. He could see no sign of modern life, no technology, no cars, no high rise buildings in the distance. And the air was so clean. He had never realized the constant smell of smog lingering faintly in the air until it was gone. The air he breathed in was so much richer and fresher, and everything was so clear, he thought that if he was high enough, he could see to the end of the world.

People dressed in clothes that belonged to the scenery peered out of the simple houses he passed, watching the guard lead him through town. His pendant thumped against his chest with his rapid pace.

Finally, they came around the corner of a two-story inn and upon the church. Jacob's eyes widened as he gazed up at the building. The architecture was incredible, patterned with statues and details around a huge stained glass window, like the cathedrals he saw in pictures of Europe.

The guard's pace quickened as he climbed the wide stone stairs up to the huge oak and iron doors leading into the church. Pulling one open, he gestured fervently for Jacob to go inside. Jacob complied, too confused to think what else to do.

Once inside, he froze. He had played this part of the game more than a dozen times since it had come out a few years ago. The church where he now stood was exactly as it appeared in the game, with its carved pillars supporting the high arched ceiling, soft light from candles and sunlight streaming through the stained glass windows, and the priestess at the altar at the back of the church, dressed in fancy white and gold robes.

This church, however, was much bigger.

The limited video processing power of the game could not portray such immense size as he saw before him. Where in the game, only about three people fit to a pew for a total of fewer than twenty rendered townspeople at this ceremony, here there were twice as many rows with four times as many people filling them. Only a handful of the more than one hundred people lining the church turned to look at him as he stumbled in. Jacob couldn't concentrate on the words the archbishop spoke beside the Grand Priestess as he gazed around at the church.

Suddenly, the archbishop's droning words stopped, and in a powerful voice, he called across the church, "Our hero approaches."

As one, the members of the congregation turned to look at Jacob.

His breath caught in his throat as he gazed out at the eyes staring back at him. The guard behind him gave him a quick shove, and Jacob walked slowly down the red carpet leading to the altar. His hands shook and he fiddled uneasily with his gloves as he passed by row after row of people, seemingly getting no closer to the waiting archbishop and priestess. His eyes rose to an enormous, round stained glass window over the dais, depicting an ancient hero that looked surprisingly like the way Jacob had made himself look now, standing at the top of a hill and holding up a sword triumphantly. Jacob gazed at it in wonder. So many times he had looked upon that window in the game, but the colors and light pouring through it had never been so rich, so filling, so warm, so very present.

He felt more unnerved and worried with each step he took. He knew exactly what he was supposed to do here, but how could he do it, when he shouldn't be here at all? He desperately wanted to believe he somehow had truly been transported into the game, but it was too far-fetched to be true.

Finally, he passed the rows of pews and arrived at the back of the church. Swallowing hard, he climbed the half flight of stairs up to the priestess, who gazed at him with piercing, yet kind eyes. Arms pressed flat against the sides of his body, Jacob bowed, consciously and uncomfortably aware of the dozens of eyes boring in to his back. The priestess nodded at him as he straightened, then her voice rang out through the church.

"Kneel, Garrett." Jacob knelt, bowing his head before the priestess. "You have come to us out of legend with the Hero's pendant, your spirit brightening the town as you passed by." *Have they mistaken me for someone else?* he wondered suddenly. *Is there a real Garrett that should be here instead of me?* The remarkable and selfless deeds the real Garrett had done in the town before the game began were hinted at after the ceremony, but never gone into detail.

"You have passed the hero's test and been chosen by the Divine Light," the priestess continued. "You are the one the legends speak of, the outsider come to save the world." The church behind him was deathly silent. Jacob's knees trembled harder with each passing moment from the discomfort of being the center of attention for so many people, and he hoped he wouldn't fall right there.

Then, the priestess laid her hand on his shoulder, and it seemed to radiate a feeling of cool calmness into him.

"Garrett. Do you accept your destiny and the blessing of the light? Do you pledge your life and vow to stop the evil threatening our world? Do you swear to bring about the new era, and return peace and light to our great land?"

"I do," Jacob answered, but he felt silly saying it, and the words came out uncertain.

"Do you?" she asked him in a quieter tone, less formal, yet somehow more meaningful. Jacob's heart raced. *What am I doing here?* The impact of the questions suddenly hit him and his mouth felt dry. He didn't even know why he was reenacting the opening of *Legend of Aurius*. Was this actually real? What was he about to agree to? And yet, standing here in a church crowded with people hoping for salvation through him, what choice did he have?

"Yes," he stated, forcing confidence into his voice.

"Then go forth with our blessing, hero." Formality solidified the priestess's voice again. "Your fate is ours, and with your success shall we thrive." Jacob raised his head as the church erupted into cheers and saw a pall of sadness fall over the priestess's eyes.

"Save Aurius," she uttered to him.

He nodded, rising, and immediately the dais swarmed with people racing from the pews to meet him. Jacob's eyes darted between the hands reaching up to him, everyone clamoring at once to greet him personally.

They think I'm a hero, he thought as he began shaking hands and offering generic blessings. *They think I'm going to save them.* Realizing it meant little to him, as he still didn't know what to make of what had happened. He glanced over his shoulder at the priestess as the crowd writhed before him, each person trying to touch him. The priestess had stepped back a few paces, quietly waiting out of the light of the stained glass window.

It took over an hour for Jacob to shake hands with everyone who had come. The sunlight streaming in the windows had grown long and golden and Jacob's legs ached from standing so long. *Are Emily and the others worrying about me?* he wondered. *I've got to get home.* And yet, even as he thought it, he found himself relishing the escape.

"Bless you, Garrett," spoke a small, portly housewife as she shook his hand, her young daughter waiting silently beside her. They were the last people left in the church. "You've given hope to our dear town. May your journey be safe." Jacob could only nod back at her, his voice hoarse from all the talking he had done already.

As the woman began walking toward the entrance of the church, the girl flashed him a broad smile, then turned and skipped after her mother. Jacob blinked, stunned by the events that had transpired that afternoon.

Whispers of footsteps drew near, and he turned to find the priestess approaching.

"Are you ready for your journey?"

Abandoning character, Jacob stated, "I'm still pretty confused…"

The priestess reached up and patted his shoulder. "I know. It will all become clear soon. Is your sword prepared for battle?"

Jacob blinked, startled by the thought of marching into battle. Taking in her serious expression, he unsheathed the prop blade. "It's… not even sharp."

The priestess took the sword gently. "That won't do at all." She turned to the archbishop. "Have Marod sharpen it." The archbishop nodded as he took the blade and shuffled softly off toward the back door of the church. Jacob watched his exit until the priestess stated, "He will put his life's blood into shaping your sword. Don't worry, he should have it back to you tonight."

Jacob shook his head, uncertainty clouding his mind. "I…" He couldn't think of what he wanted to say. The priestess laid her hand on his shoulder again.

"Rest and enjoy yourself, Garrett. Take this last chance for peace before you set out. Have dinner in the Great Hall." Jacob glanced at her, wanting to say something else, to ask questions he knew were stupid.

"Go," she stated with a sad smile. He could only manage a nod before walking down the aisle and out of the church.

The warm glow of oil lamps hanging beside the doors of buildings cast a friendly light as the town began falling into the purple shadows of dusk. Laughing children chased each other through the streets and townspeople running errands greeted each other as they passed. Jacob was no sooner out the front doors of the church before people waved and greeted him as well. His eyes passed across the clean, quaint cobbled streets, neighborly, warm, and inviting. It was a pleasant place to be, but Jacob felt very much out of place. He felt strangely voyeuristic, as if he was intruding on something to which he had no right being a part. Maybe he was supposed to be Garrett here, wherever "here" was. He thought that perhaps he should embrace this role, but a part of him still was afraid to accept it as truth, in case it somehow was a joke, or a dream.

Deciding to play along for the time being, he stepped down from the church and began walking through the streets toward the Great Hall. At least, he thought, it was easy to keep up appearances when he had played the game enough times not to need any guidance through the town. The empty scabbard thumped awkwardly against his leg as he walked, and he fiddled with the sword belt as he tried to steady it. When he caught the gaze of a shop owner watching him trying to adjust the belt, he dropped his hands and shot the man an attempt at a casual smile.

Light streamed out from the high windows of the Great Hall as Jacob approached. The entrance was crowded with people filing in for a feast which Jacob could smell from half a block away. The strong herbs used to flavor the meat perfumed the air, leaving the building with a heady scent. He followed groups of people into the hall, which was filled with loud music and pounding dancers and a huge table covered in all manner of food. It was all real food, hand-cooked from scratch with fresh ingredients, dishes unlike anything he had eaten since his last family dinner on Easter. A smile spread uncontrollably onto his face at the sight of the food and festivities. However, with it came a pang of uneasiness. *They wouldn't be celebrating if they knew what happened next like I do.* The thought made him feel so uncomfortable that he nearly turned around and left at that moment, but then, the rest of the crowd filling the large hall noticed him.

With a chorus of cheers ringing throughout the hall, he was ushered deep into the throng, and before he knew what had happened, a wooden mug of ale had been pushed into one hand and a large turkey drumstick, dripping with juices, into the other. He glanced into the mug, white foam flowing over the edges. Though he knew most of his classmates had already had at least some sort of alcoholic drink in their lives, and many boasted of breaking into their parents' liquor cabinet weekly or even nightly, he had never indulged himself before and wasn't certain he wanted to start amongst all these strangers. His decision was made for him as someone grabbed his wrist and thrust the drink up and against his mouth. Half choking as he tried to swallow the pungently bitter drink, he managed to pull his hand away and wiped foam off his upper lip with his sleeve. Cheers and laughter swelled around him at the sight. Suddenly aware of the rumbling in his stomach and eager to get his mind off the already drunken townspeople around him, he bit into the drumstick. He glanced up curiously as the crowd urged him on, and found even the smallest of women were tearing much larger mouthfuls of meat off the bones they held than he did. With a nervous smile, he bit a larger chunk off the drumstick, trying to emulate the people around him.

Before the sky outside had even drained of the remnants of daylight, Jacob found himself laughing uproariously and dancing among the villagers, his head spinning and stomach churning but never feeling so welcome, so at home, and he hoped that night would never end.

He had no idea what time it was when he left the hall, but a sky rich with stars hung huge and dark above and many oil lamps in front of houses had been extinguished. Most of the journey to the inn was a haze as he stumbled along and leaned on the innkeeper. His stomach roiled and frothed inside him, its contents constantly threatening to escape his body, but when he fell back on the bed in his room at the inn, it was so soft and his body so tired that he fell asleep almost instantly. All his worries disappeared and he forgot entirely about the events yet to pass that night.

Until a crash in the common room of the inn downstairs woke him.

The moon had risen high in the sky when a loud noise clattered downstairs, startling Jacob awake. He threw himself up into a sitting position, but immediately regretted it. His head spun and pounded with the movement, and with a groan, he leaned back onto his elbow. Panting heavily while his stomach settled, he tried to assess the situation. In the darkness permeating the room, he could see that his sword had been returned. It hung across the room in its scabbard, his sword belt draped over the door knob. A soft orange glow illuminated the thick curtains hanging over the window, and distant sounds of scuffling passed across his ears. Memories of the game came back to him.

The town was under attack.

Moving quickly but carefully to his feet, he strode over to the window, pulled the curtains aside, and gazed out. The creatures outside were barely visible, no more than shadows against the light of the fires consuming buildings. People ran from the creatures in the streets, screaming, but they were quickly pursued by their attackers. As Jacob watched, a mother carrying her child was overtaken by one of the monsters, and with a quick swipe of a clawed limb, the woman collapsed beside another body already lying in the street, the child thrown from her arms. The child cried out and scrambled backwards on hands and feet, but the creature paced forward relentlessly.

Unwilling to watch any more, Jacob let the curtain fall back into place and quickly retrieved his sword belt. He struggled to strap it around his waist in the darkness. He could barely see the outlines of his own feet against the floor in the dark room and couldn't manage to buckle the belt. His heart raced and he grew frantic. He didn't even know where the lamps in the room were, let alone how to light them, but he couldn't see. A strangled scream emanated from below, and then heavy steps began moving toward the stairs leading up to his room. Fear chilled him and his hands trembled as he wrestled with the belt. Alien, heavy footfalls rang up the stairs, each second bringing something closer to him. He had a terrifying suspicion what it was that approached as well, and it suddenly became horrifyingly clear to him that he was not a warrior.

The footsteps came to the top of the stairs. The loose end of the belt slipped out of his hand and the sword in scabbard thumped against the floor. The steps hesitated. Jacob snatched up the loose end of the belt and wrapped it around his waist again. The creature moved down the hall, ignoring the other doors on the second floor and approaching his room directly.

Just as the footsteps stopped outside his door, the buckle caught the hole. Jacob paused for a heartbeat in relief, just long enough for the door to be thrown open. He yelped, trying to move back from the door and draw his sword at the same time, but neither came easily. The sword blade seemed to be longer than he expected, and his arm swung upward as he tried to pull it out. The scabbard snagged his heel as he did, and he went tumbling backwards, sword out, just as the shadowy creature that stank of rotting meat pounced.

He screamed instinctively, though the attack never came. He only felt a sharp jab like a fist digging into his stomach as a heavy weight fell on the sword. Scrambling out to the side, he tilted the sword and let the weight fall to the floor beside him. Before he realized what had happened, he found himself standing next to the dead monster, pressed against the wall with his sword hanging awkwardly from his hand. The creature had fallen on his outstretched sword as it leaped onto him and impaled itself. He gazed at the sword, stained with darkness and now ridged in the middle, the edges sharp and the end tapering to a needle-sharp point.

Not willing to let his eyes adjust to the darkness and see the creature he had inadvertently just killed, Jacob shuffled along the wall and out the door quickly. His heart pounded against his ribcage, fear causing his whole body to tremble as he stumbled down the stairs to the common room. The pungent odor of fresh blood assaulted his senses and he felt himself growing sick again. Abandoning the innkeeper, he threw open the door and escaped the inn.

Screams, inhuman howls, and the roar of fires all around rang through the air. Jacob's eyes darted all around the street outside the inn. A monster ran across a rooftop across the street from him and another chased a man down the block. Too afraid for his own life to worry about others, Jacob turned away from them both and raced toward the edge of the town. Before long, his stomach churned worse than ever and a stitch gnawed at his side, slowing his pace. He groaned, cursing himself for not staying in shape.

He tried to force himself to keep jogging at least, but his body protested with each step and by the time the edge of the town was in sight, he could only stagger along, head spinning.

Then, another monster appeared before him, bared fangs glinting in the moonlight. Gasping, he grasped his sword in both hands and raised it, fear filling him. He held the sword before him like a baseball bat, completely ignorant of how to use it. He could only watch as the creature stalked forward hungrily, breathing in short gasps as if he was trying to inhale a lifetime of air in one terrifying moment.

All of a sudden, something whizzed past him and the monster snarled in pain, collapsing lifelessly to the street with something long and thin protruding from its head. Glancing over his shoulder, he found the archbishop from the church, bow in hand and quiver of arrows slung over his back, gesturing at him.

"Go!" he called out as he turned and ran deeper into the town after another shadowy monster that chased a family trying to flee the destruction. Jacob leaned forward and opened his mouth as if to call back, but his fear was like an invisible wall, preventing him from moving forward. Panting, he turned and began stumbling out to the forest surrounding the town, sheathing his sword as he went.

He didn't know how much time passed as he moved onward, his whole body sore, tired, and uncomfortable. All he knew was that he had to escape, and he hoped he could get far enough away that the monsters attacking the town couldn't find him. The town grew distant behind him and the light of the fires faded into pale moonlight streaming through the barren, twisted trees surrounding him. His pace slowed, his feet barely able to carry him any further, until finally, he couldn't move forward any longer.

Coughing, his stomach lurched and he emptied its contents onto the forest floor. He leaned against a tree, knees trembling, and soon collapsed to the ground beside the mess he had made. Raising his head faintly, he glanced through the trees back at the town, the fires engulfing it lighting up the night. He tried to rise and escape farther from the town, but he could only crawl forward a few paces before collapsing again, panting heavily. He was too sick and weary to be afraid, but he had never felt so alive, so mortal, as he did then.

At that moment, lying on the ground of a foreign forest, unable to move, a trail of death and fire behind him, he realized it had truly happened.

I'm really in the game.

It was the last thing he thought before everything faded to darkness.

JACOB STIRRED, MOANING, as he slowly began to awaken from a deep, dreamless sleep. His head ached fiercely, but the pain began to abate as his senses returned to him. He opened his eyes, vision focusing slowly from a blur to reveal an off-white ceiling above his head. It wasn't familiar.

Sitting upright hastily, he glanced around. He lay on a simple bed in an unadorned room. His tunic, gloves, and sword belt had been removed and hung over the endpost of the bed, boots laid beside them on the sturdy, but scuffed wood floor. A small table sat at the foot of the bed, laden with a stoneware jug and cups, but otherwise, the room was unfurnished. A window covered with gauzy curtains let in the soft glow of sunlight filling the room.

For a brief moment before he opened his eyes, he had thought that the events of the last night had been a dream. It was difficult now to picture the chaos of the battle. He had never been in this room before, but he knew exactly where he was.

Swinging his legs off the bed, he stood experimentally. His legs felt rubbery and he was light-headed, but he managed to support his weight. Ambling slowly over to the window, he drew the curtains. He took in an amazed breath as he gazed outside.

A city bustled outside the window, filled with wood and brick buildings lining cobblestone streets. People swarmed through the streets, dressed in robes and archaic outfits of tunics and cloaks. Signs hung over doorways, painted with a symbol of the goods or services provided therein. As Jacob glanced down the street, he saw a fruit stand he recognized, a small boy looking for his lost dog, and a street magician playing expensive tricks on unwary passers-by. He had never been here before, but he knew them all.

He was in the town of Shelas. He was in Aurius, the *real* Aurius.

And he was Garrett here.

Each breath he drew in as he gazed out at the town lifted his spirits. The real world was gone and he was surrounded by a world of magic, of honor, of kings and heroes and gold and all very tangible things. How many times had he daydreamed of this very thing happening? And yet, he had never dared to dream that it actually would.

The door opened behind him, and a gentle voice stated, "Oh."

Jacob turned away from the window and his heart leaped. Serina stood at the other end of the room, the real Serina, his first love. Her unusual clothes had never looked more natural as they did wrapped around the slender body of smooth, fair skin before him. Her face was perfect, exactly as it was rendered in the game, soft, light brown hair flowing down to her shoulders, wide, crystal blue eyes gazing at him. She was even more beautiful in person than she was in the game, her smooth, oval-shaped face, her delicate frame, the smooth curves of her legs. She was like an angel standing before him. And she smiled at him.

"You're already awake," she remarked. Her voice was like music in his ears, gentle and light. Even in those few words, he had heard that her voice was just faintly softer and warmer than it had sounded in the game. It was her voice, and it suited her like none other could, better than the voice actress that had portrayed her in the game.

"How are you feeling?" she asked.

"I'm..." *Ecstatic!* he thought. He could barely control himself with Serina standing just a few paces away, so real and gentle. Trying to steady his pounding heart, he recited from the game, "Better, thanks." He realized his own voice sounded nothing like the Garrett of the game. His was much higher pitched and slightly nasal, completely lacking the confident power of the real Garrett. But then, he hadn't become Garrett. Jacob had replaced him.

"My name is Serina," she stated. He loved the way it rolled off her tongue.

"I'm Garrett."

Her smile widened as she tilted her head slightly. "It's nice to meet you, Garrett." The words made him feel as if he could fly. He knew he was going to love being Garrett, far more than being Jacob Marshall.

"Where am I?" he asked, following the script of the game he had almost entirely memorized.

"Shelas," Serina answered as she stepped into the room. "Some of our city guard found you in the forest when the astronomers saw the light coming from Merakis." Her expression fell as she poured some water from the jug into a cup. Jacob walked over to her and took the proffered drink. "What happened last night?"

He averted his eyes. "The town was attacked." Serina gasped, sinking onto the bed. He held the cup absently, flashes of the previous night flitting behind his eyes. The hauntingly real features of the monsters, obscured by darkness, melded with the rendered figures from the game, creating a terrifying mental image, and even the name of the beasts sent a shiver up Jacob's spine. "Orlocs attacked the town." He hesitantly lowered himself onto the bed beside her, just like the real Garrett had done in the game, but she only gazed at him, horrified at what he'd said.

"That's awful!"

Jacob only nodded. His stomach tightened as he remembered his escape, fleeing the town alone and leaving its people to their fate like a coward.

"I should have tried to help them," he remarked, eyes on the floor at his feet.

"No! Don't say that," Serina argued, and she laid a hand on his leg. The touch sent a shiver of delight through his body. "If you had stayed behind, you might've…" The fact that she was too innocent to even admit to death caused his heart to swell, and the village of Merakis soon left his mind.

"Were there any other survivors?" he asked, realizing his voice sounded stiff and forced. Serina only shook her head, glancing away. He felt silly repeating the words she should already know, and it was obvious in his voice. He was going to have to work on his acting being here.

"It seems like there are more orlocs every day," Serina remarked sadly. "The city guard lost someone just last week fighting to keep them out of town." Jacob gazed at her despondently. She looked like a hurt child, and all he wanted to do was try to make her pain go away.

Turning his head, he concentrated hard, trying to say his lines as he always imagined he would in this situation, making them genuine and expressive.

"I'm going to stop them."

Serina glanced at him quickly, stunned. "You can't mean that!"

"It's my destiny. I passed the Divine Test and pledged my vow last night that I would save Aurius from the orlocs and darkness, just before the town was attacked." He glanced down, pulling his pendant out from beneath his shirt.

Serina drew in a breath as she glimpsed the amber teardrop. "The Hero's pendant! You're the chosen one?" Jacob nodded, gazing at the crude metal pendant. Serina shook her head. "But, nobody even knows where the orlocs are coming from."

I do, Jacob thought as he slid the pendant beneath his shirt again. *And maybe I can stop them sooner, be a bigger hero than Garrett.* Knowing the answers to the mysteries of his quest in advance could make it much easier.

"It's too dangerous."

Now Jacob shook his head, trying to summon all the emotion the words had in the game. "It's more important now than ever that I go. Someone must pay for what happened to Merakis." Silence fell over the room. The bustling streets outside could be heard through the closed window.

Jumping suddenly to her feet, Serina spun to face him and exclaimed, "Then let me go with you!" He smiled before he remembered that he was supposed to be shocked by this announcement, and he gazed wide-eyed up at her.

"You want to come with me? But why?"

"I can help," she offered hastily, sitting on the bed facing him. "I've seen too many people die from orloc attacks. I just want to see the world… healed." The last word came out hesitantly, glancing at him from the corner of her eye as if seeking his permission to say it. He knew why she had put the peculiar emphasis on the word, but disregarded it as Garrett had done.

"It will be dangerous." He couldn't give her the defying tone the words had in the game, and stated it as simply a fact.

"I know. But it will be more dangerous for all of us if the orlocs aren't stopped, soon. Please, let me come with you."

He knew he was supposed to refuse until she finally relented, but he hated the thought of hurting her feelings. More still, he knew that if he did, she would come into danger later when she snuck out of the city to follow him, and he wasn't sure he, without any knowledge of fighting, would be able to save her.

"Okay," he answered, "but only if you promise to be careful." She beamed, her smile seeming to light up the room in her joy.

"Oh, thank you!" Flashing straight, pearly white teeth, she leaned forward and hugged him quickly. A scent of lavender wafted up from her body in the moment she pressed herself against him. Sobering, she stood before him and clasped her hands together. "I swear I'll do everything I can to help you." He could only smile back at her, dizzy from her embrace and suddenly tongue-tied now that the dialogue was his to provide.

"You'd better rest," she continued. "You need to regain your strength. Whenever you're ready to go, I'll be ready."

"Okay," he replied lamely.

"If you need anything, just call me."

"Okay."

Eyes glittering, she skipped out of the room. Pausing at the door, she smiled back at him for a moment. Jacob could feel his heart pounding, still reeling from the feeling of her arms around his neck. She was like a porcelain doll with an inner glow that shone onto everything that saw her, beautiful, delicate, and fragile, to be held and admired and protected from a harsh and ugly world. He suddenly felt guilty, knowing what pains would come to her for his allowing her to join him, but he couldn't bear to leave her.

That brilliant smile stayed in view until the door closed completely behind her. Jacob leaned back on his hands and grinned up at the ceiling, overwhelmed by his first meeting with the girl he had adored for so long. He could not have asked for anything more, and he uttered a silent thanks to whatever force had brought him there.

Serina wanted Jacob to linger at the town for a few days and recover, but he found himself getting bored quickly. For two days he hung around the small house where Serina lived with the elderly woman who had found her abandoned in a forest and adopted her. He wandered the city when he had the chance, but though he marveled at the city being real, much larger than it had been in the game, he had seen it all before, and exploring the town didn't hold his interest for long. He had no money, at least none that was accepted in Aurius, and he protested when Serina spent her savings to stock up on supplies for their journey.

"It's no problem," she stated with a smile. "This is the day I've been saving up for." Jacob could only smile back and vow to repay her someday.

They left on the morning of the third day after Jacob had arrived. He stood in the sparsely furnished room where he had been staying, practicing drawing and sheathing his sword. The action wasn't natural, and it took precise arm movements to slide the blade out and back away in the scabbard smoothly and quickly. He felt embarrassed when he thought back to his stumble at the inn in Merakis, and fear tickled his mind when he thought of what might have happened if he hadn't been so lucky.

He thought briefly of the life he'd left behind and wondered what people were thinking about him. He thought of Emily, Eric, Karen, and Jasmine, the people he'd met only the day before he came here, and the people he'd met at the convention, whose names he had already forgotten. His mother might miss him, but she had his stepfather Ted to keep her company. *Christina probably doesn't miss me, and none of my friends deigned to contact me over the summer.* The thought brought a bitter frown to his face, but at that moment, the door opened behind him.

He turned and a smile grew instantly on his face as Serina stepped inside, carrying a staff just taller than her, topped with a large, ornate round design accented with shimmering crystals.

I could stay here forever, he thought. *I have everything I need right here, and nothing I left behind is worth going back to.*

"Are you ready to go?" she asked, flashing her sweet smile at him.

"Yep." He reached over to the leather backpack full of supplies hanging over the endpost of the bed and swung it over his shoulders. "Are you?"

"As ready as I'll ever be," she stated nervously. "I've never even left town before."

Jacob smiled, wanting to touch her but afraid to push her away. "Don't worry. Everything will be okay."

She smiled up at him in response. "Let's go." Turning, she walked out of the room, Jacob following close behind. Down the short hallway outside his room, they came to the common room, where the elderly woman, stooped but sharp-witted, waited for them.

"Serina, won't you reconsider?" The woman laid a leathery hand on the girl's shoulder, and Serina hugged her.

"Don't worry, Adella, everything will be fine. I can't just hide here while the world gets more dangerous every day."

"I'll protect her, ma'am," Jacob added. "I swear." As Serina leaned down to adjust her boots, Adella shot him a suspicious glare. He recoiled slightly, surprised by the animosity in her expression.

Smiling convincingly, the old woman stated in a joking tone, "You'd better, or I'll never forgive you." Jacob felt uneasy. He remembered when he returned to Serina's home later in the game, the old woman had fainted from both grief and joy to see her adopted daughter again, and only then had it become clear how Adella cared for Serina.

Does she blame me for Serina leaving, since I told her she could come?

Before either of them could say anything more, Serina stood and remarked, "Don't worry, Adella, we'll be fine. Come on, Garrett." Taking his hand, she steered him toward the front door. Adella watched him with a hard expression, but he only smiled back at her.

"Thanks for all your hospitality, ma'am," Jacob stated quickly as Serina opened the door.

"Be careful, Serina," the old woman called back.

"We will, Adella," the girl answered. "Goodbye!" The door closed behind Serina and only the busy city streets surrounded them. She glanced at him sheepishly. "I'm sorry about that. Adella's just suspicious of strangers."

He smiled at her, the old woman's sharp words and eyes fading from his mind in the light of Serina's smile. "It's okay. She cares a lot about you."

Serina brushed a lock of hair out of her eyes. "Well, shall we go?" Turning, they climbed down the stairs and out into the cobbled street.

"Serina!" came a voice to the side. A middle-aged man ran up to them. "Is it true you're leaving?"

"I'm afraid so," she answered.

"Oh, I'll dearly miss seeing you around my shop." The man's eyes drooped sadly. "The children will be so disappointed."

"I'm sorry, Mr. Potter." She took his hand in both of hers. "I'll miss your cakes and your stories." Jacob, watching the exchange quietly, couldn't even feel jealous of the man stealing her attention. She looked so sweet and caring speaking to the baker that he couldn't bear to desire anything more of her.

"Please travel safely," the baker continued. "And please come back someday."

"I will, Mr. Potter. And you take care of yourself."

"I will. Goodbye, Serina."

"Goodbye, Mr. Potter." The baker sent Jacob a brief glance before turning and continuing on his way. Jacob watched him walk off, wondering how many lives Serina had touched in this town. Little wonder Adella had been so suspicious of him.

"Sorry for the delay," Serina offered, startling him out of his reverie.

"It's okay. It looks like the people here really care about you." She didn't answer, and Jacob saw a flash of sadness pass across her eyes that wrenched his heart. If only he could tell her that he knew what bothered her, and that he understood. *But how would I know, having only met her two days ago?*

The rest of the journey out of the city was occasionally interrupted by other people offering similar blessings, but Jacob noticed that many people only gave her a curt nod or stared at her, despite the fact that they were both clearly prepared for travel. Serina appeared not to notice the reactions and walked along with a bright smile on her face, taking in everything around her for the last time.

"I can't believe I'm finally leaving Shelas," she remarked. "I'm a little nervous about it."

"Me, too," Jacob replied honestly. He had big shoes to fill, and he still had no idea how to use the sword hanging by his side.

Soon, they came upon the open gates leading out of the city, set in a fourteen foot high limestone wall. One of the guards standing post at the gate raised an eyebrow as they approached.

"You going to pick mushrooms, girl?" the guard asked skeptically. Serina and Jacob stopped before him.

"No, sir," she answered, "we're going traveling."

"Traveling?" the guard echoed incredulously, and he glanced between them with a baffled expression. "You know orlocs are everywhere, don't you?"

"We know." Serina flashed him her sweetest smile as she touched Jacob's arm. "But we'll be safe."

"I wouldn't be so sure." The guard shot Jacob a dubious look before glancing at the woods and plains beyond the city walls.

"Hey," Jacob protested, trying not to betray his uneasiness. "Do you think I carry this around for decoration?" He gestured to his sword, the guard following his gaze, and prayed that the guard wouldn't challenge his assertion. But the city guard only shrugged and stepped aside to let them pass.

"Whatever. But if I were you, I'd hold off traveling until it becomes safe."

Over her shoulder, Serina responded, "We'd be waiting a long time if we did that. Thank you, sir. Goodbye!" Waving at him, she ran forward lightly onto the dirt road leading away from town. Grinning, Jacob jogged after her. He watched her lean her head back and close her eyes as she ran down the dirt road, completely carefree, hair flowing gracefully in the wind.

At the top of the first hill overlooking the land around, she stopped, gazing around with a hand over her heart. Jacob cringed as he came up beside her, clasping a stitch tightening his side. He had yet to see Serina look so solemn as she gazed across the landscape.

"It's so big." Her eyes swept over the endless rolling plains dotted with groves of trees as a breeze whispered past them, gently rustling their hair and clothes. Jacob followed her gaze. "I never realized how huge and open the world is past the city walls." Turning, she glanced back at the town, the size of a quarter at arm's length behind them. "It looks so small. The sea always looked so close in the maps I've seen, but I can't see it at all. I can't even see the next town."

"Yeah," Jacob stated, cursing himself for being unable to say something more profound. The world seemed a lot bigger than home. It had taken less than two hours for Eric to drive to the convention, a journey that would probably take more than a day to walk. The convention seemed so far away, so long in the past now, and he felt a brief pang with the thought that he might never see any of his friends again.

The grief disappeared as soon as it had come, however, when his eyes passed across Serina. The view was spectacular, no concrete or cars or power lines or anything to mar the green hills, and unencumbered with schoolwork or cellular phones or any of the elements of modern life, he felt more free than he ever had.

Noticing his eyes on her, Serina turned and smiled at him. "So, er, where are we going?" He faced the open plains again, letting the sunlight warm his face.

"South. They'll have more information on the orlocs in Dekaal." She nodded understandingly.

"You really know a lot about the world, don't you?" she asked admiringly.

Jacob rubbed the back of his neck, chuckling nervously. "Well, I've just studied maps and stuff."

She giggled and took his hand. "Okay, then, we'll go to Dekaal. We'd better get moving, it's a long journey." Jacob nodded, unable to wipe the idiotic grin off his face as he followed her down the hill, hoping she wouldn't run with the same spring in her step as she had earlier. He dreaded her knowing how out of shape he was.

"It's so quiet," Serina stated, her voice soft as if out of respect for the silence.

"Yeah," Jacob replied, not wanting to intrude on the silence either. Having lived in a medium-sized city all of his life, he was used to some level of noise at all hours of the day. Shelas had been a reprieve for him, and even after sunset, there were still a few people out breaking the silence of night. But out here, there were no sounds aside from their own footfalls on the fading trail and the wind whispering through the trees and grasses.

And a sudden rustling of grass nearby.

Jacob and Serina spun, facing the source of the noise. He tried to draw his sword quickly, but he pulled at the wrong angle and the scabbard flailed wildly. Cursing himself, he slid the sword back in carefully, then drew it slowly, but properly. He thought of the animated movements Garrett had made in battles in the game and tried to picture himself doing them as he gazed out at the unnervingly quiet fields. Serina brandished her staff beside him, not reacting to his struggle drawing his sword. His heart thumped in his chest and his arms began to ache from holding up the steel sword.

Another rustle, and Serina pointed. "There!"

Following her gaze, he saw it. A dark spot rose over the grass, half concealed by a lone tree. It had the broad frame and sunken face of a bulldog, but its hairless skin was dark as jet and it had no visible ears. The orloc shifted, its waist-high form poorly hidden behind the tree as it studied them. It was stalking them, Jacob realized, just like a cat, and now it waited to see if they would run. Jacob shuffled his feet, heart hammering in fear. He could see two yellow orbs, eyes with no pupil gazing between the blades of grass at them.

Please don't hurt her, he prayed inwardly.

At that moment, it sprang.

4

THE ORLOC WAS upon them in seconds, leaping into the air ten feet from them. Jacob lunged to one side, Serina to the other. Landing with a thump that shook the ground beneath his feet, the creature spun toward Jacob and pounced before he had fully regained his footing. Gasping, he threw himself to the side and brought his sword down on the monster. It stumbled with a snarl of pain as the sword chopped down on its shoulder, but Jacob noticed that with the way he swung the weapon, it hadn't even broken the creature's skin. The orloc swung its head around in a blur, and before he could pull himself safely away, its teeth sank into his wrist and halfway up his arm with a grip like a vise. He howled in pain and dropped to his knees as the razor-sharp fangs dug into his flesh. He couldn't even gather the strength to raise his sword in spite of the agony.

Suddenly, a large, round blur fell down onto the top of the creature's head with a crack. Jacob barely glimpsed Serina shifting her body to swing the butt of her staff up against the underside of the orloc's jaw just as it released his arm. She hopped back as the orloc turned to bare bloodstained teeth at her. Jacob thrust his sword forward as it began to pounce, the point digging into its flesh up underneath its ribs. It stopped there, Jacob unable to drive the blade deeper on his own power, but as he pulled the weapon back, a glimmer of hope alighted in his heart. The sword tip was stained with blood.

The creature pounced as it turned back to face him, but he threw himself out of its path this time. His left arm hung limply from the elbow down, throbbing painfully, but he kept his attention defiantly on the orloc. He slipped as he tried to regain his footing and fell onto his side, knuckles smarting as he landed on the hand still gripping his sword tightly. Serina's staff whacked the orloc again before it could attack him.

"Quick! Get its neck!"

Rolling quickly into a sitting position, Jacob stabbed his sword into the creature's neck, though it still didn't penetrate far. The monster thrashed against the attack, but pinned in between Jacob's sword and Serina's staff, it couldn't escape. His hand sweated and ached inside his glove and he struggled to keep his grip on the hilt. Gathering his strength, he lunged to his feet and forward, pressing the sword against the side of the orloc's neck. Serina pulled her staff away and jumped back as Jacob's weight threw the beast over onto its side. It continued thrashing its limbs, but couldn't manage to get to its feet, and its snarls became strangled. Jacob leaned against his sword, keeping the orloc pinned down and trying to stay out of reach of its swinging claws.

Panting, he eased the pressure on the orloc, drew in close, and let his weight fall onto the sword on its neck. Finally, the blade broke through, sliding through the creature's flesh until it hit the ground on the other side. The creature shrieked pitifully, its struggle diminishing to twitches of its limbs.

After a long moment, it fell still.

Jacob collapsed to his knees, too weary to even step away from the dead creature.

"Garrett!" Serina cried as she ran around the orloc's eternally open mouth and lolling tongue to crouch beside him. "Are you alright?" He only moaned in pain, his arm throbbing anew. Putting his good arm around her shoulders, she helped him stand and led him some paces away from the orloc's body.

Gently, she lowered him onto the grass. His hands and knees trembled, and he half expected the monster to rise and attack again.

Taking his left arm gingerly in one hand, she lowered the head of her staff over the bite wound. She closed her eyes and spoke something under her breath. The crystals embedded in the head of her staff began to glow, shining brilliantly onto his bloodied sleeve.

Suddenly, Jacob felt the flesh of his arm knit back together. He gasped as the pain abated. A moment later, the crystals dimmed and Serina opened her eyes and drew back. He gazed in shock at his arm. His sleeve was torn and warmly wet, and even part of his glove had been stained, but the pain was gone, and he could feel no trace of the wound.

"That was amazing!" he breathed.

Serina looked away sadly. "It-it's nothing."

Jacob flexed his fingers, feeling the way his muscles moved. It felt no different than it ever had. "It's like it never happened. There aren't even any scars."

Serina stood abruptly and walked a few paces away, arms wrapped around her body. She didn't meet his eyes. "It's not natural, what I can do. I… I should've told you about it." Jacob glanced up, so entranced by the miraculous healing of his wound that he had forgotten about the reaction he expected Serina to have. He stood and walked over to her, remembering a line from later in the game when her healing magic had first been brought up. "I'm sorry. I just wanted…"

"What you do," he cut in, now standing beside her, "is beautiful. If you hadn't healed me, it might have taken weeks for it to recover." She gazed desperately up at him, clearly wanting to believe his words.

"You can't really mean that." Her voice sounded choked.

"Sure I do," he stated. "Your magic is amazing." She smiled sadly, then leaned forward against his chest. He clutched her bare shoulders, heart pounding as it had during the battle.

"Thank you," she uttered. "I just want to help people, but whenever they see me use magic, they get scared."

"They don't deserve your help." In Aurius, he remembered, magic came from within, passed down through bloodlines to create powerful mages. The innate power a mage had was sacred, and all care was taken to ensure that his power remained intact and that his genes were passed on and children nurtured. It was strange enough for Serina, who was abandoned at birth, to be able to use magic so powerful. But the way she cast magic through crystals, or forests, or the very ground around her, was strange and deeply suspicious to those who understood magic. And so, he thought angrily, her extraordinary and unique ability to heal, a magic lost to those who claimed to understand it, was spurned, as was she.

Sniffling, she pulled back with a faint smile. "We'd better get moving again before more of those… things show up." Jacob nodded, turning to glance at the ungainly body lying across the road several feet away. Fighting the fear that welled in his stomach just looking at the orloc, even knowing it was dead, he walked over to it and pulled his sword out.

He was about to slide the sword away when Serina suddenly asked, "Don't you have a cloth? For… for cleaning your sword?" He looked at her peculiarly and she looked bashful. "It'll rust if you don't clean it."

"Oh," he answered, "right." He glanced around, finding nothing of use, then reluctantly leaned over the foul-smelling creature and wiped the flat of his blade off on its hide. Only the wet glint of the sunlight against its dark skin showed where the blood was on its ugly body. He shivered at the sight, shaken by the life-threatening danger the orloc posed. It was something he had never experienced before. His pulse failed to slow as he recalled the hectic fight.

"I-I'm sorry. I don't mean to…"

"No, it's okay." Jacob swallowed around a lump in his throat as he gazed at the dead orloc. He decided to tell her the truth, at least part of it. "Where I come from, we don't need swords." Serina smiled sadly at him.

"Merakis must have been a really peaceful village."

"Well, actually, I'm..." Turning to face her, he paused mid-sentence. "Yeah. Yeah, it was." He walked over to her. Tilting the sword up slightly, he glanced down its smooth metal surface. "I just... don't know how to use this."

"Well, you don't want to swing it like a club." Holding her staff up and out in both hands, she moved across the ground on the balls of her feet. "The sword should be an extension of your own arm." Swinging her staff around gracefully, she pivoted and brought it down in a perfect imitation of a swordfighter's stance.

Jacob gaped at her.

She giggled, lowering her staff. "I cared for one of the city guard once and I got to watch a training practice." He grinned in response, then raised the sword to gaze at it again.

"An extension of my arm..." He tried to think of the martial arts and fantasy movies he had seen and the maneuvers the actors had performed with their swords. Trying to picture his sword as an extension of his arm, he swung the blade slowly through the air across, then down and back up.

Serina beamed at him. "And don't be afraid to move your feet. A lot of swordfighting is proper balance and countering with your footwork." He nodded, shifting positions as he practiced a few more swings. Serina pushed a lock of hair back from her eyes with an embarrassed smile. "I'm afraid that's as far as my knowledge goes, though."

"That's okay." He moved forward and backward, balancing the weapon's weight in his posture. "I feel better already." Serina's lips parted in a wide smile as he glanced back at her. Standing straight, he sheathed the sword. "We'd better keep moving, though." She nodded and walked beside him as they continued down the dirt road leading south.

The rest of the day passed uneventfully and the hours slipped slowly away as they crossed from one horizon to the next. It was strange to Jacob. In the game, the world outside of towns, landmarks, mountains, and other places of interest was nothing but a way to get from one place to another. Traveling from one town to the next took a manner of minutes frequently interspersed with random battles against monsters, designed to help increase the abilities of the characters through experience. For the journey to Dekaal to be a significant span of time, days of constant walking, was something he had never anticipated. It was wonderful to have more time alone with Serina, but it was going to be a long few days.

And his feet became sore just a few hours into the day.

At dusk, a long, quiet, dull day later, he gratefully accepted Serina's suggestion to stop and set up camp for the night. He could only imagine how many miles they had trekked that day. The world had never seemed so big.

As he set up the tent they would sleep in, worry gnawed at his heart. Sleeping in a tent at night kept the group completely safe until morning in the game, but with everything being far more real here, he wasn't sure it would be enough.

By the time he had the tent pitched, Serina had a fire going. He groaned as he dropped down cross-legged in front of it.

"Are you alright?"

"Yeah." He rubbed his feet. "Just sore."

She smiled in response. "I know how you feel." He smiled gratefully at her, but she didn't appear uncomfortable at all. Swinging his pack off his shoulders, he dug through it for some of the dried meat and biscuit they had stocked up on.

"How are you feeling?" she asked as he portioned out some food for each of them.

"I'm alright." His feet ached fiercely, but he didn't want to burden her with his complaints. "I've just never been this alone for this long."

"Me neither." She sat across the fire from him, fingers entwined at arm's length around her shins, gazing up at the night sky. She smiled. "It's kind of nice."

It was nice, he thought. Sometimes, he wondered if he only did his costuming and played video games so much just so he could be someone else. But out here in the wide, open, and empty plains, with no one to judge him and no one to impress, he could really be himself. The problem was that he wasn't entirely certain who that was.

He simply answered, "Mm." He hoped he had the survival skills to get them safely to Dekaal. Serina had assured him that they had enough food for the trip, and they had passed enough streams not to have to worry about water, but what if they ran out of either before arriving? He couldn't hunt, that was certain, and he had no way of knowing how to find wild foods or whether a type of berry or mushroom was poisonous.

At the moment, however, that was his least concern regarding food. He grimaced as he tugged with his teeth at another bite of dry, flavorless meat. Serina giggled at his attempt. He shot her a dirty look, but quickly sobered, feeling guilty for glaring at her.

"I'm sorry," she stated, trying not to smile. "Here." Reaching into a pouch on her belt, she retrieved a tiny burlap sachet. In the light of the fire, he saw her pinch her fingers in, reach over, and sprinkle a fine herb on his remaining chunk of meat. He took another bite. The meat was still tough and dry as jerky, but the herb improved its flavor immensely.

He smiled his appreciation. “Thanks.” She smiled brightly, returning to her food, and the rest of the meal passed quietly.

The last rays of daylight faded and night fully fell over the land. Stars winked to life above, forming a glittering blanket overhead. Jacob gazed up at the sky, stunned at its brightness. He was used to the night sky being a shroud of pure darkness held just at bay by the light of streetlamps. He never realized how rich and full the sky looked out in the open. Even the slim, Cheshire-cat grin of the moon illuminated the land around them so that he could see well enough.

Yawning, Serina stretched her arms over her head. “We’d better get to bed. We have a lot of traveling to do tomorrow.” Jacob rubbed his swollen feet, not looking forward to the proposition.

“Will the tent keep us safe?”

“The orlocs seem to be confused by tents. They don’t react if nothing’s happening inside, and if they hear movement, they seem to think the entire tent is some creature and usually shy away. It should keep us safe this far north. There aren’t so many orlocs up here. At least,” she glanced sidelong at him uneasily, “everyone thought so, until Merakis…” Jacob frowned. Though he was interested to find a reasonable explanation as to why the tents kept people safe, he still could only hope its psychological protection would work this night.

“Well, we only saw the one orloc today, right? And we traveled a long way.” Her expression grew distant, her voice quiet. “It was so close to town, though.” She looked worried.

Clearing his throat, Jacob stated, “I’m sure we’ll be fine.” She nodded, seeming to shake off her worry. Reluctantly rising to his feet, he kicked dirt onto the fading fire and stamped it out. As the deep blue of night fell over them, they crawled into the tent and the two bedrolls within. Serina pulled the blanket around her almost fully dressed, curling up with her back to him. He removed his gloves, boots, sword belt, headband, and tunic, laying them on the ground beside him. He thought about removing his shirt as well, but he felt strangely as if he would be imposing on her if he did. He gazed at her back for a moment before crawling into his own bedroll in his shirt and trousers. Silence fell over them, an oppressing noiselessness marked only by the distant chirping of crickets outside.

“Goodnight, Garrett,” Serina stated sleepily.

“Goodnight.” After a pause, he added, “Pleasant dreams.”

She murmured, sounding pleased, but said nothing more. Jacob lied for a long while staring at the pointed tip of the tent above him. Despite being exhausted from walking all day, he found he couldn’t fall asleep. The ground was hard and uncomfortable, the bedroll and floor of the tent offering little padding for his stiff back. He shifted onto his side, but the ground seemed to dig harder into his shoulder and hip, and his neck strained from his head lying too low. Reaching out, he grabbed his tunic, wadded it up under his head, and tried to relax. He could hear Serina breathing softly and steadily over his shoulder.

He couldn't stop thinking about the orloc attack that morning. Just the thought of it made him tremble. He could hardly imagine now the things he had done to overcome it. And once again, he was saved only by virtue of someone else's intervention. Serina had been braver than he had. In the game, the first monsters that he faced were simple, almost harmless creatures that allowed him to learn the game's unique battle system. If that creature was weak, he thought, he couldn't imagine fighting some of the beasts he would face later in his journey. He couldn't use a sword, and he had never even fired a gun in his life. He knew that fighting with his hands and feet like some characters did would be wholly ineffective. He had to learn fighting techniques, but when would he have the time, or someone to teach him?

Then, he thought of Runic Seals, the magical special attacks that the characters learned throughout the game. Would he be able to perform those attacks as well? Perhaps that was what he needed to fight effectively. The thought of learning such amazing abilities brought a smile to his face. He was Garrett here. He would find a way to fight and overcome the challenges set before him.

He fell asleep imagining his victory over the villain of the game, the celebrations and honors he would receive, and the praise from Serina for saving the world.

WHEN JACOB AWOKE, the tent glowed with light from the risen sun outside. Serina was gone, her bedroll neatly folded beside his. He hastened to slip on his tunic, gloves, boots, and sword belt, then tied the headband around his head, wishing he didn't have to wear it. It was an unfamiliar sensation having it wrapped about him.

Crawling out of the tent, he found Serina crouched in front of the reignited fire, holding over it a cast-iron pan filled with sizzling bacon, fried eggs, and slices of bread wedged against the side of the pan. She looked up and smiled as he emerged from behind the tent flap. Never had he had a more pleasant awakening.

"Good morning. I thought you might like breakfast when you woke up. Did you sleep well?"

"Great," he answered with a grin, hoping she couldn't see him rubbing the back of his hipbones. His feet felt better, though still somewhat sore. He hoped they would stiffen up as his journey progressed. How long would a journey of a few minutes in the game take in a world of painfully real proportions?

Using a meat fork, Serina removed some bacon and eggs from the pan and dropped them onto the toast he held out. It was a refreshingly familiar meal to him, and flavorful enough to more than make up for the dried meat last night. He felt energized and optimistic.

"How long have you been awake?"

"Not long. Only an hour or so."

"An…" His eyes widened incredulously. "Why didn't you wake me?"

"I thought you could use the sleep. It's okay, I don't mind."

He blinked, suddenly realizing that his sleep pattern was attuned to a different life. He had thought it strange that there had been such a stark difference in town between dusk and darkness. Shelas had seemed to shut down once daylight had faded, and the entire town awoke long before him every morning. But, he supposed that without streetlamps or cars, it was difficult to operate in the darkness. He frowned. With his sleeping schedule on summer vacation causing him to normally stay up several hours after dark and rise three or four hours after dawn, he must really seem an outsider.

"Well, we should go," she stated, shaking the grease from the pan into the fire. The flames flared and hissed, flinging sparks in all directions. Jacob tensed, worried that the sparks would catch her clothes and ignite them, but she seemed unconcerned. Together, they dismantled the tent, it folding into a lumpy bundle that tied to the top of the backpack. Hefting the pack onto his back, they began their trek into the empty world again.

Long days filled with endless walking stretched away into memory. As eager as Jacob was to learn the special moves he knew would be able to defeat their enemies easily, he was glad that they didn't run across any more orlocs. Serina told him stories of her life in Shelas and she persuaded him to conjure tales about his past in Merakis, but often, they walked in silence. He grew bored and almost wished for an encounter with another evil creature to break the monotony. Each day he awoke a little less surprised, though no less pleased, to find he was still really in Aurius, and each day it seemed more real to him.

At first, he tried keeping track of the days that passed as they traveled across the countryside, but he found himself soon losing count. It was easy to forget about the goings-on elsewhere in the world as each new day rose on a land inhabited only by they two.

By his estimate, it had been about a week by the time they finally arrived at Dekaal. The scholars' town, residence of Lord Kyutu, was larger than Shelas, and the city rose up quickly around them as they passed its entrance. The town of brick buildings lay nestled about the base of Kyutu's castle, and Jacob could see its towers, topped with pennants blowing in the gentle summer breeze, rising over the buildings on the other side of the town.

The streets bustled, people clothed in robes and tunics swarming around Jacob and Serina as soon as their feet touched cobblestone. The townspeople took little notice of the travelers as they rushed to their destinations. Jacob's eyes wandered across the town, taking in the old buildings, the clay tiled roofs, and the people. It had been so long since he was last in a city he had nearly forgotten how strange and ancient this fantastic world was. Shreds of various conversations drifted across his ears from people all around as they moved through the crowd.

"Do you think the professor will give us a quiz today?"

"I was just so tired, I could barely make dinner."

"The captain of the guard is so handsome! I wish I could get some time alone with him."

Voices murmured all around them. "Who should we ask for information on the orlocs?" Serina asked.

Jacob shook his head. "I don't know." The city was enormous. In the game, it didn't take long to talk to every individual person in town, and most of them offered information useful to their journey. He already knew everything he needed to know, but he at least needed to make a show of finding it out for Serina or she would get suspicious. Besides, he wanted to relive the game exactly as he remembered it.

"I guess we should go to the school." He had learned a lot of useful information from the various people wandering around the classrooms and hallways, and it seemed a likely place to learn about the orlocs.

Serina giggled, and he glanced at her. She smiled at him, amused. "Which school?" He blinked. "There are four here."

"Oh, um…" He realized he shouldn't have been surprised. "The biggest one, I suppose." He felt his face reddening, embarrassed.

Serina laughed. "That sounds good." Jacob nodded, suddenly wondering how they were going to get to the school. If the town was so much bigger than he was used to, there would have to be a lot of streets he didn't recognize. He didn't even know if the largest school was the one he remembered. Thinking about it, he figured the school must be a lot bigger than he knew, as well. Each classroom in the game only held about a dozen people, and there were only a handful of classrooms in the building. Suddenly, the town seemed a lot bigger and more intimidating to him. Faced with such a very real city, he had no idea how he was going to talk to anyone. It was hard enough for him to strike up a conversation with someone in the real world.

Suddenly, a conversation between three older ladies wafted across his ears, one he recognized.

"I heard he skips sword practice almost every day."

"I heard he has prophetic dreams."

"I heard he sneaks out of the castle at night."

"Oh, yes, Muriel told me she saw him at the town square, *reading* of all things. It took guards from the castle to take him back."

Serina's head turned around to gaze at the gossiping women as they passed by. "I wonder who they're talking about."

"Makaidel," Jacob blurted out before he could stop himself. He cringed at his mistake.

Serina spun, gazing wide-eyed at him. "Lord Kyutu's son? How do you know that?"

"Um…" He tried to think quickly, but he was too focused on his own slip to come up with a plausible excuse. "I heard about him from someone in Merakis. The, uh…" He mentioned the first person that came to his mind from the ravaged town. "The archbishop."

"Oh."

Together, they managed to find their way through the city to the largest school. The outside of it looked like the entrance to some huge mansion, or even, Jacob thought, a country club. A wrought-iron fence circled the huge compound, set between short, square turrets of white brick topped with oil lanterns.

"Wow," Serina remarked as they walked down the long border of the fence. "Think of how long it must take to light all those lamps every night." Jacob only nodded, not knowing how an oil lamp was lit at all.

Inside the fence, the grounds were covered by perfectly tended grass, paths of white stone cut through them between the handsome buildings. Large trees with richly green, reaching branches lay scattered across the lawn, though no leaves could be seen littering the grass. A few students, decked in uniforms colored by school year, walked down the paths to different buildings. The entire scene was pristine and ideal, a haven in the middle of a troubled world.

Finally, they came upon the wide, arched gates leading into the school. The vast courtyard within was covered in stone and mortar, a fountain of clear water set in the center of it, surrounded at several paces by benches and stone flower boxes with neat arrangements of pansies, mums, begonias, daffodils, and snapdragons. Jacob felt out of place as they passed through the gates. His clothes were much rougher and less refined than the sharp, tailored uniforms that surrounded him, and dirtied by travel, he felt like a mangy dog among the students.

He glanced around uneasily. The students ignored them utterly or gazed at them with poorly concealed disgust as they strolled along. The boys, many of whom appeared his age, were well-groomed and handsome, and the girls were all china-doll figures with long curtains of perfectly straight, glossy hair and no flaws on their fair features, large eyes, and full, pouting lips. Jacob felt small and worthless under their scrutinizing eyes. High society teeming with delicate manners and wealthy backgrounds swirled around him, and he couldn't even fight to make up for his slovenliness. His head sank into his shoulders. He regretted coming to this school, and worse, it was bringing up uncomfortable memories of school at home.

"Can I," spoke a mocking voice, "help you?"

Jacob stopped in his tracks. He had been so intent on the jeering eyes to either side of him that he hadn't noticed the young man standing a few paces ahead that now gazed down his nose at them with an air of haughty authority. Jacob's throat went dry, and he was miserably reminded of his first day at school after his mother had moved to a rich neighborhood two years ago. A school of cliques, he with no allies had been quickly spurned and soon openly harassed in the hallways. Faced with another student who clearly belonged at the school and among the student body and knew it well, he froze, wanting only to turn tail and run.

"Oh, hi," Serina answered brightly beside him. Remembering her presence brought him back to the school he wasn't even attending and the students he had no reason to fear. "We were hoping to find some information here." The boy that addressed them turned his unforgiving gaze to her, his smirk widening faintly.

"Well, *you* look like you might be able to fit in," he answered, though his voice betrayed his disbelief, "but we don't give out information for free. If you," he chuckled spitefully, "can afford to attend, you have to visit the enrollment office." He gestured toward a large building over his shoulder, the wide roof supported by white marble pillars, with an almost imperceptible jerk of his head.

"Okay, thanks." She flashed him a friendly smile, not seeming to be affected by the boy's scoffing manner at all. Taking Jacob's hand, she led him around where the student stood rooted in their path and continued toward the administration building. Jacob wanted nothing more than to leave, especially since he already knew what they sought. He tried desperately to think of an excuse to leave and a way they could hear the information for themselves in a different manner, but it was difficult to concentrate with all the students around them staring. He could hardly even take comfort in Serina's hand holding his own. She didn't seem to notice the reactions to their passage at all, and there was no less spring in her step than there ever was.

Eventually, they reached the richly detailed mahogany doors leading into the administration building. Grasping the polished brass door handle, Serina swung the door open and stepped inside. Jacob's eyes widened at the interior of the building. Even out of the harsh glares of the students outside, he felt smaller still. With the huge entrance hall rising up to an elaborate skylight several stories above them, the polished marble floor reflecting the fountain in the center of the lobby, and the gilded banisters lining the huge staircase carpeted in oriental-style rugs, he felt less like he was in a school building than a nineteenth-century opera house.

"Wow," Serina breathed. "It's so glamorous." He wished he had her optimism, but he could only feel dirty and worthless standing among such elegance. Even the janitors there must look and act nicer than he did.

Turning, Serina crossed the polished floor toward an elaborate wood desk, where a middle-aged man shuffled through a sheaf of yellow paper. She made no reaction to the way her footfalls rang around the spacious room. Jacob tried to soften his steps as he followed after her, but he couldn't seem to prevent the sounds from spreading, and he was certain he would alert the entire building of his uninvited and unwelcome presence.

"Hi," Serina greeted as she stopped before the desk. The man behind the desk looked up swiftly, assessing her through round spectacles rimmed in gold wire. He glanced peculiarly at her, but without, Jacob noted with a faint echo of relief, the arrogant attitude with which the students had treated them.

"May I help you?" The man's eyebrows knitted together in confusion.

"I hope so," Serina answered with a smile and shrug. "We were hoping to find some information here."

The man behind the desk hesitated again, glancing up and down at them. "Are you students?"

"Oh, no." Serina's smile widened with an apologetic gesture. Jacob fiddled with his gloves, glad that she was leading the conversation. "We're travelers. We're just hoping to answer some questions."

Another baffled pause followed. The man behind the desk spoke slowly and removed his glasses. "What sort of information are you looking for?"

"Actually, we were hoping to find some information on… well, the orlocs."

The man drew back, eyes widening in utter bewilderment. He blinked rapidly several times.

"Anything you can tell us about them," Jacob spoke quickly. "Where they live, what causes them, um… habitats, anything."

"We want to know everything we can," Serina added. "We want to stop them." The man's eyes widened and eyebrows lowered even further.

"Stop them?"

Serina nodded pleasantly. "Or at least try to see if we can help someone else find a way to do so. We just don't know much about them, so we were hoping such a nice school as this would have more information." The man slowly replaced his glasses on his nose, seemingly comforted by her compliment.

"Well… I suppose we would have more information than a lot of places," he stated, mostly to himself. He cleared his throat and faced them again. "You would probably want to speak with our professor Phantis. He lives in town, in the market district. He usually has dinner at the Horse and Clover, the bartender will be able to show him to you. He's… unusually interested in the orlocs."

Serina flashed him a sweet smile. "Thank you very much, sir. We really appreciate your assistance." The man still looked confused, but nodded as she bowed and turned toward the entrance of the building. Jacob nodded stiffly, then followed her. The stares resumed as they returned outside and crossed the courtyard again, and he even heard open laughter he knew was directed at them.

He frowned. None of it had passed as it was supposed to. Anyone he approached in the game was willing to speak with him, other than those that already had a clear reason to dislike him personally. Most people offered him information directly helpful to his quest, with only a few complaining about the school or talking about their own meaningless lives. It had thrown him entirely off guard to come across people that reminded him of people at home. This world was so much more startlingly real than he had ever imagined it would be, far beyond the way it was portrayed in the game.

He felt as if he stepped out of water when they finally exited through the front gates of the school, the jeering and rejection like a weight that pressed in on him from all sides. As they stepped back onto the cobbled streets beyond, however, he still felt out of place, not knowing how this world of ancient technology and society functioned. It was easy to adjust to the game, as all the small things that made up daily life were disregarded. Here, everything was foreign to him.

Serina paused a few paces beyond the school gates, hand over her chin in thought. "Hmm… he said professor Phantis lives in the market district. I wonder where that is?" She glanced at him, but he could only shrug. Despite having traveled to this city so many times in the game he had played so often, he felt like he didn't know where anything was anymore.

She smiled. "I guess we'll just have to ask someone, then." Jacob followed her without responding. He didn't want to talk to anyone anymore, and wished he could just be alone. Alone, perhaps, with Serina. He was immensely grateful to have her as his ambassador to this strange world, even if she didn't realize it.

Quietly, they continued through the streets.

JACOB'S UNEASINESS SLOWLY faded as they traveled through the city. The townspeople that weren't too busy to pay them any heed treated them with amiable nods or greetings, and the city that bustled around them was far more welcoming to strangers than the school had been. When he didn't act suspicious, the town seemed to accept him.

His feet grew sore as he passed through street after street of hard, awkwardly round cobblestones. They were far rougher on his feet than the dirt path that had brought them to Dekaal, and his feet hadn't fully recovered from the unfamiliar exercise they had endured after simply walking for so long, even on softer ground. He had no idea how Serina could withstand it.

The sun began sinking toward the western horizon when they finally reached the market district and saw the wooden sign displaying a horse's head and a clover leaf.

"This professor really lives a long way from the school, doesn't he?" Serina remarked curiously as they sifted through the late afternoon crowd toward the tavern.

"Er, yeah." Jacob hadn't considered the oddity of it before. It hadn't been more than a minute-long journey in the game, but in real-life proportions, the journey was miles long, and the other professors at the school lived on the school grounds. His heart suddenly leaped in fear. He had been so unnerved by the reception at the school that he had entirely forgotten that seeking out Professor Phantis resulted in the first major battle of the game. He had only fought one enemy in his experience in the real Aurius, and though the impending fight had been an easy one in the game, the thought of facing something far more terrifying than the orloc that had nearly torn off his arm a few days ago made his knees tremble.

Before he could suggest waiting to seek out Phantis for another night, Serina entered the Horse and Clover. Swallowing hard, he followed her inside.

The interior of the tavern was faintly smoky, its dark wood walls dimly lit by the small windows at the front and lumps of candles on each table. As with the church in Merakis, Jacob was surprised by the size of the establishment, more than twice as large as it had appeared in the game with over twenty tables laid across the floor. Most of the tables were occupied, many of them with every chair filled. The sounds of dozens of conversations being spoken at once rang throughout the room as barmaids scurried about the floor in a frantic dance, balancing large platters on each arm.

"Oh, my." Serina's voice was nearly drowned out by the crowd. "It's so busy." Jacob nodded, unable to find his voice. "We should sit down until the bartender has some free time to see us." He glanced over at the long bar lining most of one wall. The bartender and another barmaid moved quickly back and forth down the many occupied stools facing them, serving drinks to several people at once. He followed Serina, shocked by the number of people filling the tavern at this hour. It took a moment before he remembered how these medieval cities shut down at nightfall, and it occurred to him that the dinner rush was probably just beginning.

Twisting their way through the crowd, they found a free table not far from the window and sat down. He wished there weren't so many people in the tavern. The room rang with conversations, the cacophony so loud he would have to yell for Serina to hear him. People all around ate and drank and spoke loudly. Bellowing laughter roared out from a few tables away, and one of the men seated there slapped the table so hard the mugs on it jumped. Jacob began feeling out of place again and wondered when they would be able to leave. As he watched, a group of people rose and left the tavern, but two more streamed in, and the bar seemed only to get busier.

A barmaid shuffled around them to serve another table. Jacob pressed himself against the table as her arm brushed his head, the tables arranged so close together that there was little room to maneuver between them. He thought about calling for her, but she was past as quickly as she came, and she seemed never to notice they were even there.

As she passed by them again, however, Serina held up a hand. "Excuse me…"

The barmaid spun, apparently seeing them for the first time. "Oh, hi! I didn't see you come in."

"That's alright." Serina smiled as the barmaid wiped her hand off on her apron.

"What'll you have?"

"Stew, if you have any."

The barmaid nodded, hands on her hips, then turned to Jacob. "And you?"

"Uh, me, too." He wasn't in the mood for stew, but he didn't know what else to order. He couldn't see a menu anywhere.

"What was that?" The barmaid leaned over to put her ear closer to his mouth, and before he realized what happened, he found himself inadvertently gazing down her low-cut blouse.

Screwing his eyes shut and turning away rapidly, he stammered, "I-I'll have stew, too." He kept his eyes closed tightly, not wanting to see anything he shouldn't again, though the barmaid seemed unconcerned, or unaware, of his actions.

"Alright." She turned to walk away.

"Oh, ma'am?" Serina called after her. Jacob opened his eyes, gazing at Serina.

"Yes?"

"We're looking for Professor Phantis of the Twin Oaks Academy. Is he here tonight?" Jacob glanced at the barmaid, careful to keep his gaze on her face.

"Phantis? Naw, I haven't seen him around here in a few days. Heard he's down with a flu." Jacob mouthed the words as the barmaid spoke them, remembering the conversation from the game.

"Oh, okay. Thanks."

"I'll be right back with your stew." With that, the barmaid turned and retreated toward the kitchen.

"Well, that's a shame," Serina stated. "I hope he's not seriously ill."

He's not, Jacob thought uncomfortably, wishing there was a way around the events soon to pass.

"Maybe we should see if there's anything we can do for him."

Jacob didn't answer. He gazed out the window at the street painted orange outside. It was much quieter than inside the tavern, only a few people left outside scurrying home for the night. It was strange to think of all of them as real people, with families and histories and dreams. He was used to them being nameless figures milling aimlessly about to fill the town. Some of them had even been rendered using the same models, so he would often find two or three of each townsperson in every town. Here, no one looked the same, and they were all individuals, all very real people. He was supposed to be the most important person in Aurius, but here, surrounded by so many others, he felt as insignificant as he did at home. He sighed.

Suddenly, Serina's eyes widened, and she gazed curiously at the entrance to the tavern.

"What's that young boy doing here alone?"

Twisting around in his chair, Jacob followed her gaze. A boy of junior high school age had stepped into the tavern, a large book bound in red leather wedged under his arm.

Makaidel, Jacob thought, feeling somewhat relieved. It was someone he knew, a familiar aspect in a wholly foreign world. It was comforting to see him, a reminder that he still knew this world, even if it was different from what he had been expecting.

Jacob watched as Makaidel strolled casually over to a table and sat down. Laying the massive book on the table, he opened it from a ribbon bookmark and began to read.

Noise on the table made Jacob turn back around. In the clamor of the tavern, he hadn't even noticed the barmaid return. Two steaming bowls of stew lay on the table before them.

"Thank you, miss," Serina stated sweetly.

The barmaid smiled at Serina's politeness. "Do you need anything else?"

"Actually, do you know who that boy is over there in the corner?"

The barmaid glanced over at Makaidel pored over his tome, apparently oblivious of everything around him. "Why, that's Marcus. He comes in here every night, orders a glass of milk and sits there and reads for hours. Don't know how he can focus with all this ruckus in here, but he pays like he just had a five-course meal. None of us know who he is or where he lives or anything."

"Oh. Thank you, miss." Serina smiled, though her eyes were on Makaidel.

"Please, call me Bethany. Y'all enjoy your dinner now."

"Thanks, Bethany." Serina smiled up at the barmaid as she walked away. Picking up her spoon, Serina began eating delicately. Forcing his eyes away from the boy across the room, Jacob began eating as well. He was aware of his stomach rumbling from not having anything to eat since before they reached Dekaal, but he took his time swallowing the chewy chunks of meat and heavily salted broth.

"How strange," Serina remarked. "I wonder why he comes here every night."

"We should go talk to him." Jacob glanced over his shoulder at Makaidel.

"What for?"

Jacob turned, caught off-guard by the question, to find Serina's head tilted curiously. He realized he didn't have an answer. What would he even say? In the game, all he had to do was walk up to someone and press a button and they would start talking, but he clearly couldn't do that here. How would he initiate the conversation already scripted in his head?

"Um," he fumbled, cursing his inability to think clearly when he was cornered. "Well, we could ask him… you know, why he does come here. I'm sure the, uh… barmaids would like to know." He felt like hitting himself as Serina gazed at him, but after a moment, she smiled understandingly.

"Okay, that sounds good."

He felt relieved, but he wondered if she was truly so innocent that she would take him at his word against such obvious lies or if she was simply letting it slide. He returned to his stew, feeling bad about lying to her and wondering what he was going to say to Makaidel.

The tavern still teemed with life around them when they finished their dinner several minutes later and Serina stood.

"Come on, let's go say hi to… was it Marcus?"

"Ma…" Jacob began, then quickly finished, "Marcus, yeah." He wanted to stop her, but she was out of reach before he could object, and he could only stand and follow her over to Makaidel's table. The boy made no reaction to their approach as he leaned over his book in the light of the fat candle on the table.

Leaning over, Serina stated, "Hi." Makaidel looked up with a start. Serina gestured to one of the chairs pulled up against the table. "Do you mind if we sit here?"

"Uh… I guess not." The suspicion was written clear on his face. Jacob regretted ever suggesting to Serina that they speak with him. They were unwelcome to him and Jacob felt guilty, knowing how it felt to have people impose on him. Smiling, Serina sat down beside him. Jacob hesitantly lowered himself into a chair.

"What are you reading?" She seemed genuinely interested, gazing at the book curiously.

Makaidel hastily replaced the ribbon bookmark and swung the cover shut. "History." Jacob raised an eyebrow as he glanced at the gilded script on the book's cover. He caught a glimpse of the word *Bestiary* before Makaidel slid the book off the table onto his lap and shot Jacob a scowl.

"Oh, I love history," Serina replied, positively glowing with enthusiasm. "What era are you studying?" The frown deepened on Makaidel's face and Jacob grew increasingly worried. They needed Makaidel as an ally. *If we could just bring up the orlocs casually…*

"Do you want something?" The boy slid his chair back faintly, preparing to get up.

"Oh, no, we just saw you sitting alone over here and thought we'd come say hi."

"Uh huh." Makaidel shifted in his seat, poised to run. Jacob clenched his teeth. This meeting was going all wrong, and if they didn't get control of it fast, Makaidel might never trust them.

"Look, I have to…"

"Actually, we were looking for Professor Phantis," Jacob blurted out, cutting the boy off as he stood from his chair. Makaidel froze, gazing at him, and even Serina sent him a surprised look.

"Professor Phantis?"

"Er, yes, from the Twin Oaks Academy," Serina stated, regaining her composure.

"I know him." The suspicion faded faintly. "I mean, I know of him. I'm looking for him, too."

Now Serina gazed curiously at him. "You are? What for?"

Makaidel shifted, but no longer seemed desperate to flee. "I just wanted to ask him some questions."

"Well, that's wonderful!" Serina beamed at him. "We could all go see him together."

"I guess. Why do you want to see him?"

"Actually, we were hoping he might have some information on the orlocs."

"The orlocs?" Makaidel repeated incredulously. "Why do you want to know about them? Who are you?"

Serina put a hand over her heart with a horrified expression. "Oh, I'm so sorry! Marcus, was it? Bethany told us. I'm Serina and this is Garrett. We're travelers from Shelas. Well, I'm from Shelas, he's from Merakis."

Makaidel's gaze shot over to Jacob, wide-eyed. "You're from Merakis? But, it was attacked by orlocs!"

Jacob glanced away with a shiver, remembering his escape from the ravaged town. "I know."

The youth dropped into the chair he had previously occupied, gazing with awe and excitement at Jacob. "You mean you were *there*? Wh… what were they like? What happened? Why did they attack Merakis?" Jacob leaned back uncomfortably against the barrage of questions.

Reaching over the table, Serina laid a hand on Makaidel's, gripping the edge fervently. "Maybe we should talk about this another time. Where do you live? Maybe we can meet you tomorrow and go visit Professor Phantis together."

Makaidel leaned back in his chair, gazing distractedly about the table. "Um… I don't really have a home. I just sleep wherever I can. I'll meet you back here tomorrow about an hour from sunset, okay?"

Serina looked horrified again. "You don't have a home? That's awful! We could rent a room for you for the night."

"No, no," Makaidel answered, too hastily, "it's alright, I wouldn't want to impose. I'll be fine, really." He pushed his chair back and began moving toward the entrance. Serina stood, holding out a hand.

"No, wait…"

"I'll see you tomorrow, okay?" Clutching his book tightly, he jogged over to the door.

"Wait!"

Serina began moving after him, but Jacob, standing, caught her arm. It still seemed like Makaidel didn't fully trust them, and he didn't want Serina's good intentions to scare him away.

"Don't worry, I'm sure he's fine." In a sudden flash of an idea, he added, "I'm sure the barmaids have made that same offer lots of times." Serina relaxed in his grip.

"Yes, you're probably right." She gazed out the window at where Makaidel had run off down the street. "I suppose we should ask about getting rooms for ourselves tonight." Jacob followed her to the bar, quieter now than it had been earlier. She raised a hand for the bartender.

"Can I help you, miss?"

"Yes, please, do you have any rooms available tonight?"

"How many you need?"

"Two, please."

Jacob felt his stomach tighten as the bartender walked away to retrieve the keys. "Oh, no, Serina, I don't want you to spend more money on me, we can just share a room." Serina glanced curiously at him. He felt his face flood with color, realizing what he'd just said. "I-I mean I can sleep on the floor! Y-you don't have to pay for a second room!" His face felt hot. *How could I have said something that stupid!*

Serina only giggled as the bartender returned and handed her two keys.

"Thank you, sir," she told him, taking the keys and moving towards the stairs at the back of the room. Jacob followed, his head sinking into his shoulders, ashamed of how completely he had embarrassed himself. He was certain his face was still beet red.

At the top of the stairs, Serina turned and handed him a key. He averted his eyes as he gingerly took it from her hand, not wanting her to look at him at all.

"Thanks for letting me come with you," she stated. "I really feel like we can make a difference." Jacob's heart would be warmed by her words, if he was not still feeling humiliated by what he had said to her.

She touched his arm. Turning his head, he gazed at her sheepishly out of the corner of his eye.

"Goodnight, Garrett. Pleasant dreams."

"G'night," he mumbled, quickly turning down the hall as she slipped into her room. He dumped his backpack unceremoniously onto the floor and collapsed fully clothed onto the bed, an arm draped over his eyes.

"I'm such an idiot."

As usual, it took him hours to fall asleep, but for once, he wished he had frightening encounters with orlocs to fill his mind.

"YOU WANT ME to teach you how to swordfight?" Rollis, the captain of the guard at Lord Kyutu's castle, raised an eyebrow at Jacob. He was tall and confident, clearly a leader and skilled with his sword. Jacob knew he would meet him again later when Lord Kyutu caught wind of Makaidel's doings. He didn't know to whom else to turn.

"Please," Jacob stated. He gazed around the castle courtyard. The guards' barracks, a long, low building set just separated from the outer wall of the towering castle, stood imposingly to his left, the training yard where castle guards sparred with wooden swords stretching over to the castle to his right.

"I'll…" *I'll what?* Jacob thought. He couldn't pay him for the service, as he still didn't have a penny, or whatever the currency was here, to his name. "I'll do anything."

Rollis shook his head. "I'm sorry, kid, I just don't have time for private lessons." Jacob's head bowed. He tried to think of another reason to make the captain agree to give him lessons, but he had nothing to offer.

"We can pay you for teaching him," Serina piped in from beside him.

"I'm sorry, I can't…"

"No, Serina, you don't have to spend any more money on me," Jacob cut across the captain.

Rollis turned and began walking away. "Look, I'm sorry, but I've got things to…"

"Wait, Captain!" Jacob called after him in a sudden flash of inspiration. "I know you won't do it for me," he reached into his collar and pulled out his amber teardrop pendant, "but will you do it for this?" Rollis turned curiously, then started as he caught a glimpse of what Jacob held up. Some of the spars around them drew to a stop as the guards stared on in awe. Jacob forced them out of his mind, focusing only on the captain.

"But, that's the Hero's pendant! How did you…"

"I've always had it." For once, the lie came out easily, convincingly.

"And you say you don't know how to fight?" Rollis raised an eyebrow, bewildered.

"He's very resourceful," Serina stated, stepping forward to stand beside Jacob. "He killed a big orloc on the journey here from Shelas, and he survived the attack at Merakis." Hushed murmurs rippled through the crowd gathering around the scene. "We're going to stop the orlocs."

"Please," Jacob added, though he realized he shouldn't have said it. Desperate as he was for swordfighting lessons, he should have kept the air of confidence and mystique that Serina had instilled in the observers.

Rollis hesitated, gazing at him with eyes for nothing else around them. Jacob's heart raced anxiously.

"Very well." The guards circling them chattered excitedly. "I'll do what I can to teach you, though it takes years to become a true master of the sword."

"I need to know how to fight by tonight."

"Tonight?" Rollis repeated incredulously. Jacob saw Serina turn curiously toward him from the corner of his eye, but he gazed steadily at the captain of the guard, unwavering.

Rollis frowned. "I'll see what I can do." He turned to one of the guards beside him. "We need practice swords, now." The guard quickly handed his training sword over to the captain as another guard jogged forward to Jacob.

"Here, sir, you can use mine." Jacob grinned faintly at the title, realizing the guard was older than him. His arm sank as he gripped the surprising heft of the wooden sword. He realized it was weighted in the core, so it felt much like his own sword in his hand.

The ring of guards surrounding them moved aside as Rollis stepped away from the barracks, staring intently at Jacob. The guards formed a tighter border a few paces around them. Jacob followed, wondering what Rollis was going to do. The captain stopped, standing tall and erect with the wooden sword held beside him, the tip resting lightly against the ground angled away from him. The focus in his eyes betrayed his preparedness to strike, and Jacob lifted his practice sword into a ready position. A hush fell over the crowd around them, which Serina had joined. Jacob glanced hesitantly at her in the silence, her light-colored clothes exposing fair skin standing out starkly against the dark, identical uniforms of the guards. He remembered her words from the open fields a few days ago and tried to hold the sword like an extension of his arm.

Rollis did not move, gazing sharply at Jacob like a hawk.

Jacob shuffled his feet, suddenly worried that the captain's lessons would be more hands-on than he had been expecting. The sun shone down from nearly directly above them. Jacob frowned. He had only a few hours before they had to be back at the Horse and Clover to meet Makaidel. How much could he learn about fighting in so little time?

Still Rollis did not move.

Jacob shifted again and glanced to either side. Was this some sort of test? Was Rollis expecting him to do something? He received no clues from the guards surrounding them, who gazed on in interest. His arms began to ache from holding up the wooden sword.

Finally, Rollis stated in a commanding voice, "Intimidation is your strongest weapon. Use it as you would use any other. If your opponent does not believe he can defeat you, then he cannot. If you do not believe you can defeat your opponent, then you have already lost." Jacob frowned as his sword sank, feeling heavier the longer he held it in the same position. Was this a trick? He knew he had no chance of winning. He, a seasoned captain of the guard for a lord's castle, against Jacob, an ordinary and out of shape high school student.

Rollis's voice lowered, somehow conveying more depth and power in its softness. "Always fight knowing that you can win."

Suddenly, he charged, swinging his sword tip up in a horizontal swipe. Jacob raised his weapon to parry, but in two quick swings, he found himself disarmed and sprawling on the ground, his hands stinging from the crash of wooden swords.

"Spread your feet more. Maintaining your balance is essential."

Faint cheers and applause rose from the crowd as Jacob got to his feet and retrieved his sword. Rollis stood back patiently as Jacob got into position, feet spread apart and driving his center of balance downward.

Rollis charged again to wild hoots from their audience. Their wooden swords locked as they met this time, but spinning Jacob's sword around with his own, Rollis freed the sword from his grip and sent it reeling to the ground.

"Keep a firm grip on your sword. Let nothing distract you."

Jacob panted as he retrieved his sword a second time, the crowd roaring around him. He could feel his shirt growing damp and clinging to him as the midday sun beat down on him.

Once more, Rollis charged.

"Know when to give ground. There's no sense using up your strength parrying a blow you can't defend."

Jacob slipped and nearly fell over from a push by Rollis. He stood still and focused as a statue as Jacob regained his footing and raised his sword again. Nothing he held had ever felt so heavy, but he forced himself to lift it again as Rollis darted forward.

"Learn and follow the rhythm of the battle. This will only take practice."

Jacob winced as he fell onto his backside, sword slipping out of his grip after their blades clashed twice. He wouldn't be able to get much practice outside of actual battle.

The wooden swords clacked noisily together several times, Rollis's blade breaking frequently through Jacob's defenses and slapping him on the wrist, shoulder, ribs.

"Always look for an opening."

Twisting Jacob away with a swipe of his practice sword, Rollis slapped the weapon against the back of Jacob's legs, causing him to stumble, arms flailing for balance.

"And never leave one open on yourself."

Shaking his hair out of his eyes, Jacob turned to face Rollis once more, panting as he prepared to face another attack.

Once more, Rollis charged.

Jacob's arms seared with pain and aches sprouted all over his body from falling down so many times, but Rollis offered him no respite. Guards brought him water when he could barely hoist himself off the ground again, though the captain seemed never to even break a sweat. He was surprised that Rollis never showed him any actual swordfighting moves, but as the afternoon wore on, he became able to hold his own longer. The courtyard seemed suspended in time, as all the training around them had stopped, and when a guard left the circle surrounding Jacob and Rollis to take up his post, another would arrive to take his place. Dust hung in the air from their feet shuffling across the circle.

Jacob leaned heavily on his wooden sword, chipped and splintered from Rollis's relentless attacks, panting from deep in his stomach, and noticed his shadow was now as tall as him. His knees trembled, fire pumped through his arms, and he was exhausted in a way he had never known before. His head throbbed and he thought he would pass out from weariness, but he had dodged and parried Rollis's series of blows to a stalemate. He had let only two or three attacks in and had even managed to slap his sword against the captain once.

"Very good." Jacob managed to lift his head and gaze between the strands of hair plastered to his forehead. He could make out a faint pleased smile beneath Rollis's thick, well-groomed mustache. "Your form lacks style, but you're learning the basics well for such a novice. You may become a warrior yet." Jacob tried to smile, but between starving, exhaustion, and feeling sore all over, he wasn't sure he managed it.

"What is the meaning of this?"

All eyes turned to the source of the sharp voice behind Jacob. He could barely turn his head to glance over his shoulder as the circle of guards dispersed into neat rows, all standing at attention and saluting. Rollis straightened with them, wooden sword held firmly at his side, and Serina bowed her head from where she stood in a row of guards.

"Lord Kyutu. My apologies, sir. I was teaching this young man swordfighting." Jacob heard footsteps approach behind him, but couldn't gather the energy to rise from his crouch. It took all his effort simply to remain on one knee, leaning on the wooden sword.

"This… commoner?" Lord Kyutu's voice was authoritative, commanding, and harsh. "This townsperson, this *boy* not under your command, not a member of the castle guard at all?" Jacob watched as the lord strolled over to Rollis, standing at what to him would be an uncomfortable closeness. The sharp planes of Lord Kyutu's face stood out starkly in the midafternoon sunlight as his hawk-like eyes bored into the captain of the guard. Rollis didn't react to the intimidating look and straight-backed posture of the lord that stood an inch or so taller than him. Lord Kyutu's voice dropped, though Jacob could still hear him. "Don't you think that you have better things to do with your time, Captain? Especially with the rumors of a traitor in my castle floating about."

"I beg your forgiveness, My Lord. It won't happen again."

Lord Kyutu spun on his heel. "See that it doesn't. Get your men back to work. I have a job for you."

"Yes, sir."

The ranks of guards relaxed uneasily as the lord of the castle walked away from the scene.

"You heard him," Rollis ordered. "Back to your posts or your training."

With mutters of, 'yes, sir,' the guards spread out in all directions. Wincing in pain, Jacob struggled to push himself up from the ground. Before he had managed to rise to his feet, Rollis took his arm and lifted him up bodily. His arm raged in protest and he fought to suppress a whimper of pain.

"I think I've paid my debt to you." Rollis released Jacob as Serina crept in to drape his free arm over her shoulders. The captain gazed intensely at Jacob, but he could only pant as he returned the look. "See that you fulfill your end of the bargain. Stop the orlocs. And remember what I taught you."

Jacob nodded heavily, swaying as he leaned against Serina. "Thank you, sir." His voice was weak and raspy. Rollis's gaze pierced into his eyes. He could see traces of suspicion and disbelief there, but with them was a glimmer of hope.

"Good luck." With that, Rollis moved around them and strode off toward the castle entrance.

Jacob cringed as he turned, feeling every muscle in his body more acutely than he ever had. Serina helped him out of the courtyard and beyond the castle gates. Each step was agony as they crossed the span of grass beyond the outer wall of the castle before the buildings of Dekaal sprouted between cobblestone streets. A part of him wanted to feel satisfied with his progress that day, but he ached far too much to accept it.

"That was a lot of work!" Serina stated as they moved down the path toward the town. "You really learned a lot from the captain." He wheezed, his throat aching from panting so hard for so long.

Finally, they reached the edge of town. Serina helped him into an alley between two buildings and lowered him onto a barrel beside a side door leading into a carpenter's office. He faintly registered her glancing carefully about them before holding her hands out to him.

Suddenly, he felt his strength rush back to him. Gasping, he straightened, back arched as his body rippled, his aches washing over his body in waves. When the feeling subsided, he felt stronger. Dampened from sweat, his clothes felt cool in the shade of the building. He was still sore, but not nearly so much as he had been a moment ago, and walking was no longer the trial of his life.

Glancing forward with a smile, he noticed that he had grabbed Serina's hand. He released it and pulled his hand back with a twitch. Serina giggled at his reaction. He smiled nervously.

"Thanks."

"You're welcome. We should head back to the inn. We don't have too long until we meet Marcus." Nodding, he rose and followed her out of the alley. He drew his sleeve across his perspiring brow, amazed at how much stronger he felt. Glancing at her, he smiled widely, though he felt his cheeks reddening doing so.

The afternoon waned as they returned to the Horse and Clover. Jacob found it difficult to continue keeping his eyes open, and each bench, barrel, and ledge they passed looked more inviting than the last.

As they found a table inside, he laid his head down on his folded arms on the table. *Just need to rest a few moments.*

He was asleep before a barmaid had come to take their order.

"Garrett?"

Jacob felt a gentle nudge on his arm and he bolted upright with a snort. He wiped his mouth with the back of his glove, realizing embarrassingly that he had been drooling.

"What happened?" he mumbled groggily. Serina and Makaidel sat at the table with him.

"You were asleep when I got here," Makaidel stated.

Serina smiled. "You looked so tired, I didn't want to wake you." Jacob stretched his arms out in front of him. He felt thick-headed and he was still sore from his training earlier, but the nap had refreshed him. He glanced around. The street outside was fully dark and the tavern was lit by the flickering firelight of the hearth and the candles set on all the tables.

"Well, good morning, sleepyhead."

Jacob turned and found Bethany the barmaid standing beside him.

"Would you like anything?"

He ran a hand through his hair. "Um… coffee?" The barmaid grinned.

"You look like you need it. Anything to eat?"

Jacob's stomach rumbled, reminding him that he hadn't eaten since breakfast, but he was relieved that he hadn't ordered anything that didn't exist here. *Yet.* "Um… is there… do you have anything special tonight?"

"Well, we have some river trout just caught today. You want that?"

"Sure." He wasn't normally big on fish, but he was hungry enough to eat just about anything, and certainly anything that wouldn't arouse suspicion.

"Alright." Bethany turned toward the kitchen. Jacob glanced curiously at Serina and Makaidel.

"We already ate."

Serina looked bashful. "I'm sorry. I wanted to wait for you, but Marcus said we should hurry."

"Oh," Jacob responded, feeling guilty for making them wait.

Makaidel leaned conspiratorially over the table and spoke in a low voice just audible over the clamor of the tavern. "We've been talking about Professor Phantis. Apparently, a lot of people around here think he's pretty weird."

"He hasn't been to work all week," Serina added. Jacob put on a mask of confusion and curiosity.

"The problem is, nobody seems to know where he lives."

"I think I might be able to find him," Jacob replied. Serina brightened and Makaidel's eyes widened.

"You do? How?"

"I heard someone talking about him last night before I fell asleep." He'd had the excuse prepared all day, but the unscripted words still came out hesitantly. "He's in a small, black house with an apple tree in the front yard."

"All houses are going to look black now," Makaidel remarked sarcastically.

Serina giggled. "It's a lot more than we knew before. Thanks, Garrett." Jacob's proud smile was short-lived. "But why didn't you tell me earlier?"

"I… guess I forgot." He glanced sheepishly at her, feeling ashamed of using the same excuse he had given back home so many times, for everything from not doing his homework to putting off chores. "Sorry."

"It's okay." She smiled.

At that moment, Bethany returned with his dinner. The smell enticed him, stomach twisting in hunger, but when she set the plate down before him, his appetite disappeared. The fish lay flat on his plate without any side dish or garnish, whole and undressed with its dead eyes staring up at him. His hand trembled faintly as he reached across the plate to grab the coffee Bethany had deposited behind it. He cringed as he took a sip. The coffee was bitter and powerfully strong, but not enough to settle his stomach at the sight of his dinner.

"Anythin' else?"

He swallowed, the heat and pungent taste of the coffee lingering in his mouth. "No, thanks." Nodding, Bethany strolled off to another table. He stared at the fish, its open mouth mocking him. He half expected the tail to flop in front of him.

"Well? Aren't you going to eat it?" Makaidel asked impatiently. "We don't want to wake Professor Phantis."

Swallowing uncomfortably, Jacob picked up his knife and fork and sliced at the skin. The silvery scales glistened in the light of the lumpy candle on the table. Jacob felt like he was going to be sick.

"Why are you cutting it there?"

Jacob glanced up at Makaidel curiously.

"Haven't you had fish before?"

"Not like this," Jacob answered honestly, pulling his fork and knife away.

"You're supposed to slice along the belly and pull the skin back." Makaidel sent Jacob a dubious look. "You've never done this before?"

"I don't eat fish much," Jacob growled.

"Then why did you order it?"

Jacob scowled at his dinner, not answering. Reaching forward, he reluctantly poked the fork into the fish's flesh and sliced along its belly. He shivered as the pectoral fin flopped over the fork, moving with entirely too much realism for his taste.

"Hurry up. We have to find Professor Phantis."

Trying to still his churning stomach, Jacob pulled a piece of meat out from his slice and raised it to his mouth. Closing his eyes, he popped the bite into his mouth and chewed.

It was somewhat bland but overpoweringly fishy. However, if he tried to picture it as an ordinary fish fillet, it was far more tolerable and satisfying. He wished he could eat it with his eyes closed.

On Makaidel's insistence, they rose and left the tavern after he choked down about half the meat in the ribs. He was still hungry, but the aftertaste of the fish followed him for several blocks.

The streets remained eerily quiet as they strolled through the town, Jacob only hoping he could lead them successfully to Phantis's house. He was sure he would recognize the house if he saw it, but trying to find it in the town that was much bigger than he knew worried him. They walked in silence through streets bathed in the mixed light of torches, oil lamps, and the moon's pale glow. Occasionally, they passed a tavern or other building that still bustled with life, its light and noise filling the block with warmth. The farther they got from the marketplace, however, the fewer and farther between came those glimpses of activity and life.

The darkness had lain uncompromisingly over them for several minutes when Jacob suddenly stopped in his tracks.

"There."

Serina and Makaidel followed his gaze. The twisted skeleton of the apple tree loomed out of the night ahead of them, a silent, silhouetted sentinel guarding the foreboding house. The sight filled Jacob with dread.

"You're sure that's the one?" Makaidel asked, though his voice was subdued.

"Positive."

"It does look darker than the other houses," Serina stated, glancing around. "And that's definitely an apple tree." She fiddled with a canteen she held, clearly trying to hide her uneasiness. A pall of silence fell over the street.

"Well, let's go talk to him, then," Makaidel continued, louder than Jacob had been expecting. His words rang across the street as he hesitated, the next ones softer. "The lamp beside the door is still burning, so he must still be awake." Jacob reluctantly followed Makaidel and Serina up the walk to the front door. As they passed the apple tree, it whispered ominously in the breeze as if to warn them away. Jacob swallowed hard, the faint lingering aftertaste of his fish dinner and potent coffee leaving his mouth dry.

At the front door, Makaidel hesitated. He clearly looked unnerved by the twisted frame of the house in the dark, silent night. He glanced at Serina.

"You knock."

Smiling bravely, Serina raised her hand and knocked on the door. Her gentle raps were like gunshots against the quiet street. The sounds bounced off the houses around, echoing over and over again, so that Jacob swore he could still hear them half a minute later. He glanced around, hardly daring to breathe in the utter silence of the street. The world seemed dead around them, the oil lamp faintly illuminating them the only sign of life anywhere in sight.

Finally, muffled footsteps thumped toward the door from inside. Jacob jerked back around, twisting his neck. A latch released and a small panel slid open at eye level. The light of the lamp didn't even penetrate into the darkness beyond, other than to glint off a pair of suspicious eyes.

"Who are you?" The words were sharp and gruff, yet it masked a nervous, mousy voice.

"Er, Professor Phantis?"

"What do you want?"

"We were hoping we could speak with you. We heard you were ill, and we brought some soup…" Serina held up the canteen in her hands, but Phantis cut her off.

"I don't know who you are. Go away."

The panel began to slide shut, but Makaidel quickly stated, "Wait, Professor Phantis! I wanted to…" he rummaged in a bag hanging over his shoulder, "talk to you about…" he pulled out the heavy book Jacob and Serina had seen him reading at the tavern the last night, "your book!"

The panel slid open again, and the eyes widened in interest. "You've read my book?"

"Yes, it was fascinating. I wanted to ask you about…"

The panel slammed shut so rapidly Makaidel couldn't even begin to speak the next word. He stared dumbfounded at the closed door for a moment. Jacob tensed, wondering if things were going wrong again.

Before he could say anything, however, he heard a lock click on the other side and the door opened. Professor Phantis, a thin, stringy man with an aquiline nose and widow's peak, holding a burning candle in one hand, beamed at them.

"You're the first person to tell me you liked it. A-are you really interested in knowing more?"

"Yes," Makaidel answered eagerly, cradling the bestiary against his body like a baby. The professor's smile widened, teeth showing fiendish and ratlike. Jacob tried to suppress a shudder at the sight. Phantis looked twisted and untrustworthy in the game, but in person, the exaggerated features were downright disturbing. He looked half a ghost, his face sunken in for lack of sleep or food, or both.

"Come in, then! Come in!" Phantis stepped aside and held the door open wide as Makaidel crossed the threshold, followed after a nervous glance by Serina and Jacob. Phantis shut the door behind them and latched it.

"Oh, this is terribly exciting," Phantis muttered as he began moving down the cobwebbed entry hall. Jacob glanced up a dusty staircase as the professor's candlelight fell on it, but inside the house with the curtains drawn tightly against the scant moonlight, it rose into utter darkness.

"Everybody always says I'm mad for wanting to learn so much about orlocs." The professor seemed hardly to be addressing them at all as he led them toward a parlor lit only by a small hearth fire. "They don't understand, such amazing beasts. Sit down, sit down, I'll put on some tea." Phantis shuffled out of the room, leaving Jacob, Serina, and Makaidel to gaze at each other uncertainly. The unadorned parlor was furnished only with two chairs, one wrapped in leather torn in several places and the other plain wood, greyed from age. Makaidel lowered himself onto the wooden chair, glancing around awkwardly. Jacob and Serina exchanged a glance. She pulled a lock of hair back from her eyes with a nervous smile.

Phantis returned carrying a scuffed and dented metal teapot and five plain clay cups piled up on his arm.

"Remarkable creatures." He didn't react as Serina stepped in and relieved him of the cups. She handed one each to Jacob and Makaidel as Phantis hung the teapot over the hearth fire. "You wouldn't believe the things I've learned about them." He absently took a cup from Serina, leaving her with one in each hand. She sent a questioning glance to Jacob. He shifted uneasily, bothered as much by the professor's eccentric manner and unfurnished home as he was by what he knew was about to happen.

"They sleep with their eyes open, did you know that?" Phantis turned sharply to send Makaidel an intense gaze, and the boy started faintly under his scrutiny.

"Er, yes. It's in your book…"

"Ah, yes, the book. No one would scribe it for me. I had to write it myself."

Makaidel's eyes widened, surprised. "But, I found it at the library…"

"Yes, I gave it to them. People should know about the orlocs. They say it's cursed to learn about them, they say I'm cursed, but they should know." He rarely met their eyes, still seeming to talk more to himself than anyone else.

"Um, Professor…" Jacob's voice trembled as he recited the words from the game, reluctant to join the conversation. "How do you know so much about the orlocs?"

Phantis gazed at him, piercing. "I study them."

"Er, Professor," Makaidel cut in, drawing Phantis's gaze back to him. "What you wrote about their living habitats…"

Suddenly, a series of thumps emanated from below, quaking the floor beneath their feet and shaking dust loose from the ceiling, which drifted slowly down onto them. Serina gasped, leaping backwards and dropping both cups she was holding, and Makaidel sprang forward out of his chair. Jacob started at the abrupt noise, but didn't react otherwise. A deep, hissing rumble thrummed through the air from below as the cups Serina dropped shattered on the floor. Jacob felt like his stomach dropped out of his body.

"What was that?!" Makaidel crouched, poised to either fight or flee. Phantis looked somehow paler than before.

"Oh dear." He set his cup on the mantel and began shuffling out of the room. "It shouldn't be doing this. No, this shouldn't be happening at all."

"*What* shouldn't be happening?" Makaidel ran after Phantis. Serina glanced quickly and worriedly at Jacob, then followed. Jacob wanted to warn them, to tell them not to follow Phantis, but he couldn't find his voice. Heart pounding, he trailed after them.

Opening a surprisingly well-oiled door in his musty house, Phantis began descending to the cellar. He didn't seem to notice the group following him, but he left the door open as he went. Jacob, Serina, and Makaidel didn't speak as they moved, their nervous footsteps echoing in the narrow, dimly lit staircase.

Finally, Phantis reached a landing at the bottom of the stairs, ending in another door. The irregular thumps and rumbles sounded from beyond it.

"P-Professor…" Serina attempted as he grabbed a key off a hook and unlatched the door. He didn't respond.

Swinging the door open, he revealed a large, single room with dirt and natural stone walls and a high ceiling, lit by torches lining the walls. Crates lay scattered about the floor, along with a number of large clay pots, some overturned or broken. Makaidel gasped and started and Serina shrieked, turning to cling fearfully to Jacob.

In the center of the room, chained to the wall with links as big as Jacob's hands, was an eight-foot-tall orloc, flailing and snarling against its bonds.

"Professor!" Makaidel yelled. "What are you doing?!"

"Beautiful, isn't it?" Phantis gazed admiringly up at the monster. "It's the biggest one I've ever been able to capture." Jacob froze when he caught glimpses of inhuman skeletons scattered around the floor. Phantis stepped forward, grabbing a torch off the wall and swinging it toward the struggling beast. "Stop that! Down!"

"Professor!" Serina still clutched Jacob's arm with trembling hands. "You can't keep this thing chained up in here! What if it escapes?"

"Don't worry." His voice barely carried over the increasing noise of the orloc. "He's secure." He swung the torch just in front of the beast's swinging claws, but it seemed unaffected by the threat. The chains rattled as it tried to lunge forward, the fist-sized bolts against the wall loosening under its struggle.

Makaidel noticed it and pointed frantically. "Professor…!"

With a crash and a shower of rubble on the far side of the room, the metal plates holding the chains to the wall bent and broke free.

SPRINGING FORWARD WITH the momentum, the orloc swiped at Phantis, slapping him bodily aside. Phantis yelped as he sprawled on the ground, the torch he held sent spinning across the floor. Serina and Makaidel leaped aside as Jacob drew his sword, though terror filled his heart at the sight of the enraged monster.

"Fire Lance!" Makaidel's voice cut shrilly across the orloc's growls as he darted to the side and swung his arm around. A tongue of flames shot out from his hand, streaking through the air to blaze against the creature's side. The light from the torches in the room wavered as Makaidel's spell lit up the rock walls. Roaring deafeningly, the monster turned from examining Phantis's unconscious body and snarled at Makaidel. Makaidel turned and ran, but the beast sprang after him much faster than he could move.

Bolting forward in a panic, Jacob raised his sword and slashed down on the orloc's ribs as it ran by. A thrill of excitement flared in his heart when he saw his sword tip stained with blood.

He spun to confront the orloc and found it doing the same. Before he realized what happened, the chain still attached to the beast swung around, slamming into his back and throwing him forward onto the ground with a cry. He felt the creature's paws slam the ground to either side of him just before he was flung into the air from a tight grip on the back of his shirt. His tunic stretched tightly over his body as the orloc shook him back and forth in its jaws. His heart seemed to drop into his feet and his stomach into his head as he was tossed about like a rag doll. The world was a blur before him. He tried to raise the sword he thought he still held, but he couldn't feel his arms and could barely keep his grip on the weapon.

Through the nausea sweeping over him, he heard Makaidel's voice coming from everywhere at once yell out, "Lightning Blast!" A brilliant flash of light lit up the cavernous cellar. With a roar, the orloc released Jacob and sent him flying. His head swam and stomach churned so much that he didn't know which way he was falling, or if he even was. He felt like he was going to be sick all over himself.

Suddenly, something hard smashed against the front of his shoulder, spinning him around moments before he slammed into the ground. He wheezed, too ill, pained, and disoriented to even cry out. His stomach roiled and he shortly coughed its contents onto the floor beside him, unable to move. Crashes echoed around him, but he could hardly feel the danger so close to him.

All of a sudden, he felt his strength seep back and his pain abate. Gasping, he pushed himself up to his hands. Serina crouched beside him, eyes closed and palms together as she uttered something under her breath. The rocks around her trembled, resounding in Jacob's heart like some noise just lower than he could hear. Wiping his mouth with his sleeve, he glanced over his shoulder.

The orloc chased Makaidel around the room, shrugging off the spells he flung one after another at it. Though Makaidel's magic seemed to harm the beast, each spell only enraged the monster further. The entire room trembled with the fury of their battle. Jacob crouched next to a pillar of stone cut from the rock that had been hollowed away to make the room, and he realized that was what he struck in mid-air. As he glanced over to the orloc, he saw his sword lying near its feet, apparently flung from his grip from the last toss.

"I… I wish I could help more," Serina stated miserably as she watched the orloc race after Makaidel. She hadn't brought her staff and had no weapons with her.

"No, no," Jacob quickly replied. "You stay here, where it's safe." He rose, frowning at his sword, wondering how he was going to retrieve it from the middle of the cellar, where the orloc paced back and forth.

As the beast turned away from him, he darted out from behind the stone column and ran toward his fallen sword, watching the chains dragging after it carefully this time. He had only made it halfway across the room when the orloc spun around again and snarled at him. Yelping, he dove to the side and rolled as it leaped toward him. Scrambling to his feet, he fled, the orloc bounding after him. He could smell the stench of its hot breath as he raced around a pillar as thick as a tree. Just as he rounded the pillar, his foot caught against an outcropping of rock and flung him sprawling on to the ground.

Throwing himself forward into a run, he looked fearfully over his shoulder at the orloc. He caught a brief glimpse of the inside of its mouth before its sharp teeth slammed shut with a crash that would have severed Jacob in two, inches in front of his face. Shouting in terror, he lost his balance again and fell over backwards, heart hammering against his chest.

"Stone Assault!"

The entire room trembled as chunks of rock broke free of the walls, floor, and ceiling and went flying through the air to hit the orloc in all directions. Jacob crawled backwards frantically as the creature moved its head around the pillar to snarl at Makaidel. Scrabbling to his feet, Jacob raced at top speed and crouched behind the next pillar. His entire body shook with fear and his breath came out in quick gasps.

It wants to kill me, he thought, panicking. If its mouth had been any closer, he would have been beyond any help Serina could give, and here, where everything was so terrifyingly real, he couldn't start over at the last place he had saved his game. *Oh, God, I'm going to die here.*

He snuck a glance around the pillar he hid behind, but darted back behind it quickly. The room wasn't big enough to be able to keep the orloc at any safe distance. He knew he should help Makaidel, who was clearly growing tired from casting so many magic spells so fast, but he couldn't make himself join the fray. The creature was as large as an elephant and twice as fast, he had no weapon, and worse still, he didn't know how to fight.

Learn and follow the rhythm of the battle. The words of Dekaal castle's captain of the guard came unbidden to his mind. His shoulders sank. An afternoon of basic lessons did not a good swordfighter make. He was too afraid to focus on what he had been taught.

Let nothing distract you. Jacob shook his head. How could he not be distracted? His opponent was bigger, faster, and stronger than him, and in a berserk rage. He didn't stand a chance against it. Makaidel's spells didn't even seem to be hurting it much.

Suddenly, a blast shook the pillar he leaned against. Yelping, he darted away from it toward a different pillar as fragments of stone tumbled down where he had just been. Darting aside from the orloc's swinging chains, he took refuge behind a stack of crates and shivered.

Always fight knowing that you can win. He shook his head against the remembered words.

But I can't *win,* he thought. *I'm going to die here, that thing's going to maul me and no one will ever know what happened to me...*

All of a sudden, it clicked, like a light switch turning on in his mind.

"If I don't fight back with everything I've got," he said aloud, "I'll die for sure." *That's what Rollis meant!* He peered around the crates at the battle. Serina had begun throwing rocks at the orloc, trying to distract its attention away from Makaidel, who leaned on his trembling knees and panted. Jacob's sword was still beyond reach. He glanced around where he crouched. He was near where Serina had dragged Phantis's body out of harm's way, and his fallen torch lay nearby, still burning.

Darting out from behind the crates, he grabbed the torch. The orloc snapped at Serina, chains flailing in front of Jacob.

Always look for an opening.

Serina ran around to the far wall of the cellar, the orloc turning its back to him. He ran forward toward his fallen sword. With a quick swipe of its massive paw, the beast slapped Serina aside with a cry.

"Hey!" Jacob yelled angrily as he neared the giant beast, before it could lunge on Serina. It spun to face him, snarling, and Jacob swung the torch. It wasn't an empty gesture like Phantis had done, however, and he reached as far out as he could, trying to touch the scorching flames to the orloc's skin. It seemed to sense the difference in intent and drew back, but tried to snap at him around the swinging torch. Fear still gnawed at his heart, but he knew he had no choice other than to fight back.

He advanced slowly, pushing the orloc back. Its front limbs were over his sword, almost in arm's reach. Tilting its head, the monster shot forward, trying to snap Jacob in its jaws.

Follow the rhythm of the battle. Recognizing the sign, Jacob lunged safely aside before it pounced and swung. The torch smacked against the creature's jaw, and it drew back with a roar as the burning brand singed its flesh.

As the orloc stumbled backwards away from the blaze, it stepped away from Jacob's sword. Switching the torch to his left hand, he took up the sword and swung. The orloc roared so loud his ears rang as the blade slashed across its collarbone.

Before he could prepare for it, the creature swung a huge paw, slapping him bodily away to tumble across the ground.

"Energy Beam!"

Jacob raised his head to see a spiral of light streak across the room and drive into the orloc's side. It roared as it stumbled and Makaidel collapsed to his hands and knees.

Shaking off the pain of his fall, Jacob rose and lunged forward as the orloc glared over at Makaidel. He swung, slicing higher than the last attack. As the beast spun back to roar at him again, he raced around a pillar beside him. The orloc was slower rounding the pillar than he was, and he swung at the back of its leg. The sword bit into the tendon and soft flesh at the back of its knee, and with a snarl, the creature stumbled and fell.

Jacob ran forward onto the orloc's side, spreading his feet for balance as he reached its ribs. It raised its head to snap at him, but he thrust the torch forward, touching it to the roof of its open mouth. It recoiled with a roar, the body beneath his feet tossing. Throwing the torch aside, he grabbed the hilt of his sword with both hands and positioned himself. As it lunged with its head again, he thrust, driving the point into its eye.

With a belching snarl, the orloc jerked its head aside. Jacob, clinging tightly to his sword, was hurled over its head and through the air as the blade slid out. He crashed gracelessly to the ground, shoulder aching from his hard landing. Rising quickly, he held his sword out, but hesitated.

The orloc lay flat and unmoving on the ground, blood flowing from its eye. It no longer breathed.

Jacob's panting hastened as a grin grew on his face. A moment later, he laughed triumphantly.

"I did it!" Excitement and pride welled up inside him. For the first time, he had truly fought, and without assistance, defeated an enemy much larger than himself. It was euphoric. He felt powerful, unstoppable, and no longer afraid of what he had to do in this world.

He glanced across the room to where Serina helped Makaidel to his feet. She smiled faintly and tiredly at him, but Makaidel shot him a dirty look. Jacob was confused by the boy's reaction, but it couldn't dampen his elation.

"No!"

All three of them started at the sudden cry from across the room. Phantis collapsed again, panting for breath. Jacob approached the professor at a jog, Serina helping Makaidel along from the other corner of the room.

"I was so close… so close to finding out the truth… where they come from."

"Are you crazy?" Jacob snapped, filling the scripted words with very real anger. "That thing tried to kill us!"

Phantis weakly shook his head. Serina gently lowered Makaidel to the ground and crouched to inspect the professor. "No… there's so much you don't know." His voice grew faint and he moaned in pain.

"Like what?" Jacob knelt beside the professor, baffled by his lack of reaction. "Tell us!"

Serina shook her head, looking horrified. "He's bleeding internally. We have to get him to a doctor!"

"W-What? He's dying? But… can't you do anything for him?

"The wounds are too deep. We have to get him help, quickly."

Jacob shook his head, shocked. "This… this shouldn't be happening."

"Well, it happens when our only good fighter hides from the fight like a coward," Makaidel snapped.

Jacob spun to face him, stung and angered by his words. "Hey, I killed that thing."

"Oh, yeah, real heroic, wait 'til everyone else wears it down, then run in and act like you did all the work."

Jacob lunged to his feet, glaring down at Makaidel. "Hey! I attacked right from the start, and I could barely move after that thing threw me!" Their voices grew louder, bouncing with increasing ferocity off the cavernous walls of the professor's cellar.

"Oh, yeah, and you're welcome for saving your life! Not that I think it was a good idea anymore."

Jacob pointed an accusing finger at Makaidel. "You'd be dead right now if I hadn't…"

"Please, stop!" Serina cried, cutting across Jacob in a tearful voice. She hunched her shoulders, trembling. Jacob froze, gazing at her in shock and guilt.

"I-I'm sorry."

"We have to get him to a doctor, fast. I can't do anything for him." Serina stepped back. Jacob darted in and tried to pull Phantis up to a sitting position, his mind wracked with worry and guilt. His pendant slipped out from behind his shirt, swinging beneath him as he struggled to lift Phantis.

Suddenly, the professor stiffened, shooting a hand out to grasp the pendant. Jacob gasped at the action, gazing into Phantis's suddenly intense gaze.

"Find the other… element stones," the professor hissed. Jacob blinked, taken aback. Then, Phantis went limp in his arms, eyes staring unseeing up at the ceiling. Starting, Jacob dropped him.

Serina fell to her knees beside him and checked Phantis's pulse. Squinting her eyes shut against oncoming tears, she reached out and closed the professor's eyes. Jacob could only stare at the body of the professor, stunned by his untimely and entirely unexpected death.

Makaidel coughed behind them. Serina rose, arms held close to her body. "We need to tell someone what happened." Jacob sighed, gazing over his shoulder at the dead orloc. He hardly knew what to feel, overcome as he was with guilt, surprise, relief, and shame all at once.

As Serina reached down to help Makaidel up, Jacob stated, "Here, let me." Makaidel shot him another dirty look as Jacob helped him to his feet, but said nothing. Jacob half-crouched awkwardly, being too tall compared to Makaidel to support one of the boy's arms around his shoulders comfortably. Silently, they walked out of the room, ascending the dark, narrow staircase and passing through the entrance hall of the creaking house into the dark night sky.

Only as they returned outside did Jacob realize how tired and hungry he still was. The back of his throat felt sour from getting sick during the battle and his headache hadn't entirely abated from being tossed around in the orloc's jaws. His shoulder ached and he still felt sore from his sword practice that afternoon and he didn't know what to think of the evening's events.

"I'll go find a city guard and tell him what happened," Serina remarked softly, subdued. Jacob hated to see her so upset. "I'll see you back at the inn."

Jacob opened his mouth to argue, but she began jogging away before he could say anything. His stomach churned. He didn't want her to leave, not when he needed comfort so, and he didn't want to be left alone with Makaidel, who remained bitterly silent as they walked.

The night hung over Jacob and Makaidel, dark, quiet, and oppressing, and the scuffing of their feet against the ground seemed to ring throughout the sky. Jacob stole an occasional glance at Makaidel as they passed through the streets, but the young mage never looked at him. The way he so reluctantly leaned against Jacob for support told him both how angry and how tired Makaidel was. Jacob frowned, thinking about his actions in the fight. He didn't think he had cowered from the orloc for that long, but Makaidel could barely stumble along, so worn out from casting spells was he.

"Look, about the fight, I'm…"

"Just shut up, will you?" Makaidel cut in. Jacob snapped his mouth shut, feeling ashamed. The words had come out so quickly that he couldn't discern exactly how Makaidel was feeling, but he dared not ask.

He shifted uncomfortably, a knot forming in the small of his back from bending over to support the boy, and he suddenly worried that he wouldn't be able to find his way back to the tavern. They had taken so many turns to reach Phantis's house that he couldn't remember where to turn to go back the way they had come.

That fear soon abated, to be replaced by further guilt and shame, when he started to make a turn, but Makaidel stated in an annoyed voice, "Not here, it's the next left."

Finally, the familiar façade of the Horse and Clover, lit now by a single oil lamp beside the door and much quieter than it had been when they left, came into view. Feeling immensely grateful at the sight, Jacob led Makaidel inside.

Only a handful of patrons still remained in the tavern, as well as two barmaids cleaning the empty tables. Jacob helped Makaidel to the nearest table and lowered him into a chair. He frowned, thinking that Makaidel should lie down, but he still had no money to pay for a second night at the inn. It was becoming increasingly frustrating to not have money. In the game, any enemy defeated would drop gold, making money a minor concern at best, but the real orlocs he had faced so far didn't carry coins on them. How else was he supposed to make money to continue his quest?

He stood straight, gazing outside worriedly. He wished he hadn't let Serina go off on her own to find a city guard. Towns were safe in the game, but he had learned that the real Aurius was very different from the game, and there were no walls or fortifications around the city to keep orlocs from wandering in. Also, it was her first time in Dekaal, and she wasn't as familiar with it as Jacob was. Would she be able to find her way back?

"Can I get you anyth—goodness, you're a wreck!"

Jacob turned to find Bethany standing behind him, gazing in surprise at him and Makaidel. "What happened to you?"

Jacob ran a hand through his hair, mussed and tangled from the fight. "It's a long story."

Reaching into his pocket, Makaidel wearily slapped a small silver coin on the table. "Give me anything that's hot."

Bethany nodded, turning to Jacob. "And you?"

"Um," he stated, rubbing the back of his neck nervously. "Can… can I pay later?"

"Yeah, alright. What do you want?"

"Stew, please." Heavily salted and tough as it was, it was something he knew was safe to order.

"I'll be right back." Nodding, she scurried off into the kitchen. Jacob lowered himself into a chair across from Makaidel. It was restful, not having to run or hurry anywhere for what seemed the first time since they arrived in Dekaal, though he felt uneasy with the way Makaidel fixedly avoided looking at him.

Bethany returned quickly with a lamb steak, a steaming bowl of lentil soup, and a chunk of hard bread for Makaidel, then set a large bowl of stew on the table for Jacob. Makaidel ate ravenously, ignoring everything else around him. Jacob gazed at his stew, hesitating. The overly fishy taste of his earlier dinner, and the way it had felt coming back up, lingered on his mind. He frowned. He didn't get sick often, but he had already thrown up twice since he had been in Aurius.

Simply thinking of the way he had been tossed around by the orloc in Phantis's basement disoriented him, and he began eating his stew as much for a distraction as anything else. His stomach grumbled as he swallowed the thick broth and chewy meat, reminding him how the day's events and skipping lunch had famished him.

Jacob gazed absently over to the door as it opened, then sprang excitedly to his feet as Serina walked inside. Hearing the noise, she turned, and she approached their table with a faint smile.

"Is everything okay?" he asked as she arrived at the table and sat down.

She nodded. "I showed them the professor's house and told them what happened." Jacob returned to his seat. He still couldn't believe Phantis had died, and so quickly. He hadn't seemed sickly in the game, but it seemed such a small blow to have killed a grown man. A shiver ran up his spine with the realization that he could have been killed just as easily. If his head had hit that pillar instead of his shoulder…

"What did he say to you just before he… he died?" Serina asked, startling him out of his reverie.

He blinked at her. "'Find the element stones.'"

Serina cocked her head curiously, sadness abating. "Element stones? What are those?"

Jacob glanced away, wondering what to say that wouldn't give away more than he should know at this point in the game. How had Phantis even known of the element stones?

Reaching into the collar of his shirt, he pulled out the amber teardrop pendant. He gazed at it, the simple pendant he had made, part of a costume. Here, it was supposed to be the mark of a hero, a symbol of incredible power and destiny. This simple pendant he had crafted with his own hands. Clutching it, knowing its importance here, made him feel powerful. He was a hero here.

"I think he meant this."

Makaidel looked up from his dinner and his eyes widened. "The Hero's pendant? *You're* the chosen one?"

"I passed the Divine Test," Jacob lied easily, pleased with how convincing it sounded.

"Wait," Makaidel continued as if he hadn't heard, "you mean there are more of those?"

"Yeah." Jacob added quickly, "At least, that's what Phantis said."

"So that might not be the Hero's pendant."

Jacob's eyes narrowed at the insinuation. "It is."

"Why did he ask you to find those other element stones, though?" Serina cut in.

"Maybe someone else is looking for them, too. Someone bad."

"What makes you think that?" Makaidel asked suspiciously.

Jacob turned to him, pausing. *Have I given too much away?* "It's just an idea."

"We don't even know what these element stones are."

"But Professor Phantis did," Serina stated. "If he studied them, they must be in his research somewhere."

"So, all we have to do is look through his research until we find out about them." Jacob felt encouraged, despite knowing that he wasn't even supposed to hear about the element stones until much later in the game.

"Uh, hello?" Makaidel remarked sarcastically. "We don't even know how to find all of his research. Remember, I have the only copy of his bestiary, and that was in a library at a school he didn't even work for."

"The guards told me that he's been with Twin Oaks Academy for over twenty years," Serina added. "He's written more books than any other professor, but they're scattered all over town. Some aren't even signed."

Jacob's shoulders sank. Why was this so much more difficult than it was in the game?

Makaidel yawned. "Whatever we do, it'll have to wait until tomorrow. I have to go."

"Oh, Marcus, please stay here tonight." Serina reached a hand across the table to him. "I couldn't bear to think of you sleeping on the street after what happened tonight."

"I have somewhere I can stay." Pushing his chair back, he stood up. He wobbled slightly, grasping the chair for balance, then bowed to Serina. "Thanks for your help finding Professor Phantis." He gazed suspiciously at Jacob, then turned and walked out.

"Marcus…"

"Let him go." Jacob narrowed his eyes at Makaidel's dirty look. "He knows what he's doing. We should get some sleep, anyway." Reluctantly, Serina rose and followed him upstairs, back to their separate rooms.

"Goodnight, Garrett." Jacob paused, seeing her hesitation. "I… I thought you fought really well tonight."

He smiled freely for the first time that long day, it seemed. "Thanks. And thanks for your help during the fight." Guilt weighed down in the pit of his stomach for the way he'd hidden from the orloc while Serina selflessly protected Makaidel.

She returned her sweet smile, showing no hint of shame or disappointment in him. "You're welcome. Goodnight, Garrett."

"Goodnight," he answered and slipped into his room.

He slept soundly that night.

10

A SUDDEN POUNDING on the door startled Jacob awake. He sat up quickly, instinctively throwing the covers off his legs to go answer the door, but paused. He wasn't in his bedroom at home and it wasn't his stepfather outside asking for his help mowing the lawn. Someone dangerous could be out there.

"Open up, Garrett!"

Softly sliding his sword out of its scabbard, he crept over near the door, heart still pounding from the abrupt awakening. "Who's there?"

"Soldiers of Dekaal Castle. You're coming with us. Open the door or we'll open it by force."

For a split second, Jacob's heart seemed to pound so hard it cut off the air supply to his lungs as a hundred horrible scenarios played out in his mind at once. Then, a familiar voice spoke, "Wait, please!"

"Serina?" His fear rose.

"It's okay, Garrett. We've been summoned to the castle."

Cautiously, he unlatched the door and opened it a crack, hiding his bare legs and chest behind it as he peered out. Only two soldiers stood in the hallway, the one not addressing him lounging against the wall looking bored. Serina stood beside the other, tall and imposing as he stood in front of the door. She wasn't restrained, held, or even watched very closely. The nearer soldier stared commandingly at him.

"Lord Kyutu wishes to see you. Now."

Jacob gazed at the soldier, hesitating. He still didn't want to trust them, but with Serina already within their grasp, he had little choice. He didn't want to know how they would force him to go, either.

"Let me get dressed," he finally answered.

"You have five minutes."

It didn't take him that long. He quickly slipped on his clothes and strapped his sword belt on, all the time wondering what was going on. This hadn't happened in the game. *Why is everything going all wrong?*

He stepped out of the room to find Serina waiting alone at the top of the stairs. At the base of them, he could see the bored-looking soldier watching the barmaids sashaying across the tavern with a smirk.

"Ready to go?" Serina asked. Jacob could see the uneasiness trying to hide behind her smile.

He leaned in close to her as they began descending the stairs. "What's going on?"

She allowed her mask to slip, showing her fear beneath it. "I don't know. The commander said it was important, but he doesn't know anything else." Jacob frowned as he faced forward, trying to appear nonthreatening to the bored-looking soldier. "What should we do?" Jacob nodded to the bored-looking soldier as they entered the main room of the tavern. Only a few people occupied the room, all of them gazing in interest at the soldiers. The bored-looking soldier shrugged apathetically as Jacob and Serina walked past him.

"I don't think we have much choice," Jacob answered quietly. "Don't worry, I'm sure everything will be alright." He glanced around at the staring eyes, hoping Serina took his words to heart more than he did.

At the entrance to the tavern, the commander spun, gazing down at them. "You are ready?" Jacob simply nodded, a lump forming in his throat from all the eyes boring into him. "Then let's go." Turning on his heel, he walked out of the tavern, and the bored-looking soldier crossed the room to follow. Jacob stepped outside, then stopped in his tracks with a gasp.

Lining the street outside the tavern was a group of sharots, the large, ram-like creatures used as mounts in the game in place of horses. They stood as high as horses, great shaggy beasts with faces like llamas and legs as thick around as his own, ending in cloven hooves. Several of the sharots bore more soldiers, but four stood tacked and unoccupied before him. In the game, the creatures were almost comical in their oddity, but here, the texture of the long hair draping their bodies and the way they moved with such realism stunned Jacob. He had never even thought of the sharots before, but there were no horses in Aurius. To come face to face with an entirely foreign creature, one that was domesticated and useful, drove home the point of how different this world was.

"Have you ever ridden a sharot before?"

"Uh, no." Jacob tore his eyes away from the sharots to return the commander's gaze.

"Then just let it do the work." The commander walked over to a sharot tacked with a saddle and bridle fringed with red and gold cloth and with armour covering its head, neck, and hindquarters. He mounted the beast. "They'll follow the rest of us, so you don't need to guide it." The bored-looking soldier mounted a sharot beside the commander.

Slowly, Jacob approached the nearest sharot not in use. It snorted, the noise somewhat deer-like. Hesitantly, he reached out a hand and touched the long hair beside the saddle. The hair was coarse, with a texture like wool, though with the way it hung straight down almost to its knees below its belly, it reminded him of a woolly mammoth.

"Hurry up," the commander snapped. Grasping the saddle, Jacob mounted the creature. It shifted a hoof, but remained steady otherwise. He gazed over at Serina, mounted atop the other extra sharot. She smiled widely with a shrug. Jacob returned the smile, thinking that it must be her first time to ride a sharot as well.

"Move out." The commander's sharot snorted and strode forward, and with a sudden movement, the sharot Jacob rode began walking along with the others. The sounds of the many hooves traveling down the cobblestone street were strangely muffled, each cloven hoof falling with little more than a thump, rather than the clop he expected.

He gazed out at the town as they passed through, grinning from his seat atop the sharot's grey back. People stared as they passed by, but he felt almost regal, mounted on this strange creature while everyone else around him walked on their own feet.

He didn't recognize the paths they took, though he thought they must be the same he and Serina had traveled the previous day to get to the castle. The training he had received from Rollis yesterday seemed so far away already, though he noticed his arms and legs still felt sore. He couldn't imagine now how he had managed to train for so long without collapsing completely.

Finally, they reached the castle for the second time since he had arrived at Dekaal. The guards at the gate set into the twenty foot high outer wall nodded as the group passed within into a much greener and friendlier courtyard than Jacob had become familiar with the previous day.

Holding up a hand, the commander brought the procession to a halt. Jacob dismounted with the soldiers around him, uneasiness returning as he wondered why Lord Kyutu had insisted upon bringing them there.

"Glenwood, Markey." Two soldiers approached at the commander's order as the others began leading the sharots away. Jacob watched them walk off, captivated by the foreign creatures. The commander cleared his throat, and Jacob snapped his attention back to him.

"You will address Lord Kyutu as 'Sir' or 'My Lord.' You will do as he says or you will be thrown in prison. Your sword." The commander held out a hand to Jacob. Jacob put a hand to his blade's hilt protectively.

"I…"

"You will not enter the throne room armed. Hand it over."

"It's mine," Jacob argued lamely. "You can't make me get rid of it, you brought us here."

Serina moved closer to him. "Garrett…"

"It will be returned to you when you leave. Give it to me."

Serina laid a hand on Jacob's shoulder. He glanced at her, then reluctantly drew the sword and handed it hilt first to the commander. *Oh well,* he thought as the commander turned on his heel. *It's not like I still know much about using it, anyway.* A brief flash of the way he had killed the orloc in Phantis's basement blinked before his eyes. He shuddered at the memory. Jacob and Serina followed the commander inside the large doors into the castle, flanked by two other guards.

Jacob gazed around as they entered the castle. The entrance hall was even larger and more extravagant than the church in Merakis had been, though the stone surrounding him made the cavernous hall feel cool. He followed the commander down the hallway, lined with unmoving guards, towards a large double door at the other end of it.

The doors creaked as the commander opened it into an even more extravagant room lined with stained glass windows. At the other end of the long, crimson carpet leading across the floor, Lord Kyutu, dressed in a dark blue military uniform, sat ramrod straight on an elegant mahogany throne, gazing sternly at them as they approached. Beside him, draped in robes that entirely concealed his form, Jacob recognized Fahren, Lord Kyutu's advisor. And, he knew, traitor. His heart hammered in his chest, wishing Rollis was there. At least he respected Jacob and was willing to trust him. In that room, Jacob saw no friendly looks.

The commander drew to a stop in front of the throne, bowing deeply. Jacob swallowed, gazing at Lord Kyutu. He remembered how stern and imposing the lord had looked the first time he played the game. Kyutu looked far more so in person.

"Lord Kyutu, these are the ones who faced the orloc in the cellar of Professor Phantis of the Twin Oaks Academy." Jacob's eyes widened at the commander's announcement. The line was from the game, word for word. Was this simply the meeting that Kyutu had allowed them after the battle with Phantis's orloc, only expedited by the guards?

"Kneel, you idiot," hissed the soldier standing beside Jacob. He kicked Jacob in the back of the knee, the loss of support throwing him to the floor with a yelp. Serina already knelt beside him.

With a wave of his hand, Kyutu sent the commander aside. "So, you're the only ones who know what happened in that house. Why was there a giant orloc in my city?"

Jacob glanced at the soldiers around him, trying to summon the words from the game. "The professor was keeping it chained in his basement… sir," he added quickly as the commander's eyes narrowed at him. "He was studying it."

"You're the one who killed it?" Kyutu's voice was hard.

Jacob swallowed. "Yes, sir."

"And now Phantis is dead, too."

Jacob paused, his mouth feeling dry. "Yes, sir." Fahren caught his eyes, shifting under his voluminous robes.

"Phantis was an expert on orlocs. I find it hard to believe that he would have been surprised by the creatures he knew so well." Kyutu's voice grew dark. "What I think is that you foreigners killed him and released that orloc into my city."

Serina's head shot up with a gasp. "No! We didn't even know it was there. We tried to tell him it was too dangerous to keep that orloc!" Jacob felt comforted by the familiar words of the game, but dreaded the confrontation to follow.

"He thought he could control it," Jacob added.

"Where did you come from? Why have you come to Dekaal?" Kyutu demanded.

"We're just traveling. We came here from Shelas looking for information about the orlocs."

Kyutu's eyes narrowed darkly. "Why did you go to Professor Phantis's house last night?"

"We just wanted to ask him some questions. We heard that he was the foremost source for information about the orlocs."

"And now the only one who knew enough about orlocs to give us a chance at stopping them is dead. Was that what you wanted?" His voice grew more hostile each passing moment.

"No!" Serina cried, horrified. "We want to stop them! He's the chosen hero!"

"I've heard enough. You two are obviously a threat to my town. Guards, kill them." Jacob and Serina spun, finding soldiers with drawn swords circling them.

Kyutu's reaction didn't surprise Jacob, but it greatly worried him. In the game, this part involved a simple battle, but unarmed, outnumbered, and facing real swords, Jacob knew he didn't stand a chance.

"Dad, stop!"

Jacob glanced between the approaching guards to find Makaidel running into the throne room, dressed in regal clothes. Serina gasped.

"Marcus?"

"They're telling the truth! He has the Hero's pendant!"

Jacob fumbled for his pendant, thrown off guard by Makaidel's appearance, when in the game, he hadn't arrived until after the battle. He held the pendant up toward Kyutu, heart skipping a beat. In the game, the pendant had emitted a brilliant light that stunned everyone in the room and was enough to reveal Fahren. Jacob's pendant, however, was not magical, and it didn't glow.

Kyutu's response was uncomfortably expected. "Superstitious nonsense. Kill them."

Serina leaned against Jacob, quivering in terror as the soldiers advanced, despite Makaidel's objections. Jacob backed away, creeping closer to the throne, trying furiously to think of a way out. Glancing over his shoulder, he caught sight of Fahren, standing beside the throne with a sinister smirk visible beneath the large cowl of his robes as he watched the proceedings.

Jacob turned back toward the guards, sword points within arm's reach. Makaidel yelled to Kyutu to stop as he ran toward the scene, but the lord stood implacably in front of the throne. Jacob knew there was no other way to save himself and Serina.

Spinning around, he lunged, tackling Fahren and throwing him to the floor. The advisor yelped as he was slammed against the polished stone floor. The robed man tried to wrap his hands around Jacob's neck as he pinned Fahren to the floor, but Jacob shoved the reaching hands away and punched, hoping he could hit hard enough to knock out the false advisor. *I may not know how to fight with a sword,* he thought, *but I've been in enough fist fights at school to know what to do!* Yells roared around him as Fahren pushed, rolling over with Jacob.

"What is he doing?!"

"Garrett!"

"Stop him!"

"I can't get a clear hit!"

Jacob pried at the hands as Fahren choked him, crouched over him and pinning him to the floor. He gasped for air, swinging a hand wildly around. Trying with great effort to aim, he slammed his fist against the side of Fahren's head, throwing him off. Jacob knelt on the floor, coughing, as Fahren rose calmly and pointed at him.

"Kill him."

Gathering his strength, Jacob lunged to his feet and forward. He grabbed Fahren around the waist and shoved him backwards until he slammed against the arm of the throne and bent backwards over it onto the seat. Before Jacob could do anything else, Fahren raised his legs and kicked hard at his stomach, sending him sprawling several feet away. His groans were drowned out by the gasps and cries of surprise that filled the throne room.

Turning his head, Jacob saw Fahren standing beside the throne, hood thrown back from his assault. What had appeared to be shadows beneath the large cowl was scaly skin the color of dried blood. In place of hair were several lines of sharp spines running down his skull and neck. A long scorpion's tail rose from beneath the robes behind him. The sight was far more disturbing than it had been in the game, and Jacob shuddered even as he coughed for breath.

Fahren, or the creature masquerading as the lord's advisor, glanced down at himself in shock, realizing the charade had ended. Raising his head, he glared hungrily at Lord Kyutu, who held his head and leaned heavily against the throne, looking exhausted.

The guard commander raced forward just as the false advisor leapt, slicing his sword across the creature's chest. It leapt back with a hissing snarl, landing lightly on the arm of the throne before pouncing again. Jacob rose to his elbows, watching with bated breath as it rose over the swinging sword to fall down towards Kyutu, who was being dragged away by a soldier who didn't have a free hand to protect the lord.

"Flash bolt!" In a blinding flare of light, the creature shrieked. When Jacob could see again, he found the false advisor behind the throne and creeping away from the approaching guards. Its head whipped around its surroundings quickly as it backed towards the corner of the room, and it was clear from the look in its eyes that it knew it was trapped.

Crossing its forearms in front of its face, another flash of light filled the room. When the light faded, the creature was gone, with no trace of it remaining. The guards gazed around hastily, swords still drawn, but Jacob knew that the false advisor was long gone. He coughed, head hanging between his trembling arms.

"Dad? Dad!"

"Get him to the infirmary, now!"

"Wait!"

Jacob raised his head as Serina's soft voice cut across the rough voices of the soldiers. "Please, let me try."

"Sir, I don't think that's…"

"Let her," Makaidel cut in, subdued. Between the soldiers blocking his view, Jacob saw Serina crouch beside Lord Kyutu. A faint glow emanated from the floor and seemingly the very air around her. Excited and terrified murmurs rippled through the soldiers watching, and some openly called out warnings or tried to move forward to Kyutu's assistance, but Makaidel shot his arm out, stopping them from approaching.

A moment later, Lord Kyutu stirred, his body jerking with sudden coughs.

"My Lord!"

"Dad!"

The crowd scrambled around Kyutu, hiding him from Jacob's view, but as he watched, he saw Serina quietly slip out of the group, standing aside with hunched shoulders and a pained look on her face.

"Dad, are you alright?"

The murmuring of the crowd around Kyutu silenced. "Makaidel…" He moaned. "What happened?"

"It was Fahren. He was a monster. Or, a monster had replaced him. I don't know."

Jacob pictured Kyutu gazing at his own hand, as he had done in the game. "The things I've done… he must have had me under his control."

"Sir?"

"Those cruel things I've been doing… I knew, somehow, that they were wrong, but for some reason, I couldn't stop myself from making those orders. How did you…?"

As one, the crowd turned, gazing at Jacob just as he rose to his knees. He froze under the singular stare. The guards parted to allow Kyutu, leaning on Makaidel's shoulders, a glimpse of him.

"How did you know he was a monster?" Makaidel asked. Jacob pushed himself to his feet, using the pause to wrack his mind for an answer.

"I could just… feel it." He tried to make the words sound convincing. "He gave off a bad vibe." Kyutu gazed deeply at Jacob, his eyes piercing even in his weakness. Jacob held his breath, hoping they would accept the excuse.

Finally, Kyutu stated, "You see more than any of us can. I had no idea Fahren was replaced. I can only wonder…" To the soldiers around him, with as much force and command in his voice as when he was under the monster's control, he ordered, "Search the castle. Fahren must still be here somewhere. He deserves to be found, even if he's already dead. Leave no door unopened."

"Yes, sir!" Many of the soldiers, including the commander that had brought Jacob and Serina to the castle, strode out of the throne room.

"Now, where is the young lady who healed me?" Turning, everyone remaining glanced at Serina, standing behind the throne. Donning a mask of dignified control, she curtseyed to Kyutu.

"I'm glad I was able to help you, My Lord." Jacob's throat grew tight at the suffering sound to her voice.

"Sir, there's somethin' not right about the way she does magic," one of the remaining soldiers remarked suspiciously.

"I'll have none of that," Kyutu stated sharply. Standing straight and free from support, he walked over to Serina, towering head and shoulders over her. She clasped her hands together, fear touching her eyes. "This young lady just saved my life, and she will be treated with all the respect and gratitude that encompasses."

"My Lord…" Serina attempted.

Kyutu turned to face Jacob, still standing several paces away where the false Fahren had kicked him. "I don't know you two, but you risked your lives to save a man who had ordered your execution." Jacob half-smiled, not bothering to mention that he had little choice at the time. "You may stay at the castle for as long as you remain in Dekaal as a small token of my thanks. What are your names?"

"Garrett," Jacob answered, wishing strangely that he could give Kyutu his real name, "and Serina."

Kyutu nodded. "Garrett," he turned to the girl standing beside him, "and Serina. Those names will be remembered here." Jacob smiled faintly. Kyutu laid a hand on his chest, breathing deeply. "I need to rest. If there is anything you need, don't hesitate to ask one of my castle staff." He sent his piercing gaze to Jacob. "Thank you again."

Jacob could only nod as Kyutu turned and began walking out of the throne room. He glanced at Serina, but her eyes were fixated on Makaidel. Makaidel rubbed the back of his neck with an uneasy expression, looking away.

"Marcus, you're… you're really…?"

"Look, I'm," Makaidel answered quickly, "I'm sorry. I didn't mean to deceive you, I just… didn't want you to think differently of me."

"I… I'm so sorry, Lord Makaidel. I didn't mean to disrespect you."

"No, no. I don't want to be treated like I'm better than anybody else. I just want to be normal."

"I think," Jacob recited as he approached them, "that if he wanted to be treated like a lord, he wouldn't go sneaking out of the castle at night and giving strangers a fake name so we'd think he was just a regular kid." He grinned at Makaidel.

"Uh… yeah." Makaidel smiled sheepishly.

"Oh," Serina stated. "Okay. I'm sorry."

"It's okay. And thanks for saving my dad." Serina smiled sweetly as he turned to Jacob. "I still think you should have helped more in the fight last night, but… I'm sorry I said those mean things to you."

Caught off-guard by the unexpected statement, Jacob fumbled at a smile and response. "It's okay. I shouldn't have hid like that. I'm just not used to fighting."

Makaidel raised an eyebrow. "And you have the Hero's pendant?"

Jacob frowned, gazing down at the amber teardrop surrounded by the crude metal talisman hanging around his neck. For the first time, he wondered if he really had what it took to be the hero of Aurius. His pendant was only a mockery of the original, it held no special powers like the one in the game did.

"I always heard that Merakis was so peaceful." Jacob and Makaidel looked at Serina. She shook her head. "I would've been surprised if there had ever been anything to fight." Jacob glanced away, remembering in a brief flash the sight of the town engulfed in flames and ripped apart by orlocs.

Makaidel shrugged. "Well, is there anything I can get you?"

Jacob put a hand to his stomach, still twisting from the hard kick he had received from the false Fahren. "I could use some breakfast."

Serina smiled at him. "That does sound nice."

"Sure. I'll show you to the kitchen."

Then, Jacob thought, fighting down a yawn, *I could use some more sleep.*

"SO, MY SON tells me you aim to stop the orlocs."

"Yes, sir."

Jacob and Serina stood in the throne room of Dekaal again, although this time, no extra guards were present and Kyutu gazed upon them with quiet respect. Makaidel stood beside him.

"I took the Divine Test in Merakis. It's my duty." Jacob spoke and carried himself as if this was a play he was starring in, speaking, he thought, rather convincingly. "We came here hoping to find information on the orlocs."

"It's a shame that Phantis was killed. I know of no greater source on the orlocs in Dekaal, perhaps in all Aurius, than him." Jacob frowned, still taken aback by Phantis's untimely death. "However, I can tell you that the imposter that took the place of my advisor spent an inordinate amount of resources looking for something in the mountains southeast of here. You may find a clue there."

"Um, sir?" Serina stepped forward hesitantly. "Were you able to find Fahren?"

Kyutu nodded. "The monster locked him in the dungeon, altering his appearance almost beyond recognition and magically blocking his memories. He's ill from his month in a cell, but he'll recover. He wanted me to give you his thanks."

She smiled. "I'm just glad to hear he's alright."

"You're leaving soon?"

"Yes," Jacob answered. "Tomorrow morning."

"Then I bid you good luck. I can't thank you enough for freeing me from the spell of that creature. Please take this as a token of my appreciation." Kyutu held out a round pouch to Jacob that jingled as it moved. Jacob's hand sank under the surprising weight of the fist-sized pouch. He fought to suppress a grin, immensely relieved to finally have money.

"Thank you, My Lord."

"No, thank you, Garrett. You give hope to the world. Aurius is crumbling around us. I will pray for your success."

Bowing, Jacob and Serina turned to walk out, but Makaidel, watching silently up until now, called out, "Wait!"

Jacob and Serina spun as Makaidel raced forward to face Kyutu. "I want to go with them."

Kyutu's eyes widened. "What?"

"You can't mean that!" Serina exclaimed.

"Please," Makaidel continued, ignoring her reaction. "I want to find out what's going on, too. I can't ignore what's happening to the world any longer. I have to do something."

Kyutu frowned softly. "Makaidel, you belong here. You're going to be lord after I'm gone, you need to learn how to rule."

Makaidel shook his head, glancing away. "I shouldn't be. This is what I was really meant to do." Silence fell over the room. Gazing sadly at Makaidel, Kyutu laid his hands on his son's shoulders.

"You don't deserve this life, Makaidel. You're my son and first-born child, you should be lord of Dekaal after me." Kyutu raised his gaze with a weary smile at Jacob and Serina. "But, now that it's known that you're the son of a mage and not my legal heir…"

"We won't tell anyone." Serina shook her head vehemently. "We promise." Jacob nodded beside her.

"No." Kyutu gazed down at Makaidel again. "It was never meant to be. You were born to strengthen the mages' blood, and I'm proud to have raised a son as worthy as you. You're right, Makaidel, this is your path. You have to find your own way in the world." Makaidel raised his head and Jacob could see a smile on the boy's face. "But I won't let you go alone. I'll send an escort with you."

"Dad," Makaidel began to argue.

"No arguments. I won't send my only child out into a dangerous world unprotected."

"But don't you think it would be more obvious to have a bunch of guards following me around?"

Kyutu shot him a sly grin. "You are my son. But you don't think so lowly of your old man, do you? Your escort will seem as average as you."

Makaidel chuckled. "Thanks, Dad."

Kyutu's smile faded to a solemn gaze. "Be safe, Makaidel." He raised his eyes to Jacob once more. "Take care of him."

Jacob nodded. "I'll protect him with my life, sir." Jacob knew it was the last he would see of Kyutu for a long time, and now that the lord of Dekaal was freed from the monster's spell, he regretted not getting more of a chance to know him. With a bow, he turned and walked out of the throne room, followed by Serina and Makaidel.

Jacob spent a relaxing day wandering the castle, marveling at its immense size and splendor. Even after the things he had seen and done, he was still amazed by the wonders of Aurius, and the fact that it was real.

The next morning, as he, Serina, and Makaidel prepared to leave, they walked out the front doors of the castle to find, to Jacob's surprise, the captain of the castle guard waiting for them.

"Rollis!"

Rollis returned a wry grin. "I heard about what happened. It's a good thing I gave you those lessons."

You have no idea, Jacob thought, though he only smiled. Rollis shifted his attention to Makaidel.

"My Lord." He stepped aside, gesturing behind him. "These are some of my most skilled and trustworthy men." Jacob's smile faded as he gazed at the uniformed soldiers standing at attention nearby. *Well, skilled, maybe.* "Thorn and Arys."

Thorn looked like a well-dressed football player, standing a head and a half above Jacob with shoulders almost twice as broad. His bulging muscles stretched the fabric of his uniform, making his lack of any obvious weapon that much more pronounced. Beside him, Arys looked hardly impressive, though he was taller than Jacob, and better built.

Thorn bowed deeply, his baritone voice almost perfectly matching the one in the game. "It's an honor to serve you, my lord."

Arys bowed beside him. "We devote our lives to your protection." Jacob narrowed his eyes.

"Thanks," Makaidel stated, "but it'll draw too much attention if you call me 'my lord.' Please, just call me Makaidel."

"As you wish, si…" Thorn cut himself off. "Makaidel." The young mage smiled at the effort.

"Good luck, My Lord," Rollis stated. "I wish I could accompany you myself, but…"

"Your duties are here, I know." Makaidel grinned. "I can take care of myself." Rollis smiled.

"Best of luck to you all. I hope you all return here some day."

I can think of one that'd be better off not coming back, Jacob thought with a sidelong glance at their new companions.

Rollis waved a hand toward the bottom of the stairs leading into the courtyard. "I've prepared sharots for your travel. Their saddlebags contain food and supplies for your journey."

Jacob blinked in surprise at the loaded-down beasts of burden waiting patiently at the bottom of the stairs. “Thanks, Rollis.”

“Strength and fortune be with you.” Jacob turned at the captain’s solemn words and nodded. Thorn and Arys stepped aside as Jacob led the way down the stairs. He mounted a sharot, wishing he’d had more experience riding one, or any at all guiding it, but it didn’t dampen his spirits. He felt powerful remembering his encounters with orlocs so far and thought that nothing could stop him, especially with so many skilled companions. But more so, he felt important, something he never had at home. He was in command and he was going to lead his loyal company to victory. He was going to save the world. He had never felt so worthwhile, so important. For once, he truly mattered, and nothing could take that away from him.

Glancing over his shoulder, he found everyone else mounted and ready to go. Serina smiled at him. Pointing forward, he stated, “Let’s go.”

Water

12

WITH A TOSS of the reins, Jacob's sharot began moving forward through the Dekaal castle courtyard, the muffled thumps of the others following behind him. Soldiers saluted as they passed by, widening the proud grin on his face.

Through the castle gates, the sharots' cloven hooves fell with clunks onto the wooden drawbridge across the moat circling the castle. He pulled at the reins as they returned to the gravel path, intending to skirt the town to ride toward the mountains. He pulled harder in annoyance as the sharot turned to the right. It groaned and turned harder to the right.

"What are you doing?" Makaidel called out, stopped in front of the drawbridge.

"Shouldn't we be going southeast?" Thorn asked.

"That's what I'm trying to do," Jacob snapped irritably, pulling again at the reins. The sharot now walked at an angle back towards the moat on the right side of the castle.

"Pull the other way!" Makaidel called, exasperated. Jacob yanked on the reins, glaring at the sharot. With a whining snort, it turned sharply and began trotting back the way he came.

"Whoa!" Jacob bumped harshly against the saddle as he struggled to stay on the creature's back. He pulled back on the reins as it trotted past the others, bringing it to a sudden stop.

"Don't you know how to ride a sharot?" The tone of Makaidel's voice was similar to his question about Jacob's fish dinner the other night.

"No one ever taught me," Jacob snarled as he lashed the reins, wanting only to get away from the group. He felt his face grow hot, and knew annoyingly that it was red from frustration and anger.

Serina rode nimbly up beside Jacob, speaking softly. "Gentle movements. They're trained to follow your reactions." He met her shining blue eyes, anger fading but unable to smile his thanks.

He straightened, curious what the others were doing but not wanting to look at them. The muffled thumps of their sharots' hooves on the grass rang behind him. He tried to focus on the feelings he'd had a few minutes earlier, setting aside the frustration of not knowing how to ride the sharot.

Glancing over at the town, he found several people watching the procession away from the castle. The two soldiers with a boy the age of Lord Kyutu's son must indeed have looked suspicious. Carefully, he turned the sharot farther to the left, trying to move farther from sight of the town, but tugged the reins the wrong way again. He frowned, then relaxed, realizing that riding the sharot was just like pulling his sword from his scabbard. It was simply something he had to get used to.

Slowly, they pulled away from Dekaal, leaving behind the third town Jacob had seen in Aurius. He gazed around at the wide, open plains, surprised to discover how much he had missed the solitude and silence. Facing forward, he found the jagged line of the mountains rising above the horizon far in the distance. He had come to learn in his journey from Shelas that even at the top of a huge hill, he couldn't see how far he had walked in a day. He wondered how far those massive mountains must be, and how much quicker their travel would be riding on the sharots.

Jacob rode quietly most of the time, a little disappointed that his time alone with Serina had ended. Makaidel spoke often with Arys, a fact that made Jacob uncomfortable. As he could think of no reasonable way to object, however, he had to settle for simply sending the soldier an occasional warning look.

When the sun set, the group found shelter in a cluster of trees. Makaidel tied up the sharots while Jacob, Serina, and Thorn set up Jacob's tent and the two other tents that had been provided. Arys built a fire between them, using the tent walls to hide the beacon of light from predators.

"Okay," Makaidel stated as he returned to the fire. "Arys and I can take this tent, and you two…"

"Um, wait," Jacob cut in, worried by the proposition. He motioned to Thorn and Arys. "Why don't they take one tent and we'll share the other?"

Makaidel gave him a blank look. "Why?"

"Well…" Jacob stalled, trying to come up with a good excuse. "I just think… you know, you should, well, stay with people you know."

"I don't know you."

"I…" Jacob attempted, then spat out, "I'm not comfortable with people I don't know."

"You don't know me!"

"You can use my tent," Serina piped in.

"No," Jacob and Makaidel answered in unison.

"You don't have to…" Jacob began.

"Alright, whatever, I don't care," Makaidel spoke over him. "We should set up shifts for a night watch, anyway."

"Won't the tents keep us safe?"

"Well, moderately, but we have enough people so we can keep watch. It's safer that way. Anyway, I'll take first shift."

"I can take first watch," Jacob stated abruptly. "You need to get your sleep."

Makaidel sent him an annoyed look. "I'm not a kid. I can take care of myself."

Thinking furiously, Jacob continued, "It's been proven that kids… er, boys your age need more sleep to function properly. You need to be well rested."

"Since when do you care about my health?"

"Actually," Serina stated with a smile, "that sounds like a good idea. Garrett can watch over us."

Makaidel sighed, exasperated. "Fine, whatever. You guys are worse than my dad." He plopped down in front of the fire, snatching up a chunk of bread from his sharot's saddlebag. The others crouched down around the fire with him.

Serina looked at Makaidel. "By the way, what did your father mean when he said you're not his heir?"

Makaidel sighed, hunching his shoulders. "Well, I guess it's not a secret now." He glanced around at Jacob, Thorn, and Arys. "The mages in Dekaal have been inbreeding so much to try to keep the magic bloodlines strong that they've become sickly. Few of them live longer than about thirty years now."

Serina inhaled sharply. "That's awful!"

Thorn nodded from across the fire. "They're among the most powerful mages in the world, but because they're always so weak, they can't do anything more than any other mage."

"So, a group of mages approached my dad," Makaidel continued, "and they asked him to produce a child with their most powerful mage. They hoped that his strong blood and her strong magic would make a powerful, but healthy mage. And, well, it worked." He glanced away. "Although my mother died giving birth to me. Now it's up to me to make more mage offspring when I'm older, but that's not what I want to do."

Serina cocked her head. "So, what do you want to do?"

Makaidel perked up. "Adventurous stuff. I want to do amazing things with my magic, to help people and to change the world." Serina smiled.

Thorn grinned. "Well, that's what you're doing."

The young mage considered that. “Yeah… yeah, I guess it is.”

“We’re just here to make sure you stay safe,” Arys added with a smile. Jacob narrowed his eyes at the soldier, but the look went unnoticed in the flickering light of the fire. *Yeah, I’m sure you are,* he thought darkly.

“I just hope we can find out what’s causing all the orlocs to appear soon.” Makaidel gazed toward the mountains, and Jacob followed his eyes as he chewed his dinner.

You won’t have to wait long.

The night passed uneventfully, to Jacob’s relief, though tired as he was, he was reluctant to abandon his shift and entrust their safety to Arys.

When he awoke, the tent was lit brilliantly by sunlight dappled from the foliage around them and Makaidel was gone. He crawled out of the tent to find everyone gathered around the still burning fire, dressed, prepared, and almost done eating breakfast.

“About time.” Thorn grinned.

Serina giggled. “We were about to wake you up.”

“Hurry up and eat,” Makaidel stated. “We need to get moving.”

“Hang on,” Jacob grumbled, walking behind a group of trees nearby, out of sight of the rest of the group. There were certain city comforts he missed, he thought as he undid his belt, his back and shoulders aching from another night on the ground. He began to wish he would start waking up earlier. It was uncomfortable always being the last to rise.

Feeling rushed, he ate breakfast, broke down the tent, and within half an hour, they were once again on their way. He shifted uncomfortably in his saddle as he rode.

The day stretched on, long hours passing slowly as they traveled across the rolling hills. His one reprieve from the endless travel, the sore backside and Makaidel constantly conversing with Arys and Thorn, was Serina, who rode beside him all day and smiled when he glanced at her.

A few hours after they stopped for lunch, when the sun hung high overhead, Thorn said suddenly, “Look.” All eyes turned to follow his gaze as the sharots were pulled to a stop as one. In the distance, crouching in the grass, Jacob could see it.

“An orloc,” he stated.

“Look behind the rock,” Thorn’s deep voice replied. Jacob squinted, trying to peer around a large boulder in the grass near the monster.

“Two of them?” Makaidel wondered aloud, surprised. “I didn’t realize they lived in groups.” Jacob felt his lunch turn over in his stomach. Though the orlocs stalking them were not nearly as large as the one in Phantis’s basement, the thought of facing more than one at once unnerved him.

The orlocs crept forward, the grass rustling from the movement. Jacob drew his sword, trying to remember the lessons Rollis had taught him. *Follow the rhythm of the battle.* How did it move? He thought back to his battle against the orloc outside of Shelas. *By constantly attacking and leaving no opening for retaliation.* He swallowed hard, trying not to be afraid, but this was only the third real battle he'd encountered since he came to Aurius, and even these common orlocs seemed a lot more dangerous than they did in the game.

As Makaidel's sharot caught a glimpse of the approaching creatures, it snorted and shied away, bumping against Arys's mount.

"Whoa! Steady!" Makaidel hissed, tugging at the reins.

Distracted by the sight, Jacob turned back to the open fields, but could no longer see the approaching beasts. He scanned the plains, fear rising. "Where did they go?"

"Getting closer," Thorn answered softly, gazing out of the corner of his eyes. He angled his sharot to the side slightly.

Suddenly, grass rustled only a few paces away from the group. Sliding his feet out of the stirrups, Thorn lunged, grabbing the leaping orloc with a bear grip around its neck and pulling it to the ground. Brandishing his sword, Jacob kicked his sharot forward and around the others towards where Thorn grappled with the beast in the long grass.

"Look out!"

Jacob spun at the cry to find the other orloc already at eye level in the air, claws outstretched toward him. His sudden jerk in the saddle caused his sharot to turn sharply, and the orloc's muscular paw missed its mark, shoving instead against his shoulder. The blow and the sharot rearing up with a groan toppled him from the seat as the orloc landed nearby. He rolled quickly across the ground as the orloc deftly turned and leaped again. Bringing one leg under him, he pushed himself to his feet to see his sharot kick the monster hard against its shoulder as the beast snapped at the saddled creature. Darting forward, Jacob swung. The orloc snarled as his sword slammed into its chest and slit a large wound across it. He jumped aside as the creature leaped toward him, the sharp teeth and claws soaring inches past his arm.

As he watched the orloc land and spin back to face him, he caught a glimpse of the other monster several yards further away. His mouth went dry with the sight. Thorn, Arys, and Makaidel all fought it at once, leaving Jacob to face the second beast alone.

Jacob returned his gaze to the nearer enemy, which crouched and snarled at him. Though the wound he'd left was deep, it didn't seem to be affecting the beast any. He knew if he simply continued slashing at it that he would get tired before the orloc would and tried to think how he could overcome the monster quicker.

Before he had a chance to plan his attack, the beast charged. Lunging aside, he swung again, aiming for the orloc's neck. The blade slammed down on its thick hide, cutting slightly but not very deep. He tried to slash harder while the blade was still against its neck, but the orloc turned, its strength overpowering his, and bit down on his hand. Yelping in pain, he pulled his hand back, holding his sword awkwardly with his left hand.

He shuffled quickly backwards and stabbed out with his sword as the orloc swung a huge paw at him. The point of his sword somehow dug into its chest between its shoulder and ribcage, the sword wriggling in Jacob's hand from the orloc's struggling as he fell over backwards.

Suddenly, the pain in his hand abated, the bones popping back into place. Jacob spared a hasty glance to the side. Serina stood nearby, eyes closed and hand held over the crystals in her staff, which glowed brilliantly. Turning back to the orloc, he grabbed the hilt with his healed right hand and launched himself forward, driving the sword into the beast's chest. It roared in pain, staggering back as Jacob leaned his full weight against it. Pulling the sword out with effort, Jacob crouched and slashed up, slicing his sword across its throat. With a strangled cry, it collapsed, panting and moaning pitifully for a few moments before it went still. Jacob grinned, exhilarated with his victory.

"That was amazing!"

Jacob turned at Makaidel's cry and his smile faded. The boy gazed at Thorn in awe, no attention spared for Jacob.

"You don't ever use a weapon?"

Thorn brushed at a tear in his coat. "Nope. I've always just fought with my hands."

"Cool! Can you teach me some moves sometime?"

Jacob's shoulders sank as he turned away, disappointed. The orloc he had killed, without assistance, lay sprawled on the ground beside him, blood flowing into the grass from its chest and neck.

A hand lay on his shoulder. Turning, he found Serina standing beside him and smiling.

"I thought you fought very well."

He smiled, brightened by her presence alone.

"Everyone okay?" Arys called as they returned to their abandoned sharots.

"Yeah," Jacob answered shortly as he wiped his blade off on the orloc's hide. He walked over to his mount, waiting patiently a few paces away. He flexed the fingers of his right hand, frowning at the blood stain on his glove. He wished he could improve his fighting quicker. *Still,* he thought as he rode past the corpse of the orloc that had attacked him, *two weeks ago I never would've thought I could do that.* He grinned, proud of himself, even if Makaidel, Thorn, and Arys hadn't noticed.

Tossing the reins, he urged his sharot into a trot, eager to reach the next part of the story.

Jacob's fighting improved as their journey wore on. To his surprise, he found himself picking targets that the others didn't, preferring one-on-one sparring to practice his abilities, and preferring the bragging point of being able to dispatch an orloc single-handedly, even if Serina seemed to be the only one to appreciate it. Two more days of travel passed mostly uneventfully, to Jacob's relief. The land grew hilly and the monster attacks grew more frequent the closer they came to the mountains.

"Ugh!" Makaidel dusted his hands as they finished off another orloc. "This definitely stinks of that monster's influence."

"We must be getting close," Arys stated.

You would know, wouldn't you, Jacob thought, scowling at him. Arys's presence frustrated him. The soldier was friendly and charismatic, and each passing day, the rest of the group seemed to like him more. Makaidel grew increasingly irritated with him for not treating Arys with the same courtesy, but knowing the soldier's intentions, Jacob couldn't even pretend to trust him. He tried to explain his suspicions to Serina, but even she didn't believe him.

"Arys?" she replied one night when he told her out of earshot of the others. "But he seems so nice."

"He's planning something, I know it." Jacob glanced at the others gathered around the fire. Thorn and Makaidel laughed as Arys spoke. Jacob was desperate to get them to understand that Arys couldn't be trusted, so the soldier wouldn't lead them into the trap he knew was coming.

"I don't know." Her expression clearly showed that she was torn between her own experience with the soldier and her reluctance to disbelieve Jacob's words. He tried to think of some clear fuel for his own suspicions, but he realized in annoyance that Arys had not outwardly given them any reason to distrust him.

"Just be careful around him, okay?"

She smiled faintly, clearly relieved that he wasn't forcing her to choose. "I will." He half-smiled at her as they stood and returned to the camp.

Makaidel wiped a tear from his eye as his laughter faded. "Oh, you should hear the stories Arys has. You wouldn't believe them."

I'm sure I wouldn't, Jacob thought as he crouched down in front of the fire, narrowing his eyes.

"Anyway," Thorn stated, "we should reach the base of the mountains tomorrow. Do we know what we're looking for?"

"I talked to my dad before we left," Makaidel replied, sobering. "He said that Fahren imposter convinced him to keep sending people to the mountains because he said there was some treasure there."

Jacob couldn't help himself. "Maybe one of those element stones Phantis mentioned is there." All eyes turned to him.

"What makes you think that?" Jacob thought he noticed a hint of uneasiness in Arys's eyes.

Makaidel shook his head. "We don't even know what those things are."

"Whatever they are," Thorn added, "don't you think if there was one this close to Dekaal that someone would have found it?"

"Well, you've never even heard of them before," Jacob argued. "Maybe it's always been there and you just never knew."

"What, like you know about them?" Makaidel asked dubiously.

Yes! Jacob screamed inwardly. *If I could just get them to believe me, I could keep them from falling into the wrong hands.*

"Like you said, nobody's even heard of these element stones," Thorn stated. "How can we be sure they're even real?" Jacob frowned, frustrated by the way the conversation was going.

"Well," Serina offered, "Professor Phantis seemed to know a lot of things no one else did. Maybe he found some really old book about them or something." Jacob sighed, glad for her intervention.

"That still doesn't help us know what to look for," Makaidel responded. "We're not going to find any old books lying around the mountain or signs saying 'element stones this way.'"

"It might not even still be there," Arys added. "If these element stone things even exist."

"Well," Jacob attempted, "there can't be too many paths into the mountains, right?"

"Dad said that monster impersonating Fahren kept looking on that big mountain we saw," Makaidel stated musingly. "I guess we could look for whatever path's seen the most use recently." The others nodded understandingly at his statement. Makaidel yawned.

"Anyway, we should get some sleep," Serina stated with a smile.

"Yeah," Thorn answered. "'Cause we've got a lot of climbing to do tomorrow."

"And the orlocs are probably only going to get thicker," Makaidel added. Jacob gazed across the dark plains, unable to make out the nearby mountain range with the light of the fire blinding him to the scant starlight of the night sky.

"You taking first watch again?"

Jacob turned with a start back to Makaidel. "Yeah, sure." Nodding, everyone else retreated to their tents. Jacob watched Arys as he crawled into a tent behind Thorn, but the soldier gave away nothing. Jacob sighed as he gazed up at the sky, the edges of the gibbous moon misty from the gauzy curtains of clouds. He found himself enjoying taking the first night watch, as it allowed him to stay awake closer to the time he would normally go to bed if he were home.

He smiled as he glanced around at their surroundings. Despite monster attacks, a lack of certain modern-day comforts, and a foreign world he still had to learn in some aspects, he was glad to be in Aurius. It was so much more interesting and exciting than being home. He had none of the ridiculous stresses of school life, home life, or future considerations of college, career, and moving out to worry about. His concerns here seemed so much more real, so much more important, and the mild discomforts were minor issues. Even though he had such a clandestine and life-threatening mission, the world didn't seem to weigh down on him as it did back home. And beyond anything else, he knew he was important here. The thought never failed to cheer him.

He threw another branch on the fire, watching the embers flare as the fresh wood stirred the flames and shot sparks into the air. He wondered briefly if anybody missed him back home, and he felt guilty for leaving Emily and her friends the unpleasant task of letting his mother and stepfather know that he'd disappeared, but he didn't miss anyone or anything from that world, that life. He glanced over his shoulder at Serina's tent.

Not even Tina.

BEFORE THE MORNING was half over, the group had reached the base of the largest mountain on the near side of the range. The ground rose and fell sharply to either side of the path cutting across the face of the mountain, the rocky terrain interspersed with abruptly jutting ledges, scrubs, and pine trees. Jacob recognized the path as they joined it, appearing exactly as it had in the game. He wondered if the treasures laid randomly around the mountain would be here, as well.

Makaidel looked around. "This looks like the right way."

"It's definitely been used recently," Thorn added. He pointed ahead. "Look, that branch was cleared within the last week." With a toss of the reins, Jacob ushered his sharot forward, the others following behind him. He glanced all around, taking in the awe-inspiring scenery surrounding him. The mountain seemed so much bigger, so much more impressive than it had in the game.

"Incoming!" Makaidel called out. Drawing his sword, Jacob leaped off his sharot. A group of orlocs tore out of a cluster of brush ahead, charging them.

"We're definitely on the right track," Thorn commented dryly as he leaped to the ground beside Jacob.

The battle was over shortly, most of them receiving minor wounds that Serina healed afterward. Mounting their sharots, they continued climbing.

"They're getting tougher," Thorn stated.

"They'd have to be to survive up here," Arys replied.

Jacob glanced off to the side where a treasure had laid behind a bush in the game. He angled his sharot over, trying to see if anything lay past the bush.

"What is it, Garrett?" Serina asked.

"Oh, nothing." He shook his head. "I thought I saw something over there." As he came into a gap in the scrubs clinging to the rock, he started with a yelp. The mauled remains of a human body lay behind the bush.

Makaidel tried to peer around the bush. "What is it?" Thorn rode his sharot around Jacob's nearer to the bush, but didn't flinch when he saw the body.

"Looks like one of those men that Fahren imposter sent up here." Dismounting, Thorn walked over to the tattered remains. Jacob shivered with the thought of being that close to the bones and torn flesh.

Reaching down, Thorn grasped something near the body. "Good find." Turning, he tossed it to Jacob. He flinched, but caught the pouch as it fell into his hands with a jingle. Coins rattled around inside it. He dropped the pouch into one of his sharot's saddlebags, cringing at the blood splattered across it, while Thorn returned to his own mount. Jacob's stomach lurched as he wondered if all the treasures the mountain had held in the game would be found in a similar manner.

The orloc attacks came even more frequently on the mountainside than they had before the group had reached it. Jacob felt pleased with how he had improved his sword skill, fighting technique, and courage since he'd arrived in Aurius, but these monsters were clearly more intelligent than the ones they'd faced previously. It was more challenging to overcome them and he was concerned for the more difficult battles that awaited them.

An hour after they stopped for lunch, their travel became suddenly more precarious, great cliff faces rising around them in places and the ground dropping away in others. The path grew narrow, a tiny span of safety cutting through a world of deadly danger. Jacob swallowed as the terrain disappeared to the right side of the path and grew much higher to the left side. Before long, he found them traveling single file along a narrow ledge nestled against a sheer cliff face, the right side of the path only empty air.

Swallowing around a lump in his throat, Jacob glanced over the side of his sharot down the cliff face to his right. His heart leaped in terror and his entire body trembled. Not a foot from the sharot's cloven hooves, the ground fell away to a river frothing and hissing through the mountain hundreds of feet below. He jolted his body upright, quivering in fear. He felt uncertain that he could trust the sharot to keep its footing, but there was no room for him to dismount. He breathed in quick gasps, nudging the sharot closer to the cliff wall beside them. It didn't matter to him that his knee bumped harshly against the rock wall as he rode.

The river seemed to grow louder as they rode on, even though it remained so far away. Jacob could hardly hear beyond the roar of its waters and the pounding of blood in his ears.

Suddenly, as he turned a corner, the cliff wall beside them disappeared, and he pulled his sharot to a sudden stop in surprise. They had reached a ledge about twenty feet across, the path ending at its far side. The incredible roaring that seemed to fill the mountain with noise emanated from a huge waterfall several yards past where the ledge ended, falling all the way down to the distant river below.

The others squeezed past him as they reached the ledge, Jacob frozen in place.

"Where's the path?" Makaidel called over the roar of the towering waterfall.

"I think there used to be a bridge." Serina pointed. "Look." As Jacob followed her eyes, he saw the stakes in the ground with shreds of rope still tied around them, and suddenly, he recognized this place. There had been a bridge here, in the game, but for some reason, here it was gone.

"How are we going to get across?" Thorn yelled. Jacob gazed across the chasm at the far ledge, where the path resumed. It was only about twelve feet across, but it was clearly farther than any of them could jump.

"Look!" Makaidel pointed from his position near the edge of the cliff. Jacob reluctantly rode a few paces closer. "There's another ledge down there. The sharots might be able to jump it." Jacob's mouth went dry at the thought.

Thorn nodded. "I've seen a sharot jump farther." Jacob snapped his gaze over to the large man, eyes wide. His heart skipped a beat merely to think of it.

"What if they miss a step?"

"Sharots are very sure-footed," Serina stated. "They're actually used to mountains and cliffs." Jacob felt like his stomach dropped out of his body as he gazed across the chasm.

"It's our only chance," Arys added. They all glanced around at the ledge, but there was nothing that could help them cross the chasm any other way.

Suddenly getting an idea, Jacob turned to Arys. "Why don't you go first?" Makaidel shot him a dirty look from the suggestion.

Arys swallowed uncomfortably, but rolled his shoulders in preparation. "Okay." He backed his sharot up until its backside touched the cliff wall blocking the rest of the mountain from them. The others moved their mounts away, giving him plenty of room.

Kicking hard at his sharot's flanks with a cry, he galloped forward toward the cliff edge. Despite not liking him, Jacob couldn't help holding his breath as the animal leaped, nothing but open air below him. It sailed forward quickly as it fell, and with a jolt, it landed and skipped forward on the lower ledge safely. Serina, Makaidel, and Thorn cheered as Arys turned and waved back.

"Okay, my turn!" Makaidel stated eagerly. Jacob shot him an astonished look as the boy rode his mount to the cliff wall farthest from the edge. Before Jacob had time to object or ask any questions, Makaidel kicked the sharot into an immediate gallop and leaped across the chasm. He fell harshly against the beast's neck as it landed, but seemed unharmed otherwise, and waved back his assurances.

Without a word, Thorn rode his sharot to the far ledge and jumped the chasm, landing without any difficulty.

Jacob trembled, his hands shaking so hard he was surprised his own sharot didn't take the tossing reins as a cue to move forward. "I'm not afraid of heights," he uttered under his breath. "I'm not afraid of heights."

Serina smiled at him. "Shall I go now?" He snapped his gaze over to her, embarrassed at the thought that he would wait for her to jump before him.

"No, I'll go." He rode his sharot to the far cliff wall and turned it around to face the edge. On the far side of the ledge from where he stood, the chasm looked impossibly far away for the sharot to be able to make it in one bound. He couldn't even see the ledge he was aiming for this far back. Arys and Makaidel already waited on the higher ledge where the remnants of the bridge hung, beckoning him and shouting encouragements. He swallowed hard.

"I'm not afraid of heights. I'm not afraid of heights."

Of course I'm not afraid of heights, he thought. *I'm afraid of falling.*

Screwing his eyes shut, he took in a deep breath of mountain air, then another, trying to calm his frantically beating heart. *I don't have a choice.* He patted the sharot's shaggy neck.

"You can do it," he stated softly, though his voice betrayed his uneasiness. "I'm counting on you."

"Come on!" Makaidel's distant voice called over the roaring of the waterfall. Thorn had appeared beside him and Arys, adding to their calls.

Clutching the reins with an iron grip, Jacob kicked at the sharot. It lunged forward with a jolt, tearing toward the edge in a bumpy gait that wasn't fast enough for him. In the few seconds it took the sharot to reach the edge, Jacob pictured himself plummeting down the chasm, falling off the sharot as it sailed through the air, the rocks crumbling as they landed, slipping and sliding and falling down, down, so far…

Before he could stop the sharot, it gathered itself in its last step on the ledge and leapt. His heart shot up into his throat as he sailed through the air, nothing but hundreds of feet of open air and a cloud of mist below him. He grasped the hair on the sharot's neck, the jump seeming to take forever to complete. *I didn't make it, oh God, I'm going to die…*

Suddenly, the sharot's feet hit solid ground and he slammed into the saddle. Unprepared for the landing, he slipped at the sharot's step forward for balance and fell off. In the second it took him to drop down beside the sharot, he saw himself making the jump only to fall off on his own down to the river so far below.

As unexpectedly as the first landing was, Jacob smashed against the rock ledge, his entire body on solid ground. He lied still for a moment, panting rapidly. Cheers floated down from above along with Serina's voice calling his name frantically from the other side. The sharot waited silently beside him.

Finally, still trembling all over, he pushed himself up to his knees and glanced over his shoulder. The chasm stretched away behind him, as huge and intimidating as it had been from the other side. Serina gazed down at him worriedly, the ledge where she still waited about as high above as it was far from the one he lied on.

He slowly rose, knees trembling and entire body aching from his landing. Grasping the sharot's reins, he led it up the path along the cliff wall to the ledge where the bridge should have been. His mind was empty of thought as he stumbled up the path. Turning around when he reached the top of the ledge, he saw Thorn give him a thumbs-up. Arys and Makaidel were focused on the other side of the chasm.

Looking across, Jacob watched Serina gallop to the edge and leap towards the ledge just below him. His heart skipped a beat again, but her jump seemed to pass much quicker than his did, and not two seconds later, she landed roughly but safely on the ledge. He let out his breath as she rode up the path toward him.

Makaidel and Arys cheered and began slowly moving their sharots deeper into the mountain, Thorn following behind them. Jacob waited as he watched Serina climb the path toward him.

She smiled as she drew near to him. "Are you alright?"

"Yeah," he answered, his voice hoarse. As he shifted his weight, he cringed, his hipbones stinging from his hard landing. Serina closed her eyes and held her hands together. The rocks around them rumbled faintly and Jacob's pain faded. He weakly smiled his thanks. Mounting his sharot again, he rode forward at a trot to catch up with the others. His heart still pounded in his chest. He would sooner face a hundred orlocs at once than have to do that again.

For the rest of the day, they climbed up through the mountain, Jacob's fear from the jump across the chasm slowly fading as the hours passed by. Most of the scenery was similar and yet unfamiliar to him, the immense size of the mountain making the travel through it much longer than it had been in the game. He frowned when the sun disappeared behind the peaks around them, so many hours of climbing later. Despite that throughout the game, he'd spent a significantly longer time in mountains, caves, temples, and various dungeons than he had traveling over open country, he'd always thought of a place such as where he stood as a single location, and its trials something to overcome in a manner of a few hours. As he gazed up at the still towering summit of the mountain, he wondered how long it would take them to reach their destination. More concerning to him, with the frequency of the orloc attacks, was the question of whether the tents would keep them safe for a restful night of sleep.

He kept his worries silent as they set up camp and ate dinner, but grew uneasy when everyone retreated into their tents, leaving him alone for the first watch of the night. With the firelight blinding him to the darkness that surrounded them, he feared he wouldn't be able to spot any approaching danger until it was too late.

Owls hooted as he crouched in front of the fire, eyes constantly roving around in search of any sign that something was amiss. They had found a small alcove to set up camp that was out of the way and hid the light of their fire well, but he didn't fool himself into thinking that it would keep them entirely safe. He wished the real Aurius had the glowing portals of light scattered throughout the game where the party could rest safely, the special areas where he could save his game and start over if his party died later on. The thought made him uncomfortable. Once more, the overwhelming reality of this world weighed down on him.

Eventually, the moon rose over the peaks, allowing him a slightly better view of his surroundings. Having had to use the moon's position as a guide for the length of his watch, he realized that he had spent two nerve-wracking hours on watch. He relaxed slightly, glad that nothing had happened yet.

To his utter relief, nothing else did when he woke Thorn for his shift and crawled into the tent he shared with Makaidel. The stony floor of the mountain was even harder on his shoulders and hips than the dirt and grasses of the open fields. He didn't know how Makaidel could sleep soundly through it. For once, however, Jacob was glad to be sharing a tent with him and not Serina. Jacob pulled off his shirt without pause and folded it under his shoulder for additional padding. Exhausted as he was from all the dangers and stresses they'd faced from the mountain that day, it didn't take him long to fall asleep.

The next morning, things took a turn for the worse.

IT WASN'T UNTIL Jacob awoke that he realized how much thinner the air had become in their trek. He breathed heavily, trying to fill his lungs with less satisfying air. He was pleased that the light against the tent walls was still orangish from the sunrise. As he rose, however, he heard anxious mutterings outside. Dressing quickly, he stepped out of the tent to find everyone else standing near the fire, talking worriedly.

He stepped forward, appraising their expressions. "What's going on?"

Serina rubbed her arm as she gazed uncertainly at him. "The sharots are gone."

Jacob's eyes widened. "What?"

"They got loose in the night somehow," Makaidel explained. "We even looked as far back as that waterfall yesterday. They're gone."

"But how…" Jacob slowly looked around at their surroundings, trying to find some clue as to what happened to their mounts. Off to the side, his gaze halted. Arys stood at the trees where the sharots had been tied, the ropes holding them now dangling uselessly off the tree trunks.

"You!" Jacob pointed an accusing finger at Arys. "You set them loose!"

Arys blinked in confusion. "What?"

"What are you talking about?" Makaidel asked suspiciously.

"He set them loose, he had to have!" Jacob repeated.

"That's crazy! Why would he even do that?"

"I don't know," Serina's soft voice chimed in.

"That doesn't make sense," Thorn added.

"Thorn," Jacob stated, turning to the large man. "You had second watch, were the sharots here when you were keeping watch?"

"I assumed so, but I never actually saw them." He narrowed his eyes at Jacob. "For all I know, they were gone on your watch."

"Yeah, maybe you're the one who set them loose," Arys snapped.

"Me?" Jacob cried. "Why would I have any reason to do that?"

"Why would Arys?" Makaidel replied.

"He's up to something. He's not one of us!"

Makaidel's voice rose. "One of 'us'? What do you mean '*us*'?"

"Guys," Serina attempted. Jacob glanced over at her worried voice, but Makaidel, Thorn, and Arys continued arguing.

"How do we know we can trust *you?* You're a stranger to all of us!" Arys stated.

"Like you can talk to us about trust," Jacob snarled, spinning to face him.

"You're out of your mind," Makaidel responded. "Arys hasn't given us any reason not to trust him."

"Yeah, how convenient," Jacob hissed.

"You got a problem with me?" Arys growled, stepping forward.

"Yeah, I do!"

"Alright, that's enough!" Thorn's voice rose over all the others as he stepped between Jacob and Arys, spreading his arms to distance them. "Neither of you has given any of the rest of us any reason to distrust you. We're all stuck here, so we might as well work together, all right?" Jacob and Arys simply glared at each other, the bickering silenced with Thorn's intervention.

"We're here for a reason." Makaidel narrowed his eyes at Jacob. "Let's just get moving." Silently, they all returned to their tents and broke them down.

"Well, now we have another problem," Arys remarked as they regrouped. They all followed his gaze to the pile of saddles, bridles, and saddlebags lying on the ground, removed from the sharots when they were tied up the previous night.

"There's no point in bringing the saddles," Thorn stated.

"It's a lot of saddlebags, though," Makaidel commented as he crouched down and examined one. "And we're going to need the food and water."

"We can probably repack them so we don't have to carry so many," Serina stated pleasantly. "We should be able to fit some more in Garrett's backpack, too." Jacob frowned, adjusting the straps of his backpack over his shoulders. He had gotten used to supporting some of the pack's weight on the sharot's back, and to having less in it from eating his own supplies first.

"Well, it's not like we have a choice." Makaidel opened up another bag and began shifting supplies. Thorn, Arys, and Serina knelt beside him to help, and Jacob crouched down nearby and stuffed more food into his own backpack.

"I just hope this'll last us until we get to the next town without the sharots," Thorn stated as he stood up, a saddlebag slung over his shoulder. Jacob glanced at Arys out of the corner of his eye. Irritatingly, the soldier betrayed nothing.

"I'd be more worried about getting off this mountain."

Jacob glanced over his shoulder as the young mage looked back the way they came, but the path twisted and turned around so many ledges and cliff faces that they could only see a few hundred feet back. Jacob had only the thin air to convince him of how far they'd climbed the previous day, and his memory of the jump over the chasm the previous day to remind him how treacherous the travel had become.

Serina flashed them an optimistic smile. "We should get moving." Hefting his backpack, Jacob walked up the ledge out of the alcove where they had camped. The pack was noticeably heavier from the added weight of more supplies and especially the coins he had been carrying in his sharot's saddlebag. The money, important as it was, added the most weight to his burden, and yet it meant nothing in the thick of the mountain. Grunting from effort, he began leading the way down the trail again.

The path became more difficult to follow that day. It was less defined, the flat areas even more riddled with orlocs than the lower part of the mountain had been, and often they would travel down what appeared to be part of the trail, only to find it taper and end suddenly, and they would have to backtrack to find it again. The mountain also rose sharper, and frequently they had to climb ledges up to twenty feet high to continue. Jacob's pack and sword weighed down on him, cumbersome and the straps digging into him. His feet grew sore from traveling the hard, stony ground and he became winded easily from the sparse mountain air. More frustrating still was how the rest of the group always had to wait for him to catch his breath, not seemingly bothered by the harsher travel at all. Cold air from the higher altitude seeped into his lungs and his cheeks reddened from the effort.

Slowly, the sun crept up into the sky until it became visible above the peaks surrounding them, shining onto the inclined mountainside they traveled.

Serina brightened as she shaded her eyes and glanced up into the radiant blue sky above. "Oh, that's so nice and warm."

"Yeah, great, we can see how we're stumbling along even better now," Makaidel remarked. Jacob stopped, breathing deeply a few paces ahead of the others. He frowned. *He's right,* he thought glumly. The path had all but disappeared and they could only guess as they continued up the increasingly treacherous mountain face.

"I don't know how we're going to find anything up here," Thorn stated from several paces back. "Maybe we should turn back." Jacob shook his head, unable to come up with a good reason to keep going. He knew what they sought lay ahead, but he couldn't fathom a guess how far, nor did he have any idea if they were even going the right way.

"Why don't we stop for lunch?" Serina smiled hopefully.

"Where?" Makaidel stated in a flat voice. He was only a few feet behind Jacob, but the terrain they crossed was so steeply inclined that his head was level with Jacob's ankles.

Jacob pointed ahead. "Up here, the ground looks a little flatter." Taking some relief from Serina's optimism, he continued climbing, though his muscles ached from the hard trek. He wondered grimly how they were going to get down after they reached their destination. Even encounters with orlocs had become less frequent, as the terrain was so difficult to navigate.

Reaching the ledge he had seen, he dropped his backpack gracelessly to the ground, panting for air, and soon collapsed beside it. The others climbed up after him. Setting his saddlebag down nearby, Makaidel continued forward, eyes exploring. Thorn, Arys, and Serina crouched around Jacob, digging into the saddlebags they carried for food. Jacob tore into the dried meat he pulled out of his backpack, so famished from the climb that he didn't mind the bland taste.

"Oh, wow!" Makaidel's voice came across the ledge. Jacob turned, finding him gazing out from where the path turned a corner with a wide grin on his face. Open sky framed his form, the emptiness of the air standing out starkly against the craggy mountain face. Makaidel glanced back. "Hey guys, come look at this!"

As one, the group rose and approached Makaidel, peering around the corner of the ledge with him. Jacob's eyes widened at the sight now before him.

"Wow!" Serina breathed.

"Now that's something," Thorn remarked.

The mountain opened up before them. They could see great valleys leading to other peaks, and off in the distance, the land falling and flattening out, stretching out to a horizon Jacob thought must be a hundred miles distant.

Jacob recognized this sight. It was in the game, near the end of the mountain passage. Turning his gaze downward, he scanned the mountainside below.

"Look!" he cried, pointing down and to the left.

Serina leaned forward, shading her eyes as she followed his gaze. "What's that?"

Even Makaidel seemed suitably impressed. "Is that…"

"That's what we're looking for!" Jacob exclaimed. As the ledge they stood on curved around the mountainside, it angled down into a clear path toward a flat span of stone. In its center rose a pedestal surrounded by a circle of crumbling pillars, and he could make out large stones lining the ledge, carved with foreign glyphs.

"Let's go!" Jacob felt rejuvenated by the discovery, excited to finally find their destination ahead of them.

"Slow down, hotfoot," Thorn remarked in an amused voice as he laid a hand on Jacob's shoulder. "Whatever that is, it'll still be there after lunch." Jacob hardly wanted to take his eyes off the familiar landmark, but he turned and followed the group back to the ledge where they had left their packs. He couldn't ignore his own grumbling stomach, but choked down his food hastily in his excitement.

A few minutes later, Jacob stood and hoisted his backpack onto his shoulders, feeling refreshed. Excitement to finally be reaching this major point of the story filled him with energy, and he even grinned at Arys as they began walking again. Arys smiled back, not realizing, Jacob thought, that he knew what the soldier had planned.

The altar remained in view the entire time they approached it, even as the path curved, rose, and fell.

"I can't believe that place is here." Makaidel's eyes fixed on the altar as they followed the path.

"And to think that nobody's found it all this time," Thorn added.

"Well, considering how high up we are, you probably can't see it unless you go through the mountain like we did. And those orlocs weren't easy."

"It looks old," Serina remarked. "I wonder who built it."

"The Alorians, maybe," Makaidel answered.

"We'll know more when we can see those runes," Arys piped in.

They walked on in silence, all eyes staring and wondering. Jacob played over the events at the altar in his mind, preparing himself for what was about to come. At one point, his attention was diverted as the ground dropped away on either side of their feet, the path reduced to a single column of stone cutting through the immense, pine forested valleys stretching out between the mountains. He tried to still his trembling knees and furiously beating heart, knowing that one misstep could be the end of his journey.

Finally, the path rose and spread out into the ledge they had seen from above. They all drew up short, awed. The rock ledge was perfectly smooth, scattered with dust, pebbles, and pine needles, but sanded to a flat floor. The crumbling pillars were ornate and expertly carved clearly a long time ago. Weathered statues lined the ledge with the engraved stones, depicting fantastic creatures and beautiful human-like figures.

"Look!" Makaidel ran over to one of the stones. "I've seen this exact symbol in ancient texts from the Dekaal library. This *was* built by the Alorians!" The others murmured in excitement. Jacob paused, expecting an explanation, but he realized that the Alorians, the ancient, advanced, and beautiful elf-like people that had grown scarce and disappeared only a generation ago, were probably common knowledge to this real Aurius.

Serina pointed to the pedestal in the center of the broken pillars. "What's up there?" A green glow seemed to emanate from the top of the pedestal, bathing it in soft light. Slowly, they approached, passing between the ancient pillars and climbing the stairs leading up to it.

Lying in the center of the pedestal and the green glow illuminating it was a triangular silver talisman with a teardrop-shaped emerald cabochon in the center of it.

"What is that?" Makaidel breathed, stunned. At the words, Jacob glanced over his shoulder.

"It looks just like…" Serina began.

Jacob caught only a glimpse of Arys, standing behind them with raised arms and a sinister grin on his face.

"Look out!" Jacob lunged aside and pulled Serina with him. A flash of light flared behind him. Makaidel and Thorn cried out as they stumbled down the stairs. Finding his balance on the smooth floor, Jacob turned, seeing Arys facing him with sword drawn. He spun, drawing his own blade.

Arys grinned at him. "I don't know how you figured me out, but it doesn't matter. I can take you down without breathing hard, and then, that talisman's mine."

Jacob narrowed his eyes. "You did release the sharots, didn't you?" Arys looked completely different with the sinister look on his face.

"Precisely." He grinned wider, proud of his accomplishment. "I even persuaded them to jump back over that waterfall we passed yesterday. It's a shame two of them didn't make it, but the rest have at least a fifty percent chance of finding their way back down the mountain." Jacob clenched his teeth, infuriated by the casual way he'd spoken of sending the loyal sharots to their doom.

"W… what are you doing?" Serina uttered from behind Jacob.

"Poor, innocent Serina. It's a shame we never got to know each other better. Of course, once I kill your boyfriend, maybe I'll take you with me and get to know you *real* well."

Jacob's hands trembled, hate boiling in his heart at the thought. Arys laughed as Jacob glared at him.

Suddenly, Arys charged, bringing his sword up with a yell. Jacob pushed Serina out of the way, raising his own sword to block the blow. Sparks shot out as the blades clashed together, jarring Jacob's arms from the force of the attack. Pulling back, Arys swung again. Jacob brought his sword up to parry again, the clang of blades ringing over the altar. Again and again their swords met, Jacob barely keeping Arys's sword at bay. He stepped backward against the onslaught, drawn slowly toward the outer circle of the crumbling pillars. His heart pounded, realizing that with the strength and skill Arys had with the sword, he was a far more dangerous opponent than he had faced yet, but the fear that normally filled Jacob when he faced orlocs was not there. Every time he had played the game, he pictured this battle that never happened. He had been preparing for this confrontation for a long time, and Arys's taunts about Serina only fueled his rage.

Their swords locked together and Arys spun his, intending to twist Jacob's weapon out of his grip. Jacob suddenly remembered a maneuver Rollis had used against him in the exact same situation. Using Arys's own momentum, Jacob pushed his blade down, throwing both sword tips to the ground. As he did, he released his left hand from the hilt and raised his arm, slamming his elbow against Arys's face. Arys yelped as he stumbled backward from the blow. While he was distracted, Jacob charged, but Arys brought his sword up and parried the blow. Now Jacob advanced, swinging vehemently and driving Arys back.

Arys had nearly backed up against one of the pillars when Jacob miscalculated an attack. He lunged aside quickly, but Arys's sword slashed against his arm. He cried out in pain, grasping the wound, but he was allowed no respite. He jumped back from the false soldier's next attack, then brought his blade up to parry the next. His grip was weak, however, and the locked swords pushed toward his neck.

Suddenly, the pain faded and he felt the wound close. Vowing to thank Serina later, he pushed out with all his strength, then turned the blade. Swords still locked together, Jacob guided Arys's weapon around to the side and back down to the ground. Before he could move, however, Arys brought his leg up, driving his knee into Jacob's stomach. Jacob coughed as he doubled over from the blow. Then, Arys grabbed the back of Jacob's head, slamming it down onto his still raised knee. He stumbled back with a moan, just barely lunging clear of Arys's next swing. Face pounding, Jacob slashed out blindly, his sword tearing into the soldier's chest. Jacob shuffled back as Arys recoiled from the blow. In that moment, Jacob felt his pain abate and he blinked as he glimpsed Arys. Shaking off the pain of the wound Jacob had inflicted, the soldier charged, and Jacob raised his sword to parry.

The clangs of swords clashing rang across the altar, bouncing off the steeply rising mountainsides bordering it. What happened beyond the space Arys occupied, Jacob didn't know. For all he knew, they were the only people there.

His parries began to slow, his arms aching from the effort, and more slashes began to creep inside his defenses. Serina was always quick to heal him, but if he didn't defeat Arys soon, he might receive a wound too deep for her magic to work.

As their swords crashed together again, before Jacob could prepare for it, Arys kicked him hard in the stomach, throwing him to the ground. Jacob rolled away as he saw Arys approach, but knew he wasn't fast enough to get away from the false soldier.

Then, a blinding flash of white-gold light lit up the altar. Arys cried out as he was thrown away. Jacob turned quickly to face Makaidel, but the boy was still lying where he had fallen in front of the pedestal, slowly beginning to stir. Jacob glanced over his shoulder and found Serina leaning heavily on her staff, hair falling over her face. His eyes widened, realizing that she had just performed the first Runic Seal of the game, the magical special attacks that the characters learned as they grew stronger.

"Hurry," she uttered weakly.

Setting aside her incredible attack, Jacob threw himself to his feet and engaged Arys again. Jacob fought harder than before, knowing that everything depended on him. He still struggled to parry all of Arys's swings, but his aggressive attack pushed the soldier back until he was pinned against a pillar. Jacob leaned his whole body weight against his sword, inching closer to Arys's neck.

"You're not a swordfighter!" the soldier coughed out defiantly.

Jacob grinned. "No, but I'm a hero. We always win." Summoning a reserve of strength Jacob hadn't anticipated, Arys shoved out, pushing him away. As Jacob stepped back, however, he kicked out, knocking Arys to the ground, the soldier's sword flinging away out of reach. Before he could recover, Jacob stepped forward, raising his sword point down over Arys's back.

Then, he hesitated. Traitor or no, what he was about to do was murder.

In his heartbeat of indecision, he lost his chance. Something exploded against his back, hurtling him through the air with a cry echoed by Serina. Slamming into the ground, he heard the clang of his sword landing several paces away.

"Arys, you pathetic fool," stated a malevolent, hissing voice. Glancing over his shoulder, Jacob saw the scorpion-like monster that had replaced Fahren in Lord Kyutu's castle standing within the ring of ancient pillars. It grinned sadistically at Jacob. "Lucky for you I came to make sure you succeeded."

Roused, Makaidel and Thorn stood beside the pedestal in the center of the pillars.

"You!" Makaidel shouted. "What are you doing here?" The monster turned its amused grin to the young mage.

"Only finishing the job this lout couldn't handle." Spinning around in a blur, the monster slammed its segmented tail against Makaidel and Thorn, tossing them aside with matched yelps. Jacob pushed himself to his hands and knees, desperately fighting to stand. *It's not supposed to happen this way!*

Climbing nimbly up to the pedestal, the monster snatched the talisman off it without ceremony. "Master should reward *me* well for this."

"No, you can't…" Arys desperately held out a hand to the monster. Rising to his feet, Jacob began running back towards the pedestal.

"Farewell, hero*sss*," the monster hissed, grinning at him.

"Wait!" Jacob yelled as he neared the pillars. A sudden lurch threw Jacob off his feet, flung toward Arys. In a blinding flare of light, Arys and monster disappeared, and Jacob fell to the ground, the talisman gone.

The mountain trembled, a deep, penetrating rumble ringing through the air all around them.

"What's going on?" Makaidel glanced around wildly from where he stood next to the pedestal. He screamed as a pillar toppled over behind him, the stone crashing and breaking into chunks near his feet.

"The mountain's collapsing!" Rising to his feet, Jacob ran back to retrieve his sword, then over to help Serina up. He pointed to the far end of the altar, where the path resumed. "Hurry, this way!"

"Wait! Let's just go back the way we came!" Makaidel raced back towards the path they had taken to arrive at the altar, Thorn on his heels. Jacob turned to watch them, but didn't move. Makaidel skidded to a stop with a gasp at the end of the platform. The mountain's tremors had shattered the raised path across the valley.

"This way! Come on!" Sheathing his sword, Jacob ran forward through the pillars as the pedestal toppled over and shattered against the stairs leading up to it. The mountain roared around them, huge boulders breaking free and tumbling down the mountainsides towards the altar.

"Look out!" Jacob called over his shoulder as a shower of rubble rained down near the edge of the platform. The path narrowed, weaving through trees, boulders, and ledges. Jacob ran without abandon, barely keeping his balance against the quaking ground. He skidded down a rocky slope, hearing the rattling of stones against the feet of the others behind him. Huge boulders thudded down the slope after them.

As they darted through another wooded area, Jacob heard Serina cry out behind him.

"Serina!" He stopped in his tracks and glanced back at her. Makaidel and Thorn paused as they came up beside him. He waved his arm at them. "Go!" They hesitantly continued as Jacob raced back toward Serina. She raised herself to her hands as he crouched beside her.

"I'm okay," she stated, though her voice was strained.

"Can you stand?" He took her arm and helped her up.

"I think so." She cringed as she put weight on her left leg and sank down again. Inhaling deeply, Jacob slipped a hand beneath her knees and lifted her into his arms. He shifted, arms still sore from the battle and entirely unused to carrying so much weight, little though it was in her delicate body.

Hearing a series of crashes trailing down the mountain near him, he turned and ran. Serina wrapped her arms around his neck, bouncing in his arms with his gait. Trees snapped around him as the mountain face itself rained down upon them, each stone jolting the ground beneath Jacob's feet. His heart pounded. He could hear boulders crash onto the path ahead of him as well as behind.

Finally, they came around a bend to a long, flat ledge. It ended in a chasm with a natural bridge arcing over it. Makaidel and Thorn were already near the bridge. Jacob ran after them, struggling to continue holding Serina in his trembling arms. His chest constricted from their escape and he gasped in huge lungfuls of thin air.

He had slowed to a modest trot by the time he reached the natural bridge. It was the last obstacle, he realized, as the ledge on the far side attached to a different mountain that remained steady and solid. Groaning, he climbed the arch of the natural bridge, the ground dropping away to either side of him even farther than the waterfall had. The natural bridge's incline seemed tremendous, but the top of the arch loomed near, beckoning. Sweat poured over his brow and clung to his shirt even as the thin, cool air of the mountain pierced at his lungs. *Almost there,* he thought.

A shadow fell over the far cliff wall. Quickly, he gazed up, and his eyes widened.

"Look out!" he yelled, throwing himself backwards. Catching the faintest glimpse of the shadow, Thorn grabbed Makaidel and lunged forward across the natural bridge. A boulder the size of a car crashed down onto the bridge, breaking free a chunk of it eight feet across. Jacob gazed over the side, watching the boulder and section of bridge plummet into the fathomless depths below. He swallowed hard.

Looking up, he saw Thorn and Makaidel standing on the other side of the gap, gazing back at him.

"Come on!" Makaidel called out.

"Jump!" Thorn stated, his deep voice only just registering in Jacob's ears over the roar of the mountain. Jacob's heart turned to ice at the sight. Arms trembling, he set Serina on her feet again.

"It's okay," she stated, her voice sweet and gentle even as she spoke so loudly. She smiled at him. "We can make it." He didn't answer and simply gazed back at the break in the natural bridge. Flecks of stone still crumbled down from the jagged edges. He remembered this scene in the game, but he hadn't played through it. The jump across the natural bridge had been a fully rendered, movie-like scene in the game. It had been exciting to watch, but gazing across the gap in the bridge, Jacob quailed, certain he couldn't jump that far.

"Hurry!" Thorn and Makaidel yelled over to him. Falling boulders pounded the ledge behind Jacob, causing tremors beneath his feet. Serina grasped his hand, her gaze imploring. He shook his head, the cracking and thuds of boulders behind him deafening. He couldn't risk her not making the jump. Remembering how Serina had crossed in the game, he crouched, lacing his fingers together into a cup at knee height. He gestured at his hands. Serina looked tearful at the suggestion, but glancing over her shoulder, she stepped back several paces.

Taking in a deep breath, she raced toward the broken edge of the natural bridge as fast as she could. At the last step, she lifted her foot onto his cupped hands. With all the force he could muster, he pulled his hands up as she leaped out of them, flinging her towards the far side of the bridge. He spun quickly, balancing himself with his hand. She landed lightly onto the other side of the natural bridge, Makaidel and Thorn steadying her. Turning, they waved madly at him, yelling words he could no longer hear.

Rising, he stepped back a few paces. He feinted back and forth several times, terrified of missing the jump. It was the waterfall all over again, except this time, he had no sharot to trust or to jump off if he didn't make it. His heart pounded against his ribs. The other side seemed impossibly far away. Finally, holding his breath, he ran forward, trying to make his feet carry him faster than they ever had before.

Suddenly, the stone beneath his feet jolted, throwing him off balance. As he struggled to stop before he flew over the edge, he realized the angle of the bridge was growing sharper and the far end was sinking. A boulder had struck the natural bridge further back and broken it free of the ledge that was still assaulted by falling rocks.

Racing forward, he leaped off the edge desperately, reaching his arms out. Thorn stretched out his hand as far as he could reach. It felt like time stood still as Jacob sailed through the air, reaching for Thorn's huge hand. His heart skipped a beat as he began falling before he came near it. In a spasm of relief, he felt his gloved hand touch Thorn's. The relief was immediately replaced with horror as their fingertips brushed each other, Thorn not getting enough grip to grab Jacob's hand. Jacob felt his fingers brush the stone of the natural bridge as he fell, but not a breath later, it was gone, and there was nothing anywhere around him but open air, cliff walls, and a chasm so deep he couldn't see the bottom.

He couldn't even hear his own scream as he plummeted down into the darkness.

SUDDENLY, A WHIRRING sound and metallic clang rang across Jacob's ears as he fell into the chasm. In that moment, a hand wrapped around his wrist in a tight grasp.

He opened his eyes with a start as his weight fell onto his wrist and he was swung to the side. Glancing up in surprise, he found himself supported by a woman holding a coil of rope hanging down from the natural bridge where Serina, Makaidel, and Thorn waited. Her long ponytail of lavender hair, strangely natural despite the unusual shade, streamed behind her as she swung on the rope. She grinned at him.

"Better watch that last step."

"Kalista?" Jacob exclaimed, shocked to find her here, well before he was supposed to meet her in the game. Her smile faded instantly to a suspicious look as they swung back underneath the natural bridge.

"How do you know my name?"

Crap! he thought, realizing too late his mistake. He wracked his mind quickly for an answer.

"Uh, word of your exploits travels far."

Her face lit up at his words, eyes glittering enthusiastically. "Really?"

Oh, great, he thought, remembering the character's inflated ego in the game.

Kalista smirked. "Well, you're definitely worth saving." She pulled him up with surprising ease until his hand was as high as hers.

He reached his other hand up and grabbed the rope that supported them. He leaned his head back, uncomfortable with the way his body pressed up against hers as they hung down from the remnants of the natural bridge. She grinned at him, nodding upward.

"Climb up, the end's attached to me." Jacob glanced up, frowning at the distance he had to climb. He had never been very good at climbing the rope in gym class, and that was with knots to help him. Swinging his body to the side, he reached a hand above the other. Swinging the other way, he repeated the action, increasingly uncomfortable with being so close to her. He grunted as he struggled to reach hand over hand, his arms still aching from the fight with Arys and from carrying Serina down the path.

Slowly, he advanced up the rope, growing more tired with each hand up. Several feet up, he paused for breath and looked down. Vertigo swam over him as he gazed into the abyss of the chasm, descending into shadows. He still couldn't see the bottom of it. He tightened his fingers around the rope reflexively. Turning his gaze, he glanced at Kalista, hanging below him, but immediately regretted it. Her eyes roamed over his body as she grinned at him.

Leaning his head back, he gazed upward and began climbing again. His arms ached fiercely from the effort and each movement felt like it would be the last he could manage. Every gasp of breath rang through the immense chasm, the rumbling of the mountain on the other side finally stopped. Glancing at the far side, he saw the ledge they had come from buried in rocks over a story high. There was no trace of the natural bridge remaining on the far side.

Groaning, he threw one hand over the other. Only five feet of rope remained between him and the remaining part of the natural bridge, but his strength was spent and it took all his energy simply to hold on. To his relief, Thorn reached down to grab the hanging rope and pulled it up almost effortlessly. Jacob gratefully held his trembling arm out for Thorn's outstretched hand. Still holding the rope securely, Thorn lifted Jacob up onto the natural bridge. Solid ground beneath his feet had never felt so good. His legs felt rubbery, and shortly he fell to his knees.

"Garrett!" Serina raced over and threw her arms around his neck. "Oh, I was so scared!" He couldn't answer, his lungs burning with each breath he took. He could hardly believe so little time had passed with all that had happened. Only half an hour had passed since they had finished their lunch.

Behind him, Thorn pulled Kalista up onto the natural bridge. She stood calmly, seemingly unaffected by the climb up the rope.

Pulling back from Jacob, Serina stated, "Thank you so much for saving him."

"It was no problem." Kalista brushed dust off her arms. "Of course, a rescue like that is worth two silvers, at least." She grinned at Jacob. "I'm giving you a discount because I think you're cute."

"What?" Makaidel stated in a flat voice.

"Well, I'm a rogue. I make my living this way. I can't just go around giving out freebies, no matter how much I like my client." Jacob frowned, remembering that line from later in the game, but couldn't muster the energy to respond.

Makaidel's eyes narrowed. "That is the shallowest..."

"Here," Serina cut in, digging a few coins out of her pouch. "It's the least I can do for you for saving him." Jacob raised his head to gaze at her. She smiled at him, eyes glistening wetly. The sight warmed him and he felt slightly energized thinking that she cared so much about him.

"My pleasure," Kalista answered with a grin, though she eagerly pocketed the money.

"Well, let's get off this rock before it decides to fall, too," Thorn stated. Serina lifted Jacob's arm around her shoulders. He cringed, the movement causing his exhausted arm to throb, but he relished the attention.

"So, what were you doing up here?" Makaidel asked, giving Kalista a suspicious look.

"I travel all over Aurius," she answered, apparently proud of that fact. "It just so happens I was up on this path when I heard the mountain start to collapse. Good thing I decided to come check it out, or it would've been bad news for red here."

"His name's Garrett," Serina stated. "This is Thorn and Makaidel. I'm Serina."

Kalista struck a pose. "And I'm Kalista, journeywoman and rogue for hire! I'm sure you've heard of me."

"No," Makaidel and Thorn answered in unison. Serina shook her head.

"What?" Kalista spun on Jacob. "I thought you said word of my exploits traveled this far north!" Jacob didn't answer, but grinned off to the side. She was every bit as conceited and self-centered as she had been in the game and he enjoyed tearing her down. He coughed, knees trembling.

"He needs to rest," Serina stated.

"Let's stop up here," Makaidel added, pointing to a cluster of trees at the end of the ledge before the path resumed. "I could use some more food myself."

Hope alighted in Kalista's voice. "Food?"

Serina lowered Jacob gently onto a mossy patch of ground at the base of one of the trees. Crouching over him, she held her staff out. His strength seeped back as the crystals on her staff glowed. He felt as exhausted as he had after a full afternoon of sparring with Rollis.

Makaidel and Thorn sat down near Jacob and Serina, digging food out of their packs. Kalista stood at the edge of the trees, fiddling with her hands.

"Do… do you have any food you could spare?" Makaidel narrowed his eyes at her.

"Sure," Serina began to answer, but Jacob held a hand up to her, silencing her.

"This stuff isn't free." He gazed expectantly at Kalista. She blinked, not catching his meaning for a moment. Then, her eyes widened in realization.

She growled, balling her hands into fists as her shoulders shook. "Fine."

She tossed the silver coins she'd taken from Serina at his feet. He tossed her an apple, grinning at his victory. Makaidel snickered.

"There, I'd say we're even now, wouldn't you?" Grunting, she dropped down to eat. Thorn and Makaidel smiled. Jacob glanced at Serina beside him, but his smile faded when he saw a disappointed look on her face. He ate quietly, feeling guilty.

A few bites later, Makaidel asked, "So, what was that thing on the pedestal?"

"Must've been important, the way those guys were after it," Thorn stated.

"It looked just like Garrett's pendant," Serina remarked, turning to gaze at the amber teardrop hanging around Jacob's neck. Kalista glanced back and forth, curiously listening to the conversation as she ate.

"Maybe it's one of those element stones Phantis mentioned," Jacob stated.

"But what are they?" Makaidel asked, his eyes on Jacob's pendant as well. "If that thing was an element stone, then your pendant is, too. Does it do anything special?"

"No." Jacob glanced away, more disappointed than they realized.

"That monster mentioned a master," Thorn stated. "You think it's working for someone?"

"It's got to be," Makaidel responded. "Maybe whoever that thing's master is caused all the orlocs to appear." Jacob frowned, knowing the truth was far more complicated, but he remembered this conversation from the game and knew he couldn't help them.

"Caused the orlocs to appear?" Serina looked as hurt by the thought as if it had been a close friend of hers to do so. "Why would anybody want to do that?"

Jacob felt guilty saying things he knew to be lies, but he recited his lines from the game. "It makes sense. If these element stones were made by the Alorians, then they probably have enough power to stop whoever released the orlocs. And he wouldn't want that."

Makaidel folded his arms over his knees with a frustrated sigh. "I just wish we knew more." Serina and Thorn nodded and murmured in agreement, but Jacob thought, *You won't when you do know the truth.*

Suddenly, Makaidel glanced up at Jacob. "So, what happened at the altar?"

"Um…" Jacob fumbled for words as the conversation drifted outside of the script he had memorized.

"Arys betrayed us." Serina looked away. "He attacked you and Thorn and then fought Garrett."

Makaidel shook his head. "I can't believe it. He was really a traitor all along."

Jacob turned suddenly to Serina. “And you did a Runic Seal.”

The young mage’s eyes lit up. “You did? Really?” Even Kalista gazed over in surprise.

To Jacob’s relief, Serina smiled again. “I guess I did.”

“Wow,” Makaidel breathed. “Nobody’s known how to do a Runic Seal for years! How did you do it?”

Serina shrugged with an uncertain smile. “I don’t know. I just wished really hard that I could help Garrett, and the next thing I knew, I was casting a spell I’ve never done before.” The others murmured in amazement at this revelation.

“Maybe that’s what the Hero’s pendant does,” Thorn offered. All eyes turned to the talisman hanging around Jacob’s neck. “Allows us to perform Runic Seals.”

Jacob blinked, surprised and pleased with the thought that his homemade pendant could do something in this world after all. “You think so?”

“It could be. Not much is known about the Hero’s pendant.” Makaidel beamed. “I hope I get to learn a Runic Seal next!” Thorn grinned in amusement.

“If the legends about the Hero’s pendant are true,” Serina added, “then we should all be able to learn Runic Seals.” Jacob examined the amber teardrop. A thrill of excitement rose in his heart as he imagined being able to perform Runic Seals as well.

Thorn stood. “Well, I suppose we’ll find out soon enough. In the meantime, where do we go now?” He was looking at Jacob. Jacob hesitated, the words from the game momentarily forgotten.

“We should keep going south. There seem to be more orlocs the further south you go. We might be able to find out more where there’s more of them.” The others nodded assent and began to rise.

Kalista stood up. “Well, it looks like you guys are on a pretty big quest.”

“Thank you again for saving Garrett.” Serina beamed at the rogue. “It was nice meeting you.”

Kalista cleared her throat. “Yes, you, too… but anyway, you guys are going to need a guide if you go south, and it just so happens I’m free.”

“I’m sure we can find our way fine,” Makaidel stated flatly. “We have a map.”

“I think it’s a wonderful idea,” Serina stated.

“I’ll even give you a discount,” Kalista added. “For… no, fifty gold.”

Thorn’s eyebrows rose. “Fifty gold?”

“That’s a ripoff!” Jacob exclaimed.

“Hey! I’m very skilled! There are people who would kill to hire me that cheap.”

“So go find them,” Makaidel snapped.

"Guys…" Serina looked hurt.

"We're not getting *paid* to do this," Makaidel continued. "We're trying to save the world."

"But…" Kalista began desperately.

"We should go," Thorn stated.

"But…"

"Makaidel," Serina stated. "You must have…"

"Forget it," the boy snapped. "If we need the help, we can find someone who will come with us just for the sake of helping. I'm not paying for someone to accompany us."

"Garrett," Serina pleaded. Jacob frowned. Makaidel was the one to dislike Kalista in the game, but he couldn't help finding himself agreeing with the young mage. He had never liked the Kalista he knew, and he didn't find himself liking her any more in person.

"I don't have fifty gold," he stated simply, not wanting to hurt Serina's feelings, though he never understood why she was so kind to Kalista. He hoisted his backpack over his aching shoulders.

"Okay, okay, how about this," Kalista attempted. "You can pay me half now, and then…"

"We have to go," Makaidel cut in shortly, to Jacob's relief. Avoiding Kalista's eyes, Jacob moved onto the path and began walking. The others followed after him silently.

Jacob glanced back, finding Serina laying a hand on Kalista's shoulder. "I'm sorry." Turning, she jogged down the path until she came up alongside Jacob quietly. Guilt wracked his heart at the upset look on her face. Somehow, he felt bad about refusing Kalista, even though he didn't like her. Shifting, he increased his pace, wanting only to leave the rogue behind.

The group walked in silence, the path winding peacefully through the mountain. Jacob wondered why he hadn't thought to try taking this path up to the altar. It would, he realized, have made a much easier climb.

A few minutes into their trek, Thorn stated just loud enough for them to hear, "She's following us, you know." All eyes turned to look behind them. Kalista, some few dozen paces back, immediately tried to look casual, examining a tree branch as she passed by.

Makaidel stepped in front of Thorn. "We're not going to change our minds! Stop following us!"

Kalista looked indignant. "Hey, I have to get off this mountain, too! You don't own it!"

"Actually…" Makaidel muttered under his breath, but clearly thought better of saying anything more.

"Guys, please." Serina stepped forward. "Why don't you travel with us, Kalista?"

"Really?" Kalista perked up. She jogged down the path toward them.

"I'm sure it would be alright." Serina smiled brightly at Jacob. "Garrett?" He frowned, knowing he couldn't refuse her.

"Thanks! It's always more fun traveling with people. I always said…"

"Just be quiet, would you?" Makaidel snapped as he passed by Thorn again.

"Quiet. Right. Gotcha. No problem." Jacob turned with an inaudible frustrated sigh and began leading the way down the path again.

They had only walked a handful of steps before Kalista stated, "So, where do you guys…"

"Quiet!" Makaidel interrupted.

"Sorry." Kalista fell silent. Serina giggled softly. Jacob managed a grin as he glanced at her.

The afternoon passed quietly, and Jacob often forgot Kalista was even there. The trek was comfortable, the path descending gently, always well maintained, and the mountain was rich with the scent of the pine trees blanketing it. Birds twittered in the trees and the air was clean and rich.

The journey was so peaceful that it came as a complete surprise when an orloc crashed out of the trees to attack them.

They scattered, Jacob drawing his sword as he spun to face the monster. It hesitated, snarling at each of them in turn. Running forward, Jacob slashed at its neck, then leaped to the side as it spun to snap at him.

Before he could swing at it again, a pair of legs flew in, slamming against the beast's head and throwing it aside. Jacob faltered, watching in surprise as Kalista flipped over it, brandishing two short, arcing blades with a handle jutting out from the inside curve, the blades running parallel to her forearms. The orloc snapped at her with a snarl, but she spun away in a blur, slashing at it with her weapons. The orloc's attention was entirely on Kalista, but with the way she darted around and leaped over it, Jacob knew he couldn't get in a clear hit. He frowned in annoyance. He had, to his surprise, come to enjoy his confrontations with orlocs, and Kalista was clearly only showing off.

She ducked underneath the orloc as it leaped toward her, slashing both blades across its throat. It jerked in mid-air and began to fall. Lunging forward under the creature's falling body, she somersaulted on the ground, coming up on one knee and striking a pose with her blades. The orloc crashed limply to the ground behind her.

"Wow!" Serina clapped her hands together as she gazed admiringly at Kalista. "That was amazing!" Jacob glared at Kalista, even more irritated for her stealing Serina's adoration away from him. Makaidel grumbled something off to the side.

Ignoring their reactions, Kalista rose with a grin and tossed her hip-length ponytail over her shoulder. "Now that you've seen what I can do, I'm sure you…"

"We're not paying you!" Makaidel snapped.

"Makaidel…" Serina attempted.

"No. We need this money."

"But," Kalista began, looking heartbroken, but trailed off before she said anything more. She gazed at Jacob imploringly. He glanced away, wishing they wouldn't leave such a difficult decision on his shoulders. He rubbed the back of his neck.

"I'm sorry, but we just don't have that much money to spare."

"That's okay," she replied, desperation clear in her voice. "You can pay me later."

"Ugh!" Makaidel stormed off down the path. Jacob was about to echo his sentiments, but as he turned to face Kalista, he saw Serina with a pleading look on her face. He cringed, knowing he would regret either choice.

"We'll have to talk about it."

Kalista smiled eagerly. "Okay."

"But we haven't agreed to anything yet," Jacob added. Clasping her hands behind her back, she nodded meekly. He turned and began walking down the path again. Serina ran lightly up beside him and smiled.

"Thanks, Garrett."

He gave her a weak grin in return as they continued down the mountainside.

AFTERNOON FADED INTO evening, and as the sun began to set, they set up camp for the night. The mountain grew dark quickly after the sun disappeared behind the peaks surrounding them. Kalista stood several paces separated from the group, fiddling with her hands as Makaidel built a fire and Jacob, Serina, and Thorn set up their tents.

"So, I guess you guys are going to have your own camp…"

Serina smiled and held a hand out to her. "Why don't you join us?"

"Really?" Kalista brightened. "You wouldn't mind?" Jacob was glad for the darkness to hide him rolling his eyes. The way she manipulated emotions, using guilt and humility at once to get anything she wanted, reminded him annoyingly of his first girlfriend. He had showered gifts on her because of the way she would point out something she wanted, act like it wasn't important, then mope the rest of the day if he didn't buy it for her right then. He had felt fortunate to meet Tina, who not only shared his interests and liked him for who he was, but was decidedly more direct and didn't play those games with him.

He paused as he finished pitching his tent. It had been a while since he had thought about Tina. The mere thought of her caused a brief pang of longing in his heart. He wondered how she was doing. A sigh escaped from him. She was probably better off without him.

Shaking off the thought, he rose and approached the fire. Makaidel dug through his pack, clearly as unimpressed with Kalista's antics as Jacob had been. Serina, Makaidel, Thorn, and Kalista circled the fire so closely that there was little room for him to join them.

"Here, Garrett," Serina offered with a smile and edged aside. Kalista did likewise and he sat down between them. He fought an idiotic grin from spreading on his face. *How many guys my age would do anything to be here right now?* He allowed a smile, knowing there was nowhere else he would rather be at that moment.

Kalista gazed longingly at his pack as he opened it and retrieved some food from within. His appetite raged after the hectic day.

"Say, do you have any extra...?" Makaidel glared at her across the fire and Jacob shot her a frown.

Thorn raised an eyebrow at Kalista. "Don't you have any food?"

Kalista shifted uncomfortably. "I... haven't resupplied recently."

"What kind of rogue can't get her own food?" Makaidel asked dubiously.

"I... I was robbed."

Serina gasped. "That's awful!"

Jacob narrowed his eyes, remembering the same excuse from the game. "No, you weren't." It wasn't a question. She trembled under his hard gaze.

Hunching her shoulders, she admitted, "You're right. I just... haven't been able to get food lately."

"I'm so sorry to hear that." Serina dug in the saddlebag she carried. "Here, you can have this." Jacob made a small noise of protest, but before he could stop her, she had handed a chunk of bread and a strip of meat across him to Kalista.

"Thanks!" Kalista ravenously tore into the food. Jacob chewed his own dinner, surprised at the ferocity with which Kalista ate.

When she finished, she glanced around at the group. "So, you're trying to save the world, huh?" Jacob and Makaidel shared a glance before looking away, annoyed.

"Yes." Serina smiled across Jacob. "We're going to stop the orlocs."

"Wow. How are you going to do that?"

Serina brushed a lock of hair away from her eyes bashfully. "Well, we're not entirely sure yet. We need to find out why they've appeared, and why they seem to be multiplying so quickly first."

"Oh."

The camp fell silent but for the snaps and crackles of the fire. Darkness blanketed the mountainside, though the sky was still painted pink and violet from the sunset. Glowing streaks of fireflies floated slowly around the forest, tiny green sparks alight on the wind like the sparks of the fire.

"We should get to sleep," Makaidel stated, voice calm for the first time since they reached the altar that afternoon.

"Good idea." Thorn stood and stretched, then moved toward his tent. Makaidel and Serina did the same.

Kalista looked dejected. "Oh. Yeah, sleep... that sounds good."

"Don't you have a tent, Kalista?" Serina asked.

"N-not really." Kalista fiddled with her hands. Jacob made a face at her manipulation.

"That's okay, you can share mine."

"So, who's going to take third watch tonight?" Thorn asked. Jacob paused, realizing he hadn't thought of who would take Arys's place.

In a flash of ingenuity, he glanced over his shoulder. "What about Kalista?"

Kalista turned, halfway into Serina's tent. "What?"

Makaidel grinned widely. "That's a great idea!"

Jacob smirked at her. "Since you're staying in our camp, you can take the third shift of the night watch." Serina smiled her approval.

"Okay," Kalista stated hesitantly. Then, she donned a confident smile. "But that's rogue's work."

Makaidel gave her a hard gaze. "Consider it repayment for the food." Her eyes widened, then she nodded, subdued.

Thorn stretched. "Well, I'm looking forward to having my tent all to myself tonight." Jacob half-smiled, wishing he could enjoy the same solitude.

He glanced over at his tent hopefully. "Makaidel?"

The boy smirked. "No, I'm good here. You said you'd rather stay in a tent with me, anyway." Jacob frowned, though he said nothing.

Thorn chuckled. "'Night."

A chorus of 'goodnight' rang around the group as everyone but Jacob retreated into their tents. He grinned at the fire, thinking that he had handled Kalista well that day. Shortly, his smile faded. *Maybe I should've been nicer to her.* If she hadn't been at the natural bridge when she was, he would be dead now. He shuddered from the memory of falling into the chasm.

Shaking off the thought, he reached for another branch to put on the fire. The air filled with the tangy scent of burning pine as stars winked to life above.

Jacob awoke with Makaidel the next morning and emerged from the tent when the sky was painted red and orange from the sunrise.

"Morning, guys," Kalista greeted a little too enthusiastically, crouched in front of the fire. Jacob opened his backpack for breakfast, but paused. His supplies had been rearranged.

Kalista looked sheepish. "I'm sorry." Jacob glared at her. "I got hungry earlier, so I had an early breakfast."

"It's okay." Serina opened her saddlebag. "Here, Garrett, you can…"

"No, that's alright," he grumbled.

Grabbing Jacob's sleeve, Makaidel said to Kalista, "We have to talk." Jacob walked off to the side as Makaidel pulled him away, Serina and Thorn following. They passed outside of the clearing where they had camped, still in view of Kalista but out of earshot. Makaidel's eyes were firm.

"This can't go on. She has to go."

"But she just wants to help us," Serina stated.

"No, she just wants us to pay her. You can never trust anyone who's in it just for the money."

"But she seems so nice." Serina glanced back through the trees at Kalista.

"So did Arys," Thorn remarked.

Makaidel nodded. "We can't afford to keep her around."

"She seems pretty skilled." Thorn stroked his goatee thoughtfully. "But if she's just going to mooch off our supplies, we're going to end up with problems."

"Yeah," Makaidel stated, "and what kind of rogue is she that she can't even get her own food?"

"She's probably just had some back luck," Serina offered.

"She thinks we're suckers. She even admitted to stealing food this morning."

Jacob listened quietly to the conversation, frowning. He never thought he would feel sympathetic towards Kalista, but knowing her true history, he couldn't bring himself to dismiss her like Makaidel wanted.

"Garrett?" Serina asked, and all eyes turned to him. "What do you think?"

He shifted. "I agree that we can't let her continue to mooch off us, and we can't afford to pay her to come with us. But," he stated quickly, seeing Serina's hurt expression, "if she wants to join us without being paid, I won't tell her no."

"And," Makaidel added, "if she's going to be using our supplies, *she* should pay *us*." Jacob nodded.

Serina smiled. "I guess that's fair."

"Everyone needs to pull their own weight," Makaidel stated. "We all do." Jacob nodded again.

Thorn nodded. "She's handy to have around."

"You're okay with this?" Jacob asked Makaidel.

The mage made a face. "I'd sooner she just leave. But as long as she understands clearly that we're not paying her, I'll put up with it."

Jacob nodded. "Alright." Turning, he led the group back to their campsite.

Kalista glanced up from the fire as they neared. "Hi! Are we getting ready to go?" Jacob frowned, annoyed with the way she already included herself in their group.

"Listen," he said. "We can't pay you to accompany us. If you're coming with us, you're doing so for free." His hands trembled, wishing someone else would speak to her. He hated confronting people.

"But…"

"No buts," Makaidel cut across her. "If you want to come, you can, but we're not going to pay you. And if you're not joining us, then leave us alone." Serina shot him a hurt look, but he didn't notice. "We're not just going to let you eat our food and then disappear once we get off the mountain. In fact, we're not just going to let you eat our food, period. We need it and we paid for it with our money. If you want some, you have to pay for it." Kalista looked crestfallen, but nodded understandingly.

"So?" Jacob's voice strengthened, relieved that Makaidel had taken charge of the conversation. "Do you want to join us or not?" She glanced away, clearly torn by the decision. Birds chirped around them as the forest fell silent, everyone waiting for her answer. She winced as if in pain.

Finally, she stood, grinning once more. "Okay. I'll go with you. But I get a portion of the profits." Jacob rolled his eyes with an irritated sigh, his earlier compassion quickly faded.

Makaidel narrowed his eyes at her. "You'll get a *fair* portion of whatever profits we *might* receive on this altruistic mission."

"Okay," Kalista stated, though she seemed disappointed.

Serina smiled at her. "Welcome to the group." Kalista smiled widely.

"Now help us break down the tents," Makaidel ordered, wiping the smile off her face. "We need to get moving." Jacob followed Makaidel over to their shared tent. He felt ashamed of letting the young mage command the discussion with Kalista, but he knew he couldn't have given her those ultimatums with enough confidence. Silently, he helped Makaidel break down their tent and prepared to leave once more.

Soon, they were packed and on their way again. The descent down the mountain passed much easier than the climb up had been. They had all become so skilled at facing the orlocs that everyone but Serina began to take turns fighting them as they appeared. Jacob was disappointed that he had to watch three encounters pass by before he could face one again himself, but he knew it was only fair to let the others fight the orlocs as well. It was a startling thought, when he stopped to think about it.

"What's on your mind?"

Jacob glanced up suddenly. They had stopped for lunch on a ledge overlooking the rest of the mountain, less than half as high as they had stopped the previous day, and Jacob had been staring thoughtfully into space. He hadn't noticed Serina approach.

"Oh, nothing." He gazed off into the trees again. "Just thinking about how far I've come—we've come."

"Yeah. It seems like just yesterday that I left Shelas." Jacob nodded slowly. He guessed that about three weeks had passed since he arrived in Aurius. *Has it been that long?* he wondered, thinking back on his journey so far. He was about a third of the way through the game. He wished it would never end. The action and excitement, meeting new people, being away from home and all the stresses associated with it, and with no one he knew around, it was like a vacation. He grinned at the thought, briefly trying to count how many times he had nearly died here, and the deadly dangers still to come. He still missed the people he had left behind, but he was enjoying himself so much in Aurius that it was only a faint spell of grief soon relieved by a simple glimpse of Serina.

Jacob glanced over at Makaidel and Thorn, talking and laughing among themselves. Kalista sat near them, quiet and subdued since they had set out that morning. The mere sight of her, clothed in a revealing outfit over her curvaceous figure, brought a pang of annoyance for all the fans of the game who seemed to prefer her over Serina. He turned to Serina, who smiled at him. How anyone could think that Serina, the sweet, innocent, and beautiful girl sitting beside him, was not as attractive as Kalista, he couldn't imagine.

He shook off the thought, standing and shouldering his backpack. "Everyone ready?" The others agreed and stood, and they set out again.

Halfway through the afternoon, they stepped onto the last grassy slope leading off the mountain and returned to the open plains and gently rolling hills filling the landscape. It had, Jacob thought, been a long two days since they had first started climbing the mountain.

"You know," Makaidel began as they descended the slope. "If the talisman that monster took was really made by the Alorians, we might get some clues if we visited the ruins to the south." Jacob simply nodded, knowing already that they had to go there next. As worrisome as the fight with Arys had been, he found he had been relieved for the unexpected nature of it. Knowing everything that was going to happen before it did got boring, even if he did love the story he was living.

Kalista's eyes widened. "But you have to go through the Serpent Forest to get to the ruins!"

Makaidel sent her a suspicious glance. "I thought you said you'd traveled all over Aurius."

Kalista returned a frustrated 'harrumph.' "I've been in the forest, but no one's seen the ruins since the Alorians disappeared. All the expeditions sent to find it never return."

"Well, we're no wimpy archaeologists. I'll bet we can make it there."

Jacob grinned at the exchange, enjoying it more in person than he had playing the game.

"We need to resupply first," Thorn remarked. "I saw a town to the southwest from the ledge yesterday."

"Quinlan," Jacob stated without thinking.

Serina smiled at him. "You really do know a lot about Aurius." He smiled nervously, cursing himself for letting something slip again.

"I wish we still had the sharots," Makaidel remarked. "My feet are killing me."

"Never did find out what happened to them," Thorn added.

Serina glanced away sadly. "Y-yes we did."

"Arys released them," Jacob finished for her. He decided not to mention Arys telling them how some of their loyal mounts had jumped to their deaths. "He admitted it just before he attacked me."

Thorn shook his head. "Can't believe he was really a traitor. He had us all fooled."

"Almost all of us." Makaidel gazed sharply at Jacob, reminding him of the boy's father, Lord Kyutu. "How did you know he was a traitor?"

Jacob glanced away from the boy's piercing gaze. "I could just tell." He wracked his mind frantically, trying to come up with a convincing answer. Suddenly, he remembered what he had told Kyutu about the false Fahren. "He gave off a bad vibe." Makaidel's eyes narrowed briefly, but he said nothing more. Clearing his throat, Jacob faced forward again as they continued traveling across the plains, the group falling silent as they followed the slowly setting sun.

A FEW DAYS later, they arrived in Quinlan, a much quieter town than Dekaal and even than Shelas. Little more than a waystation for travelers and market for the surrounding farmers, the streets appeared more as Jacob imagined a typical medieval town would look. Small, plain houses with thatched roofs lined the cobblestone street, and few people wandered around the edge of town. Down the main road several blocks ahead, they could see an outdoor market filled with booths selling various types of foods, tools, nails, leather, cloth, and other goods. A sharot-drawn cart traveled down the street ahead of them, heading for the market.

Makaidel gazed down the road they walked. "Well, this looks like a good place to stock up on supplies."

"Maybe we can even rent new sharots," Jacob stated hopefully.

"I wouldn't count on it," Thorn replied. "Place like this won't have 'em to spare." Jacob frowned briefly and adjusted his backpack on his shoulders.

"Maybe we should look for an inn first," Serina offered.

"Yeah, that's a good idea," Makaidel answered.

"I'm starving," Kalista added.

Thorn grinned as he glanced at her out of the corner of his eye. "How are you going to pay for lunch?" Kalista's eyes widened, then she bowed her head with a sigh.

"Don't worry." Serina laid a hand on the other girl's shoulder. "I'll pay for your lunch."

Kalista smiled. "Thanks." Jacob frowned, reminded again of his ex-girlfriend, but said nothing.

Soon, they found an inn and retreated inside, helping themselves to a table. Jacob glanced around at the group that accompanied him, surprised suddenly at its size. Though it was no bigger than it had been when he left Dekaal, this was the first time he'd sat at a table in a tavern since the night he had fought the giant orloc in Phantis's basement, when only Makaidel and Serina accompanied him. Now, his group filled the heavy table, a crowd in a sea of mostly empty tables.

A barmaid quickly strolled over to their table as they seated themselves, smiling eagerly at them. "'Afternoon, travelers. What can I get you?"

Jacob buried his face in his hands, elbows resting on the table, as orders circled the table. The rations he had been surviving on since they left Dekaal were not the types of foods served in a tavern, and with the memory of his last disastrous meals at the Horse and Clover in Dekaal in his mind, he still didn't know what to order. *What I wouldn't give for a cheeseburger right now,* he thought wearily.

"And you, sir?"

Jacob pulled his hands away as the barmaid addressed him, thinking furiously. He shook his head. "Anything but fish."

The barmaid chuckled, smiling. "I'll bring you something nice." Jacob tried to smile in response, but inwardly dreaded the dish she would serve him.

"So, how are we going to get to the ruins?" Makaidel asked, interrupting Jacob's thoughts.

"I told you, it's suicide," Kalista argued. "Something in the Serpent Forest kills everyone who enters it."

"What's the big deal? We can handle a few orlocs, or one big one. There can't be too many there or they wouldn't all be able to survive. The forest isn't that big."

"It's not orlocs." Kalista's voice grew uncharacteristically serious. "That forest is alive. People say it moves, so that you think you're going straight, but you're really walking in circles. That's how it traps people. No one gets out of it alive."

Makaidel raised an eyebrow. "If no one ever comes back, then how do you know that's what happens?" Snickers rose up from the others.

Kalista fumed. "Nobody still returns from there! Isn't that enough?"

Makaidel grinned. "Some rogue you are."

"Hey!"

"Maybe there's something amazing in there," Thorn offered. "And people don't want to leave once they've been there."

Kalista shifted uncomfortably. "I don't think I'd want to see that, either."

"Me, neither." Serina smiled. "There's too much I'd miss out here." She turned to Jacob. He smiled, warmed by her sweet manner.

The barmaid returned with a second waitress, both laden down with the table's orders. Jacob boggled at the plate set before him. A whole roast duck lay steaming on the plate, baked yams and collard greens surrounding it. He couldn't imagine eating so much in a single meal, but it looked, and smelled, far more palatable than the last meals he'd eaten in a tavern. Coins emerged from pouches as everyone started eating.

"Oh, ma'am?" Makaidel asked as the barmaid that had served them began to walk away. She turned, gazing at him as she wiped her hands on her apron. "What can you tell us about the ruins to the south?"

The barmaid half chuckled as everyone looked at her. "Not much. Nobody's seen them in over three hundred years, not even the Alorians."

"You still have Alorians here?" Kalista leaned forward excitedly.

Now the barmaid laughed openly. "No, but whatever's to the south was ruins to them for fifteen hundred years already. Supposedly, the builders protected it with traps that no one can get past now, but all we had to say that was the remaining Alorians and even they've been gone near a century now."

"So, they might not even be there anymore for all you know," Thorn stated. Makaidel sank down in his chair, disappointed.

The barmaid nodded. "I wish someone would just prove they're not there. Kids here are always daring each other to go deeper and deeper into the forest. We lose one or two almost every year."

Serina gasped. "That's awful!" The barmaid nodded again, slowly.

"So, you don't think it's possible to find the ruins?" Makaidel asked hopelessly.

"Me, no. But if you really want to find them, you can talk to Morrie Deacon." Jacob's throat constricted and he struggled to swallow a bite of his duck.

"Who's that?"

"He goes into the forest all the time. Studies the ruins, says he's determined to find them. He's a little touched, but a sweet guy."

"Where can we find him?" Serina's smile reflected Makaidel's renewed hope.

"He lives in the southwest part of town. People in that area know him, they should be able to tell you how to find him from there."

"Thanks!" Makaidel beamed. Nodding, the barmaid turned and walked away.

Jacob turned back to his companions. "Shouldn't we ask about rooms for the night?"

"Let's see if we can find an inn closer to this Morrie Deacon," Thorn stated.

"Let's hurry." Makaidel leaned over his food eagerly. "I want to find him as soon as we can." Jacob frowned as he returned to his lunch. Knowing what would happen next made him feel terribly uneasy. The others spent the rest of their meal immersed in excited conversation, but Jacob ate silently, anxious about the events soon to pass.

It didn't take long to cross Quinlan, and before much time had passed, the five of them came upon Morrie Deacon's house. It stood on the edge of town, the back stretching off into open fields and distant forest. The front yard was fenced in, circling well tended flowers and trees on the verdant lawn. A garden was portioned off to the side, where a woman knelt and picked vegetables. Jacob recognized her as Morrie's wife from the game. Two young boys chased each other through the yard, giggling as they ran.

"Are you sure this is it?" Makaidel blinked at the sight. Even though he had seen this view many times before, Jacob couldn't help but nod in agreement. It didn't strike him as the home of a man obsessed with ruins, someone who rarely left his house but to explore the Serpent Forest.

As they neared the whitewashed fence, the younger of the children ran up to it, swinging a stick like it was a staff. He pointed it at Jacob and made a sound like an explosion, then laughed. "I got you with my magic!" Jacob glanced back at his companions as the boy ran off. Makaidel responded with a shrug. Beside him, Serina giggled softly.

Morrie's wife, hearing the child's reaction, raised her head to glance at the group gathered about the gate leading into the yard. "Oh, hi!" She walked over towards them, her arms full of potatoes, carrots, radishes, and cabbage. "Can I help you?"

"Uh, yeah." Jacob rubbed the back of his neck. He glanced back at his companions, but their expressions and gestures urged him to speak. He cleared his throat, which was suddenly dry. "We're looking for Morrie Deacon?"

"Oh, sure! Come in." She opened the gate. They all filed in, nodding or uttering their thanks, and followed her to the house.

"Morrie!" the woman called out as she stepped inside. "You have some visitors." They waited in front of the door into the house, facing a large room holding kitchen, dining room, and common room all in one. Jacob shifted uncomfortably while Morrie's wife walked into the kitchen and deposited her vegetables on the counter.

Presently, footsteps could be heard below, moving towards the stairway to the basement visible across the room. The timbers of the house rattled as the heavy footfalls thudded up the stairs. Makaidel tensed, thinking, Jacob knew, about their fight against the orloc in Phantis's basement. Jacob couldn't help being reminded of it as well, though he remained calm, knowing that nothing out of the ordinary was about to happen.

Nothing particularly *out of the ordinary, anyway,* he added silently.

Jacob noticed surprised reactions around him as Morrie Deacon emerged from the stairs to the basement. When he had first played the game, he had expected a small, wiry person like Phantis as well, but the bearded and red-haired man that grinned broadly at them was built like a logger. He was nearly as large and muscular as Thorn, his well-formed muscles stretching the fabric of his shirt.

"Welcome, welcome!" His deep, rich voice reverberated around the room. "Come in! Sit down! Would you like anything to drink?" Jacob walked with the others over to the table and sat down, slipping his backpack to the floor beside his chair. Morrie glanced toward the kitchen as he lowered into a chair with a creak. "Darling, would you put on some tea?"

"Oh, no," Makaidel stated. "You don't have to…"

"Nonsense!" Morrie flashed them a wide smile. "You came all the way out here, the least I can do is make you comfortable. Travelers, eh? Well, I'm Morrie, and that's my wife, Cassandra. She just goes by Cassie, though."

"Uh, well." Jacob shifted in his chair. He glanced briefly at his companions seated around the table with him. "I'm Garrett. This is Makaidel, Thorn, Kalista, and Serina." Morrie gazed intensely at each of them, mouthing the names after Jacob. When his gaze returned to Jacob, he smiled again.

"So, what brings you folks here?"

"Uh, well…"

Serina leaned forward. "We heard you go through the Serpent Forest often."

He grinned. "Yes, I make an expedition there at least once a week." Cassandra appeared at the table and set down a teapot spewing steam from its spout, along with a tray of mugs. "Thank you, dear."

"We want to find the southern ruins," Makaidel stated abruptly. Morrie sat up straighter, eyebrows rising.

"That's pretty ambitious. I've been searching the forest for ten years and haven't found them yet."

"It's really important that we get to them. If they're still there."

Morrie smiled, amused. "Whatever for?"

Without hesitation, Makaidel began to explain the altar in the mountains, and they all told Morrie of their quest. The large man listened intently, not saying a word while they spoke.

"Well," he remarked when they finished. "You certainly do seem to have a very great need to find the ruins." He leaned back in his chair, sipping his tea. "The truth is, a few weeks ago, I reached the end of the forest."

Collectively, they cried, "You what?" Jacob forced himself to look surprised with the others.

Morrie nodded. "Mm-hm. It ends at a great big wall, clearly Alorian built.

There doesn't seem to be an opening in it as far as I've seen, and it's built in a way so that it can't be scaled. That's why I haven't told anyone else yet."

"Can you take us to it?" Makaidel leaned forward in his chair, barely containing his excitement.

"Of course."

"Great!"

"Thank you very much, Mr. Deacon." Serina smiled.

"Well, it's my pleasure. But please, just call me Morrie." Serina's smile widened. "Why don't you all stay here tonight so we can leave first thing in the morning?" They all glanced at each other questioningly.

"Ah, are you sure…" Kalista attempted.

"Of course! There's lots of room. You'd be welcome, wouldn't they, dear?"

"Of course," Cassandra echoed pleasantly. "I'll make dinner for all of us."

"Oh, you really don't…" Jacob began.

"Nonsense, it would be our pleasure," Morrie stated. "Would you like to come see my notes on the forest?"

"Sure." Makaidel stood to follow Morrie into the basement. The others rose, glancing around uncertainly.

"Just makes yourselves at home," Cassandra stated from the kitchen. "Dinner will be ready in a few hours."

"Would you like some help with that?" Serina asked, approaching the kitchen. She took up some of the potatoes Cassandra had brought and began peeling them, despite Cassandra's objection, as the others dispersed, trying to make themselves useful.

The afternoon passed so peacefully that Jacob forgot about the journey to come. Despite Cassandra's protests, they kept themselves busy helping around the Deacons' house. Makaidel remained in the basement, poring over the archaeologist's notes and maps. Serina helped Cassandra prepare dinner for them all while Kalista tended the garden and brought in more vegetables. Around the back of the house, Thorn split wood while Jacob played with Morrie's children. Jacob had never been too fond of kids, so he wondered how he had ended up there, but the children were friendly and well-behaved, and soon he found himself having fun as chased them around the yard and wrestled with them.

"You're going to the forest tomorrow?" asked Elias, the seven-year-old boy.

"Yep." Jacob grunted as the five-year-old boy, Shane, climbed up his back and on to his shoulders.

"Daddy said he'd take me to the ruins when he found them. He's going to be the first human to see them and he'll be famous for it." Jacob's smile faded as he gazed away. He was struck with a dilemma new to him. He was the only person to know that if nothing changed from the game, Morrie Deacon would die the next day.

"My turn!" Elias shouted suddenly. Before Jacob could prepare for it, the boy launched himself up and grabbed Jacob's shoulders, still bent from carrying Shane.

"Ow!" Jacob sank under the additional weight. "Okay, okay, I need a break." Elias and Shane groaned in disappointment as they slid down to the ground, but soon laughed again as they ran off. Jacob rubbed the back of his neck as he watched them play. If he didn't do anything, those boys would lose their father. But he didn't know if he could do anything about it or, more still, if he had a right to.

But then, he thought, *what kind of a person would I be if I just let him die when I could stop it?*

"They're cute at that age, aren't they?"

"Huh?" Jacob blinked, startled out of his reverie. Kalista stood beside him, watching Shane and Elias play. He turned to the face them again. "Yeah, I guess."

Her smile faded. "Do you remember what it was like to be that age?"

Jacob sighed. "Yeah." He thought back to the time before his parents divorced, when they lived on the coast, and at the children's age, he had no cares at all. That time seemed so distant now, as did the family and home he still had. For the first time since he had arrived in Aurius, he felt a pang of loneliness for the people he had left behind. He didn't even have anyone here he could talk to about it. He turned to her.

"What about you?" He knew what her answer was going to be, remembering this conversation from the game.

Kalista shook her head. "I wish I'd gotten the chance to run around and play like that. All I ever wanted to do was please my parents, but nothing I did ever seemed good enough for them."

Jacob gazed at Elias and Shane again, thinking about Renaldo, a friend he'd had before his family moved. Kalista's words had reminded Jacob of him, and he had spent his childhood trying to make Renaldo feel better. Jacob hadn't spoken to him since his family had moved.

Kalista's voice grew faintly choked. "The last thing they said to me was that I'd never amount to anything." Jacob glanced at her in surprise as she sniffled. Though he knew everything she was saying already, this part of the game hadn't been voiced, and hearing the emotion in her words shook him. "All I ever wanted to do was prove them wrong, but I guess Makaidel's right, I'm not much of a rogue."

Here, in the game, Jacob had been given a choice as to how to react to Kalista's admission. It was one of the things he liked about *Legend of Aurius*, that it let him interact with the characters. Yet, the last time he had chosen a response, it had only affected a fictional character, not a real person like the one that stood before him, on the verge of tears.

He chose the gentler response. "That's not true. You fight better than any of us and you know your way around real well."

Kalista sniffled again. "You don't really mean that."

"Sure I do." He shifted, uncomfortable with how distressed she looked. "You just…" He stalled, uncertain what to say. "Need to stock up better."

She chuckled faintly, wiping at her eyes with the back of her hand. Leaning forward, she laid her head against his shoulder. He hesitated, stunned at the outcome of the conversation. In the game, even when he had responded positively to her, her initial arrogance and the way she seemed to be preferred over Serina by other fans of the game stuck in his mind too much to warm up to her. And, he thought, only so much could be conveyed through text. From the way she leaned against him now, he could truly feel how inwardly fragile she was, as so many other fans of the game had said. He felt guilty for judging her so harshly.

Hesitantly, he raised his arm and laid it against her back. He couldn't think of anything else to say to her.

She sniffled again. "Thanks, Garrett." He smiled faintly in response.

Suddenly, among Elias and Shane's laughter, Thorn's voice called out, "Whoa! Careful there, kids."

Stepping back quickly, Jacob cleared his throat. He glanced over his shoulder as Thorn rounded the corner of the house, firewood piled up under each massive arm.

"Hey, Thorn." He raised an eyebrow. "You, uh, got enough wood there?"

"Ah, this is nothing." Thorn deposited the logs onto a pile stacked waist high all along the side of the house.

"Looks like they'll be set for firewood for a month." Kalista smiled in amusement, though Jacob could see the sadness lingering in her eyes.

"Yeah, well, it's fair repayment for a free night's sleep." Thorn leaned against the pile of firewood, gazing out across the open plains. "It's nice out here, nice and quiet." Jacob nodded. It had taken a while for him to get used to the utter silence of the open fields and even the towns, which were much quieter than he was used to, but over the past weeks, it had become relaxing to him.

"I think this is the kind of place I'd like to be."

Jacob grinned. "Never figured you for a bumpkin."

Thorn chuckled. "I don't know. I still don't know what I want to do with my life. I joined the Dekaal guard because it seemed like a good thing for me to do, but it's not what I want to keep doing. I haven't figured out what I want to do yet." Jacob smiled, reminded of the way everyone in the game seemed to understand him in one way or another.

The front door of the house opened, and they all turned to face it. Serina gazed around until she saw them and smiled. "Oh, there you are. Dinner's ready. Will you bring the children in, please?"

Jacob glanced over his shoulder. "Hey, dinner's ready." Elias and Shane cheered as they ran inside, followed by Jacob, Thorn, and Kalista.

"Hey, Garrett?"

Jacob turned as Kalista grabbed his sleeve, stopping him. She fiddled with her hands.

"… Thanks."

He rubbed the back of his neck, her upset expression etched uncomfortably into his mind. "Don't mention it." He glanced at the open front door. "We'd, uh, better go inside." Nodding, she followed him in to the house that bustled from the activity of all the people within.

With the welcoming way Morrie and Cassandra treated their guests around the table of home-cooked food, Jacob felt more like he was at a family gathering than a meeting between a group of adventurers and their guide. The children ate on the floor as conversation filled the large common room of the house. Jacob spoke little but listened contentedly to the others talk. He ate heartily, feeling at home and comfortable among his companions and the Deacons.

After the meal, he escaped outside for some peace. He stood on the back porch, gazing out at the setting sun. The door opened behind him, emitting light and continued conversation from within. Turning, he found Morrie stepping outside and closing the door after him, a lit pipe in his hand.

"Oh, hi, Garrett. Didn't see you slip out here." Jacob only smiled in response. Morrie brought the pipe to his mouth and took a drag. As he let out the smoke, he offered Jacob the pipe.

"Oh, no, thanks."

Morrie nodded and brought the pipe back to his lips. "It's a nice night." Jacob nodded, gazing out at the painted sky with Morrie. "I have a good feeling about tomorrow. You're the first people in a long time to be interested in my research, you know."

"Yeah…" Jacob stated distractedly. "Um, about tomorrow… are you sure you want to go?"

"Of course." Morrie smiled at Jacob. "I'm so excited to finally show someone the wall. Cassie's seen my drawings, of course, but I haven't taken anyone to see it yet."

"Well..." Jacob struggled to find a way to say what he wanted. "Maybe you should stay here with your family. We could just borrow your maps and..."

"Nonsense!" Morrie replied, dismissing the suggestion with a smile. "You're looking at no better guide through the forest. I'd be honored to take you. Unless..." He turned with a concerned glance at Jacob. "You don't want me to come."

"No, no, that's not it."

Morrie's smile returned. "Then I'd be glad to guide you. Wild sharots couldn't drag me away." Jacob glanced away with a frown, reliving the next events in the game and wondering how, or if, he could prevent them.

"This is my life's work, Garrett." Morrie took another drag on his pipe. "I used to be a farmer, you know. So unfulfilling. But this... when I first made an expedition into the forest, it changed my life. I loved it. But more than that, studying the forest and the Alorians made me special. People know me because of what I do." Jacob gazed at him, his heart wrenching. "Ah, don't mind me. I'm just rambling to myself, I'm sure it makes no sense to you."

"No," Jacob answered quietly. "I know just how you feel." His throat constricted, feeling even more guilty hearing Morrie say the very things he himself had once thought about his own passion. He knew he couldn't stop the large man from accompanying them through the forest, but to allow him to do so without complaint would lead Morrie to his death.

Maybe I can do something to save him there.

He glanced up, finding Morrie examining him. But the archaeologist's gaze was lowered, focusing on his pendant.

"Yes, that's definitely Alorian made. I've seen the very same symbol on the wall." He laughed eagerly. "Tomorrow is going to be great!"

"Yeah," Jacob replied uneasily as Morrie tapped out his pipe and retreated inside. "Great."

18

JACOB AWOKE TO orange light glowing against the curtains as Elias and Shane stomped around the floor and giggled. He sat up groggily, not well rested after an uneasy night's sleep. Thoughts of how to prevent the disaster to come had kept him awake much later than normal, even without having to keep watch for danger.

"Get going, you scamps." The children giggled as Morrie shooed them out the door. "Sorry they woke you."

"'S okay." Jacob stood and stretched.

"Were you comfortable?" Morrie put a pan on the stove. "I'm sorry you had to sleep on the floor."

"No, it's alright, it was fine." The others echoed Jacob as they stood around him. The additional blankets Morrie had given them as padding had been decidedly more comfortable than sleeping on the ground, even inside a tent. They began packing as Morrie prepared breakfast. While they ate, Morrie gathered his maps, notebook, and other supplies. The sun rose over the distant mountains from which they'd come, Morrie's house soon lighting up as the day began.

Before long, they had all gathered on Morrie's back porch, waving their goodbyes to Cassandra, Elias, and Shane.

Serina bowed to Morrie's wife. "Thank you again for all your hospitality, ma'am."

Cassandra smiled. "It was my pleasure, and I can't thank you enough for all your hard work. Especially you, Thorn."

"It was the least I could do," Thorn answered. Turning, they began to walk away from the house towards the forest.

"Take care of Morrie." Cassandra grinned. "He tends to get a little reckless in his excitement when he goes exploring."

"Don't listen to her," Morrie called over his shoulder in amusement. "I am the epitome of caution on my expeditions."

"Right, to the historical artifacts you find," Cassandra added. A round of chuckles circled the two groups. “Goodbye, Morrie. Be careful!”

“I will. Goodbye, darling. We should be back tomorrow at the latest.” Elias and Shane bounced up and down as they waved madly to the group.

“Come back soon, Daddy!”

“G’bye, Garrett! You can come back and play anytime!” Jacob waved briefly to Morrie’s sons, feeling uneasy with their departure.

With a final goodbye, the Deacons disappeared into the house and Morrie began leading the way across the plains. Jacob heard conversations ahead of him as he walked, eyes on the ground in front of him.

“So, you use sidearm blades, eh? You know, there’s a very interesting history behind those…”

“I hope we can find the ruins. This is so exciting.”

“Yeah, I never thought I’d be making an expedition like this. Got to say, I’m pretty interested…”

“What’s wrong, Garrett?”

He glanced up at the question directed to him. Serina had fallen back into step with him. “You’ve been so quiet and distracted since we got to Quinlan. What’s bothering you?”

“Nothing, really. I’m just… worried about this trip.”

“Is it…” She hesitated. “Morrie? Are you getting a bad vibe…?”

“No, no,” he stated quickly. “It’s not that. I’m just worried something will happen.”

“It is pretty scary. Going through the Serpent Forest, I mean.” Jacob simply nodded in response, and they walked on in silence.

Within two hours, they had reached the edge of the Serpent Forest. The trees loomed off into the distance, obscuring entirely from view anything that might hide on the other side.

Kalista shuffled nervously. “Is it true the forest changes shape and traps people inside?”

“Nah, that’s just a story women tell to keep their children from wandering in,” Morrie answered. “But there’s no path, and the forest is deceiving, so it’s entirely possible that people have been trapped by losing their sense of direction.”

“What about orlocs?” Makaidel asked.

Morrie chuckled. “There’re more orlocs before you get to the forest than there are in it. They’re sprinters, they don’t hunt so well in an enclosed forest.”

“Is it really all that safe and no one knows?” Thorn asked.

“Oh, make no mistake. This forest is ancient and treacherous, and I do believe there are strange things lurking in it. But it's nothing like all the stories if you take the time to learn your way through it. You just have to respect this forest. It's been around a lot longer than any of us, and maybe even longer than the ruins it protects."

As he finished, he took the first step into the forest. Already the atmosphere seemed different. A rich scent hung in the air, heavy and cloying. The foliage was thick and green and the undergrowth dense. It felt very close and crowded after the long journey across towering mountains and open plains, but it felt somehow more comfortable to Jacob. He was still unused to such openness as they had been traveling.

Morrie led the way through the forest, walking through the ferns and weeds littering the forest floor and across uneven ground with ease. The rest of the group followed in single file, the gaps in the wild trees not wide enough to allow more than one person through side by side.

"You're sure you know where you're going?" Kalista sounded far away to Jacob, who trailed at the rear behind Serina.

"Without question," Morrie answered. "I've been through this very route a dozen times since I found that wall."

"Do you ever find anything new there?" Makaidel picked up his feet over some protruding roots.

"Every time. I've studied the glyphs, the construction, the texture, the dimensions. There's always something new to learn about it."

"But you've never been able to see over it? Not even if you climb a tree?"

"That's just it. The trees by the wall are all very young. And the ones that are high enough are too far out to see over it."

"How is that possible?" Thorn asked. "There's no one around to tend the forest."

"It shouldn't be possible. I've been studying the trees since I made that discovery. I think there might be an enchantment around the wall."

"An enchantment," Makaidel echoed, amazed.

"Well, I guess if the Alorians wanted to protect it," Kalista began, trailing off to let them draw their own conclusions.

"It must have been really sacred to the Alorians if they kept it guarded so well," Serina added.

"That's what I figure," Morrie replied. "And why I'm so interested in finding them. I can only imagine the secrets those ruins must hold."

"Well, with those symbols you showed me, we're bound to find out about those talismans here," Makaidel stated.

"Provided we can get in," Thorn added. Jacob saw nods of agreement ahead of him, then the conversation fell silent.

They walked on quietly, the shuffling of their footsteps across the increasingly treacherous ground ringing through the forest with the scufflings of birds, squirrels, and other creatures around them. They stopped some time later for rest and food at a small clear patch, then soon continued on their way.

All of a sudden, a few hours later, Morrie stated, "We're coming up on it."

"Really?" Makaidel gazed around curiously. "I don't see anything." Jacob glanced ahead as well, but he could see nothing but more trees.

No sooner were the words out of Makaidel's mouth than he stopped in his place with a gasp.

Morrie grinned, hands on his hips. "Yeah, it sneaks up on you."

As Jacob reached the spot where the group had halted, he couldn't help his eyes widening. The trees dropped away suddenly, the wall looming not twenty feet ahead. He gazed up at three stories of sandstone rising over the forest without blemish, seeming hardly to be weathered at all in all its age. Large glyphs were carved across the face of the stone. Jacob recognized them from the game, though like everything else, the wall seemed so much larger and more real in person.

"Wow!" Serina breathed as she gazed at it. Kalista marveled at it, leaning her head back to take in its full height. Makaidel, however, was already examining it with intellectual curiosity. He glanced off to one side, then the other.

"Does it have an end?"

"Logically, it should," Morrie stated. "But east and west of here, after a time, the ground gets so treacherous and the trees grow so close together that I can't get to its side."

"And you can't go around another way?"

Morrie shook his head. "I can't even find it from the side and the back opens up onto a cliff and a huge waterfall. There's no scaling it."

Jacob watched Serina step forward slowly while the others discussed the wall with Morrie. She examined the glyphs, tilting her head as she gazed at them. Jacob stepped forward, captivated. She reached her hand out and laid it against a symbol centered around a ring of others, the same one on Jacob's pendant. Her eyes closed.

Suddenly, the crystals on her staff began to glow. The others stopped talking and turned as the land resonated around her, thrumming in a way Jacob could sense, though he could neither hear nor feel it. Then, the circle of glyphs on the wall began to glow as well. A hairline fracture, emitting light like the glyphs, ran around the circle. Everyone but Serina yelped as, with a great rumble, the circle of stone receded back into the wall, then rolled slowly to the side, opening a passage through the great wall.

Slowly, Serina opened her eyes and dropped her hand.

"How did you do that?" Makaidel asked incredulously.

"I… I don't know." She stared at the wall, bewildered at the change before her. "It asked me to cast a spell, so I did."

"It *asked* you?"

She shook her head, stepping back. "I didn't recognize the words, but somehow, I know that's what it was saying." She looked fearful, shaken by what had happened.

"How…" Kalista attempted. "That's impossible."

"It's incredible," Morrie stated, staring at the gaping circle where there had once been solid stone. "You actually opened the wall!"

Makaidel reached out and touched the wall, eyebrows knitting together in concentration. "There's definitely magic in there, but it feels so… foreign. I would never have been able to do that." He laughed excitedly. "You're amazing, Serina!" Morrie pulled out his notebook and a piece of charcoal and began writing furiously as he approached the opening. Makaidel, Kalista, and Thorn followed him inside, chattering excitedly. Serina stood rooted to the spot, gazing anxiously at the wall.

Jacob walked over to her. "Serina?" She snapped her gaze to him with a gasp, then glanced away.

"I… I shouldn't have been able to do that. It's not right."

"Nobody's even seen this wall for hundreds of years," Jacob replied softly. "That might've been something anyone could do."

She sniffled. "I guess." He frowned, his heart wrenching at the sight of her so upset.

"Come on. We'd better catch up to the others." Nodding, she followed him through the opening. Jacob tensed as he quickened his pace, dreading the revelations about to occur.

The gap in the wall opened up on a clear path through another forest. Exotic twitters and chirps rang around them as they fell into step behind Morrie and the others. The trees were ancient but rich with life, the forest floor almost clear of fallen leaves and undergrowth.

They walked in silence, Morrie's charcoal stick scribbling furiously as their eyes roamed all around, taking in the scenery. A strange feeling permeated the air, like some unidentifiable perfume. Jacob remembered going through this part in the game, riddled with orlocs as was every place in the game, but here, something felt indefinably alive. He felt like he was being watched, and he shifted uncomfortably at the thought. None of the others seemed affected as he was, and they continued strolling slowly through the forest until at last, they found the ruins.

The group stopped with a collective gasp as they came to the end of the forest. The ruins lay before them, as huge and preserved as the wall protecting them. With its domes and pillars, statues and courtyards, all constructed of sandstone blocks, it looked like a mixture between ancient Greek and Mayan architecture. Most of the structure was open to the sky with canals intersecting across the ground, separated by causeways over the water. Glyphs were carved into the walls, and Jacob recognized predominantly the symbol on his own pendant, as well as others that had been on the mountaintop altar.

"This is amazing!" Morrie's voice quavered in excitement. He stepped forward, charcoal flying over the page in his notebook. The others followed slowly, speechless. They crossed the first causeway leading to the ruins and were soon surrounded by them.

"I can't believe we're standing in the remnants of ancient Alorian civilization," Kalista stated softly.

"It looks just like the altar on the mountains," Makaidel remarked. They entered a central courtyard ringed by pillars in precisely the same way as the mountaintop altar. Instead of a pedestal, in its center was a life-size statue of a beautiful woman with long, pointed ears, rising above a pool of clear water. Pathways split off in many directions from the circle. Morrie stepped to the side, glancing between the statue and his notebook as he sketched it. The rest of them wandered off slowly in all directions, gazing at the ruins around them.

Jacob's eyes fell on Serina. He watched her curiously as she approached a symbol on a wall nearby, wide-eyed. She reached a hand up and ran her fingers along it. After a moment, she raised her staff and held it up. The round design at its top perfectly matched the symbol carved into the wall. Jacob's eyes widened. He had never noticed the similarity before.

Makaidel saw her in that moment. "Serina, where did you get that staff?"

"I… I don't know. Adella said it was with me when she found me in the forest outside Shelas."

"Incredible," Morrie remarked as he walked over to sketch the design. Serina stepped back uneasily, shaking her head. Jacob frowned, heart aching to see her so upset.

"Whoa," Thorn stated suddenly from across the courtyard. Jacob, Serina, and Makaidel glanced over to him. Kalista stood beside Thorn, gazing through a doorway on the opposite side of the circle from where they'd entered.

She glanced over her shoulder at them. "Guys, I think you should see this." Anxiously, they all crossed the circular pavillion to where Kalista and Thorn stood. Morrie stepped backwards slowly, putting the finishing touches on his sketch, then followed them.

Through the doorway, a large, empty room opened up, completely walled in with no other exit than the one they came in. At the far end of the room, the floor rose a few steps and a pedestal stood in the center, bathed in light from a circular cut in the ceiling above. A book lay on top of it.

They all stepped slowly inside and gazed around. The walls, floor, and ceiling were covered in runes and images. Morrie stopped a few paces in, gazing down at a great circular design on the floor with four symbols and strange drawings and writing surrounding a symbol that matched the one on Jacob's pendant. The others stepped quickly off it as Morrie began sketching it in his notebook.

Walking around the design, Makaidel approached the pedestal. Jacob followed after him, Serina by his side. Makaidel crept quietly up the stairs and laid his hands delicately on the ancient leather cover of the book.

"What is this?" He opened the book and gazed at its pages. Jacob glanced over his shoulder anxiously. Kalista and Thorn still gazed at the walls while Morrie sketched the design on the floor.

"Look!" Makaidel exclaimed. Jacob turned to find him pointing at a page in the book.

He shifted nervously. "Guys, I think we should get out of here." Serina glanced curiously at him, but none of the others seemed even to hear him.

"This is the same design as on the floor there." Makaidel examined the page. "And that's the symbol on your pendant and that talisman…"

"Guys," Jacob stated louder, feeling frantic. "We need to go." Heads turned curiously and suspiciously toward him.

"Huh?" Thorn stated.

"What's going on?" Kalista asked.

"What's your problem?" Makaidel snapped.

Desperate to flee before it was too late, Jacob grabbed Serina's arm and strode forward. "It's not safe here! We have to hurry…"

He stopped and lurched back with a gasp. As his foot fell on the edge of the design in the floor, the symbol on the outside of the circle emitted a sharp light. Morrie stepped back hastily as the glyph by his feet began to glow as well, followed by the other two surrounding the central symbol.

The others gasped and uttered amazed exclamations, but Jacob back-stepped in horror. Serina moved with him, clutching his arm. As the entire circle began to emit a brilliant light, he called out, "Morrie!" He hesitated. If he told Morrie to run, would the archaeologist's fate be theirs?

"Everyone, stay calm!" Morrie called back. Kalista and Makaidel murmured anxiously.

Suddenly, the glowing symbols flared, filling the room with an incredible light. Everyone cried out in unison and looked away, shielding their eyes. A collective gasp echoed around the room as the light faded and they turned back to the design on the floor. A figure stood in the center of the glowing circle, clad neck to toe in black clothes and glossy black armour trimmed in gold, shimmering in the light of the stone beneath his feet. The face was human, strikingly handsome, but his ears were long and pointed, stretching away from his head.

Jacob stepped back another pace, his stomach twisting in fear. Somehow, he could feel extraordinary power radiating out from the man now in the room with them.

The elf-like man tossed his head, throwing strands of long, black hair over his shoulder. "I must say, I'm impressed you people made it this far." There was a faint hint of scorn in the way he said 'people.' His surprisingly deep voice was silky smooth, the elegant enunciations rippling off the stone walls of the chamber.

"It's…" Morrie began.

"An Alorian," Thorn finished for him, shocked.

The Alorian glanced at Thorn from the corner of his eye with an amused grin. "How astute of you."

"Is… is this an apparition?" Kalista asked incredulously, staring at the Alorian. He turned his head, grinning at her. Raising an arm from beneath the black cloak that trailed the ground around him, he held his hand palm out to her. With a flash and a roar, Kalista was blown back against the wall with a cry and crumpled to the floor. Everyone shouted and moved forward as if to help her, but the Alorian stopped them all with a hard look.

"Oh, I'm quite real."

Jacob tensed, and he noticed Thorn and Morrie did as well.

"W-who are you?" Serina asked, still clutching Jacob's arm, though she had moved forward when the Alorian attacked Kalista. In the game, the line had been Garrett's, but Jacob was frozen as he gazed at the Alorian. He glanced at Serina, the sinister grin widening.

"I am Lord Dharius." He gazed past Serina. "And I have come for that book."

"What?" Makaidel protested. "What are you…" He stopped himself short with a gasp. "The talisman!" The teardrop-shaped emerald set in silver hung on a chain around Dharius's neck. "You're the master of that monster that replaced Fahren!"

"So, you're those troublemakers who uncovered Graxis." Jacob, Serina, and Makaidel backed away as Dharius approached them. "I guess I'll kill two birds with one stone." Behind Dharius, Morrie helped Kalista to her feet as Thorn edged closer to the Alorian's other side. Jacob tensed, knowing that behind him, Makaidel lowered the book he held, hiding his glowing hand beneath it.

"Give me that book."

"Okay," Makaidel stated. "Catch!" He hurled the ancient book across the room, aiming high. As he released it, he threw his arm forward and yelled,

"Lightning Blast!"

Dharius held out a hand, easily repelling the spell with a sneer, but as he watched the book fly over his head, Thorn slammed his shoulder against the Alorian and Kalista leaped in to a kick that landed on Dharius's armoured side. Morrie, standing by the entrance to the room, caught the falling book. As Dharius stumbled forward, he spun, a flare of energy sending Thorn and Kalista flying. Jacob, Serina, and Makaidel began to run forward, but with a sweep of his arm, Dharius blasted them to the floor as well. Jacob groaned, his entire body searing.

"Morrie, run!" Makaidel coughed out.

The archaeologist hesitated by the doorway as the others were slammed with powerful spells, but roused himself and turned to flee at Makaidel's cry. Jacob managed to raise his head against the paralyzing pain wracking his body and watched in horror. Flinging his arm out, Dharius shot a blast of magic over to Morrie. Morrie cried out as he flew forward and hit the wall. The others struggled to rise to their hands and knees as Dharius approached Morrie, drawing a long, elegant sword from a scabbard on his hip.

Morrie turned to face the Alorian as he towered overhead, his dark-clad form shadowing the prone archaeologist.

"No!" Serina cried.

Without pause, Dharius ran the blade through Morrie.

Turning, the Alorian strode back to the center of the design in the floor, the book in his hand. Holding his hand out to the doorway, he shattered the stone above it with a blast. Chunks of the wall fell into the entrance, blocking all escape.

He turned to Jacob, Makaidel, and Serina, still sprawled on the floor from their harsh landing. The grin was gone, and he gazed out at them with a perfectly calm expression that was full of malice.

"You don't know what it is you seek."

Slamming the point of his sword to the floor, he sent out a shockwave that rippled across the floor throughout the ruins. All around, the stone trembled and cracked, threatening to collapse in a great quake. With a flash of light, the Alorian was gone. Everyone quickly rose to their feet.

Serina covered her mouth. "Morrie…"

"This way!" Kalista cried over the rumbling of stone around them. She ran towards the pedestal, pulling her rope and grappling hook from her belt. Makaidel backed away as she drew up beside him. Hesitating, he raced across the room.

"Makaidel!" Serina yelped as he neared Morrie's lifeless body. Chunks of stone from the ceiling began raining down around him as he snatched up Morrie's notebook.

"Come on!" Kalista exclaimed. Jacob turned to find her crouching over the opening in the ceiling, her long ponytail streaming through it as she gazed back into the room.

"Go!" Jacob exclaimed, pushing Serina towards the hanging rope. Kalista pulled the rope up as Serina climbed and lifted her onto the roof quickly. Jacob gestured furiously for Makaidel to go next as he arrived back at the pedestal, followed by Thorn. Thorn and Kalista pulled Jacob up through the hole swiftly as the floor began to quake so ferociously he could barely stand. The pedestal toppled over and shattered as they pulled him up through the hole.

Makaidel stood at the edge of the roof, shaking his head as he looked over the side. "We'll have to jump." Jacob felt slightly less dread knowing that they would be jumping into a canal circling the ruins, but it was still an uncomfortable reminder of the mountaintop altar.

Suddenly, the floor lurched beneath his feet as a chunk of rock he stood on broke free and plummeted down to the floor of the room below. He tried to put his weight on his other foot, but felt himself falling towards the missing stone, arms flailing.

Reaching out, Thorn grabbed his arm and flung him back onto more solid ground. They both tore across the roof towards the edge where Makaidel, Serina, and Kalista had already disappeared. Taking in a deep breath, Jacob stepped onto the corner of the roof and leaped, the ruins crackling and roaring behind him. His heart sailed up into his throat as he fell through the air.

After a long moment, he plunged into the canal, slamming harshly against the surface of the clear water and sinking several feet below. The crumbling of the ruins reverberated muffled through the chill water as he struggled to swim to the surface, his sword and backpack weighing him down.

Dust filled the air when he broke the surface of the water and gasped for breath. His heart pounded as he brushed his wet hair back and watched the entire ruins collapse, burying everything in twenty feet of rubble. The thought made his throat constrict. In the game, the crumbling of the ruins was shown from above. Once again, the action seemed so much closer, the danger so much more real and terrifying, and once more, he had been inches from death.

Worse still was the thought of Morrie.

They all treaded water in silence as the last pillars and blocks tumbled to the ground. Some stones fell into the canal they occupied, but they remained safe. Finally, more than a minute later, the ruins fell still, and silence lay oppressingly over the scene.

Wordlessly, Jacob turned and swam to the far side of the canal, followed by the others. They emerged on the edge of the forest that surrounded what remained of the ruins. Makaidel walked over and retrieved Morrie's notebook, thrown safely over the canal as he had leaped from the crumbling building. Kalista gazed back at the ruins miserably while Serina stared unseeing at the ground, arms wrapped around her body.

"We should go," Thorn stated softly.

Leaves shuffled under Kalista's feet as she turned. "Maybe we should wait and dry off a bit first."

"No."

Everyone turned to Makaidel at his soft-spoken, but firm response. He gazed at the notebook in his hands, running his thumb over the leather cover.

"Cassie deserves to know what happened."

Kalista and Thorn glanced questioningly at Jacob. He looked at Serina. Goosebumps rose on her damp arms. She didn't look at him. Nodding faintly, he turned and began leading the way around the canal. He heard footsteps behind him, but didn't turn to see if they all followed him. His heart wrenched and his throat constricted as he walked, though his mind was blank.

The trek passed in silence as they circled around the ruins and back through the entrance they had created in the wall. Jacob paused outside the wall, gazing around at the wild forest. He glanced at Makaidel, preparing to ask him if he could navigate through the forest with Morrie's notes. Before he could speak a word, Makaidel strode forward, the notebook already open in his hands, and began walking into the trees. The others followed silently.

None of them spoke a word as they passed back through the forest. Jacob felt miserable, his wet clothes clinging coldly to him, but it was a much more tolerable pain than the one lingering at the back of his mind. The sun crawled slowly across the sky, the afternoon seeming to take forever to pass.

Hours later, they reached the end of the forest. Far in the distance, they could see Quinlan. The tension in the air seemed palpable as they began approaching the town.

Makaidel continued leading them as they neared the familiar house. Jacob could barely breathe around the lump in his throat. Without a word or any hesitation, Makaidel climbed the stairs leading up to the back door and knocked.

The door opened swiftly and Cassandra beamed at them.

"You're back already! I'm so relieved… what is it?" Her smile faded as she gazed on all the forlorn and guilty faces looking back at her. Jacob could see a hint of horrified understanding alight in her eyes. He wished he was anywhere but there.

Makaidel held up the notebook. "I'm sorry." Cassandra put a hand over her mouth and shook her head. "We found the ruins... so did an Alorian who was after something there." Cassandra drew in a shuddering breath and glanced away, her eyes welling with tears. Looking at her, Jacob's heart had never felt so small and hollow. He watched, worried, as Serina turned abruptly and began walking away. He gazed at her in desperation, but hesitated to follow.

"Mrs. Deacon," Makaidel continued. "I know this is hard for you, but I need to see Morrie's notes."

"Makaidel," Kalista protested, gazing at him in shock.

"Please," he continued, ignoring her. "We have to find out what that Alorian is after... so Morrie's death won't be in vain."

Jacob caught only the briefest glimpse of Cassandra's reaction before he turned and walked away as well. One thought circled his mind as he strode quickly around the house, unable to outrun it.

I took her husband away. Because of me, a good man is dead.

Rounding the corner, he spun and kicked out, toppling several logs off the wood pile. A gasp drew his attention to the side. Serina perched atop the wood pile further down, hand over her heart as she gazed at him in surprise. He dropped to the ground, covering his face with his hands.

"I should've stopped him. I should've done something." He heard Serina approach and crouch beside him.

"There wasn't anything you could do. It's not your fault." She laid a reassuring hand on his shoulder, but he shook his head against it.

It's a lie, he thought. *They're all lies. It's my fault.* He heard Elias and Shane cry from inside the house and clutched his head tighter. Serina's hand trembled on his shoulder.

"Let's go for a walk." He didn't answer, but stood and followed as she returned to the town.

Making their way to an inn, they whittled away the rest of the day. Thorn and Kalista caught up to them, but Jacob rarely said anything. He thought he would explode in a fury of guilt if he said anything about Morrie, and so remained silent, even as the others talked about him.

"Let's just hope Makaidel figures out something," Kalista stated as they sat around a table in the common room of the inn.

"I should've stayed with him," Thorn remarked, gazing absently into his drink. "But..."

Kalista shook her head. "We stayed there about an hour, but she never said a word. Never even looked at us."

"The kids did, though."

Kalista's head sank. Thinking about how the boys he had played with the previous day would grow up without a father because of his inaction, Jacob stood abruptly and went up to his room. He pounded his pillow in frustration and misery before his strength faded and he collapsed onto it.

He fell asleep thinking that Aurius would have been better off if he had never come to it.

19

JACOB AWOKE BEFORE everyone else and went down to sit alone in the inn's common room while it was still lit by candles and the hearth fire. He felt calmer after the night of sleep, but thoughts of Morrie still weighed on his mind.

I'm the hero, he thought. *And this isn't a video game. Real people have died because of my actions. I can change things. I have to.*

"I can't let that happen again," he said aloud.

"Let what happen?"

He started and looked up to find Serina standing beside him.

"I'm sorry." She sat down. "I didn't mean to startle you."

"It's okay." He was about to answer 'nothing,' but as he gazed into her delicate, oval-shaped face and wide blue eyes, he knew he couldn't lie to her. "I… had a bad feeling about yesterday. I had told Morrie that he should stay home. I should've insisted on it. Maybe then…" He trailed off, his voice choked.

Serina sighed. "You always seem to know when danger's coming." Jacob felt a small amount of relief that she wasn't suspicious of the way he had predicted trouble so far.

At that moment, the door to the inn opened. Makaidel stood in the golden light streaming in through the doorway, a notebook under his arm. He strode over to their table, a stoic look on his face tinged with a determined hardness. Once again, Jacob was reminded of Lord Kyutu.

"Makaidel." Serina tried to smile.

The young mage set the notebook on their table. "Professor Phantis was right. The orlocs are connected to the element stones."

"What?" Serina asked, baffled. Jacob simply watched Makaidel, unable to feign the surprise he knew he was supposed to be showing.

"The ruins were a temple devoted to the element stones. Humans were never meant to know about them. That's why it was so well guarded."

"But what are these element stones?" Serina asked.

Makaidel shook his head. "I don't know exactly. I saw a lot of runes for 'divine,' 'magic,' and 'nature' related to them, but what exactly they are appeared to be common knowledge among the Alorians, and they didn't write it down, at least in what I found." He gazed at Jacob. "I can tell you that your pendant is one of them, as is that talisman we found on the mountain."

"How many are there?"

Makaidel opened the notebook to a sketch of the floor in the room where they had met Dharius the previous day. "Four." He pointed at the symbols surrounding the central glyph. "Air, water, fire, earth."

Serina pointed at the central symbol. "What does this one mean?"

"It's almost identical to the ancient Alorian rune for 'heart,' but it's modified. I don't understand precisely what it means, but the whole design suggests that the element stones represent incredible power." He raised his head from the page and gazed sharply at them. "Enough to kill thousands if that Alorian got hold of them." Jacob didn't react, expecting the announcement, and knowing full well what Dharius was capable of.

Serina shuddered at the reminder of the mysterious Alorian. "What does he want with the element stones?"

"I don't know, but I do know why he followed us to the ruins. Knowledge of the stones seemed to be lost even among the Alorians. Even though they're kept safe elsewhere, the ruins were the only place with any information on them at all."

"But he got that book," Serina pointed out disappointedly. "There must have been lots of information about the element stones in it."

"All the information available would be my guess," Makaidel replied. "Except for one thing." He flipped the page in the notebook. "The design on the floor of that room in the ruins had more detail than the image in the book. And these extra images Morrie drew from the floor show where the element stones rest."

Serina's eyes widened. "So, you mean…"

"We know how to find the other stones and that Alorian doesn't." Makaidel straightened as Serina beamed. "But we need to hurry. The stones are related to the elements, so all he has to do is search in very watery or fiery places to find the last two."

"Do you know how to find them?"

Makaidel flipped to the last page in the notebook, displaying a map. "Here's the water stone. It resides west of here, in the middle of Darkwater Lake."

"Darkwater Lake?" Serina's eyes widened.

Makaidel nodded. "There's no mistaking it. Obviously, we'll have to do something special to get there."

"Well, let's start going right away!" Smiling, she stood.

"There's one thing I still don't understand, though." She stopped as he focused on her. "By all accounts, only an Alorian should have been able to open the door to the ruins." He gazed at Serina. "I don't know how you could've done it."

Serina glanced away uncertainly and Jacob quickly offered, "Maybe the magic in it just got old."

Makaidel looked skeptical, though he said, "I guess." Serina gave Jacob a faint smile of thanks. "Well, we'd better rouse Thorn and Kalista." Jacob nodded and followed Makaidel upstairs, deep in thought.

Soon, the group packed and left the inn, joining the morning traffic of the town. Jacob frowned at the people strolling calmly through the streets. Everything was the same as it had been when they arrived in town two days ago, the normality of the townspeople mocking the darkness of Morrie's death hanging over him. The sentiment appeared to be shared among the group, as they all remained quiet and subdued as they set out.

Before they had passed two blocks, Elias suddenly darted through the crowd in front of them, a glare marking his small face. Jacob gazed down at the boy, surprised at his appearance.

"Mom wants to talk to you. I hope I never see you again, but she told me to come find you."

Jacob glanced questioningly back at his companions as Elias ran off. His stomach twisted at the thought of facing Cassandra again. "Maybe we should leave her alone." Makaidel frowned uncomfortably in agreement.

"I don't think so," Thorn stated.

Kalista nodded. "If she wants to talk to us, we should at least hear her out."

"I agree," Serina added. She smiled faintly at Jacob. He frowned as he turned and began walking towards the Deacons' house.

All too soon, he reached the familiar house. He paused at the gate, gazing uncertainly at the house. He turned as Serina laid a hand on his arm. She smiled reassuringly. Taking in a deep breath, he opened the gate, crossed the front yard, and knocked on the door.

He heard footsteps approach from inside. The door opened and Cassandra smiled sadly at them. "Oh, good, Elias found you. Please, come inside." They all walked in silently, Thorn and Serina nodding to her while the rest avoided her eyes. As Cassandra closed the door, her smile faded. "I want to apologize for the way I acted yesterday."

"Y-you don't have to…" Jacob attempted.

"No," Cassandra cut in. "I feel bad about treating you that way, and I'm sorry. I know it's not your fault Morrie died." Jacob hung his head, ashamed. She chuckled faintly. "I'm sure even as he was dying, he was grinning from ear to ear for finally getting to the ruins." She faced them. "And you said you actually met an Alorian?"

Makaidel nodded. "Yes."

"Please," she stated as she lowered herself onto a chair. "Tell me what happened." All eyes turned to Jacob. He felt himself reddening under the collective stare. He glanced at Makaidel, but the young mage only shrugged imploringly at him.

Clearing his throat, Jacob awkwardly told Cassandra what had happened at the ruins, looking everywhere but at her. She listened intently, never speaking a word while he talked. He stole a quick glance at her as he finished. Her gaze grew distant.

"I see." She stood and drew in a deep, steadying breath. "You did the right thing. I'm sure Morrie agrees with you."

Serina stepped forward. "Mrs. Deacon, I'm so sorry for your loss."

"He was a good man," Thorn remarked.

"If there's anything we can do, just ask," Kalista stated.

"We'll do everything we can to avenge him," Makaidel added.

Jacob's gaze dropped. "I wish I had done more to try to save him. I'm sorry."

Cassandra smiled at them, her eyes brimming with tears. "Thank you, everyone. I'm glad Morrie had such good company… for his final moments." She walked into the kitchen and returned carrying something. "Garrett, I want you to have this."

Jacob looked up, startled. "What?" She held a dagger out to him, plain in design, but engraved with Alorian runes on the hilt.

"He found it near the ruins and paid to have the blade re-forged and the hilt cleaned and polished," she explained. "It was his prized possession, the closest he'd ever come to being inside the ruins."

"Oh, no, I can't…"

"Please. He would have wanted you to have it." She slipped it into a leather scabbard with a short strap attached to it.

He gazed uneasily at the dagger as she handed it to him. "Are you sure you want to give me this?"

"Yes. It will do more for you than it will for me. It's the least I can do for you for bringing such joy to my home." The lump in Jacob's throat grew larger, but he took the dagger.

He gazed curiously at the strap. "What's this for?"

Makaidel elbowed him. "It's to hide it in your boot, dummy." Jacob frowned, embarrassed.

"Garrett!"

They all turned as young Shane raced into the room. He threw his arms up around Jacob's waist, pressing his head against Jacob's stomach. Jacob leaned back in surprise and patted the boy's back awkwardly.

"You aren't leaving, are you?" Shane's muffled voice came out from Jacob's stomach.

"I…" Jacob began, uncertain what to say.

"Shane," Cassandra stated, but Serina stepped forward and crouched to eye level with the boy.

"We're going to make the orlocs go away." Shane hesitantly turned his head to glance at her. Reaching out a hand, she stroked his hair. "But I promise we'll come back to visit once we're done. Can you be strong for us and take care of your mother until then?" He paused, sniffling. After a moment, he pulled back and nodded.

"I'm gonna miss you. But I'll be strong." Smiling, Cassandra stepped closer to the boy and laid her arm around his shoulders.

"We should get moving," Thorn stated gently. Jacob nodded, unable to speak.

Cassandra glanced up at them. "Thank you again for all you did, and for telling me what happened. Good luck on your journey."

"Thank you very much, Mrs. Deacon," Serina answered.

"Take care," Kalista added. Jacob simply nodded and turned to walk out of the house. He turned back while he was on the path to find Cassandra and Shane waving at him from the open doorway. He attempted to smile as he waved back, feeling even more guilty for their kindness than their anger. Facing forward again, he led the group back into the town.

Soon, they were restocked and on their way again. Jacob felt more at ease as they began traveling across the plains. It was easier to forget about the mistakes he'd made when their greatest challenge was defeating monsters, and he enjoyed the quiet time together with his companions.

And yet, he found it was in those moments that feelings of isolation most often fell over him.

He sat apart from the others that night, the light of the campfire just touching him some paces away. He rubbed his thumb over his pendant, the crude talisman with the amber teardrop that he had crafted with his own hands.

"My name is Jacob." The word sounded foreign, it had been so long since he had heard it. He had never been very fond of his name, but he realized it was his, and he couldn't accept any other as his identity. It was something he hadn't realized he was losing, and he found himself thinking more often recently about the life he had left behind.

Will I ever be able to return there? To go home?

"Are you alright?"

He looked up to find Serina standing beside him. She sat in the grass facing him.

"Yeah." He slipped the pendant behind his shirt. He hadn't intended to say anything more, but once again, he unexpectedly continued. "Just remembering where I came from."

She smiled sadly at him. "You must really miss Merakis."

"Yeah." Lying had become so easy for him. He frowned. "I just wonder if I'm really all everyone seems to think I am. If I'm really much of a hero."

"Of course you are. You're going to save the world."

Jacob frowned, fiddling with his gloves. *Does doing a good deed by itself make me a hero?* He didn't feel that he was anything special, and trying to remember the world he had left behind, he thought that there wasn't anything to him that made him better suited to be a hero than anyone else. He had come this far simply playing the part, and it felt to him that was all he was doing. To consider the full responsibility of his quest weighing on his shoulders intimidated him and made him feel small.

"I've just made so many mistakes." His throat constricted as he thought of the people who had died because of him.

Serina shook her head. "Everyone does, it doesn't make you any less of a hero."

"But…" Jacob sighed, trailing off.

Serina scooted closer to him. "You've done things that no one else has. You've defeated orlocs, saved lives, and now you're going to save the world, using talismans no one else even knows about."

"Yeah," he stated slowly, thinking about all the battles he'd won, the encounters with friends and foes, the danger and victory. "Yeah, I guess I have." Even if the only thing that made him better prepared to play the role of Garrett was to be so familiar with the video game, it still put him in a better position for it than many people. He glanced at her smiling at him and couldn't help smiling back. Regardless of his reasons and his origins, he had indeed done remarkable things in this world. Seeing the respect reflected in Serina's glistening blue eyes, he felt more confident in what he had done. He ached to reach out and hold her, but at the same time, she was so sweet and innocent that she seemed untouchable.

She shrugged her shoulders. "We should probably get back to camp." Nodding, he rose with her and returned to the fire where Makaidel, Thorn, and Kalista talked. Jacob gazed around at the group accompanying him with renewed joy. The biggest surprise to him was that he had become so accustomed to their presence that it no longer astounded him that he was living out his greatest fantasy.

The smile that Serina had reignited in him remained on his face for the rest of that evening.

Two more weeks passed into memory as they traveled across Aurius. Orloc attacks became more dangerous and more frequent, and Kalista protested their destination every day.

"Darkwater Lake? The Serpent Forest is one thing, but ships go down every time they try to sail Darkwater Lake, and that's a fact!"

"Then that must be the right place," Makaidel replied. "The altar in the mountains and the ruins were also dangerous to get to. The Alorians must have protected the element stones that way."

Kalista groaned. "I don't know why I stay with you guys."

Thorn grinned sidelong at her. "You've said that every day since we left Quinlan." Serina giggled as Kalista fumed.

A day before they arrived at the lakeside town of Belford, when they began to see the silvery line of Darkwater Lake spreading out in the distance, a deep, rumbling roar rang through the sky from behind them.

"What's that?" Thorn asked over the growing noise. They all looked over their shoulders and gasped. A great wooden boat sailed through the sky, suspended by a huge, oblong balloon with rotors spinning around it.

"Wow!" Serina watched as it roared over their heads and continued flying through the sky.

"That's the grandson of Charis, the man who built it," Kalista explained. "It's still the only fully operational airship in Aurius."

"Hey!" Makaidel perked up. "We could get him to fly us over the lake and see if we can find where the water stone is."

Kalista looked uncertain. "I don't know. I've heard some strange things about him."

Jacob grinned at her. "What kinds of things?"

She flushed. "Um, well… I guess we'll find out, he seems to be going to Belford, too." Makaidel raised an eyebrow at her vague response, but said nothing. With a shrug, Jacob continued leading them on.

They arrived at the town late the next day, just after the sun set. The moderately quiet feel of Belford, lit by oil lamps and torches, reminded him of Shelas. He thought briefly of the town so far away where he had met

Serina. It seemed so long ago now. As he stopped to think, he realized that he had been in Aurius for over two months. The thought was shocking. His home seemed so distant.

Makaidel yawned loudly, interrupting his thoughts. "Let's just look for an inn. We can find that airship guy tomorrow."

Serina smiled. "That sounds like a good idea." Jacob nodded, still thinking about how long he had been in Aurius. Some of the trees they had passed on their way to the town were now touched with yellow and the air had grown cooler, even though he had traveled so far south from Merakis. He could hardly believe that all that surrounded him had once been a video game to him. His feet were only mildly sore from their journey from Quinlan, whereas they had been covered with blisters on his first day out of Shelas. He felt more nimble and agile than he had in years, and though he had never been trained how to properly wield a sword, swinging it had become a natural action to him. Orlocs no longer scared him. He had spent so much time admiring and trying to fit in to the world around him that it didn't occur to him how different it was, or how different he had become.

They spoke little on their way to an inn, all of them tired from a hard day's travel to arrive at the town that day. Jacob retired silently to his room and decided to take a bath before going to bed. He longed for a hot shower, but it was enough for him just to wash off the dirt of his journey.

He emerged to find the room generously lit by candles and oil lamps, their light all that stood between him and utter darkness. Yawning, he stepped across the room toward the bed, looking forward to a restful night's sleep.

Suddenly, he caught a glimpse of movement out of the corner of his eye. He spun, crouching into a defensive stance, but paused. The movement had been his reflection in a full-length mirror against the wall. He gazed at his image, blinking in surprise. The reflection hardly looked like him. He had lost weight since he arrived in Aurius, the extra flesh on his stomach having receded into shaped abdominals, and his muscles were more toned. His chest and arms were more defined than perhaps they had ever been. Grinning, he flexed his biceps, marveling at how they bulged and trembled. His hair had grown out so long that he had to tie it back in a tail. All the travel outside had tanned his skin as well, and his freckles were all but gone. Even his face seemed better defined, more masculine. Older.

He moved closer to the mirror curiously, examining a strange shadow on his face. The realization hit him suddenly, and he laughed aloud in excitement. Peach fuzz flecked his jaw, the beginnings of a beard.

I've grown my first beard!

As soon as the thought crossed his mind, however, his smile faded and his expression fell. For the past few years, he had wondered when he would grow his first beard. It was an occasion he had been awaiting, a symbol of adulthood and the freedom that went along with it. He had eagerly anticipated showing his friends and family when it finally began to grow. Seeing the hair around his chin now, he had never felt so far away from home.

With a sigh, he snuffed the candles and oil lamps and flopped onto a strange bed. He had always thought he wanted to travel, but he knew now that he was not a wanderer. He missed the familiarity of home, something he realized he no longer had. He longed for his old house on the coast, in the town where his father still lived, and hadn't yet grown to feel at home in his mother and stepfather's new house.

He rolled onto his back and shook his head. *What is my problem? Here I am having the adventure of a lifetime and I'm thinking about my house!* He chuckled, though the smile didn't last in his longing. Rolling over, he settled into the pillow and relaxed, soon falling asleep.

20

NOISE ASSAULTED THEIR ears as they opened the door. The tavern teemed with life, people crowding its smoky and warm interior. Jacob stepped inside, followed by the rest of the group. Their eyes roamed slowly around the bustling common room, dozens of conversations buffeting their ears at once.

"So, which one is he?" Makaidel called over the noise.

"We don't even know for sure he's in here," Thorn stated.

Serina turned to Kalista. "Do you see him in here?"

Kalista flushed. "I've only heard about him, I've never actually met him."

"I guess we'll just have to ask around," Jacob stated, completely uncertain how he was going to go about that.

The bartender proved immediately helpful. They all turned as one to follow his pointing finger.

Makaidel's upper lip curled distastefully. "Him?"

A suave and rugged-looking man grinned from the middle of a group of women fawning over him halfway across the room. The only man nearby sat across the table from him, looking disheveled.

As they approached the table, they saw the man surrounded by women shrug. "Sorry," he stated to the man who sat across from him, a handful of playing cards lying on the table before him. "I guess it's just my lucky day." The women giggled, one hanging off each arm. Groaning, the other man rose from his chair and walked away. Makaidel grimaced as the man they approached crooned to the women around him.

He glanced up as they neared, grinning as his gaze fixed solely on Kalista. "This must be my lucky day. Hello there, gorgeous. Have we met before?" Kalista stuttered, but the man continued before she could answer, "No, I definitely would've remembered a beautiful face like yours. What's your name?"

"Um, Kalista." Jacob thought inanely how completely the tough and self-confident visage she had projected when they first met had disappeared.

"Well, have a seat, Kalista." The man gestured to the now vacated chair across from him. "My name's Thayer." Kalista lowered herself uncertainly into the chair, Thayer following her with his eyes the entire way. "What can I do for you?"

Makaidel stepped forward, clearing his throat. "We need to…"

"Ah," Thayer cut in sharply, holding up a hand to silence Makaidel. "Wait your turn, kid. I asked her." Makaidel glared at Thayer while Kalista turned to glance uncertainly at Jacob. He shrugged, holding out his hands encouragingly.

She shifted. "Well, um, we wanted to ask if you could take us somewhere in your airship."

Raucous laughter rang up from the women around him as his grin widened.

"Thayer doesn't let *anyone* fly on his airship," one of the girls responded bitingly.

"Not even us." The girl to his right rubbed her hand over his chest.

Thayer grinned. "Sorry, gorgeous, but the girls are right. But if you want, I can take you on a tour of it later." Kalista visibly shrank in her chair at the tone of his voice. Jacob's heart wrenched at the sight.

Makaidel stepped forward and slammed his hands on the table. "This is important!"

A round of giggles circled the women surrounding Thayer. He grinned. "Everyone's business always is."

"Please, Mr. Thayer."

Everyone turned as Serina stepped forward. Thayer's eyebrows rose.

"Well, where were you hiding, beautiful?"

Serina smiled pleasantly at him as she reached her hand across the table. "My name is Serina." He took her hand, bringing it up to his mouth to kiss it. Jacob frowned, annoyed, but Serina seemed unaffected by the gesture. "Please, Mr. Thayer, we have to go over the lake in your airship."

One of the women on the other side of the table put her hands on her hips, glaring at Serina. "Listen, girl…"

Thayer held up a hand, silencing her. "Sorry, Serina, but I'm the only one who's ever flown in my airship. I can't make exceptions now. But I'll tell you what, let me finish my drink here and I'll take you both on a special tour of it." Kalista looked uneasy, but Serina only smiled at Thayer.

"No, thank you, I'd rather stay with Garrett." Her words made Jacob's heart swell, even though he had been expecting them.

"What, this pipsqueak?" Thayer answered with a disbelieving look.

Jacob fumed. That hadn't been in the game. He supposed it had to do with the fact that he was shorter than the real Garrett appeared to be.

Makaidel stepped forward before Jacob could say anything. "We don't have time for your flirting. The fate of Aurius depends on us using your airship!"

"I'm sorry, but…"

"Hey," Thorn cut in unexpectedly, laying a steadying hand on Makaidel's shoulder. "You look like a gambling man. How about a round of five-card draw? If we win, you let us use your airship."

Thayer's eyes narrowed, but he grinned. "And if I win?"

The group hesitated. Kalista turned around in her chair and winked at Jacob.

Facing Thayer again, she answered, "I'll go with you on that airship tour… alone." She draped an arm casually over the back of the chair. Thayer's eyes widened with the proposition.

The women surrounding Thayer sputtered in anger. "Just who do you think…"

"Take it easy, girls," Thayer interrupted, silencing their protests. He leaned forward, leering at Kalista. "There's always room for one more. Alright, you've got a deal. Who's taking me on?"

"I think Garrett should play." Serina steered Jacob toward the chair across from Thayer. Kalista stood as Jacob uncomfortably lowered himself onto her chair.

In the game, if he hadn't won either of the first two rounds against Thayer, the third would always win, the victory seemingly programmed in. But here, there was no such fail-safe, and he was not an experienced poker player like his opponent. He uneasily considered his chances as Thayer dealt each of them a hand.

His cards were worthless. As soon as he glanced at them, the rest of the group leaned over his shoulders, uttering suggestions. Shrinking away from the closeness of their presence, he picked three cards to trade in. He tried to keep a straight face as he received his replacement cards. His new hand still wasn't worth much, but he hoped that the odds were against Thayer to get much better in a single round.

Jacob laid his hand on the table. "Two pair."

Thayer's grin didn't waver as he spread his cards on the table. "Three of a kind." Jacob frowned, hoping he would have better luck in the next round. To his surprise, however, Thayer leaned back in his chair, ignoring the deck of cards. "Sorry, kid. Just the luck of the cards."

Jacob glanced up with a start. "Wait, you have to give me a second chance!"

The women around Thayer laughed mockingly. He smirked at Jacob. "You don't get a second chance in the real world."

"But…" Jacob stood abruptly, taken aback. He trailed off, thinking dismally that this was another difference between the game and the real

Aurius.

Thayer stood, gazing at Kalista. "Shall we go on that tour now?" Jacob didn't meet her eyes.

"Come on!" Makaidel argued. "We need your help!"

Annoyance tinged Thayer's voice. "I'm sorry, kid, but you had your chance, and you lost. I know you're young, but you'll have to learn that losing is part of life." Makaidel glared daggers and even Jacob's blood boiled at the condescending tone to his words, but Thayer didn't react as he rounded the table and put his arm around Kalista's waist. "Deal with it."

"Let's just go," Jacob growled as he stalked across the tavern floor ahead of Thayer and Kalista. He had found Thayer amusing in the game, but he wasn't so fond of the real one.

"Well, great," Makaidel remarked as they stepped outside. He glanced over his shoulder as Thayer and Kalista turned down the street. Kalista looked uncomfortable with Thayer's touch. "Now what?" Jacob was at a loss. They couldn't get where they needed to go next without Thayer's airship, but without being given a chance to win a game of poker against him, he didn't know what to do.

"Should we follow them?" Serina asked, watching Kalista and Thayer walk away.

Thorn shook his head. "He won an exclusive tour with her fair and square. Don't think it would endear us to him if we followed."

"Do you have any ideas?" Makaidel asked Jacob. Jacob only frowned.

Suddenly, a crash rumbled through the air, followed by screams. A cloud of dust rose from a building a few blocks away.

Serina tensed. "What was that?" Drawing his sword, Jacob broke into a run, followed by Serina, Makaidel, and Thorn.

"What the hell?" Thayer yelped as they passed by him. Kalista had already drawn her sidearm blades and fell into step beside them.

Jacob drew to a stop, the others following suit behind him. A great, shapeless creature, seemingly made of water, rose over the buildings the next street over. The top of its proboscis-like extension swirled around as if to face them. Jacob could see a red nucleus about the size of a small car floating in the creature.

"What is that?" Thorn stated.

The creature rushed forward in a flood of water, the tip of the proboscis foaming white from the movement. With a collective yelp, they scattered, the proboscis crashing into the ground and spraying them all. Spinning around, Jacob swung at the tower of water now rising beside him. His eyes widened as he lost his balance, thrown to the side from the force of his swing as his sword passed right through the creature.

An arm of water stretched out of the creature. Before Jacob could react, it slapped him bodily through the air with a cry. He shouted in pain as he slammed into the support beam for an overhanging roof on a nearby building. The wood cracked and bent as he hit it, showering him with splinters. He lay ragged with pain only a moment before a familiar warmth passed over him and the aches abated.

"Fire Lance!"

Jacob glanced up as a stream of flames shot out from Makaidel's outstretched hands. The mage's eyes widened as the fire fizzled harmlessly against the creature's watery body. He barely lunged out of the way as it slammed an arm of water down towards him, the entire extension white and frothing viciously.

Remembering the logic of the game, Jacob yelled, "Cast lightning on it!" As he lunged to his feet to rejoin the battle, he saw Kalista slashing at an extension of the creature, though her blades splashed harmlessly through it. Thorn charged the main tower of water, his body crashing clear through it. As the creature fell, however, it rejoined the water it had been separated from, rising back to its previous height.

"The nucleus!" Jacob slashed off an extension of the creature's shifting body. "Aim for the nu…"

A shriek cut him off. Turning, he found the creature had grabbed Thayer and rose into the air, its watery body coiling over and enveloping him. The airship owner's eyes were huge with fear. He tried to push the encroaching water away, but his hands merely sank into it.

Running around the creature, Kalista swung up onto an overhanging roof and leaped off, rising toward the nucleus floating below the proboscis that slowly engulfed Thayer. She slashed, her blades passing through the layer of water and slicing into the nucleus.

An ear-splitting hiss rent the air as the creature dropped Thayer. He crashed gracelessly to the ground as Kalista landed in a somersault, coming up on one knee.

The air fairly crackled with the palpable fury of the water creature. Spreading itself out, it slammed fountains of water like enormous raindrops all over the street. Jacob lunged aside from the pelting fountains, struggling to stay clear of their crushing force.

"Lightning Blast!"

An orb of crackling energy that lit up the street flew out from Makaidel's hands. As it collided with the tower of water, the creature stiffened, its various extensions paralyzed as lightning sparked over it.

Jacob ran past Kalista and Thayer as the proboscis sank towards the ground. Leaping into the air, he slashed at the nucleus, satisfied with how the blade dug into the red orb. With a foaming hiss, the creature swatted him away again, but the blow was much weaker this time. Jacob regained his footing as he tumbled along the street. He paused before returning to the creature.

As Kalista swung her arms back, her blades began to emit a shimmering, iridescent light. She spun gracefully away from the creature's swinging arm of water, her hair twirling behind her like a ribbon of violet between the twin glowing streaks trailing after her weapons. Jacob's eyes widened, recognizing the signs of a Runic Seal. Turning, she leaped into the air far higher than seemed possible, raising the weapons over her head. At the peak of her jump, she swung, her blades cutting deeply into the throbbing nucleus.

The creature hissed, its watery body trembling as it began dripping on the street. Kalista landed lightly before it, poised to strike again. The creature lost shape as its body gurgled and melted and the extensions splashed off it.

The creature paused, quavering, when it had shrunk to half its size. The street was silent, watching, cobblestones glistening wetly where parts of its shifting form used to be.

Suddenly, in a single release, the creature broke. Kalista leaped nimbly up onto an overhanging roof behind her as water gushed out from the meaty nucleus and ran down the street. Jacob stepped backwards hastily, but the water, now entirely unremarkable, spread out down the gutters and troughs between cobblestones, diminishing to a trickle by the time it reached his feet. The only one who had gotten wet from the creature's death throes was Thayer, now drenched from where he had crouched not far from Kalista.

Jacob glanced sharply at the airship owner, but before he could say anything, Makaidel's voice called from across the street, "Now do you see why we need to use your airship?" Thayer glanced between Makaidel and Jacob, his face still white with shock. The nucleus lay unmoving in the street not far from him like a disgorged heart.

Slowly, he nodded. "Alright, you have a deal." Sighing, Jacob sheathed his sword as they regrouped.

"Thayer!"

The shrieks of the women who had surrounded Thayer in the tavern filled the street as they raced over to him.

"Are you okay?"

"We were so worried!"

Thayer donned a confident smile as he stood, his wet clothes clinging to him. He laughed nonchalantly. "Of course I'm fine. It would take something much worse than that do me in." The women giggled while beside Jacob, Makaidel groaned.

"We have to leave in the morning."

The women turned to glare at Makaidel. "He's not actually going with you."

"Sorry, ladies," Thayer stated, drawing their attention back to him, "but I'm afraid it's time for me to move on." He tried to cool their immediate protests, then turned to glance at Kalista. "Which reminds me, shall we go on that tour now?"

"Hmph." Kalista stepped closer to Jacob. "I'm with Serina, I'd rather stay with Garrett. At least he wasn't afraid of that thing." Jacob felt his face grow warm, but he grinned and shrugged triumphantly at Thayer.

One of the women turned to Thayer, wide-eyed. "You weren't actually afraid of it, were you?"

"Of course not!" Thayer replied a little too quickly. "I just didn't get a chance to fight back."

Jacob, Makaidel, Thorn, and Kalista all groaned in exasperation. Jacob turned to find the others walking back towards the inn where they had stayed the night. He glanced at Serina, still standing beside him. She smiled and shrugged. He smiled back, then faced Thayer again.

"We're leaving first thing in the morning."

"Yeah, alright." Thayer's gaze didn't leave his admirers.

Rolling his eyes, Jacob turned and followed after the others, Serina by his side.

Jacob's head leaned back to take in the sight as he walked.

"Wow," Serina remarked. "I've never seen a real airship before."

Thayer grinned over his shoulder at her. "That's because this is the only one in Aurius, and nobody goes on it but me."

Jacob heard Makaidel grumble, "Elitist."

The wooden ship towered over them as they approached, enormous to behold, and the balloon seemed to rise halfway to the clouds as it was.

"If you don't let anyone else on it," Thorn stated, "then what do you do if something goes wrong?"

"I fix it. My granddad taught me everything there is to know about this ship." Thayer approached the side of the ship, opened a panel, and flipped some switches. "Get ready to experience something no one else has."

"We've been to the southern ruins," Makaidel stated dryly. "It would take a lot to impress us." Serina giggled.

Thayer grinned at her as a gangplank swung down from the side of the ship with a series of clanks. "You've got a beautiful laugh, you know that?"

Serina smiled at him. "Thank you." Jacob frowned, annoyed that Thayer only liked her for her appearance.

"Follow me." Thayer strode up the gangplank into the ship.

The interior was much brighter than Jacob had been expecting, due to the many windows set into the side of the ship. The ground floor of the ship opened onto a large room cluttered with coils of rope, crates and barrels of food and drink, and various tools scattered about the floor and walls. A staircase rose along the far wall and the room ended at a hallway leading away to the left.

Thayer chuckled. "You'll have to excuse the mess. I don't really have a store room, so I just throw everything here."

"Some tour," Kalista scoffed. Thayer shot her a piercing smile, but Makaidel spoke before he could.

"What's down there?" The mage pointed at the rows of doors down the hallway.

"The engine room, kitchen, bathroom," Thayer answered. He gazed deeply at Kalista. "Bedrooms." Kalista rolled her eyes.

"Bedrooms?" Makaidel cut in oddly. "Why do you need bedrooms if you don't let anyone on?"

Ignoring him, Thayer laid his arm around Kalista's waist. "Maybe I could show them to you later." She pulled his hand away with a disinterested look.

Jacob cleared his throat. "We were going over the lake?"

Thayer shrugged. "Alright, let's go above deck." They followed as he approached and climbed the stairs to the upper deck.

Jacob was the last to climb onto the upper deck, shadowed by the enormous balloon floating some twenty feet over their heads. He glanced about in surprise. The airship had looked enormous as they approached, but it was only as wide as his backyard at home, and only about as long as the yard and house put together. He had thought that most of the lower deck was in the rooms they had passed by, but the entry room seemed to be half the size of the ship. He strode over to the gunwale and looked down, finding himself about two stories off the ground. He realized then that ordinary boats were probably as large as well, but most of it lay underwater.

"Anyone afraid of heights should go below deck." Thayer shot Makaidel a pointed look. The young mage narrowed his eyes. "Here we go." Thayer flipped a lever beside the helm. With a *chunk* and a series of clacking sounds, the floor beneath their feet began to vibrate. The group gravitated towards the railing, clinging to it with nervous and excited looks.

The whirring sound of a propeller emanated from the stern of the airship as the other noises grew louder. Jacob wondered what powered the airship in a world without batteries or gasoline. He glanced up at the balloon, which creaked as it stretched at the ropes holding it to the ship.

Presently, the boat swayed beneath their feet. Jacob grabbed the railing to steady himself as the airship lifted off the ground. He glanced around, finding Makaidel gazing over the edge in awe while Serina and Thorn listened intently to the sounds of the airship. Kalista's eyes were wide as she clenched her fingers around the gunwale, knuckles white.

Jacob glanced over the side as the wind caught his long hair. Already he could see the entirety of the airship's shadow on the ground, and the far side of Belford where it disappeared into open grass. His heart pounded in exhilaration.

"A-are you sure this is safe?" Kalista called over the roar of the propeller and gears below deck.

Thayer laughed. "Undoubtedly."

Jacob gazed out across the land stretching away below them as they rose still higher into the air. The airship's shadow was faint from distance, no larger than an eraser.

"Here we go!"

All heads turned toward Thayer as the ship tilted backwards. Kalista yelped as they all stumbled back, clutching the railing. Jacob shot a foot back for balance, but it was less of a lurch than on a subway car or even a school bus.

He leaned against the gunwale with a smile as the world rotated slowly beneath him. The others marveled at the sight, awestruck. He glanced oddly over at their reactions. Serina seemed close to tears in her amazement and even Thorn was speechless, shaking his head in wonder at the sight. On the other side of the ship, Kalista trembled as she crouched, still gripping the railing tightly. Makaidel leaned over the railing, quiet and subdued, but eyes huge as he gazed out. It was an incredible sight, Jacob thought as he gazed across the silvery sheet of Darkwater Lake, but the rest of the group seemed nearly hysterical.

Then, it occurred to him how wholly unique this experience was for them. He had flown much higher in an airplane, but in this world, rising above ground outside of a tall building or mountain was unheard of. They had never even seen anything in the sky aside from birds. He wondered why no video game ever thought to mention that fact.

"So, you know where we're going?"

Thayer's raised voice jostled everyone out of their reverie. Makaidel shook his head under the pilot's gaze.

"Yeah," he stated, clearly still dazed from the experience of being on a flying airship. He stepped away from the gunwale uncertainly, then walked slowly over to the helm.

Thayer laughed. "Don't worry, she's smooth as butter in flight." Jacob looked to the wooden planks on which he stood, but the airship swayed less beneath his feet than any land vehicle he had been on.

Standing beside Thayer, Makaidel opened a map. "The entrance should be here."

"Entrance to what?" Thayer turned the wheel.

"I'm not sure exactly." Makaidel gazed at his map, as if hoping to glean answers from his own pen strokes. "Probably an altar or temple where the water element stone is kept."

"Element stones, huh?" Thayer shrugged. "Well, I've never heard of 'em."

Makaidel glanced up at Thayer. "Hey, did you ever fly over the southern ruins?"

"Sure. I always wanted to be the first one to discover them, but there isn't enough room to land for miles around." Jacob glanced away, thinking of Morrie.

"Why don't you let anyone else on this ship?" Thorn asked abruptly.

Thayer blinked at him. "Huh?"

"It seems a shame to be the only one to enjoy this remarkable view," Serina added. "Don't you get lonely up here?"

Thayer smiled wistfully. "All the time. But my granddad told me never to let anyone else on it, as long as I lived. He's probably rolling over in his grave now that you're on it."

"Why?" Makaidel asked. "You could charge people for trips and make a fortune."

"And never get it to myself again." Thayer shook his head. "If I let tourists on now, I couldn't reject them later, and it would never stop. It's the same with the military. My granddad was commissioned to make this as a weapon of war, but then every kingdom in the world wanted to either make him build one for them or sabotage or destroy it. That's why he kept it to himself and never let anyone on it again, except me." He sighed, closing his eyes as the breeze tossed his hair about. "This ship is my freedom. If I share it, it won't be anymore. That's the most important lesson my granddad taught me." The group fell silent, surprised at his words.

"I'm sorry," Makaidel ventured softly. "I'm sorry for the things I said. I didn't realize…"

"Nah, it's okay. I don't expect anyone to understand. To be honest, it's kind of nice getting to tell you guys this." He tossed his head, the distant expression on his face replaced with a confident grin. "So, is that map to scale?"

"Uh…" Makaidel blinked, clearly thrown off guard by the sudden change of subject. "Yeah, it should be."

"How long will it take to get there?" Thorn asked.

Thayer gazed over at the map in Makaidel's hands. "Well, if it's in the middle of the lake, it should be about two hours." Kalista, still crouched against the gunwale, groaned at his response.

Thayer grinned over his shoulder at her, but before he could say anything, Serina stated, "This is amazing. No one else has even seen this far over the lake in centuries."

"You wouldn't believe the places we can go on this ship," Thayer replied. *I would,* Jacob thought, but he simply gazed over the edge at the blanket of rolling waves below. The view, he had to admit, was spectacular. The conversation fell silent as the land drifted away behind them and the water below shimmered in the sun.

21

THE JOURNEY PASSED quietly, the lake unchanging beneath them. Makaidel barraged Thayer with questions about the mechanics of the airship, and though the pilot often answered that it was a secret, he seemed eager to show off the ship's workings to the mage. Kalista eventually retreated below deck, accompanied by Thorn. To Jacob's delight, Thayer allowed him to man the helm, though he he had no idea how to operate the airship aside from steering the wheel. Serina stood at the bow of the ship, gazing over the edge in search of their destination.

"Wow." Her gaze swung over the endless plain of water below. "There's no way that awful Alorian could follow us now." Jacob's smile faded as he watched her. The problem, he thought, with knowing what was going to happen next was that when he knew to expect trouble, he couldn't warn the others without raising suspicion, and so far, he hadn't been able to prevent disaster himself. He had known exactly what was going to happen in the southern ruins, but Morrie had still died. Dharius still had the element stone of earth. Even Phantis had died, and that hadn't happened in the game. His influence, Jacob thought morosely, had only made things worse. And something far worse was about to happen if he didn't do anything this time.

"Hey, look!" Serina exclaimed suddenly, pointing ahead. "There's an island!"

Her cry brought Thayer and Makaidel up from below deck.

"Let me see." Makaidel ran up to the bow of the ship and leaned over the railing. "That's got to be it!" Jacob craned his neck from where he stood, but he could see little over the gunwale some paces away.

Thayer took the wheel. As he examined some instruments built into the steering column, Jacob strode over to the railing and followed Serina and Makaidel's eyes. An island rose out of the lake below, no larger than a football field and seemingly adorned only with a few trees and boulders. Even from a new angle and this far away, Jacob knew the island immediately. He felt a pang of excitement, as well as uneasiness, with the sight.

"Yeah, that's the spot." Thayer adjusted some switches around the wheel.

"Can you land this thing down there?" Makaidel peered over the edge at the island nearly directly beneath them.

Thayer laughed. "I can land her on a dime. Just watch." Jacob blinked, wondering how the phrase 'turn on a dime' had come into Aurius when there was no such currency here. A faint movement in the ship was all the indication that it stopped moving forward.

Thayer pulled down what looked like the mouthpiece of a trumpet attached to a long brass tube spiraling below deck. "All passengers, prepare to land." He grinned, replacing the tube. "I've always wanted to use that thing." Thorn emerged as the airship began sinking towards the island.

"Careful," Makaidel remarked as he gazed over the edge.

"Where's Kalista?" Thayer glanced quickly between Thorn and the instruments at the helm.

"She said she'd come up after we landed," Thorn answered.

"Is she okay?" Serina asked.

"A little seasick, but she'll be fine. She just wanted to stay below."

Thayer grinned. "It's called airsick when you're up this high."

"You're too far up," Makaidel remarked. "You'll hit the water."

"I know what I'm doing," Thayer replied.

Jacob glanced at him, finding himself agreeing with Makaidel. "How can you even see where we're landing?"

Thayer's grin faded. "Okay, it's quiet time now. I need concentration." Jacob exchanged concerned glances with the others.

To his surprise, the island emerged as they dropped closer to the ground until they touched down safely.

"Here we are," Thayer remarked as the noise of the propeller and machinery died down. "Isla de… uh, I guess it doesn't have a name, since we seem to be the first people here."

"Hey," Makaidel stated. "Why don't we call it Isla de Lamanis, for the Alorian word for 'water'?" Jacob grinned as the others agreed with the name of the island in the game.

Kalista crept up from below, pale-faced and wide-eyed. "Are we here?"

Thayer grinned. "Yeah, we're here."

"Well, let's go already!" Makaidel exclaimed as he ran over to the stairs below deck.

Thayer chuckled and shook his head at Jacob. "Kids." Jacob sent him a wry grin, knowing that Makaidel was only a handful of years younger than him. Saying nothing, he strode toward the stairs leading below deck, the others following behind him.

By the time they got to the open gangplank leading out onto the island, Makaidel was already looking about in wonder.

"Huh," Thayer stated. "I never knew this island was here. I always went around the lake."

"Why?" Serina cocked her head curiously.

Thayer shrugged. "Superstition, I guess. It's not like I'd ever try to land in the water."

"I can see how it's easy to overlook," Thorn stated. "You really think the element stone is on this tiny chunk of rock?"

Jacob rubbed the back of his neck. "Well, uh…"

"Hey, guys!" Makaidel waved fervently from the top of a rise some paces ahead. "Come look at this!" Jacob strode up the incline, followed by the others.

"Oh!" Kalista exclaimed as she gazed down the other side of the hill.

A wide, circular platform of stone sat on the bottom of the island, surrounded by boulders and the crumbling ruins of old pillars.

Thayer's eyes widened. "Amazing."

"It looks just like the altar on the mountain," Thorn stated. Makaidel was already examining the island altar. The others descended the hill to join him.

"Isn't this amazing?" the young mage stated. "It's just like the mountaintop altar. Look! There's the symbol on the talisman."

"But where's the talisman?" Kalista asked.

"On the mountain, it was on a pedestal in the middle of the altar." Thorn gazed at the designs carved into the floor at the center of the circle. "But it doesn't look like there was ever anything here."

"It's got to be here somewhere." Makaidel peered around the boulders marked with Alorian runes.

Jacob glanced at Serina. Her gaze looked distant, her eyes glassy as she stared ahead, unseeing. He watched as she strode slowly forward until she stood at the center of the platform, then closed her eyes.

"Whoa!"

Jacob snapped his gaze over at Makaidel's outcry. He lunged backwards from the rock he had been inspecting, which now emitted a faint blue light.

"What the hell?" Thayer glanced frantically about at the boulders surrounding the altar, all glowing softly.

"Serina," Kalista uttered. Turning back to Serina, Jacob found her standing calmly at the center of the platform, eyes still shut. The stones beneath her feet shone light onto her and her hair and clothes flowed in some otherworldly breeze. Jacob caught his breath as he glimpsed her ears beneath her hair.

Then, the platform began to move. Everyone but Serina let out a collective yelp as the stone sank beneath their feet.

"What's going on?" Thayer exclaimed. Jacob saw Makaidel gazing strangely at Serina.

The group gasped in unison as the stone platform sank beneath the ground, dropping slowly down like an elevator. A cavern opened up around them, a great cylindrical chamber of stone below the altar. Everyone let out exclamations of wonder as they slowly fell farther and farther down.

Thorn strode over to the edge and gazed down. "Well, I guess now we know where the talisman is."

The group remained silent, glancing about at the mysterious cavern, as they dropped ever downward, the light of the opening where they had entered growing fainter and fainter. Finally, the movement stopped as the platform reached the bottom of the chamber. None of the light from the quarter-sized opening to the world above touched the smooth stone walls. Ripples of blue light like reflections of flowing water illuminated the chamber, though where the light source was, or the water, they couldn't tell.

Serina's eyes fluttered open.

"How... Did you do that?" Makaidel's soft voice rang around the chamber.

"*You* did that?" Thayer echoed suspiciously.

Serina shook her head, confused and fearful. "I don't know. It asked me to cast a spell, so I did."

"What asked you?" Thorn stated.

Tears welled in Serina's eyes as she trembled. "... The altar."

"What?" Thayer snapped, disturbed and angry. "And how are we going to get back up?"

Serina hugged herself, clearly terrified of what she had just done. Unable to contain himself with the sight, Jacob reached forward and laid a hand on her shoulder. She smiled weakly at him, sniffling.

"Look, we need to find that talisman anyway," Makaidel cut in, his leader's voice cutting across the silence gripping the chamber. "We can worry about how to get out of here after that." Thorn followed the young mage across and off the platform toward an opening in the chamber leading into a hallway. Reluctantly, Thayer followed, giving Serina a suspicious look as he passed by. Jacob glared at the pilot in response. Kalista smiled encouragingly to Serina before trailing after Thayer. Jacob smiled, glad for her presence, before turning his gaze to Serina. She glanced uncertainly at him.

"Hey," he offered, hoping he could cheer her. "We never would have been able to come here if it wasn't for you."

She smiled faintly. "I guess we should catch up with the others."

"Yeah," he answered lamely as they approached the hallway where the others had disappeared.

Jacob and Serina soon caught up to where Makaidel, Thorn, Kalista, and Thayer walked through the hall.

"And what if we see another of those water-monsters?" Makaidel asked, apparently continuing a conversation Jacob and Serina had missed.

"I know what to do now," Thayer answered confidently. "In fact, I'm probably better equipped to handle it than you." He held up an arm-mounted crossbow, which Jacob knew was armed with small needles rather than full-size bolts.

"Yeah, your pants will already be wet before it even touches you," Kalista remarked. Everyone but Thayer roared in laughter, the sounds echoing off the walls of the passage they walked. Jacob caught an annoyed frown on Thayer's face mixed with amused admiration of Kalista.

Soon, they turned a corner and halted, gasping. An enormous chamber opened up before them, the rocky ceiling like the distant rafters of a concert hall. The floor was uneven, dotted as it was with raised platforms and narrow ledges. It was a puzzle, Jacob knew, to get to the three-story-high entrance opposite the one where they stood, but he had it memorized.

"Wow!" Kalista exclaimed. "I wasn't expecting this." The others agreed. Jacob stood silently, gazing out at the cavernous chamber. In the game, this area had his favorite music. It had seemed so long since he had heard any music he knew, or much at all aside from the occasional minstrel in town. At first, he had missed the sounds that had accompanied him everywhere he went, but over the weeks that had passed since he came to Aurius, he had become accustomed to the silence. As he gazed at the cavern before him, however, the tune rang through his mind as if it played now, a distant memory resurrected by the rippling blue light shining off the walls.

"Garrett?"

Startled out of his reverie, Jacob found the group already moving into the chamber. Thorn glanced back at him curiously. Shaking his head, he followed them.

Suddenly, an orloc dropped down from above with a snarl. The group scattered with a collective yelp and Jacob drew his sword. The battle was quick and frantic in the closeness of the chamber crowded with raised stone platforms. Within a few minutes, the orloc was dispatched and collapsed across the floor awkwardly.

Thayer chuckled. "That wasn't so hard." Makaidel grumbled something as Serina healed the few wounds in the group from the encounter.

"We'd better get moving before that thing starts to smell," Thorn remarked, turning to continue on their path. Jacob wrinkled his nose as he gazed at the ugly body of the orloc. That was a difference in the real Aurius that he hadn't anticipated. In the game, monsters simply disappeared once they were killed, and the ones he had faced here on the openness of plain and mountain they had been able to leave behind. But in an enclosed chamber like this, there would be little escaping the body. He hoped that not too many more orlocs would appear before they left the room.

They encountered several more as they made their way across the steep ledges and narrow crevasses towards the exit, but to Jacob's relief, the air never grew foul.

"I sure hope we're going the right way." Thayer balanced precariously on a stepping stone raised twenty feet off the ground. "Because if we're doing all this for nothing, I'm going to be pissed."

"It's got to be here." Makaidel hopped to a ledge some way ahead. "All these glyphs are Alorian, and I recognize most of them from the ruins."

Jacob glanced over his shoulder as Kalista secured her grappling hook on a high ledge above. He knew they were in the right place, and he knew exactly what was going to happen here, and that was what worried him.

Finally, they reached the ledge that connected to a hallway into the next room. As they came to the far end of the hall, all thoughts of the end of the temple disappeared from Jacob's mind. The group pulled up short at a small chamber with three exits, each leading out to a twisting hallway with various other paths branching off.

It was a maze.

"Oh, great." Makaidel made a face, clearly seeing the entrances for what they were.

"Which way do we go?" Serina peered into the openings. None of them went more than ten feet before turning a corner out of sight.

"Maybe we should split up and take each path." Thayer put an arm around Kalista's waist. "I'll go with Kalista."

Kalista pushed him away with a disgusted look. "You can split up, I'll stay with everyone else."

"I think we should stay together," Serina stated.

Thorn nodded. "I agree. We don't know what we might find in there, or what might be at the other end." Jacob did, and he wondered briefly if splitting up and allowing some of the others to become lost in the maze while he continued on would be better. He shook the thought from his mind.

He pointed to the right-hand entrance. "Let's go in here."

"Why that way?" Makaidel asked.

Jacob grinned over his shoulder at him. "Call it a hunch." He had this maze committed to memory and he was eager to impress them all as he guided them easily through the twisting paths. Serina smiled at him as he led the way into the third entrance.

He strode forward confidently, bypassing paths he knew to be dead ends. The maze was familiar, exactly as he remembered it, though even in his confidence in being able to lead them through it successfully, he felt a pang of claustrophobia in the narrow, fully enclosed hallways.

At a junction of paths several turns in, a snarl and a large, black body streaked past. With a yelp, Jacob darted ahead, the orloc scattering the group a few paces into different hallways. Maneuvering was difficult in the narrow passages, but the orloc had less space to evade and was quickly defeated.

Jacob stood with a sigh, wiping his sword off on the orloc and sliding it into his scabbard. He glanced around, trying to get his bearings as the others recovered. "Which way did we come from?"

Makaidel, Kalista, and Thorn pointed down the hallway where they stood.

Jacob turned around, trying to orient himself as the game had depicted this part of the maze. He pointed down the left passage. "Then we should go that way."

"You want to go towards where that orloc came from?" Makaidel asked.

"Yeah." At the uncertain and dubious looks given him, Jacob continued, "Well, if there's orlocs that way, they must be guarding the talisman."

"Orlocs don't *guard* things," Thayer remarked, arms folded.

"I guess they did guard the ruins," Kalista mused. "And the mountain."

Serina smiled at Jacob. "I'll follow you whichever way you think is best."

Jacob smiled back, but Makaidel stated, "I don't know why you think you can find your way better than the rest of us."

"I'm good at mazes." It wasn't true, Jacob had to admit, but he knew his way through this one. Without another word, he continued on.

Some minutes and turns later, they came upon a dead end. Jacob stood, gazing dumbly at the unbroken joining of walls.

"Some hunch," Makaidel stated.

Serina smiled pleasantly at him. "I think we're doing pretty well if this is the first wrong turn we've taken."

"Uh, yeah." Jacob tried to remember the turns they had taken to arrive there.

"At least we'll know where we went wrong if we end up back at that orloc," Thorn stated, amused.

They didn't find the dead orloc again. Jacob backtracked to another passage that looked familiar, but his pace slowed as he continued, trying to remember where he was.

"You still know where you're going, right?" Thayer asked.

"Of course," Jacob snapped, trying to focus on the maze and remember how he got through it in the game.

"How could you?" Makaidel asked suspiciously. "We never even knew this place existed." Jacob didn't answer.

They strolled quietly through the maze for a long while. Jacob wondered idly how much time had passed since they entered. Without even the movement of clouds or passage of the sun as a reference, there was no way to know how long they had been there. Time seemed to stand still in the rippling blue light of the maze.

"It feels like we've gotten turned around," Makaidel stated.

"This is the right way." Jacob was acutely aware of how pathetic he sounded. "I know it is."

They marched on in silence for another span of time. They encountered two more orlocs, each battle disorienting Jacob further, but he wouldn't allow any self-doubt to mar his leadership.

Finally, Jacob could see open space down the turns of the path ahead. He straightened, excited.

"Look! There's the exit!"

"Hurray!" Serina clapped. The others murmured, some relieved, some dubious. Jacob ran forward, all his enthusiasm rushing back with the exit looming so close.

As he passed out of the maze, he stopped in his tracks, his smile fading. He was in a small chamber with two entrances to the maze to his left and a hallway stretching away ahead.

It was the room where they had come from.

"What the…" Makaidel paused as he came into the chamber behind Jacob. "We're back where we started!"

"No, we're not." Serina's voice betrayed her uncertainty.

"Yes, we are!" Makaidel pointed down the hallway. "I can see the room we were in before!" Jacob screwed his eyes shut, trying to remember the turns they had taken in the maze.

"You mean we just went in a circle?" Kalista stated in disbelief.

Thayer moved towards her. "Well, we could still try splitting up."

Kalista groaned in exasperation, moving away from the pilot. "*Please* get us out of here, Garrett."

"Hang on, be quiet," Jacob snapped, trying to picture the maze from the game. "We took a left turn, was it two pathways down?"

"Forget this," Makaidel cut in. "There's one surefire way to get through a maze." He turned to face the left entrance.

"But that's where we just came from!" Jacob protested, knowing that they could reach the other end quicker through the right entrance.

Makaidel shot him a sharp look as he laid his left hand on the wall. "Follow the left wall. It'll take us down a lot of dead ends, but we won't miss any turns and we'll eventually get there." Thorn, Kalista, and Thayer sent Jacob a glance as they followed Makaidel back into the left-hand passage. Jacob glared at the entrance, as though it mocked him. Serina laid a hand on his shoulder with a sympathetic frown. Sighing, he followed the others, Serina by his side.

As predicted, they came across numerous dead ends along their way, and encountered more orlocs. They walked on in silence while Makaidel led the way, dragging his hand along the wall. Jacob trailed at the back of the group, feeling humiliated.

At long last, they came to a long, straight passage with no more branching off. Ahead at the end of the passage, they saw an entirely new room.

"Finally!" Kalista exclaimed.

"*There's* the exit." Makaidel let his hand drop as they continued toward the end.

The group murmured as they reached the next room. They entered a cavernous chamber like the one they had crossed before the maze, but this room was far more open. Pools of clear water seemingly lit from below surrounded a series of large platforms connected by arching bridges leading up to an altar that looked like the one on the island above. Trickles of water ran glistening down the walls into the pools surrounding them. A shining blue light glowed from a pedestal set in the center of the altar on the highest platform.

"What's that light?" Thayer asked while the others still uttered exclamations in hushed voices.

"It's the talisman," Makaidel answered excitedly. "We made it!"

"Careful," Thorn admonished, amused, as Makaidel ran across the ledge and over a stone arch to the next platform. The others followed and a sense of dread filled Jacob. He increased his pace to catch up with Makaidel.

"Well, well," came a malevolent voice as Jacob and Makaidel reached the center of the next platform. They skidded to a stop as the air shimmered before them. Then, the scorpion-like creature that had been Fahren's doppelganger in Dekaal appeared. It grinned darkly at them. "Took you long enough."

"YOU!" MAKAIDEL CROUCHED into a defensive position. Jacob drew his sword as the rest of the group ran up behind him, blue light from the pools of water rippling over them.

"Yes, me," the scorpion-monster, Graxis, replied. "You people really messed up our plan*ss* when you expo*ss*ed me in Dekaal. But, fortunately, master was so plea*sss*ed that we got the earth stone anyway that he let me come take care of you here, too." Jacob brandished his sword uneasily. This had been by far the hardest battle in the game. Nearly every time he had played, his characters had died at least once when facing Graxis. Without even being able to perform Runic Seals, he feared for his life.

"Why are you working for that horrible Alorian?" Serina asked, clearly disturbed at even having to mention Dharius.

Graxis fixed her with his gaze. "You have no idea what's going on, do you." It wasn't a question.

"We know your master wants to destroy everything!" Makaidel replied.

Graxis scoffed at the mage's words. "You are as dumb as you look. But I don't suppose it matters, because you'll die here now!" The monster lunged with an abruptness that startled Jacob. Before he could react, Graxis slapped him away like he was made of straw, flinging him several feet away across the platform. He yelped as he rolled across the floor, but forced himself to his feet quickly. Graxis was incredibly fast, darting across the platform after the others often quicker than Jacob could see. Focusing on the monster, he raced forward, swinging his sword over his head.

As he neared Graxis, the monster spun, its huge tail slamming into him and throwing him back. He wheezed as he hit the ground, the breath torn from his lungs. He had only enough time to gasp as the scorpion-creature leaped over him, football-sized barb on the segmented tail flung forward to pierce his heart. Before the huge spike came down, Kalista flew in, kicking Graxis off Jacob. Heart hammering against his chest from nearly being killed, Jacob rolled to his feet, his breath feeling weak in his lungs.

Jacob held his sword out as the battle spun around him, glowing weapons swirling through the air with magic spells from Makaidel as Graxis darted about. Wherever one person attacked the scorpion-creature, another came in from a different angle, but Graxis always leaped out of range as they approached.

Trying to still his trembling hands, Jacob moved towards Graxis, careful this time to watch the segmented tail. His body still ached from his harsh landings, but frequent flashes of light against Kalista, Thorn, and Thayer showed him that Serina was too busy healing the others' wounds to notice his trouble. He charged when Graxis seemed distracted by Thorn's attack while Kalista came in from his other side, but the monster leaped clear of them all.

The battle was frantic as everyone tried to keep pace with Graxis, who seemed to be everywhere at once. Jacob's mind was blank, so governed by instinct in trying to stay alive and attack Graxis that he couldn't even feel fear. Again and again he approached, but he came closer to slashing Thorn and Kalista than Graxis. His sword never touched the monster. Makaidel's spells and Thayer's needles whizzed past his head as flashes of light from Runic Seals lit up the platform.

Jacob yelped and lunged backwards as Graxis slashed open his arm with long claws on the ends of his fingers. He distanced himself from the battle while he waited for Serina to heal him. It didn't seem like any of them had touched Graxis yet. He was quickly growing tired and disoriented from racing in circles around the platform, and Graxis continued landing powerful blows against the others. Jacob felt it was only a matter of time before that poisonous tail impaled someone, and here, there was no potion to restore life. The thought sent a chill down his spine. He cursed himself for being unable to learn how to perform a Runic Seal.

Presently, his arm knitted back together and the pain abated. Raising his sword, he charged into battle again. He realized absently that he was learning how to avoid the scorpion-creature's attacks better, but he still seemed no closer to being able to land a blow himself.

Suddenly, as Graxis darted away from Thorn's direct attack and Jacob's attempted attack from behind, Kalista feinted, at first seeming to attack with Jacob, then spun, her glowing sidearm blades streaking around seemingly to open air beside her. As her blades swung in front of her, however, Graxis seemed to leap directly in their path, and the blades slashed across his torso. Graxis screeched inhumanly and stumbled backwards, distracted by the pain just long enough for Thorn to race forward and send a fist barreling into the monster's shoulder. Jacob swung as Graxis was pushed towards him, his sword slashing across the scorpion-creature's side. Graxis howled in pain as a stream of glowing needles flew in and embedded into the monster's chest.

Seizing the opportunity, Jacob, Kalista, and Thorn raced toward the suffering minion. As they neared, Graxis spun, slamming them all away with his huge tail.

As he tumbled along the floor, Jacob heard Makaidel cry out, "Magma Rain!"

The platform trembled as cracks opened up in the floor beneath Graxis, spewing molten lava into the air. Graxis's roar of pain rang through the chamber as the lava rained down over his dark skin. The chamber dimmed around them as the lava illuminated the platform. Smoke wafted up from the scorpion-creature's body where the burning magma touched him. Jacob couldn't suppress a cringe in revulsion, greatly disturbed by the painful sight of the spell that in the game had only affected a number representing the enemy's health.

The ground fell still, the cracks Makaidel's spell had opened permanently cut through the platform, as the red glow of the lava faded to black. Rousing himself, Jacob charged forward again as Thorn and Kalista approached Graxis. The scorpion-creature leaped into the air as they converged, landing several feet away from everyone else. As they turned to approach, he slammed his tail into the ground, sending quakes across the platform that threw everyone to the floor. He glared at the group as they all collapsed against the rocking ground. Blood glistened over his body with dark patches of dried magma. He panted, one eye shut.

"This isn't over, heroe*sss*," he snarled scornfully. In a flash of light, Graxis was gone and the rumbling stopped. Jacob gazed at the spot where the monster had disappeared, panting. His heart still raced, his hands trembling from the deadly pace of the battle. He could scarcely believe it was over already.

A flare of white light washed over the platform. Jacob felt his last wounds healed. He stood, gazing at the others. Their faces were mostly blank, also clearly surprised by the sudden end to the battle.

Makaidel moved first, shaking his head. "We did it. We have the talisman." The others nodded and breathed sighs of relief as they approached the stone paths leading to the highest platform.

The blue glow of the talisman seemed to light up the altar as they reached it. Makaidel sent Jacob a strangely subdued glance as he reached the edge of the pillars, mossy but still intact from being kept underground. Jacob approached the pedestal where the talisman rested, uncertain about what would happen next.

The talisman looked just like the element stone of earth, a rounded teardrop of sapphire set in the familiar silver triangle rendered crudely around his neck. Without ceremony, Jacob snatched up the talisman. He hesitated with a gasp as a warm shiver spread up his arm and through his body.

Shaking his head, he turned and strode toward the lower platform. "Let's get out of here." The others were clearly baffled by his abruptness, but they fell into step behind him without complaint. He tried to slide the talisman into the pocket of his trousers, but he couldn't reach it properly with his sword belt over his hips.

Suddenly, a thrum of energy rippled through the air, followed by a deep, echoing laugh. The group drew in a collective gasp. Jacob raced forward, hoping desperately that he could reach the lower platform first.

Before he made it to the edge of the altar, however, a flash of light before him lit up the room. He skidded to a stop as Dharius appeared before him, grinning darkly.

"So, you defeated Graxis, did you? You people are better than I thought." Jacob backed away as Dharius approached. With the rest of the group behind him, he felt alone against the Alorian, small and weak compared to the incredible power radiating out from Dharius.

"But that talisman's mine."

"Why do you want the element stones?" Makaidel barked, his high voice ringing through the chamber.

Dharius smirked. "They're Alorian. They belong more to me than they do to any of you."

Switching the talisman to his left hand, Jacob quickly grabbed the hilt of his sword. Before he could draw it, however, Dharius swung his arm forward, and a blast of energy threw him backwards. He groaned as he hit the ground, dark magic seeming to seep into his body from the attack. He heard a metallic ring. Opening his eyes, he found Dharius approaching with drawn sword. He couldn't move, helpless as the dark-clad Alorian approached. Despite knowing how this scene ended, he couldn't help his eyes widening in fear.

"No!" Serina cried from behind him. A flash of light flared against Dharius's chest. Jacob felt the evil energy swarming over him dissipate as the Alorian stumbled back with a snarl. Jacob threw himself to his feet, but felt torn whether to run toward Serina or toward the exit.

Before he had moved, he felt his body gripped with a stifling sensation, like the air had suddenly become too heavy to allow movement. He caught a glimpse of Dharius gazing strangely at Serina as Jacob's knees buckled and he dropped to the ground.

"That magic… Who are you?"

Jacob tried to cry out to Serina, scream for her to run, but all he could manage was a choked, "No…"

Ignoring his protest, Dharius strode over to Serina, still standing, but twitching as she struggled to move. Her eyes widened in terror as Dharius stood over her, nearly as tall as Thorn.

"No," she pleaded as Dharius raised a hand to her chin, tilting her face up.

"You cast magic like an Alorian," he stated.

"W-what?"

"Leave her alone," Jacob coughed out, though he doubt his struggled voice even carried over to Dharius. He tried to drag himself over to Serina, but his arms barely moved. The suffocating spell lay over him like a lead cloak.

Moving his hand from her chin, Dharius brushed Serina's shoulder-length hair away from her face. The group gasped as he grinned, exposing ears that were elongated and pointed at the tip. Jacob bowed his head, disappointed that he had been unable to prevent this revelation.

"Half Alorian?" Dharius mused, grinning widely.

"S… Serina?" Makaidel sputtered, shocked.

"Serina?" Dharius took her chin in his hand again and chuckled in amusement. "It really is. You look so much like that human girl all those years ago." Jacob clenched his teeth, fighting with all his energy to break free of the encroaching spell holding him to the ground. *After all this time,* he thought, *I still can't change anything.*

"Wh… who are you?" Serina asked almost in a whimper.

Dharius chuckled darkly. "Isn't it obvious, my dear? You're my daughter." Serina gasped, her eyes growing even wider in horror.

Angrily and desperately, Jacob grasped the talisman in his hand tighter. In a wash of energy, the spell gripping him faded. Yelling out, he charged Dharius, swinging his sword as he did. Releasing Serina, Dharius leaped back from the attack, clearly startled. Before Jacob could swing again, Dharius threw his hand forward, blasting the entire group back again.

While Jacob lied groaning in pain on the ground, Dharius strode casually over to him and took the talisman from his hand.

"Why ally yourself with these filthy humans?" Dharius asked Serina. "Your magic could actually heal the world if you joined me."

"I am healing the world, not trying to destroy it like you!"

"Hm." Dharius turned, his long cloak swirling around him as he strode toward the edge of the platform. "Have it your way. After I get the last two element stones, there won't be anyone left but you and me." Serina raised her head, gazing in horror at the Alorian.

Dharius spun, facing them again as he stood between two pillars. He idly twisted the talisman around in his hand. "You people may have escaped last time, but it's a lot further to the surface from here. Alorian magic will destroy your filthy human interference." With a flash of light, Dharius disappeared. A shockwave boomed out from the spot where he had stood, and the walls and floor trembled, stone cracking above.

Jacob stood as the dark spell that had held them disappeared. "We have to get out of here!"

"Hurry!" Makaidel raced across the altar to the lower platform, Thorn, Kalista, and Thayer in tow. Serina still crouched on the floor, a horrified look etched onto her face. Jacob raced over to her and grabbed her shoulder. She glanced up at him, dazed.

"Come on!" Pulling her to her feet, he ran after the rest of the group, now on the second platform. Huge chunks of rock from the ceiling and walls splashed into the pools. As cracks opened up at the back of the room, water rushed through. The cracks widened against the flooding water and the pools surrounding the platforms began to rise.

"We'll never make it through the maze in time!" Kalista cried as they reached the hallway leading into the maze.

"Leave it to me." Thorn increased his pace to overtake Makaidel. As he stretched his arm back, his gauntlet glowed with the power of a Runic Seal. He swung as he reached the first bend in the maze, his fist breaking through the wall and crumbling a hole in it large enough to step through.

"Why didn't you do that when we were coming through the first time?" Thayer yelled out as he followed Kalista through the opening.

"Couldn't know if the walls were supporting the ceiling," Thorn replied as he crashed through the next wall, "but I don't think it matters now." Jacob agreed silently as the overflowing pools in the altar room flowed into the maze, splashing about his and Serina's feet.

The temple roared and trembled around them as Thorn crashed through walls, assisted by spells Makaidel cast. They could hear huge boulders crashing to the floor elsewhere in the maze as water gushed in to the altar room. Jacob's heart raced. This part had not been shown in the game, and their escape had cut from the altar room to the island outside without any indication of how they had gotten there so quickly.

Finally, they reached the chamber where they had entered the maze and raced into the next room. Orlocs snarled at them as they leaped onto ledges recklessly, desperate to escape the flooding water now pouring into the chamber through the gaps in the maze. Makaidel blasted the orlocs away as they ran past, quickly running out of time to escape the temple. Jacob's legs stung as he jumped down from a ledge seven feet up near the exit, but he ignored the pain as he continued after the others.

"Now how do we get out?" Thayer yelled as they ran into the entry chamber with the stone platform that had brought them down into the temple.

"Serina!" Makaidel cried as they stepped up onto the platform. Uncertainly, Serina stepped to the middle of the platform and closed her eyes.

"Hurry," Kalista stated as water began flowing quickly into the chamber. With a lurch, the platform began rising back toward the surface, the stones around the edges glowing.

"Faster." Thayer gazed over the edge at the rising water. "Faster would be good." Serina's eyes screwed shut in concentration as the platform increased speed. The entire island seemed to quake around them.

Finally, they reached the surface again. Jacob could only faintly appreciate the warmth and light of daylight as he led Serina across the platform towards the airship. They climbed on, chunks of the island falling down into the lake behind them.

Thayer was already at the helm and powering up the airship when Jacob reached the top of the stairs above deck. The propeller thrummed to life slowly and the airship struggled to lift off the ground.

Suddenly, the island crumbled below them. Everyone cried out as the airship tilted, falling into the water of the lake. Thayer kept a tight grip on the helm, though the ship listed madly from side to side in the frothing water.

"Hang on!" Thayer called out, flipping some switches. The airship slowly gained stability as it lifted out of the water.

Then, Kalista screamed. They all turned to find the tip of an enormous tentacle reaching over the railing near where she crouched.

"Look out!" Serina pulled Jacob away as another tentacle swung over the gunwale next to him. Two more tentacles thumped against the sides of the airship, and they could hear the wood creaking under the creature's grip.

Undaunted, Thayer pulled at a hanging switch, then flipped some more switches. "Fire in the hole!"

A deafening boom ripped through the air. Everyone but Thayer was thrown to the floor as the airship lurched and began rising into the air again. Jacob rose and glanced over the edge, finding the disembodied tentacles sinking down around a patch of frothing water. The airship lifted quickly into the air and began moving forward even before they had reached their highest altitude. Jacob turned to sit against the railing of the ship, breathing hard. He glanced to Serina, sitting next to him. Her arms wrapped around her knees, drawn up against her chest, and her expression was pained. His heart ached with the sight.

Makaidel sent Thayer a wide-eyed look. Thayer simply shrugged. “I told you this was built as a war machine.”

Jacob panted as he leaned his head back against the gunwale, feeling exhausted by the afternoon’s events.

THE AIRSHIP HUMMED around Jacob as he stepped into one of the small rooms below deck. He frowned as he gazed at Serina, huddled on the small bed bolted to the wall with her knees pulled up to her chest and her arms around them. She didn't bother to brush her hair back, and the pointed tips of her ears peeked out from the sides of her head. Jacob repressed a shudder at the sight and promptly felt ashamed of it. They hadn't bothered him in the game, but seeing them on a real person, she seemed somewhat alien to him.

She glanced up as he stepped into the room. He caught a glimpse of tears flowing down her face before she turned away. Uncomfortably, he took a seat in a chair beside the bed, knowing he should be here and wanting to comfort her, but uncertain what to say.

"I can't believe that awful Alorian is my father." She shuddered at the mere mention of Dharius. "No wonder people were always afraid of me, of the way I do magic. They were right all along."

"Don't say that," Jacob quickly replied before he remembered what he was supposed to say. "There's nothing wrong with being half Alorian. Heck, half the people in Aurius would give their right arm just to meet you." The words from the game sounded stiff and forced. He cursed himself for being unable to think of anything better to say to her.

Serina sniffled. "But he's done such terrible things. My own father…"

Jacob tried to put more emotion into his scripted words, wishing she wasn't so upset. "Who he is doesn't change who you are. You're nothing like him."

She glanced absently out the window at the clouds rolling by. "I always wondered who my parents were. Why my ears looked like this and I could cast magic the way I do. But now that I know… how can I hate him, even after what he's done? He's the only family I have."

Jacob swallowed the next line from the game before it could come out of his mouth. He thought of the dysfunctional families of some of his friends.

His childhood friend Renaldo's overbearing father, the disapproving father of Eric, who had driven him to the convention where he had entered Aurius, and his own father, whom he hadn't seen since he turned sixteen. His eyes narrowed.

"Just because he's your father doesn't mean you have to like him. He should have to earn your respect just like everyone else." Serina glanced up at him in surprise, but he couldn't keep the anger out of his voice. "After all, he was never there for you while you were growing up. Why should you be so nice to him? You don't owe him anything." He realized he was nearly yelling, frustrated as he was by the reminder of his own father. He huffed out a sigh.

Serina seemed startled by the vehemence in his words, but slowly bowed her head in understanding. "I guess you're right." She smiled weakly. "Adella always told me I looked Alorian. I always said she'd have no way to tell." Her head raised and her smile widened, though sadness still touched it. "Thanks, Garrett."

Jacob rubbed the back of his neck, feeling embarrassed by his outburst. "No problem."

She brushed her hair over her ears, seemingly out of habit. "I'm sorry I never told you about this. I was just afraid…" Her voice lowered meekly. "That you wouldn't like me."

Jacob felt his face flush. "O-of course I like you. Who your parents were doesn't change that."

Her smile widened as she stretched her legs out in front of her. He had to force his gaze up to her face, certain his cheeks were as red as his tunic. "I'm glad I met you, Garrett. You're so sweet and kind." Standing, she stepped forward and wrapped her arms around him. His heart hammered in his chest as he put his arms around her as well.

"I'm glad I met you, too," he replied, barely keeping enough control of his voice not to stutter. His heart pounded, yet he felt a strange sense of disappointment as he held her close. He had dreamed of being in this very spot in this very scene so many times, yet every time he had imagined it, he had been suave and romantic, whispering sweet comforts in her elegant ears as he gently wiped away the tears. Now that he actually stood on the airship, alone in a room with her, however, he felt nervous simply touching her, even though she had reached for him first, and he couldn't work up the courage to say anything more to her. In that moment, more than any other in the months since he had come to Aurius, he felt more profoundly how very real this world was. The thought brought a flood of mixed emotions to him.

Still, he wanted to touch her, to feel her body more intimately than he did now, and he knew this was the best opportunity he would ever have. He tried to work himself up to it as she buried her head against his shoulder.

Suddenly, footsteps approached the room and Makaidel appeared in the doorway. "Hey, guys, we should… oh, I'm sorry." His face reddened faintly as he glanced quickly away. Jacob hastily let go of Serina, though she didn't seem bothered by the interruption and pulled back calmly.

Makaidel continued gazing at the wall beside the door. "Um, if you want me to come back later…"

"No, it's okay," Serina stated, still holding Jacob's hands. "What is it?"

"Er, Thayer wanted to know if you wanted to do anything before we go find the last element stone." Makaidel was still clearly embarrassed. Jacob hated him for his timing, but had to admit to himself that even if the mage had arrived later, it probably would have changed little.

"I don't think so.," Smiling, she turned to Jacob. "Garrett?"

"No," he stated distractedly.

"Okay," Makaidel replied, eager to leave. "Sorry." With that, he shuffled off.

Jacob faced Serina to find her looking at him. "Should we go join them?"

"If you want to." It wasn't what he wanted to say. He followed her out of the room and above deck, cursing his insecurity as he watched her walk in front of him, having lost the best chance he would ever have to grow closer to her. He sighed, realizing that being in Aurius didn't change the fact that he was just an uncomfortable teenager who was awkward around girls he liked.

"In the volcano?" Thayer exclaimed. "Are you out of your mind?" Serina cocked her head as she and Jacob approached Makaidel, Thorn, and Thayer at the helm of the airship.

"It makes sense," Thorn remarked. "It's a good place for a fire stone, and that moat of lava around its base makes it hard for anyone to get to it."

"But you can fly this thing over it and land on the mountain," Makaidel added.

Thayer shook his head. "Heat like that could melt the tar holding it together. I can keep it up and lower you guys down with a ladder, but I'll have to stay up here. Frankly, I think it's suicide."

"The Alorians had to have gotten in there somehow," Makaidel replied. "I just hope we can get there before Dharius."

"You know," Thorn mused, "he said in the water temple that he was still looking for two other element stones."

"Do you think he doesn't know about Garrett's pendant?" Serina looked at Jacob.

"It's possible," Makaidel stated. "According to everything I've seen, there should be a wind temple somewhere, but apparently someone got the talisman and passed it down through the years." Jacob frowned as he fiddled with the pendant normally hiding beneath his shirt and tunic. Was there a real air talisman somewhere in this real Aurius? He thought back to the water talisman he had held for such a brief time. He had never felt anything like it. That talisman was true magic, unlike his worthless pendant. Or did it mean something more here, and he simply had no way of knowing? He gazed down at the amber teardrop around his neck. It seemed so coarse and crude compared to the other talismans.

"How long will it take to get there?" Thorn asked, cutting across Jacob's thoughts.

Thayer glanced at Makaidel's map. "At least a day, maybe two, depending on wind."

"Guess we should settle in, then." Makaidel wandered over to the edge of the deck and glanced down.

"I'll go check on Kalista," Serina stated. Jacob hadn't realized she wasn't on deck, though he wasn't surprised. He watched Serina disappear down the stairs, then strolled over to the gunwale beside Makaidel.

"So, you learned Magma Rain, huh?" It was an advanced spell in the game, and it struck Jacob how far they had come for Makaidel to have learned it.

"Yeah!" The perked up at the memory. As soon as the smile appeared, however, it faded. "But I didn't realize it would be so… violent." He shuddered. Jacob nodded, disturbed himself by the way the drops of glowing lava had scorched Graxis's flesh.

"And how about Thorn breaking down walls?" The mage grinned over his shoulder at the large man. Thorn chuckled. "We're really learning some powerful Runic Seals." Makaidel glanced curiously at Jacob. "I wonder why you haven't been able to do any yet."

Jacob frowned, not answering. *Is it because I'm not from Aurius?* He hoped not, or that meant he would never be able to learn Runic Seals. By the end of the game, battle occurred almost exclusively with Runic Seals, regular attacks doing little damage against the more difficult enemies. It had already become clear from their encounters in the water temple that he had grown much weaker than the rest of the group for being unable to attack with Runic Seals. He still didn't fully know how to use a sword, and already they were moving past that. If he couldn't learn to use Runic Seals, he would soon be worthless to the group. He glanced away, dismayed at the thought.

Thought of the talismans gave him hope, but he knew that if nothing changed from the game, they wouldn't get the element stone of fire, either. And his greatest trial yet was about to come.

The journey to the volcano passed peacefully. They each manned the helm, slept, navigated, cooked, and helped to tidy the main room below deck in shifts. Despite keeping busy, Jacob couldn't shake the thoughts of what would happen in the volcano. There were too many unanswered questions. If Jacob's handmade amulet had taken the place of the real Hero's pendant, then all four element stones would be gathered in one room. He'd be bringing it right to Dharius.

He stepped down below deck the next night as twilight reigned over the sky, deep in thought.

"Oh, hi, Garrett."

Jacob looked up with a start and found he had nearly run into Serina. She stood in the main room, mopping the floor. "H-hi. How are you?"

"Good, thanks." She smiled. "How are you?"

"Good," he answered, though his tone of voice betrayed otherwise. "Are you ready for tomorrow?"

"As ready as I'm going to be, I guess." She shrugged. "I can't believe we're already going to find the last element stone. It's almost over."

Jacob glanced away, rubbing the back of his neck. "Yeah. About that… here." He pulled his pendant up over his head. "I want you to have this."

Serina's eyes widened. "Your pendant? I couldn't…"

"Please." He dropped the pendant into her hand. "I want you to hold on to it and keep it safe."

She clutched the pendant to her chest, fear touching her eyes. "Why?" His heart raced as he remembered what she had said to him in Quinlan. *She knows that I know something's going to happen.*

Trying to smile convincingly, he shrugged. "Just in case. I'm sure everything will be fine."

After a moment, she smiled again. "Okay."

The volcano came into view in the distance an hour before they reached it. Jacob stood at the bow of the ship, gazing out at the approaching mountain. He dreaded reaching it and had wondered at one point over the last two days if he should stay on board the ship rather than go in. As much as he wished he could, he felt embarrassed simply picturing everyone's reaction to the suggestion.

The rest of the group, even Kalista, trickled up above deck as the volcano grew before them. Jacob fidgeted with the tails of his tunic, shifting his weight from foot to foot.

"Excited to reach the last element stone?" Makaidel asked.

"Yeah." How could he tell them what truly frightened him?

It's all part of being in the game, Jacob told himself. *This is what I always wanted.*

Thayer flipped switches around the helm as they passed over the river of glowing lava circling the volcano's base. The mountain dwarfed the airship as it floated through a hazy sky tarnished by wisps of smoke rising off the blackened surface.

"We'll make for that ledge." Thayer nodded towards the mountain. "That's as close as I can get you."

"How are we going to get in?" Serina peered uncertainly over the edge.

"I don't..." Thorn attempted.

"Look!" Makaidel cut in. Jacob followed the mage's pointing finger. "There's an altar down there!" Jacob recognized the structure from the game as the others recognized it from Darkwater Lake. The stones were blackened by soot, but there was no mistaking the pillars and platform. It sat nestled against a thirty foot high cliff face.

Finally, the airship came to a steady hover thirty feet over a ledge. Pulling a lever to keep the airship suspended in the air, Thayer led the way below deck. While the gangplank lowered, he tied the ends of a rope ladder to hooks in the floor.

"I don't want to keep this open. When you want to come back up, shoot a spell past me." Makaidel nodded in response. "There." Tugging on the sides of the ladder to tighten the knots, Thayer threw it out over the gangplank. It unraveled as it sailed through the air before disappearing beneath the gangplank.

Everyone looked at Jacob.

He frowned. In the game, he had been given an option of which four characters he wanted to take down to the volcano, though the game wouldn't allow him to leave Garrett behind. There would be one more person to face the dangers below with him, but he felt like he was still being forced to go.

Clearing his throat, he edged his way sideways down the angled gangplank, sliding his hands down the rope ladder. At the edge, he crouched down, grasping the last handhold on the ladder while he reached his legs over. He struggled to find a foothold as he dangled over the edge of the gangplank. Finally, his foot caught. He reached his other foot below to the next step and climbed beneath the airship.

Heat radiated up from the surface of the mountain as he climbed down. He glanced down at the streams of lava crisscrossing the mountain and wondered how they were going to get to the altar. Slowly, he descended, uncomfortable with the way the ladder swayed with his weight and how his legs reached so far forward to lean on the step.

Halfway down, the ladder began to twist and sway in the strong breeze wafting up from the mountain. Jacob yelped as he spun right around, clutching the ladder tightly as the stifling, hot gust passed over him.

"Hurry up!" came a yell from above.

Jacob glanced up to find Makaidel descending the ladder, already only six feet or so above him. Grumbling, Jacob continued climbing down carefully. The further down he went, the more wild the ladder's movements became.

Finally, he came within a few feet of the bottom and jumped down, relieved to touch solid ground. As soon as he let go of the ladder, it slid away from him, pushed by the hot wind. Makaidel yelped, spun around on the ladder. Darting after the tail of the ladder, Jacob grabbed it and stepped on the lowest rung, steadying it. Makaidel gave him a dirty look as he hopped down. Jacob returned it.

One by one, the others climbed down.

"Whew." Serina wiped her brow. "It's warm."

As Thorn hopped off the ladder after everyone else, he gave the ladder a toss, a ripple of movement rolling all the way up to the open gangplank. A moment later, the ladder began sliding back up towards the hovering airship.

"Okay, the altar's this way," Makaidel stated and began leading the way across the blackened ground.

The air was heavy with smoke that darkened the sky, casting the mountain into a permanent twilight. They walked silently across the rocky ground while the rivers of lava flowed steadily, though the mountain seemed solid beneath their feet. Hot breezes blew over them, heavy and sulfurous. Jacob's clothes weighed heavily on him and he felt like he was in an oven.

Crossing the streams of lava proved less difficult than he had been expecting, as they often found narrow bends or overhanging edges they could jump. Once, Makaidel summoned large stones to hover over a glowing river.

Eventually, they reached the altar. Though the tops of the pillars were dusted with soot, most of the altar, constructed of black granite to match the charred mountainside, remained clean. Jacob realized why as he stepped onto the platform and the suffocating breeze died down. The cliff face the altar was placed against blocked most of the wind.

Everyone spread out over the platform, gazing about. Like Isla de Lamanis, the altar lacked a pedestal in its center, and there was no element stone in sight.

"So, where's the talisman?" Kalista asked. Makaidel glanced at Serina. With an uncertain frown, she stepped towards the center of the altar and closed her eyes. The stones surrounding the platform began to emit crimson light. The group spun around as the cliff wall at the edge of the altar rumbled. Three cracks spread up the cliff from the ground, joining together halfway up the wall. As they watched, the two broken halves of the wall swung inward like a door, opening onto a shadowy passage leading into the mountain.

A moment later, the rock walls fell still against the sides of the passage, the sounds of their movement fallen silent. They all stared at the gaping hole in the cliff wall, black as pitch within. A breath of stifling air whooshed out of the cavern, rushing hotly over them. Makaidel coughed.

The carved stones around the altar dimmed and Serina opened her eyes.

"Don't tell me we have to go in there," Kalista complained. Jacob couldn't help agreeing with her.

"Is that the way in?" Serina asked. "I can't see a thing."

Makaidel, standing closest to the opening, held up his hands. A sphere of glowing light flared to life above his palms, illuminating the entrance. The cavern was wide and dark, stretching away into the distance beyond where the light touched it.

"Well, let's go." With that, he walked forward. The others reluctantly followed.

As they stepped into the cavern, they stopped, some of them gasping.

"Oh!" Serina exclaimed.

When they crossed the great entrance, stones embedded into the walls at intervals lit up with red light. Makaidel dropped his hands, the sphere of light winking out. The cavern continued into the inside of the mountain, narrowing and turning a corner several hundred feet in. An orangish glow emanated from the bend in the hall.

Without a word, Makaidel continued walking. Jacob trailed at the back, feeling more uneasy as they strode into the cavern.

"Ugh." Kalista shook her arms. "This is unbearable." The air in the cavern was still and oppressing, the heat beating down on Jacob like sunburn. He could barely breathe. Makaidel panted as he strode down the cavern and Thorn's dark skin glistened in the red light.

When they got to the end and around the corner of the entrance hall, they came upon an enormous room seemingly carved from the entire inside of the mountain. The far side wasn't even visible from where they stood. The cavern was filled with a labyrinth of crossing stone paths and platforms over a lake of molten lava. The heat was even more stifling in this room than the entry cavern, and Jacob felt he could hardly move. The ash in the air stung his eyes with the sweat that trickled down his head and all over his body.

"How could the Alorians stand this?" Kalista fanned herself with her hand, breathing heavily.

"I think the bigger question is how can they?" Thorn nodded ahead to the next platform.

Makaidel wilted as he caught a glance of dark movement. "There are orlocs down here? Where *haven't* they reached?" Jacob and Serina exchanged a worried glance, thinking of the quiet and relatively unprotected towns of Shelas and Merakis.

Setting his shoulders back, Makaidel strode forward toward the next ledge. "Well, let's get moving. The sooner we can get the fire talisman, the sooner we can get out." Thorn walked silently after him, followed by Serina and a grumbling Kalista. Jacob frowned as he fell into step behind them, almost welcoming the encounter to come at the end of the temple so he could get out of the heat.

The orlocs they faced seemed weakened by the heat as well, and were no more difficult than the ones at the water temple. Each passing moment, Jacob felt he was going to pass out from the encroaching heat, but he managed to keep staggering forward with the others. Every now and then, Makaidel would summon water for them all to drink. Jacob relished every drop.

In the game, the greatest challenge to the fire temple had been the more difficult orlocs present, but in the real Aurius, it was the heat. Navigating their way through the temple was not nearly as confusing as it was in the water temple, though the sheer size of the underground cavern was mind-boggling.

"Why is there such a big hole in the mountain like this?" Kalista snapped as they crawled up onto a higher platform. As Jacob reached the top with the others, Makaidel drenched them with a torrent of cool water. It was heaven to Jacob, and he delighted in the way it felt as it ran down his body and the back of his throat. In the heat of the cavern, however, it soon evaporated.

"This isn't natural," Makaidel remarked testily as he turned to continue.

"The Alorians must have some kind of heat resistance to be able to bury a talisman so deep in here," Thorn mused.

"I wish we did, too," Kalista added. In a flare of white light, Serina cast a healing spell over them. It didn't refresh like Makaidel's water spell did, but it helped restore their strength.

"She probably does," Makaidel replied, glaring in envy at Serina. She glanced away with an uncomfortable look, brushing a lock of damp hair over a pointed ear. She had seemed less affected by the heat than the rest of them, Jacob had noticed, but he couldn't help laying a hand comfortingly on her shoulder at the dismayed expression on her face.

Always so beautiful and delicate, he thought. The sweat didn't cling to her chest and underarms as it did with the others, but gave her skin a glistening glow. Even suffering under the heat as he was, he couldn't help but admire how she never seemed less than perfect.

Jacob suspected it took them less time to get through the fire temple than it had the water temple, but each second stretched on in agony.

"At least the room's so big," Thorn stated. "We probably wouldn't even be able to move if all this heat was closed in a tiny space." He seemed little comforted by the fact himself. Though he didn't seem on the edge of his temper like Makaidel, Kalista, and Jacob, the large man had abandoned the careless, easily amused manner he normally displayed. The heat bore down on all of them as they continued through the cavern.

At long last, the walls drew together and connected ahead of them, marking the end of the tunnel. Makaidel pointed ahead, two platforms above them. "Look!" Exhausted, drenched with sweat, and his skin feeling like it was going to burn right off his body, Jacob raised his head to follow the mage's pointing finger. Not a hundred feet away, Jacob saw what Makaidel did, the unmistakable rising pillars of the real altar. And visible in the center of the altar was a crimson glow brighter than the illumination provided by the lava beneath them.

"Finally!" Kalista wheezed, spying the altar from beneath her drooping bangs. With a splash of water and another healing spell, the group charged forward, refreshed by the sight of their target.

Then, as they all stepped onto the platform below the altar, the ground rumbled.

24

KALISTA YELPED AS she struggled to remain standing, the group glancing quickly around as the tremors spread through the volcanic cavern.

"What's going on?" Makaidel cried.

As if in response to his question, a fountain of lava shot into the air from off the far edge of the platform. Jacob drew his sword, knowing what was coming, and the others drew their weapons in response.

With a roar, a great beast leaped up onto the platform, shaking the ground beneath their feet. It looked like an enormous lizard, but it was covered in glowing magma.

"What's that?!" Kalista shrieked.

"The Alorians must have put it here to guard the talisman." Thorn was clearly unimpressed with the idea.

Roaring, the beast charged, and with a collective yelp, the group scattered. Jacob spun as he ran around the lizard and slashed his sword across its side. Lava splashed off it, but whether he broke the creature's skin, if it even had any, he couldn't say. As he pulled his sword back, he gasped. Magma cooled quickly on his blade, darkening to black patches that clung to the metal like glue. He shook his sword, but the tar-like magma didn't budge.

"Ice Daggers!"

The lizard roared and diverted its attention to Makaidel as shards of ice shot out from the mage's hands. The fragments sizzled and melted as they dug into the lizard's molten body. The group danced around the charging lizard. Jacob caught an uncertain look from Thorn.

"I can't get near it," the large man yelled.

"Neither can I!" Kalista added, her short blades held at the ready.

Don't tell me I'm on my own against this thing! Jacob thought desperately. He ducked under the huge, swinging tail and slashed, digging his sword into the creature's leg. It responded with a satisfying roar of pain. Jacob's sword glowed briefly before more magma cooled on the blade. He wouldn't be able to hurt it much longer at this rate. It was a problem that hadn't been addressed in the game.

"Where's Thayer when you actually need him?!" Makaidel snapped. "Water Cascade!" A flood of water rushed up out of nowhere and bore down on the lizard. A deafening roar filled the cavern as steam poured off its body. The cloud of mist obscured the platform entirely, and Jacob couldn't see his own hand in front of his face.

He heard a cough and someone yell, "I can't see it!" Behind him, he could hear the lava frothing and boiling, and distant growls and roars rang through the cavern.

Finally, the steam cleared enough to show the lizard, its body covered in scales of cooled, black magma. It lurched slowly, crackling as it moved. Jacob charged and began slashing the lizard without abandon. Kalista and Thorn joined in and Makaidel slung more ice spells at it. The lizard roared plaintively, frozen by its own cooled body.

Sweat poured down the back of Jacob's neck as he attacked, growing dizzy and lightheaded from exhaustion. His limbs burned as he continued slashing at the lizard. The heat pressed in on him, forgotten in the battle, stifling his breath and searing his skin.

Finally, with a lunge, the lizard leaped off the platform and back into the lava below. Serina held up her staff, crystals glowing, and a healing spell washed over the group. Jacob's strength returned, but the heat was still overpowering.

A moment later, the lizard reappeared. With a roar, it leaped back onto the platform, raining drops of magma onto the ground beneath it. The group fled until Makaidel cast the water spell again. It took two waves of water to cool the lizard this time, and the others barraged it with attacks until it leaped into the lava again, noticeably weaker this time. Jacob's mind was in a haze from the heat and exertion. He couldn't even get relief from Makaidel's water spell. Exhausted as the mage was, he didn't have energy to spare for it.

The entire group seemed ready to collapse by the lizard's third appearance. Jacob hardly knew what he was doing, but after another barrage of attacks when Makaidel cooled the creature's skin, it collapsed in the center of the platform. Its form spread out into a mound, losing definition as it cooled fully.

Finally, nothing remained of the lizard but a shapeless pile of cooled lava.

Jacob collapsed. His lungs burned with every breath and he had never felt so drained. He heard Makaidel cough out, "Ice Pellets."

Jacob groaned as tiny pebbles of ice rained down over his body like hail. He felt bruised by the attack, but as the fragments of ice melted against him, the cool air they emitted refreshed him immensely. Following Makaidel's spell, Serina sent out another wave of healing energy. Jacob let out a relieved sigh, feeling only as uncomfortable as he had when they first stepped into the cavern, though his clothes remained drenched from sweat.

He stood, finding the others rising from the ground as well. Makaidel coughed.

"I don't think they needed that lizard," Kalista remarked. "People aren't meant to survive down here."

"No kidding," Thorn replied. Feeling the hot air in the cavern anew, Jacob glanced over at the highest platform. The talisman glowed from the pedestal, beckoning. He looked over his shoulder. He could see nothing in the cavern but rock platforms and ledges and the bodies of the orlocs they had encountered along their way. He tried to hurry as he approached the altar, but his lungs constricted painfully at the effort.

The others fell into step behind him as they walked up to the altar.

"We made it," Serina stated breathily, smiling.

Jacob approached the pedestal, glancing over his shoulder again. Still no other beings inhabited the cavern. He gazed down at the glowing talisman. As soon as he grabbed it, everything would begin. He wondered fleetingly what would happen if he picked up the talisman and hurled it into the lava surrounding them.

Closing his eyes, he laid his hand over the talisman. He gasped as a wave of energy passed through his body as had happened with the water element stone. The heat of the cavern seemed to bother him no longer and he felt more aware, more able.

"Garrett?" Thorn asked.

Jacob opened his eyes. He felt more powerful with the talisman in his hand, yet Runic Seals still seemed beyond his reach. He pulled the talisman off the pedestal, letting his arm hang beside him.

"Guys," he stated with a calmness he didn't entirely feel. The cavern loomed silently around them. "Get ready."

"For what?" Makaidel asked oddly. Jacob turned around and his eyes narrowed. As the others turned, they gasped and started.

Dharius stood beside the remains of the lizard on the lower platform.

"Not bad." The Alorian gazed at them with a sinister grin. "And here I was hoping to sneak up on you. More's the pity. I'll just have to take that talisman the hard way."

"It's not yours!" Makaidel retaliated. "We're not going to let you use it to kill everyone!"

Dharius sneered at him. "You would dare spite me, you with your filthy human magic."

Jacob examined the altar and the platform below it as they argued, trying to find a way out.

"Us?" Kalista shot back. "We're using our magic to save the world, not destroy it!"

Dharius held out his sword, his gaze growing darker. "You haven't the faintest idea what's going on."

"We know you're trying to destroy everything," Serina replied. "And we won't let you do that!"

"Are you so dense that you haven't seen how the monsters you fight grow more powerful when that boy uses his magic against them?" Dharius shook his head. "You of all people should realize it's the humans that are ruining Aurius. It's their dirty magic poisoning the earth that's destroying the land and causing all the orlocs to appear."

"What?" Makaidel exclaimed. Jacob tensed, knowing the end of the conversation drew close.

"Guys," he attempted softly.

"You blame me for everything," Dharius continued, "but all I'm trying to do is save the world from the destruction your filthy human magic is creating. Alorian magic is natural magic, at peace with the world, not the chaotic, destructive force of your human spells."

"Guys," Jacob hissed, grabbing Makaidel and Serina's arms for their attention. "We don't stand a chance against him. The first chance you get, *run*." Serina blinked, perplexed by the abrupt statement. Makaidel seemed hardly to hear him.

Dharius crouched into a ready position. "And I won't let you use Alorian artifacts to destroy this land further!" He shot his hand forward and a blast shook the entire platform supporting the altar. The group yelped as most of them fell to the floor. The altar trembled and cracked, large chunks breaking off it to plummet into the lava. In a frenzy, the five of them raced across the platform and down to the previous one just as the altar crumbled and splashed into the molten lava.

And then the group was left on the platform with Dharius.

Casually, the Alorian slung a blast of magic at them too quick and large to evade, and it struck them almost instantly. They all cried out in fear, but as Jacob held his hands out to protect his face, one holding his sword and the other the talisman, the ruby teardrop glowed bright crimson. A wall of flame shot out of the talisman, blocking Dharius's spell from hitting them. Before Jacob could even recover from the shock of the talisman's protection, another spell flew across the platform and the group fled.

"I've had to watch for centuries while your disgusting magic slowly poisoned this once beautiful land." The group scattered as Dharius flung spell after spell at them, speaking and moving calmly as though nothing was going on around him. Jacob dodged and darted across the platform at top speed, barely staying ahead of the crippling spells pummeling the ground. Streaks of flame and shards of stones ripped regularly across his body, burning, bruising, and stabbing him. Serina's healing spell was never too far behind the attacks, but the pain intensified with each blow.

"My people failed to make you stop. The rest of them were content with leaving, with abandoning our home." Makaidel's shrill voice called out occasionally, but his spells seemed to disappear when they got near to Dharius. Only the lava around them reacted, boiling and churning stronger with each spell as the walls of the cavern began to tremble.

"They were cowards, too afraid of what had to be done." The entire group raced across and around the platform, Dharius attacking and warding off all of them at once. None of them could even get close to him.

"It's gone on too long. Once I get all four talismans, their combined power will allow me to eliminate the threat of your poisonous magic forever. And finally, this world will be able to rebuild."

Thorn charged Dharius, darting around the spells flung back at him, so Kalista could approach from the Alorian's other side. She raced quietly across the floor, but by the time she drew close enough to hit him, he spun, blasting her away with one hand.

"Enough of this." Dharius He raised his free hand into the air above him. The light in the air above his upraised palm faded. The battle fell still as the others gazed on, worried and uncertain.

Jacob slowly rose from where he stood behind the Alorian. Clutching the talisman, he approached carefully, sword held at the ready.

"You're lying." Makaidel panted as he watched Dharius. "It was the Alorians who taught humans how to use magic in the first place!"

Dharius scoffed. "Yes, you could use magic properly, in the beginning. But all you ever wanted was power. You twisted and warped the gift we gave you into something grotesque, something unnatural." Jacob drew near to the Alorian, hoping the fire talisman could keep him hidden. His heart pounded in fear, yet there was no hesitation in his steps.

"What's the big difference, anyway?" Thorn added. "It all looks like magic."

"The difference is that pure magic works in harmony with nature." He fixed his gaze on Serina. "With rocks, with grass, with water, with air, with the earth itself." Jacob tightened his grip on his sword as he came within a few feet of Dharius. "You ask it to help you and it answers. It doesn't steal power from a place where the element doesn't exist or…"

Jacob realized he had made too much noise as he began to charge, as Dharius spun just as he began to swing his sword. Distracted by the pall of darkness he clutched, Dharius attempted to bring up his own sword to parry, but Jacob's sword fell before he could reach it. The spell shot into the air as Jacob's blade crashed against the Alorian's armour. Jacob darted aside as Dharius swung in retaliation, ignoring the boom and rumble overhead where the dark spell hit the ceiling.

Jacob faced the Alorian with sword out, feeling a rush of excitement. In the game, none of the characters had been able to land a hit on Dharius, and the dark spell had hit them. He grinned.

"I know the truth about Alorian magic. The real reason you haven't defeated us yet is because you can't kill people with your magic." Dharius's eyes widened, startled by Jacob's knowledge. Jacob saw the others start in surprise over the Alorian's shoulder. A flash of inspiration hit him. "You want to talk about eliminating magic? Then let's fight *mano a mano*. Swords only."

Dharius laughed darkly. "You think you can beat me in a swordfight, either? Fine." Jacob shot a pointed gaze to Serina before returning his eyes to Dharius. She seemed to take the hint, as she began leading the others around the edge of the platform towards the next ledge. The ceiling rumbled and quaked overhead. Stalactites broke free from the distant ceiling and plummeted into the lava below, sending splashes of boiling magma into the air.

Without warning, Dharius charged. Jacob barely had enough time to raise his sword to parry before the Alorian spun and slashed again. He stepped backwards, desperately struggling to repel the barrage of attacks coming at him. Flakes of cooled magma sprayed out from Jacob's sword as the blades clashed again and again. With a two-handed swipe, Dharius sent him reeling off to the side, stumbling for balance.

Dharius laughed. "*You* people beat Graxis? This is pathetic." Jacob spared a split-second glance to the other side of the platform, finding the rest of the group on the next platform, watching anxiously. The entire mountain rumbled around them.

Paying no heed to any of it, Dharius charged again. With a yelp, Jacob raised his sword to block. Dharius didn't allow enough opening between his swings for Jacob to even attempt to fight back. He realized worriedly how little he truly knew of using a sword. Orlocs were one thing, but he had no hope against a skilled swordsman.

Dharius pushed him back across the platform from his relentless attacks. Jacob thought the Alorian could lead him straight off the edge and he wouldn't realize it until it was too late. More and more frequently, Dharius's sword broke through Jacob's defenses. He groaned as the beautiful Alorian sword slashed his arm, his cheek, his ribs, the point digging into his shoulder before pulling out. Dharius didn't press any attack, even when he drew blood, and simply continued with more blindingly fast swings of his sword. Jacob got the impression, with the way his opponent allowed Serina to heal the wounds he suffered, that Dharius was toying with him.

The rumbling around them grew to a roar that made Jacob's ears ring. The lava below frothed and churned, spewing columns of magma high into the air at intervals. Boulders crashed down from the distant ceiling, shattering pillars of stone that rose out of the magma and breaking huge chunks off the platforms spreading out across the cavern. Jacob struggled to keep his balance against the quaking floor as Dharius continued slamming him with attacks. His fear rose as his arms grew tired, the heat of the volcano finally beginning to resonate in him despite the talisman he somehow continued to hold. Dharius, however, seemed only to increase the speed and ferocity of his attacks.

Suddenly, Makaidel and Kalista yelled, "Look out!"

Dharius paused, and in that instant, he and Jacob both glanced up. A stalactite the size of a car fell down not twenty feet above them. Yelping, Jacob lunged out of the way just as Dharius leaped gracefully aside. Shards of stone flew into the air as the boulder slammed into the platform, knocking Jacob off balance.

Before he realized the Alorian was even close, Dharius darted around the fallen boulder and slashed. In two quick swipes, Dharius's sword ripped open Jacob's chest. Jacob screamed as he fell over backwards, his sword clanging weakly to the floor over the roar of the crumbling volcano.

"Garrett!" Serina shrieked. Jacob managed to raise his head through the sharp, stinging pain in his chest and found the point of Dharius's sword hovering over the wounds. He drew in a terrified breath as Dharius pulled his sword back to strike.

Before he could swing, another scream came from the lower platform, the edge of which they had neared in their battle. Jacob found another boulder plummeting towards where he lied. Rolling onto his side, he lunged to his feet and away from the falling stone. The pain in his chest faded as he felt the flesh knit back together.

Another jolt shook the ground as the boulder crashed onto the platform where Jacob had just been, throwing him to the floor. He rose to his knees, but froze. The tip of his own sword, still splashed with cooled magma, hovered in front of his throat, Dharius's elegant blade sheathed at his side. Fear gripped Jacob, but as he glanced up, he saw that the Alorian's attention was fixed where he had just escaped. Carefully turning his head, Jacob glanced back. A large chunk of the platform had broken free as the boulder had fallen, and the natural bridge between it and the lower platform had shattered.

They were trapped.

Glancing back over the gaping hole where the connecting bridge had been, Jacob saw the rest of the group running away. More and bigger boulders fell down all around them. Serina gazed back at him in horror, pulled along by Makaidel.

"Garrett!" Her cry was almost drowned out by the roaring of the collapsing mountain. Jacob had never felt so alone and helpless.

"Hm." Dharius grinned. Jacob turned back as the Alorian fixed his silver eyes on him. "I suppose I could just leave you here and that would be the end of that." Jacob knew that Dharius wouldn't, but he wasn't certain which option he preferred. "But I think you're much more useful alive. Now, the talisman." Dharius held out his free hand, undaunted by the crumbling mountain around him. Jacob hesitated, clinging tightly to the talisman like a beacon of strength. The sword reached forward, the flat of the blade sliding up under Jacob's chin with the sharp edge resting against his throat. Swallowing uncomfortably, Jacob held the talisman out. His arm trembled.

The cold metal of the Alorian's gauntlet swiped Jacob's hand as he snatched up the talisman. Jacob quickly let his arm drop, exhausted and suddenly burning up from the heat in the cavern. It took all his strength just to remain on his knees and his vision grew hazy.

"Beautiful." Dharius held up the talisman to admire it. As his cloak pulled back over his raised arm, Jacob saw the earth and water stones hanging around Dharius's neck. Jacob's eyes roved frantically around as another boulder smashed a chunk off the other side of the platform where they stood. It sounded like the entire ceiling was about to cave in. Clenching his fingers around the talisman, Dharius grinned darkly at Jacob.

Suddenly, all of the breath seemed to be sucked out of Jacob's lungs. His body lurched and it felt like he was being pulled along behind a jet, leaving his insides behind in the cavern. He couldn't see anything.

As soon as it began, it ended. He collapsed to his hands and knees, gasping for breath. He found himself leaning on a red marble floor, the stone cool beneath him. The air was mercifully mild, finally relieving him of the stifling heat of the volcano. His skin still burned from the residual heat.

Glancing up, he faced Dharius as before, though the Alorian had lowered his sword. Jacob recognized the immense, elegant chamber around him as the room where he faced, or would face, Dharius in the final battle. His breath came up short.

"Ma*ss*ster," came a familiar, hissing voice. Jacob turned his head to find Graxis approaching them. It was difficult to discern on the scorpion-creature's dark skin, but Jacob could make out scars where Makaidel's Magma Rain had hit him in the water temple. "Welcome back. I tru*s*st you were *sss*uccessful?"

Dharius opened his hand, showing his minion the fire talisman. Graxis screeched in glee. "Get me a chain for this, and put this into storage." Jacob watched in dismay as the scorpion-creature crept forward to take his own sword from Dharius's hands.

"And what of this *human*, ma*sss*ter?" Graxis gazed down at Jacob scornfully.

Dharius grinned in a way that made Jacob exceedingly uncomfortable. "We'll make an example of him." Jacob opened his mouth to speak, but before he could say a word, Dharius held his hand palm out to him and a blast of magic struck him full in the face. Dharius's malicious laughter faded into silence as everything went dark.

Fire

25

JACOB GROANED AS he awakened. As soon as he was aware of it, his head pounded as hard as it ever had, though the pain began to fade as feeling tingled through his body. Slowly, he opened his eyes. A haze of dull colors spread before him. As his vision focused, he found he was lying on the floor of a small, dirty cell. He shifted, trying to assess his surroundings, but found it difficult to move, as his hands were bound behind his back. He discovered that his tunic had been removed, as well as his sword belt and gloves, and his backpack was gone. Also, he could not feel the familiar weight of Morrie Deacon's Alorian dagger in his boot. His skin stretched uncomfortably over his body, dry and cracked. He cringed at the pain and lied still.

The heat of the volcano that had dried out his skin felt like a distant memory as the chill of the stone cell set in over his body. He shivered. The only light came from a window cut into the wall several feet up, ground level outside, crisscrossed with iron bars. Dreary light from what seemed to be an overcast sky outside illuminated the rough, dewy stone walls surrounding him.

Jacob swallowed, his throat burning from dryness. This part in the game, after Dharius captured Garrett, had not been shown in detail. It had vaguely hinted that the game's hero had suffered greatly, and by the end of the ordeal, he had changed. Garrett's character had become dark and cynical and he lost the will to fight Dharius.

Jacob knew the secret of the Alorian's dark, but natural magic, however, and he vowed that no matter what happened, he wouldn't change. Dharius still had to be stopped, even if he was trying to heal Aurius.

Suddenly, a loud *clack* sounded behind him. He strained his neck to glance over his shoulder, but caught only a brief glimpse of the riveted metal door before his head fell again. The door opened with a loud squeal of protest.

"Get up."

Jacob yelped as he felt a sharp kick to the small of his back. He tried to slide his legs under him, but found it more difficult than he had been expecting without the assistance of his arms. He pushed himself up on his elbow, struggling to get his feet under him.

"Hurry up." The guard kicked him again.

"I'm trying!" Jacob turned to glare at his assailant. His eyes widened before narrowing again. "Arys."

The traitor grinned. "My, how the mighty have fallen. I'm going to enjoy watching Dharius tear you apart."

Jacob managed to stand in front of Arys. "Why do you work for him, anyway? You know he's going to kill everyone if he succeeds."

Arys chuckled, amused. "No big loss. Besides, he's teaching me the proper way to use magic." Holding out his hand, a pall of darkness fell over it. Jacob's eyes widened. "Now get moving before I show you what I can really do." Jacob stumbled as Arys shoved him backwards towards the door. He turned as the guard fell into step behind him, walking into the hall outside his cell.

Jacob glanced down the row of cells stretching down the dungeon. Like his, they were all walled in with solid iron doors shut tight, so he didn't know if anyone was in them. Arys pushed him through the castle, yanking on his collar roughly when he wanted Jacob to turn. Jacob glanced around, once more impressed with how much larger everything was in the real Aurius than it had seemed in the game.

After the fourth strangling jerk on his collar, Jacob spun to face Arys. "Knock that off! Just tell me where we're going!"

Arys laughed, shoving him backwards so hard Jacob struggled to stay on his feet. "You don't get to make demands. Don't you get it? You're not leaving here alive."

That's what you think, Jacob thought, the knowledge of how this sequence ended giving him strength.

"If you know what's good for you, you'll get moving." Arys shoved Jacob again. Jacob glanced at the guard, bracing himself as Arys approached again. It was just like how he had been treated at school, and he was tired of being pushed around.

Arys drew near, but before he could push again, Jacob leaned back and kicked him in the stomach. Arys coughed, doubling over under the attack. Jacob stood tall, even with his hands tied behind his back.

Suddenly, while he crouched and held his stomach, Arys threw his arm around. A wave of energy barreled into Jacob, knocking him flat on his back. He wheezed, eyes bulging, as it felt like his very life was being drained out of him. It was an encroaching and utterly hopeless feeling, drowning him. His heart pounded in terror, feeling his limbs go numb and his lungs stop working.

Just as darkness threatened to overwhelm him, Arys grabbed his collar and the spell slowly faded. Panting from fear, Jacob glanced up into Arys's narrowed eyes.

"You're out of your element," the guard snarled. "I'm in control here, and you *will* do as I say." Still reeling from what seemed like his closest brush with death yet, Jacob just gazed up at the guard complacently. He could only follow Arys's commands as the guard pulled him to his feet by his collar. Jacob realized his knees were trembling as he began marching through the elegant castle once more, subdued.

Jacob was silent as Arys led him the rest of the way through the castle. The halls were huge and grand, bright and airy, yet as distant and cold as their inhabitants. Aside from a few guards, the cavernous halls were empty. Jacob and Arys's footfalls rang throughout as they strode down the elegant hallways.

Finally, they came to a gilded double door, held open, and entered a throne room. Jacob swallowed, his pace slowing as he glimpsed Dharius sitting on the ornate chair at the back of the room, Graxis standing beside him. At Arys's harsh prodding, he continued forward.

Dharius grinned darkly as they approached. Jacob felt uncomfortable with the look, still reeling from the spell Arys had cast on him. The Alorian chuckled when they drew near. Jacob slowed again. Suddenly, Arys kicked him hard in the back. Jacob tried to reach his hands under him as he fell, forgetting that they were tied together. He turned his head as he crashed against the floor, his cheekbone slamming against the granite and whipping his neck back sharply. He grunted from the impact, shoulder aching with his face. Stars swam in his vision.

"So nice you could join us, Garrett," Dharius stated. Jacob tried to move, but found it even more difficult lying face down on the floor than it had been on his side.

"Or, should I say, Jacob Tobias Marshall."

Jacob leaned his head back with a gasp. His stomach trembled as he struggled to hold his shoulders up and face Dharius. The Alorian grinned darkly at him. Leaning on his side, Jacob pushed up on his elbow and rose to his knees. Dharius gazed at a small plastic card in his hand. Jacob recognized it as his student identification card. His eyes widened.

"It's amazing what things people keep on their person where no one else is supposed to see it." Dharius grinned, amused with Jacob's reaction. Jacob then noticed his old, brown leather wallet lying on the arm of Dharius's throne. He had forgotten entirely that he had it in his pants pocket all this time, all these months, hidden beneath the tails of his tunic.

"A student." Dharius flipped the card over in his hand. "After all the trouble you've caused me, it turns out you're just a schoolboy." Jacob said nothing, terrified and dismayed with Dharius knowing the truth about him. Knowing that, the Alorian seemed to hold some additional power over him, and he felt small and weak against his powerful adversary. Just a high school student, as the card in Dharius's hand attested.

"Such foreign things." Dharius's attention still lay on the card. "You're not from Aurius, are you?" Jacob's head sank. He felt violated, watching Dharius rifle through the only remnants of his real life, so far distant. Kneeling prone before the Alorian, it was also an uncomfortable reminder of the truth that he was no warrior, no hero. *Just a guy who likes video games.*

"Answer him!" Arys snapped and kicked Jacob in the back, knocking him onto his face again. He simply lied there, despair settling over him and unwanted tears gathering beneath his eyes. What horrors was he about to face in this castle, alone and helpless against the greatest villain in this world?

Jacob swallowed around a lump in his throat, eyes closed as his aching face leaned against the cold granite floor. "No. I'm not."

Dharius laughed aloud. "So, my greatest challenge is nothing but a schoolboy from another world." Graxis and Arys laughed along with the Alorian. Jacob felt Arys grab the back of his collar and pull him harshly up to his knees again.

"Well, no matter." Dharius carelessly tossed the card over his shoulder. Jacob watched the card as it fluttered to the floor several feet away. His throat constricted. Seeing his only remaining link to home, without even the familiarity of his homemade pendant around his neck, being discarded so casually was a poignant symbol of his own hopelessness to ever return there.

Dharius stood. "You can still suffer and die like anyone else." Jacob took in a deep, steadying breath as he raised his gaze to the Alorian. No matter what happened here, he knew he would still escape. Whether he would be able to return home hadn't bothered him yet, and there was no reason for it to do so now. He stared Dharius firmly in the eyes, his fear not fully abated yet.

Dharius approached, his tall, lean form towering over Jacob. "And I want the world to know what happens when you defy me."

Jacob held his chin up defiantly. "You'll never win. You'll be stopped before you do."

Before he even realized Dharius had moved, the back of his armoured gauntlet slammed into Jacob's face, harder than he had ever been hit before. He couldn't help crying out as the jolting blow hit the side of his face that still ached from falling onto the floor. Pain throbbed over his cheek. He leaned forward, panting from the attack.

Dharius laughed. Jacob moaned in pain again as the Alorian grabbed his hair and yanked his head back to face him.

"Oh, how I've longed to do this. I'm going to keep you alive long enough so you can watch me succeed. Nothing will stand in my way."

Jacob just gazed at him, panting through his severely aching mouth. Once more, Dharius hit him in the face, on the other side. He groaned, head whipped aside though held in place by the Alorian's tight grip on his hair. He struggled at his bonds, but the rope holding his hands together was secure.

Dharius continued laughing as he pulled Jacob's head back. Jacob cringed from the last yank on his hair, but the reaction caused his aching face to pound even harder.

"Graxis."

Jacob opened his eyes at Dharius's command and found the scorpion-creature had left his master's side. He began to turn his head to look for Graxis, but before he had moved far, an ear-splitting crack rent the air. As it did, his back ripped open, a huge gash tearing through his shirt and scoring his flesh with searing heat. He screamed, the pain throbbing over his back worse than anything he'd ever felt. Leaning forward away from the pain, he fell to the floor again.

The hall erupted in uproarious laughter. Jacob felt he could barely breathe, the pain was so intense, but the mocking laughs surrounding him infuriated him.

"Shut up!" His face ached harder as he clenched his teeth from pain.

"This is pathetic," Arys stated, the sadistic smile clear in his voice.

"Shall we get *ss*omething *sss*tronger, ma*sss*ter?" Graxis hissed.

"No." Dharius's laughter faded. "I want him to know pain such as he has never dreamed before." Jacob weakly tried to roll onto his side. "I want the remainder of his life to be nothing but suffering." His back flared in a surge of pain as he rose on his elbow. "I want him to believe that he will never know anything but despair again." Trembling, his back and face throbbing, he struggled to push himself off the floor. "I want him to beg me for death." Biting back a scream, he raised himself to his knees and glanced up at Dharius. The Alorian grinned triumphantly down at him.

"And if a simple whip is going to cause him this much pain, I want to get as much out of it as I can."

Jacob gazed desperately at his captor, but a moment later, the whip cracked again and the pain seared over his back anew. Screaming at the top of his lungs, he fell to the floor once more. His legs curled beside him, tears breaking free of his eyes and running down his swelling face. Laughter filled the room once more, but Jacob hurt so much he couldn't even be affected by it.

"Take him back to his cell."

Jacob faintly felt the tail of Dharius's cloak brush over his face as the Alorian returned to his throne. Arys stepped in front of him and kicked him in the shin.

"Get up."

Jacob only moaned, uncertain he could move against the pain.

Arys kicked him in the shin again, harder. "I said get up!" Groaning, Jacob struggled to get to his feet. His head pounded from the pain in his face, back, and leg all at once and it was all he could do to stagger along in front of the guard. He limped as he walked, his bruised shin sending a spike of pain through his leg with each step.

Eventually, they reached the cell where Jacob had awoken not an hour ago. Opening the door, Arys shoved Jacob inside. He stumbled and fell once more to the floor as Arys closed the heavy metal door, his laughter ringing around the cell.

Alone, Jacob allowed himself a weak moan and more tears, his back pounding with every beat of his heart. He coughed as he inhaled dust from the floor of the cell. His stomach twisted and cramped up with hunger, his throat burned with thirst, his limbs were stiff and sore, and the chill in the air made him shiver as soon as he had set foot inside the cell.

He swallowed back a sob as he tried to console himself. It hurt now, but he knew something that Dharius and his minions didn't. His friends were going to break into the castle and free him. He hoped it wouldn't be long before they did.

Letting out a shuddering sigh, he tried to relax his body, splayed awkwardly across the floor on his side as it was, and closed his eyes, weariness taking over him.

26

THE CHILL HAD taken over Jacob by the time he awakened, and he found himself shivering constantly, his body stiff from it. Each tremble sent a wave of pain through his body, though he could feel that the blood had dried on his back. His face was tender and swollen and his shin still throbbed from Arys's savage kicks. He swallowed with difficulty, coughing from all the dust hanging in his mouth.

Despair threatened to overwhelm him in his agony. He took several deep breaths in an attempt to calm himself, his back pounding each time his chest expanded.

I just have to last until the others come.

Opening his eyes, he gazed around, but the cell looked the same as it had before. The light of the outside world seemed somehow more distant than before. He shifted, the hard stone floor rough against his hipbones, but each movement he made throbbed over his body. Cringing, he lied still.

To think this was ever just a video game. He thought of his companions, probably seeking out Dharius's castle in Thayer's airship even as he lied there. What were they thinking? What were they doing? The game, again, had not gone into detail. There had been a short scene showing the characters' reactions to Garrett's capture, but it was a glimpse at best. Knowing that they were real people here, who were always thinking and feeling, made Jacob wonder how they were reacting.

He thought then of home. His family, his friends, and Tina. He let out a sigh. It had been so long since he had seen any of them. He wondered how they were coping with his disappearance. Were they searching for him? Did they even care? He frowned uncomfortably as he thought of the hard job of breaking the news to his mother and stepfather that must have fallen on his companions at the convention.

Thought of the convention gave him pause. It was hard to believe that his biggest concern so recently had been how his costume would be received. Half of it was gone now, and his shirt was already torn badly from

Dharius's attacks in the volcano and the lashes he received earlier. He no longer had his pendant, and he may never recover the sword his stepfather's coworker had so graciously made for him.

None of it seemed to matter much, as he now lied on the floor of a dungeon cell, beaten, bloody, and starved, wholly at the mercy of his captors. He thought of Merakis, where his prop sword had been sharpened into a true weapon. Guilt weighed on his shoulders. He had known precisely what was going to happen the night that he went into the town, yet it never even occurred to him to try to warn or protect the people there. So many people had died because of him, because of his inaction when he could have prevented disaster. He pulled his legs closer to his body, even though the flesh on his back stretched painfully with the action.

He sighed, shifting again. The silence of the cell would have been unbearable a few months ago, but it was little different from the silence of the open plains he had traveled so far across. On the plains, however, there had been things to do and to see. The solitude and unchanging scenery of his small stone cell was terribly dull.

Minutes dragged on as he lied still on the floor, wishing he was able to do something to stave off boredom and get his mind off the pain that plagued him.

He rolled over his stomach onto his other side when he became too uncomfortable to remain in the same position, though it ached his back further to do so. It didn't take long for that position to grow uncomfortable, however, and he struggled to rise to his feet. He paced around the cell shortly before sitting down against the wall, leaning his shoulder into it. Boredom and restlessness weighed on him, irritating him, and he yelled at the closed door of the cell, but nothing ever happened.

Growling in exasperation, he leaned his head back against the wall. He tried to calm himself by thinking of something else. He closed his eyes, picturing clearly in his mind the last time he went to a party with Tina. She had been invited to a party at a friend's house celebrating the end of their junior year of high school. He had stayed close by her side even when he grew bored of her chatting with her friends, too unnerved by the fact that he didn't know anyone to want to leave her. With her encouragement, however, he had managed to stray into the crowd and speak with some of the people he didn't know, and had ended up enjoying himself. His head sank as he thought of all the things Tina had done for him. And yet, his last memory of her had been their fight.

More memories of home surfaced, of his friends and family, places he had been and things he had done, and he grew more homesick than he had ever been in his life. He thought the summer he had gone to camp when he was nine years old was the loneliest experience he had ever had, but he had been among two dozen other kids his age and he received letters from his parents every week. No one here even knew who he really was.

Except, he thought with a shiver, for Dharius.

The minutes dragged on into hours as he lay in his cell, staring at the wall and struggling to keep his mind busy for something to do. The cold, hunger, and thirst grew stronger with each passing moment, and his head began to ache fiercely. He curled up against the wall, wondering if Dharius meant to simply leave him in there.

Finally, late in the afternoon when the sky outside his cell took on a yellowish hue, the lock for the door turned. He started, the sound cutting sharply across the silence. The heavy door squealed as it swung open, Arys standing behind it. Jacob was standing by the time the guard stepped into the cell.

Arys grinned. "That ready to go, are you?"

Jacob said nothing. His back stung with his movement, but he was so desperate for release from the tedium and solitude of the cell that he even preferred to follow Arys to whatever Dharius had in store for him this time.

He began to follow the same path as he had taken before, but Arys turned him with a sharp tug on his collar. "Not this time. This way." Jacob wondered where the guard was leading him as he took him to a long flight of stairs. They climbed for several minutes up a spiraling staircase coiling around the inside wall of a wide tower. He glanced around, but received no indication of where they went.

Finally, they came out a trapdoor. Jacob's eyes widened as he discovered they were on the top of the castle. He had only a brief moment to take in the sight of a large, square wooden frame with ropes tied to each corner before Arys shoved him on toward it. Dharius stood to one side of the frame while Graxis stood to the other side, clutching a leather whip. Jacob swallowed uncomfortably, his back still aching from his lashing earlier.

He could see far over the land from where they stood, a dark forest surrounding the castle before fading into grass fields. He glanced briefly over his shoulder and found open sea shortly beyond the forest behind the castle. The entire land was bathed in golden light from the drooping sun, hanging at eye level to Jacob over the ocean.

As he came near the edge of the platform where the frame was set up, Jacob's eyes widened. A vision of a bustling town with a castle in the distance appeared before him like a shimmering mirror. It seemed like he stood just outside the town, and he could see the castle that made him realize he was gazing at Vanimar, the capitol of Aurius. Townspeople were scattered over the street in the vision, but none of them moved. They all gazed uncertainly and fearfully toward him.

Arys kicked him. His back flared in pain as he stumbled onto his knees beneath the frame.

"I know you have been defying me," Dharius spoke darkly to the crowd in the vision. "And I will not tolerate dissent." He sent a sharp look to Arys. The guard untied Jacob's hands, yanking him to his feet. He and Graxis pulled Jacob's arms up and out harshly as they tied his wrists to the frame, tightening the ropes so hard Jacob felt his hands tingle from the loss of blood flow.

"Let this be a lesson to you." Dharius glared at the crowd. The malice in his expression sent a shiver up Jacob's spine. "If you try to fight me, you will know pain beyond any nightmare you have experienced."

Graxis laughed as he unwound the whip behind Jacob.

"Oh, no," Jacob uttered, struggling against his bonds. "Oh, God, please don't…" He cut himself short with a scream as the whip cracked, the sound echoing over the forest and plains below.

"This is your *hero*," Dharius spat. Jacob shrieked in pain as the whip tore open his back again, digging into and searing his flesh. "He is powerless against me, as are you all. Obey me, or you will all meet his fate." Spinning around, Dharius disappeared back into the castle, but Graxis continued cracking the whip at Jacob. The wood creaked as Jacob pulled at his bonds so hard they cut into his skin, blood trickling down his arms with the river cutting a stinging trail down his back. He couldn't feel it over the incredible pain on his back.

Again and again the whip lashed, each time driving Jacob blind with pain. Tears rolled freely down his eyes as his voice grew hoarse from screaming. He could feel nothing beyond the lacerations across his back and thought that there must surely be no flesh left there. Occasionally the whip swung wide, slashing open his shoulder or thighs, and once the back of his neck. He screamed and pleaded for mercy, his body hanging from the ropes that held his arms up as his knees buckled. He sobbed, so in agony that he hardly realized anyone else was there. The lashes never ceased, and each one seemed to hurt more than the last.

The sun had nearly disappeared beneath the horizon by the time Graxis finally stopped. It was hardly a relief for Jacob. His back throbbed so much from the flogging he had suffered that his vision swam. He hung limply against the ropes holding him to the frame, unable to support his weight. He was only faintly aware of Arys and Graxis untying him and dragging him back to his cell. Pain filled his awareness, allowing nothing else into his mind. At one point, a canteen was thrust against his lips and water ran down the back of his throat, but he received no comfort from it. The salty taste of his own tears lingered in his mouth as he lied on the floor of his cell, unable to move.

Several hours passed before he could even fall asleep, and the throbbing pain covering his back followed him into his dreams. The only thought that crossed his mind as he finally drifted to sleep was a desperate hope that his companions would come for him soon.

The next day, Jacob never left his cell. His back throbbed constantly, the pain roaring with every move he made. He lied face down in his cell all day, never daring to move. A longer day he had never known.

He grew steadily more uncomfortable as the day after stretched into memory. A guard once brought him food, which he struggled to eat though his hands were no longer tied. It wasn't enough to sate his hunger, nor the water brought for him enough to quench his thirst. He lay on the floor in agony, each tiny movement sending a wave of pain through his body. He shivered constantly, colder than before with his flesh open and his shirt torn to shreds in the back, and his parched throat burned and his stomach twisted in hunger. His hands were swollen and sore from his struggles against his bonds. Mostly he lay in silence, nothing but his heavy breathing breaking the unending stillness of his confinement, but occasionally the pain became too much to bear and he moaned or sobbed plaintively.

As the sun sank towards the horizon the second day after his flogging, the door to the cell opened and Arys returned, grinning sadistically. He kicked Jacob hard in the ribs three times before he was able to rise, even with the assistance of his hands. His back flared in pain with the movement and it was all he could do to stumble along ahead of Arys. So dazed from pain was he that he didn't even realize where he was going. When he came to the top of the castle and saw the same vision of Vanimar, the same frame with the ropes, and Graxis standing ready with the whip, he leaned back, begging to be spared. He shrieked as Arys ground his boot into his still open wounds, shoving him forward.

Jacob pleaded with his captors, but didn't have the strength to fight as he was tied to the frame again. He tried to brace himself as Graxis and Arys stepped away, but the pain was even worse than before. His screaming rang through the night. The lashes opened up his wounds fresh and the blood stung viciously as it flowed down his back. His wrists bled fiercely from the struggles against his bonds, but he didn't even feel it.

The agony never seemed to end. Twice the whip flew high, sailed over his head, and split his face open. The pain was unbearable. He didn't know how his body could hurt so much. Once more, what seemed hours later, he was finally released and dragged back to his cell in a haze of pain.

The pattern continued for several horrible days, each worse than the last. His wounds never healed and the ones he received every other night grew steadily worse. Not only did Dharius, Graxis, and Arys continue beating him in the same ways every time, but they found ways to make the pain even worse. Every night when he was brought to the castle roof, he thought he would die from his wounds, yet every night, he suffered further. Once, a dull sword, glowing red from the forge, was drawn slowly across the small of his back, the searing metal flaying him alive as it sliced into his skin. He pleaded to every deity he could think of and begged for help from everyone he knew, yet he never received any relief. He screamed louder and longer than he ever had in his life and rubbed his wrists down to the bone against the ropes that held him up. He had never imagined that he could suffer so much pain, yet every time he was brought to the top of the castle, it was worse.

Pain filled his consciousness so much that he hardly even recognized his own name when spoken and couldn't understand anything that was said to him. The thought had idly crossed his mind at difficult times during his high school years, but for the first time in his life, he truly wished he would die.

His mind, it seemed, had lost the capability for conscious thought, but one night as he lay in utter agony on the floor of his cell, the realization hit him harder than any of the pain afflicting him.

They're not coming.

27

JACOB'S EARS RANG as he lay on the floor of his cell, unable to feel his body beyond the pain. Even the hunger, thirst, cold, weariness, and stiffness from lying on the stone floor failed to affect him anymore. Faint light drooped into the room through his barred window, a sign of the late afternoon sun. He didn't react when the door unlatched and opened.

"Get up." Arys kicked him hard in the ribs. Jacob didn't react. Now a frequent occurrence, Arys didn't hesitate to kick him again and again with all his strength in the same spot. Jacob heard a crack, but he barely felt the blows. The movement resonated over his back more than his side hurt. He didn't think he could move even if he wanted to. He tried to flex his fingers as an experiment, but couldn't see if he was successful.

Growling impatiently, Arys laid his boot on Jacob's back and ground his heel down on the tattered flesh. Jacob groaned as pain surged over his back, but he still couldn't gather enough energy to rise and face his next round of torture.

Frustrated, Arys rolled Jacob onto his back and grabbed his arms. It was another tactic that had gotten Jacob to rise, dragging his wounded back along the rough ground. Even that wasn't enough to move him, though he felt his stiff knees bend as his back flared. For the first time, Jacob felt anger creep into his mind. Anger at what had been done to him, anger that he had been left to endure this suffering alone, and anger that Arys complained of the inconvenience of dragging him through the castle to beat him further.

"Ugh." Arys dropped Jacob on the stone. "This is hopeless. I need Graxis here."

Suddenly, a blind rage swept over Jacob, fury like he had never felt before. He rolled onto his side to gaze at Arys turning his back and wanted nothing more than to see the guard suffer as he had. He saw Arys in his mind's eye howling with pain as he was torn apart piece by piece. The sight filled Jacob with such fury and desire that the pain no longer hindered him.

Before the guard could walk away, Jacob shot an arm out and yanked Arys's foot out from under him. Grabbing a shredded strip of cloth that used to be part of his shirt, Jacob crawled quickly forward, leaning his knees with all his weight on Arys's back. The guard struggled, but before he could do anything, Jacob wrapped the strip of cloth around Arys's neck and yanked as hard as he could. The action shoved Arys's Adam's apple back into his neck and a snap sounded out. Arys let out a strangled noise before falling lifeless below him.

Jacob panted, feeling nothing but pain. He didn't react to Arys's death, the action methodical and distant. His back raged with his mind, his fury consuming him completely. He drew Arys's sword and rose, stumbling into the hall outside his cell. His vision faded to red through his right eye, the left swollen shut from the untended lashes over his face. Pain fueled him on through the dungeon into the castle proper.

Without knowing what he was doing, he followed a path towards a hidden side entrance to the castle. He staggered as he walked, barely able to feel his legs over his pounding back. Panting out of burning lungs, he moved forward, feeding on his own rage and moving on out of instinct. No conscious thought came to his mind as he made his way through the castle.

Guards appeared every now and then, but Jacob ran the stolen sword through them without thought, without feeling, and without mercy. His wrists flamed from the ropes that had held him up while he was beaten, the crippling pain only making his blows stronger.

He left the castle into the dark forest surrounding it. How long he stumbled through the forest, cutting down anything in his way, he never knew. He had made it to the plains beyond when a familiar roar rumbled through the sky. Wind buffeted him as the airship sank down nearby, but he didn't react to it. He staggered on towards the airship, weariness finally weighing down his steps. The gangplank lowered as soon as the ship touched the ground and everyone but Thayer ran towards him.

"Garrett!"

"Oh, Garrett, I'm so glad you're alright!"

Jacob said nothing, their words barely registering in his mind. Some inner sense bade him not to attack them, though he hardly recognized them for who they were. As they neared him, they all drew up short, eyes widening with horrified gasps. Makaidel emitted an intensely disturbed noise before Thorn pushed him out of sight. The young mage retched.

"My god," Thorn uttered, his eyes huge.

"Garrett," Serina whimpered.

Jacob didn't react. He ignored them as he continued on towards the airship, the naked sword still in his hand.

"Garrett, what happened to you?" Kalista laid a hand on his shoulder.

Jacob spun, slapping her arm off roughly. He glared at all of them, full of hatred.

"*Where were you?*"

Turning, he continued towards the lowered gangplank, but before long, everything went dark.

28

FOR WEEKS, JACOB didn't speak a word. He lied on a bed on the airship, facing the wall, and refused to move. He rose occasionally to eat, but only when he was certain no one was around. Serina spent several hours a day using her healing magic and more conventional medicine on him. The wounds were so deep and untended that his recovery was lengthy and painful. His back became covered in crisscrossing scars, the largest and most uncomfortable from the red-hot sword that was drawn across the small of his back, and scar tissue circled his wrists, as well as other places where the whips and other weapons had strayed. Though Serina was able to fight off infection and he could see well out of his left eye, he was left with disfiguring scars crossing his face. The scar tissue felt strange and unfamiliar, stretching at his skin in a way that was impossible to ignore, even at rest. On his face, he could constantly feel the new flesh passing down over his left eye and cheek, his nose, and even over his mouth. How it appeared, he neither knew nor cared. He never looked in a mirror.

At first, the others came in frequently, trying to reach out to him. Despite Makaidel's berating, Thorn's logic and understanding, Kalista's pleading and encouragement, and Thayer's teasing, Jacob never looked at any of them. He would often feel his rage build and a desire to throttle his companions came over him, but he refused to react to anything they said. They came to see him less and less as they received no response, nor even a glance, time after time. Eventually, they gave up trying to speak with Jacob.

Only Serina remained silent with him. For all the hours she spent with him that he never spoke to her, she never did, either. He respected her for it, and occasionally nurtured a desire to say something, but all it took was the twinge of fresh scar tissue for him to keep his mouth shut. Even when she had to minister attention to his injured face, he gazed blankly at the ceiling without looking at her.

Several nights after they had found him, as Serina left his room and his treatment for the night, Jacob heard metal jingling on the bed behind him.

He gazed at the closed door before turning around. His pendant lay on the pillow, the amber teardrop he had given to her before he was captured by Dharius. Clipping it around his neck, he lied down again, still facing the wall.

Jacob didn't know where they went and he didn't care. The others would sometimes try to consult him or seek his approval for their next destination, but their words passed vacantly through his ears. They stopped by towns and flew over and around landmarks of every kind. Jacob never left his room and rarely even sat up from bed.

Throughout his recovery, he remained immersed in dark thoughts. He felt betrayed and abandoned by the people with whom he had been through so much in this strange world. They had left him alone to suffer such agony as he could no longer even fathom. Every time he moved, a ripple of a foreign sensation spread up his back, a shadowy reminder of the suffering he had endured at the hands of Dharius.

And the people he had considered his friends had never even tried to go after him.

Without considering his choices, he knew his next course of action one night when the airship landed west of Vanimar. A mountain range loomed in the distance, the same range that stretched south from the volcano where the fire temple had been, a jagged shadow obscuring the stars in the clear night sky. While the ship lay silent around him, he rose, sheathing his stolen sword in a scabbard Serina had brought silently to him, and left the airship. He met no one as he left and didn't look back as he strode across the plains in the deep of night, an autumn chill biting the air. The new shirt, pants, tunic, and gloves he had been given rippled in the night breeze with the long grasses surrounding him.

He felt no emotion as he strode across the plains toward the tallest mountain. Orlocs darted out of the long grass toward him throughout the night. He fought the beasts off casually and methodically, not feeling any excitement or fear from their appearance. He no longer feared dying by their claws and attacked without hesitation. The first few wounds he received from the battles he simply let flow, not bothering to look for the healing potions in his backpack.

No thoughts crossed his mind as he traveled on, his focus solely on his mission. At the top of the mountain he approached lived a hermit who had been one of the greatest warriors in Aurius. In the game, visiting the hermit was an optional quest that, if taken, gained Garrett the ultimate Runic Seal skill. It was a difficult journey climbing the mountain, but Jacob knew that the hermit was the one person who would be able to teach him to use Runic Seals.

Jacob traveled throughout the night, pitching his tent and building a fire alone shortly after sunrise. The solitude neither comforted nor bothered him. He slept until the middle of the afternoon and continued on his way.

The orlocs he faced as he came to the base of the mountain were the most difficult he had fought yet in Aurius, each battle a narrow escape from a quick death or having a limb torn off. The danger never affected him, and he fought calmly and carefully. Unlike the last time he had climbed a mountain, he grew winded only every few hours or after a particularly challenging battle. He followed the path he knew, shutting out any thoughts that might distract or hinder him on his way.

It was a three-day journey up the mountain towards the hermit's shack. He faced dangers such as he had never known and crossed treacherous terrain, brushing with death more than a dozen times on his way. He never thought of his companions, or of home, or of anything but his mission.

Finally, Jacob came to the last rise leading up to the hermit's shack. The mountain peak continued climbing up to his right, but to his left, the land dropped away and he could see down the mountainside and off into the distance. The ocean lined the base of the mountain along a short stretch of flat grassland.

As he turned a corner onto a wide ledge, the hermit's home came into view. It was a simple log cabin, nothing adorning the walls and thick windows, the back of it sitting along a cliff wall that fell thousands of feet down to the open sea. The hermit himself stood out front, chopping wood against a hardened tree stump. He glanced up suddenly as Jacob appeared, brandishing his axe. Though his face was lined and his beard peppered with grey hairs, the hermit was a muscular man on par with Morrie Deacon, and there was no fear or surprise in his hard gaze and experienced posture.

"Who are you?"

Jacob stood with his shoulders back, unaffected by the hermit's coarseness. "My name is Garrett. I'm a warrior and the owner of the Hero's pendant."

The hermit didn't react. "What are you doing here?"

Jacob stepped forward. "You're Rath, once the commander of the king's army and the greatest warrior in Aurius."

"And?"

"I need you to teach me how to do Runic Seals."

Rath's eyes narrowed, though he didn't move. "And why should I do that?"

"Because an Alorian is going to destroy all of Aurius otherwise."

Rath turned back to his wood dismissively. "That's what the king's army is for."

Jacob moved forward a few more paces. "They can't do anything this time. Only I can."

"And what makes you so special?" Rath split another log.

"I have the Hero's pendant."

The wood fell to either side of the stump with a *clunk*. "Sorry, kid. I don't give lessons."

Frustration hardened Jacob's voice. "There's more going on than you realize. This Alorian holds power you can't even dream of. If he succeeds, there won't be anyone left in Aurius, and that includes you."

Rath didn't react. "Sorry."

"Listen!" Jacob snapped, moving closer. His throat constricted as he allowed emotion to color his mind for the first time in days. "I have to stop him, and I can't do it without Runic Seals."

"And you think I can just give you the ability to do them like a gift?"

Jacob's voice rose. "There has to be something you can do!"

Rath raised an eyebrow. "What makes you so sure?"

"Because I can't do this anymore!" Jacob's voice broke as the mask he had put up inside himself came down. Misery, loneliness, and hopelessness washed over him in a flood. "I'm *not* a hero, I'm just a teenager. I don't really know how to swordfight, I don't know how I'm going to beat Dharius, and… God, I just want to go *home*."

And suddenly, like a dam bursting, it all came out. Jacob was so desperate for release at long last that he told Rath everything without a second thought. He spoke of the things he had done, and hadn't done, in this real Aurius, the struggles he had faced being an ordinary teenager thrust into the role of a hero, and the torture he had so recently suffered at Dharius's hands. He spoke of how the entire world he now traveled used to be nothing but a video game to him, how he had dreamed for years that he would be in this place, and how the real thing had become a nightmare. He spoke of his home, his family and friends, and how very different this world was to the one he had come from. He spoke of his fears that he could never return, that he would die in this foreign place and never see the people he cared about again.

He paced around the ledge as he spoke, waving his arms for emphasis. Rath sat on the tree stump quietly, though how he reacted to the admissions, Jacob didn't know. He barely looked at the hermit, so desperate to let out all that he had kept hidden over the past months that it didn't even seem to matter who listened.

The afternoon grew late as Jacob talked, the sun dipping down towards the ocean and painting the ledge in gold light. Finally, after having let out everything, Jacob dropped onto a boulder beside the log cabin with a deep sigh. He ran a hand through his long hair.

"I'm so tired of this." His throat was dry and sore from talking so long, and from the choking emotion that his words had built in him. "So tired. I don't belong here. I can't be the hero, especially if I can't count on my friends. I just want to go home. I'm tired of everything being so different, I just want to see something familiar again. I miss my home, my room, the things that make me *me*. I miss my friends and my girlfriend, and my mom and stepdad and even my stepsister." He let out a sigh. "I miss my *dad*. I haven't even seen him since my last birthday." Tears gathered beneath his eyes. Sniffling, he wiped them away roughly with the back of his hand. Through his leather glove, he could feel the raised skin of the scars crossing his face.

"I-I'm sorry." Jacob shook his head, bringing himself back to the mountain. "I shouldn't have dumped all that on you. I just… I need to beat Dharius so I can go home." He sighed. "If I can." Silence fell over the ledge. A breeze whispered down the mountainside, gently rustling the pine trees growing along the path.

Finally, Rath stated, "Think you're going to have some explaining to do before you do that." Jacob glanced at him curiously, but the hermit's gaze was fixed across the ledge where he had come from. Jacob followed Rath's gaze. His eyes widened.

Serina stood beside a tree at the edge of the path, gazing uncertainly at him.

Jacob rose, blinking in surprise. "Serina?"

She shook her head, her hair rolling over her elongated ears. Running across the ledge, she threw her arms around him.

"Oh, Garrett! I'm so sorry!"

Jacob laid his hands against her back, his mind reeling from conflicting emotions. "Why didn't you stay with the others?"

She shook her head, her face buried against his shoulder. "It was you I pledged to help, not them. I just wanted to be with you."

Jacob's heart swelled with her words, filling him with warmth and comfort he had not known in almost two months. He wrapped his arms around her, smiling as he inhaled the lavender scent of her skin and felt her soft hair against his cheek. Everything he had suffered seemed so far away in her embrace as to have never happened. In her touch, everything felt like it would be alright.

"I'm so sorry, Garrett. I told them we should go after you, I always knew we should have. They said they couldn't risk it because no one would be able to stop Dharius if we were caught, but I knew we should have gone after you. We shouldn't have just left you there. Please forgive me, Garrett!"

As quickly as it came, the beautiful moment was gone. Jacob's eyes widened as his breath caught in his throat, his chest constricting like it was in a vise. Her words echoed in his head, berating and chastising him. He had never felt so small.

Serina drew back, gazing at him curiously as his grip on her slackened.

"Oh, my God," he uttered, staring past her. He slowly lowered himself back onto the boulder behind him, his heart weighing down in his chest. The messily healed flesh of his back tingled with the movement, but it seemed insignificant now.

"They're right."

Serina crouched down before him and took his hands. "Garrett? What's wrong?"

He shook his head slowly before raising his gaze to her eyes. "Don't you see? They were right. We're the only ones who know about the element stones. If you guys had been caught trying to rescue me, Aurius would've been doomed for sure." He bent over, burying his face in his hands. "I can't believe I was so selfish."

"No, no! You weren't…"

"Yes, I was," he cut in. "We're Aurius's best hope, all of us." He thought of how he had treated his companions after they found him on the plains. "I had no right blaming you for doing…" His voice broke as his thoughts turned to what would have happened had he not been able to escape Dharius's castle, and what would have happened to Aurius had the group failed in an attempt to rescue him. "For doing the right thing." Serina squeezed his hands, saying nothing.

He raised his eyes to her. "You didn't even have any way of knowing if I was alive." It wasn't a question, but she shook her head almost imperceptibly in response. Her eyes glistened wetly as she gazed at him. Jacob let out an exhausted sigh.

"I'm no hero."

He had thought it before, but the words truly sank in for the first time since he had come to Aurius. He knew he had made a poor imitation of the real Garrett, but felt he was still saving the land by taking on the role. All the good deeds he had done had been following the game's guide, and he had enjoyed doing them only for the acclaim he received. Until this moment, he never realized what it truly took to be a hero, and how severely he lacked it.

"That's not true," Serina attempted to argue.

"Please," Jacob stated wearily, silencing her. She simply gazed at him, upset, but he couldn't bring himself to be comforted by her words.

A rustle to the side caused Jacob to turn. Rath stood from where he had sat on the tree stump. Jacob had entirely forgotten the hermit was there.

"You need more help than I can give you." Jacob nodded slowly in agreement as Rath gathered up his axe and the wood he had split. "You can stay the night on the ledge. Orlocs don't bother me so much here."

"Thank you," Serina stated quickly as the hermit disappeared into his home. She crouched to look into Jacob's eyes, her hair illuminated in fiery colors from the setting sun.

He rubbed at his eyes, the scar tissue aching like a bruise as his hand passed over it. "I guess we'd better set up the tent." Serina nodded as he stood and removed his backpack. They built a fire and ate dinner silently, Jacob swallowing around a lump in his throat that never faded that night.

"So, was it true?" Serina ventured. Jacob glanced at her. "What you said."

"You heard that?" He wasn't surprised.

She nodded bashfully. "I didn't mean to eavesdrop. I just didn't want to interrupt."

He nodded slowly. "Yeah, it's true."

Serina hunched her shoulders. "So, you're not from Aurius. I never would've thought." Jacob couldn't help half grinning at her innocence. "Though I guess it does explain a few things. Like how you knew what would happen. So… you said this was all a game?"

"Yeah." He frowned, wondering how he could explain video games to a world that lacked even electricity. "It's… kind of like a play, except you control what happens."

Serina's brow knitted in confusion. "I don't understand."

Jacob waved a hand dismissively. "Never mind. It's not important." She wrapped her arms around her knees, drawn up to her chest.

"So, what should we do now?"

Jacob glanced at her, then followed her eyes to Rath's house.

"I don't know. We may as well go back down the mountain tomorrow. There's no point staying here."

She shrugged her shoulders. "What happened next in the… in the game?"

He sighed. "We go to Dharius's castle and fight him once and for all." His head sank. "But I can't do it. I'm just not cut out for this." He paused. "You should go back to the others. They're going to need you."

She shook her head. "I came here for you. All I ever wanted was to be with you."

Jacob raised his gaze to her. Though she still looked upset, chin resting on her arms, a determined spark lit her eyes. For the first time, he saw Serina not as the girl he had desired for years, but as someone closer to him, more special. A true friend.

"Even knowing the truth about me?"

She nodded. "It doesn't change who you are. You didn't care that I'm half Alorian. I don't care that you're not from Aurius. I still believe in you."

He tried to chuckle, but failed. "That makes one of us."

The campsite fell silent as darkness descended over the mountain. The temperature dropped and the wind grew bitterly cold. They soon retreated into their tent, the same one they had shared at the beginning of their journey. How she had come up the mountain after him without a tent, he didn't know, but he was glad for her company then.

"Serina?"

"Yes?" She rolled over on her elbow to glance at him. He gazed into her crystalline blue eyes, wanting to smile but knowing that he couldn't.

"Thanks."

Her radiant smile lit up her face. "You're welcome. I'm just glad to be with you." He sighed as she curled up under her bedroll, some of the heaviness lifting off his heart. He lied down on his own bedroll, much harder than the bed where he had spent so much time on the airship, but much more comfortable than the stone cell where he had spent the time before. The canvas walls of the tent rippled in a breeze that howled down the path. Closing his eyes, he drifted to sleep, much easier than he had the last time he shared a tent with Serina, despite the dark thoughts clouding his mind.

The next morning, they woke with the sunrise and began their descent back down the mountain. Though the orlocs they faced were still difficult, it was easier with Serina's assistance. The three-day journey was just over two traveling by daylight, and soon, they reached the base of the mountain, flat grasslands stretching away into the distance before them. The airship was gone.

"So, where do you want to go now?" Serina asked as they stepped off the last rocky ledge.

Jacob shook his head. "I don't know. We don't have too much food, so I guess we should go to a town."

"I think Vanimar lies east of here." Serina gazed across the open grasses, though there was no civilization in sight. Jacob nodded, knowing she was right.

Another week slipped away into memory as they crossed the open fields. In ways, Jacob enjoyed the travel. He liked the solitude and the time alone with Serina, and it was refreshing not to have the pressures of their mission weighing them down. They traveled as they had when they first set out from

Shelas, making their way easily across the plains, not doing anything in particular.

And yet, Jacob could never forget the shame of realizing how selfish he had been. People like Lord Kyutu and Cassandra Deacon had been counting on him to set Aurius to rights, but they had put their faith in a self-centered coward.

He spoke to Serina about his life as they traveled, now that she knew the truth about him. It was a relief to finally have someone he could talk to about all the things he had kept inside since he arrived in Aurius, and she was a more than willing audience. She marveled at his stories of the foreign world he had come from and listened intently to him talk of his friends and family. At her request, he also told her details of what he had suffered at Dharius's castle. She looked horrified as he spoke and immediately tried to use her healing magic again, but the scars marking his body were too set in his skin. It was like trying to heal a rift in stone. He didn't know how he was going to explain it, especially to Christina.

Serina smiled wistfully when he mentioned his girlfriend's name. "She must be really lucky."

Jacob shook his head, his expression falling. "No, she really isn't. I don't know why she stayed with me as long as she did." He let out a sigh. "She was so nice to me, and I took that for granted so much. And she was right. She was right about everything. I should have put more effort into getting a summer job and applying for colleges, and stop trying to be a kid forever. I'm selfish and stubborn and I was obsessed with costuming." He sighed again. "None of it seems to matter anymore. College, work… definitely not costumes. I'll be lucky if I can get out of this alive and go home again." Serina laid a hand on his shoulder. He had argued against her reassurances enough times as they traveled that she remained silent, despite how she clearly wanted to protest. Jacob's heart felt heavy when he saw Serina holding back from complimenting him and trying to convince him that he was a good person. He had lied to her so much that she still believed it.

Throughout the journey, dark thoughts and shame clouded his mind. Even suffering the torture Dharius had inflicted upon him, he had never been so miserable, because now, he had no one to blame but himself.

SEVERAL DAYS AFTER they left the mountain behind them, Jacob and Serina spied the sprawling city of Vanimar in the distance, the king's castle rising over the buildings on the northern end of town. He had been to the city countless times as he played the game, but looking at it now, he could only see it as he had seen the town from the vision atop Dharius's castle. The reminder sent a shiver up his spine. Jacob wished that there was another town nearer by where they could restock their supplies. He thought of how Serina had told him that he had become famous for his pursuits, which, he supposed, was why the Alorian had tortured him as publicly as he had.

"People really think so much of me?" he asked as they strolled down the side of a hill from which they could see the far end of the city.

Serina smiled. "Yes, word has spread all over Aurius about what you've done. I know you don't think you are, but everyone calls you a hero." Jacob's gaze fell, guilt weighing down on his mind. *How can I face people who think I'm a hero?* Slowly, they drew closer to the city.

"M-maybe I should just wait out here while you get what we need." A lump grew in his throat and he wanted to be anywhere but there.

Serina smiled brightly as she laid a hand on his arm. "It's okay. You should get some rest in a nice bed after all this time outside." He frowned, relishing the idea of a long night's sleep in a soft bed, but too uneasy about the reactions he would face in Vanimar to be comforted by it.

The grass faded into a tended dirt path as they came near to the edge of town. Before they had even reached the buildings on the outskirts of the city, cries rang up, "It's Garrett!"

Jacob drew back, stopping in his tracks with an uncomfortable look. Serina took his arm with an encouraging smile and led him on. Ahead, some people yelled his arrival down the streets and a crowd began to form on the edge of town.

People spoke all at once as he stepped onto the cobblestone street into the city. Everyone waved for his attention as they shouted greetings, relief that he had escaped from Dharius, and requests for blessings. All manners of items from corn to shoes to hammers were thrust at him in offering. He tried to shy away from the attention, but the crowd surrounded him, penning him and Serina in.

He spun anxiously as someone grabbed his sleeve. A middle-aged man spoke over the roar of voices surrounding him, "Sir, I'd be honored if you'd stay at my inn." Jacob hesitated, knowing that he would only receive more attention if he took the innkeeper's offer.

Suddenly, a sharp voice shouted over the crowd, "Enough of this!"

The crowd silenced and parted to reveal a man in uniform gazing at Jacob. "Garrett, the king requests your presence at the castle." The crowd murmured in approval and spread out, allowing Jacob and Serina room to follow the guard. Jacob glanced uneasily at Serina. She shrugged with a smile. Shifting, he followed after the guard.

Townspeople lined the streets as they passed through, waving and cheering and shouting praise. People frequently ran up to offer Jacob some gift, but to his relief, the guard gestured them away. It was a long journey through the cobblestone streets and Jacob felt like a fraud with each admiring gaze he caught. He wished he could simply stock up and leave, but he wasn't certain he could refuse a king's request.

He swallowed uncomfortably when they drew near to the castle. It was twice as big as Lord Kyutu's castle, and that one had intimidated him. He felt small gazing up at the towering outer wall and the castle rising high into the sky.

Guards posted at the raised portcullis stood at attention as they came to the gate. Before they could speak, the guard leading Jacob and Serina stated, "Bringing the hero Garrett to the king." The castle guards relaxed and gazed in admiration as they passed through. Jacob hunched his shoulders.

Every guard they passed as they crossed the castle grounds saluted to Jacob. He had never felt more ashamed of himself. The guard that had met them in town led them through the two-story-high doors and into the castle. Jacob glanced around as they walked through the cavernous halls, huge tapestries and pennants hanging down at intervals with the fluted pillars that supported the ceiling. The castle seemed larger than any building he had ever been in, wide halls leading off into the distance everywhere he walked. How many rooms the castle held, he could only guess. And yet, he realized, it wasn't even as extravagant as Dharius's castle. The reminder of his time with the Alorian sent a shiver up his spine.

Finally, Jacob and Serina arrived at the throne room. It was large and airy, as big as a ballroom and just as elegant. Stained glass windows lined either side of the room, the light passing through them painting the room in jeweled colors. A herald announced their arrival as the guard led them down the plush red carpet towards the throne. King Lunas awaited their arrival, sitting straight with his shoulders back. He was a proud-looking man with waves of straw-colored hair and a neatly trimmed beard, perhaps only ten years Jacob's senior.

The guard that led them knelt as he came before the king. Jacob and Serina dropped to one knee behind him.

"Your Majesty, I bring the hero Garrett and Serina."

Lunas nodded. "Thank you, soldier. The comforts of the castle are yours today. Garrett and Serina, you need not kneel. I am honored to finally meet with you." Jacob opened his mouth to protest, but on seeing Serina rise beside him, he did so as well with a frown. He glanced over his shoulder as the guard that had brought them to the castle walked out of the throne room, leaving them alone with the king.

"I am intensely relieved to see you alive and free." Lunas's voice drew Jacob's attention back to him. "Like the people here, I had to watch the terrible things done to you. It was despicable." Jacob shifted, the scars on his back stretching uncomfortably.

"Dharius has this city in a vise. We can do nothing to defy him or he will kill innocent victims." The king's gaze became distant. "I have seen too many people die. I am powerless against him."

"How long as he been doing this, Your Majesty?" Serina asked.

Lunas shook his head. "It has been long since I have had to watch him gather an army of demons and orlocs in the forest to the south."

Serina's brow wrinkled in confusion. "But how is it we never even knew an Alorian was still in Aurius until recently?"

"By his design. He allows none to leave town, I assume so he can take the rest of the kingdom by storm. Messengers are killed before they can escape. We are utterly trapped here. That is why it gives me hope to see someone challenge him."

Jacob shook his head, avoiding the king's eyes. "Sir, I'm not…"

"Anything in my power to give is yours in thanks for what you've done," Lunas cut in.

Jacob shook his head harder, his voice rising. "I'm not what everyone says I am."

Lunas smiled in amusement. "Yes, I find people rarely are." Jacob glanced at him in surprise. "But you have still challenged Dharius and lived to tell the tale, and you have brought hope to my people. For that, I wish to reward you. I would like…"

"No," Jacob snapped, silencing the king. Serina gasped and Lunas's eyes widened at the interruption. "I'm a fraud, okay?"

"Garrett," Serina uttered, shocked, but Jacob kept his gaze on the king.

"I only did what I did for the fame. I'm not a great hero and I can't face Dharius or try to be something I'm not anymore. I don't deserve your praise or your rewards." Jacob's hands trembled, but he felt relieved for having said it.

Silence fell over the throne room. Lunas gazed solemnly at Jacob. Jacob's knees felt weak. He wished the king would let him leave. After a long, nerve-wracking moment, Lunas bowed his head with a sigh.

The king glanced to Jacob's side. "Miss Serina, would you please excuse us? One of the guards outside will help you with anything you need."

Serina seemed taken aback by the question, but nodded. "O-of course, Your Majesty." She exchanged a quick glance with Jacob before turning back the way they had come. He watched her uneasily, afraid of what the king was going to do with him. Had he gone too far in his outburst?

"Garrett."

Jacob snapped his attention back to Lunas as he rose from the throne.

"Take a walk with me."

Jacob swallowed nervously, afraid to refuse. "Okay, sir." He fell into step behind the king as he led Jacob out a back door of the throne room into a hall lined with windows. Jacob glanced outside to find the city stretching away beyond the castle walls. He wondered uncomfortably what Lunas had planned.

"So, you did it all for the fame, did you?" The king's voice was sharp and intimidating.

Jacob swallowed. "Y-yes, sir."

Lunas stopped, facing the windows. His voice softened. "If that were the case, then you would have relished the attention you received here, wouldn't you?"

Jacob fumbled for words, startled by the statement. "Um…"

"And you wouldn't have done half the things I've heard in the stories circulating the kingdom now."

"Well, I…"

Lunas grinned over his shoulder at Jacob. "And you certainly wouldn't have admitted to it in front of the King of Aurius." Jacob just stared back at him, uncertain what to say.

Lunas faced outside again, the smile fading. His next words were so faint Jacob barely heard them. "You didn't want this, did you?"

Jacob opened his mouth to answer, but closed it as he considered his response. He sighed. "I thought I did. But I'm just not cut out for this."

Lunas nodded slowly. "It always seems more glamorous from the outside."

"Yeah." Jacob gazed outside distractedly. "I just can't be a hero to people. I'm not what all those people think I am."

"Aren't you? They don't necessarily need a savior, just something to believe in. You've given them that." Jacob paused, absorbing the king's words. The reputation he had to live up to was still a heavier burden than he was prepared to bear anymore.

"I took the throne when I was twelve."

Jacob blinked, taken aback by the change of subject. "Oh?"

Lunas's gaze was distant. "I thought it was incredible, at that age, being the most powerful person in the kingdom." His eyes narrowed faintly. "The reality was far more trying than I had expected. I made a lot of stupid mistakes and caused some dark times to fall on the kingdom. Some people wanted me stripped of the crown, or even beheaded."

Jacob's eyes widened. "What did you do?"

The king didn't move his eyes. "The only thing I could do. I faced my errors and did what I could to correct them. It wasn't easy. To this day, I regret some of the decisions I made when I was first crowned." He turned, gazing meaningfully at Jacob. "I understand how it feels to take on responsibilities you didn't ask for, and to have to face consequences for actions you weren't prepared to take." Jacob could only stare back at the king, uncertain what to say. A surge of relief and exhaustion overcame him with the thought that someone understood, at least in some part, what he had done.

Lunas spun on his heel and continued down the hall, Jacob falling into step beside him.

"I still think you're worthy of praise, even mine. You've done better than most people would against the things you've faced."

Jacob sighed, glancing away. "But I'm not anything special."

They left the hall behind the throne room and journeyed down small and quiet corridors of the castle. "True heroes generally aren't. They're just the people who are able to rise to the challenges presented to them." Jacob frowned, still not convinced.

A guard strolling down a quiet hallway saluted to them as they passed by. Lunas nodded in turn, walking towards a small door at the end of the hall. Jacob blinked in confusion when the king opened the door into a storeroom. There was no other exit from the room.

"Um, where are we…"

"Do you know why this kingdom is called Aurius?" Lunas cut in as he strolled between crates and barrels of various foods.

"Uh, no." Jacob followed the king, wondering what they were doing.

"It's named after the first hero of our kingdom, back when our people were nomads struggling to survive against the orlocs that roamed the land then." Jacob looked up, surprised at the revelation. "He assembled the tribes, fought back against the menace that threatened us, and united the people as the kingdom was formed." Lunas laid his hand along the wall as he came to the back of the room. "He was the first owner of the Hero's pendant. Legend has it the Alorians gave it to him in recognition of his efforts." Jacob's eyes widened. He remembered the stained-glass window at the church in Merakis when he first accepted his quest. His head sank as he recalled the ceremony, so long ago. He hadn't understood then what he was getting into. If he had the choice again, would he take it?

Lunas paused, pushing against the back wall. Turning, he slammed his shoulder against it. A section of wall sank into the rest before swinging inward, revealing a narrow, winding staircase.

Jacob gasped. He hadn't even seen any seam in the mortar between the stone blocks of the wall. "Wh… where are we…"

"Come," Lunas stated simply as he entered the staircase. Jacob blinked, still surprised by the secret passage being shown him, then followed. He started as the section of wall swung shut behind him, casting them into utter darkness.

"The staircase is short, but be careful." The king's voice was already several feet ahead and below him. Jacob grasped the walls, feeling his way slowly down each stair. The complete darkness unnerved him.

He had come full circle on the staircase when he heard a door open below, and a faint glow illuminated a few stairs beneath where he stood. He hurried eagerly toward the light, uncomfortable with the encroaching darkness. Lunas waited at the base of the stairs, holding the door open. Jacob stepped through, then halted with a gasp.

They entered a huge, empty room, lit by pillars of cool light that shone down from small gaps in the ceiling. The walls were covered with runes and images strikingly similar to the ones at the southern Alorian ruins. At the far side of the room rose a pedestal bathed in bluish light from a hole in the ceiling, on top of which lay a sword.

It can't be, Jacob thought as his eyes widened. The sword of Aurius, the best weapon in the game for Garrett, was rumored to be hidden in Vanimar castle, but no one had ever been able to find it. He himself had explored the storeroom from which they'd come numerous times in the game to no avail.

"Much of this kingdom has forgotten its history." Lunas spoke calmly as he strolled across the room toward the sword. "But its kings have been instructed to remember the struggles and sacrifices Aurius and the other founders of the kingdom made in the beginning. It has been the duty of each king to protect his most sacred possession until the day it is needed again."

Jacob held his breath as they neared the pedestal. He had never thought much of swords, but he couldn't deny that the weapon before him was extraordinary. Not a speck of dust touched the blade, razor-sharp and polished to a mirror shine. The hilt was forged of intricately engraved brass that shimmered like gold. Beside it lay a fine leather scabbard painted red and black and attached to a belt that had clearly seen some use. As a show piece alone, the sword had to be worth a fortune. He reached toward it, but paused.

Shaking his head, he withdrew. "I can't take this. It isn't right."

Lunas raised an eyebrow. "What's not right about it? It belongs to you."

Jacob stepped back another pace, sighing despondently. *How can I tell him the truth?* He didn't think he could even tell Serina where he had come from if he had to do so again. "I can't face Dharius again."

"No one is asking you to. I put no obligations on you, Garrett. I wish to reward you well for what you have done, but the quest you have taken up is not something I could ask anyone to do."

Jacob shook his head. "Then why show me the sword?"

The king laid a hand on the pedestal, running his fingers down the stone beside the crystalline blade. "Because this sword's owner is the destined one, the owner of the Hero's pendant. It's been my task to hold it and to guard it until this day comes."

Jacob let out a sigh, feeling weary. "But I'm not a hero."

"You still could be."

Jacob turned to Lunas, startled. The king returned a steady gaze.

After a moment, Lunas shrugged noncommittally and turned, walking back towards the door they had entered. "The sword is yours. It's up to you whether to take it or not."

Jacob turned back to the blade on the pedestal, bathed in cool light. Lunas was right, he realized. He may not have had a choice before whether to accept the quest that he had taken, but he did now.

Do I really have what it takes to be a hero?

Carefully, he reached forward and picked up the sword. The blade rang harmoniously as it slid across the stone pedestal. The grip was comfortable, easy to swing. It was a little lighter than his own sword and far better balanced. He ran a finger delicately down the flat of the blade, his gloved hand gliding along the metal like ice.

Sighing, he lowered the sword. He knew what it would take to defeat Dharius, and he knew he was so close to reaching the end of his adventure. Yet, he still wasn't certain if he could truly do what must be done.

"How do you do it?" he stated softly to himself.

Lunas's voice responded from across the room. "You do or you don't. Sometimes, it's not about how. It's just about moving on." Opening the door, he stepped out, leaving Jacob alone in the chamber.

Jacob glanced down the length of the blade in his hand. It shimmered in the light shining down on the pedestal. Inhaling deeply, he took the scabbard and sword belt off the pedestal and sheathed the blade. Turning, he followed after the king, his footfalls echoing throughout the chamber around him. He climbed the winding staircase in the dark until he reached the section of wall, which hung open a crack and let in warm light onto the last few stairs.

When he stepped back into the storeroom, he found Lunas smiling at him. "I'm glad you took it."

Jacob glanced away. "I'm still not sure I can do this."

"Of course not." Lunas's voice was amused. "If you were, then it would have been an easy decision." Jacob smiled faintly. He turned as he heard a crumbling sound behind him. The section of wall pushed back into place seamlessly, leaving no evidence that there had ever been anything out of the ordinary in this storeroom. Jacob followed Lunas out of the storeroom and down the hall outside it. There the king paused and faced him.

"I must return to my duties, but I wish you the best of luck in your journey. Whatever you decide to do, please return here. You will always be welcome in my castle."

"Thanks." Jacob smiled genuinely for the first time since he had been captured by Dharius. "Thanks for everything."

Lunas turned and began walking away. "It was nothing. And if you need anything else, don't hesitate to ask." Jacob simply smiled, knowing he couldn't ask the king for anything more after what he had given already. He watched Lunas walk away down the hall, then turned and walked the other way towards the entry hall to the castle.

30

JACOB REMAINED SILENT as he wandered the castle halls, nodding distractedly to any who greeted him. For once, the thoughts that flooded his mind were nothing but fleeting hints of words he couldn't grasp even if he wanted. His mind was blank, though his path was still clouded to him. He gripped the sword of Aurius tenderly, pondering the things the king had said to him.

When he reached the grand entrance hall to the castle leading towards the open front doors, a voice called out behind him, "Garrett!"

Turning, he found Serina skipping towards him, smiling brightly.

"How did it go?" Before he could answer, she added, "Oh, you got a new sword?"

"Yeah." He held up the sword in scabbard in his hand. "The king gave it to me." He grinned softly at his own omission, deciding to keep the sword's origin a secret for now.

"So, what do you want to do?"

"Well, what I want to do is just go home." He gazed down the spectacular castle hall towards the daylight streaming in through the doors. "But I have to go back to Dharius's castle. I think I'm the only one who can." A lump formed in his throat even as he said it.

Serina's smile widened and she took his hand. "Whatever you decide, I'll stay with you."

He smiled gratefully at her. "Thanks. It's really meant a lot to me to have you with me." They gazed at each other for a long moment. For the first time in weeks, he felt hopeful.

Suddenly, a voice called from the doorway leading out of the castle, "Garrett!" Turning, he glimpsed Makaidel running toward him, followed by Thorn, Kalista, and Thayer. Strangely, he found himself unsurprised to see them there.

"You idiot," the mage stated as he came up before Jacob. "We were all worried sick."

"Are you okay?" Kalista asked uncertainly.

Jacob nodded slowly. "Yeah, I think so."

"Where'd you go, anyway?" Thayer grinned. "There wasn't anything out there."

Jacob half smiled. "No, there wasn't."

"Hey, you got a new sword?" Makaidel gazed with interest at the sword of Aurius. Jacob simply nodded, holding it out so the mage could look at it.

"So, what should we do now?" Thorn asked.

Jacob sighed. "We have to go to Dharius's castle."

"Are you sure you want to do that?" Kalista asked.

Thayer bumped his elbow against her side. "Don't tell me you're chickening out now."

Kalista huffed at him. "I just wanted to make sure he wanted to!"

"I really don't." Jacob replaced the sword hanging around his hips with the one Lunas had given him. All eyes turned to him. "But I have to. We're the only ones who can stop him." The playful and teasing looks around him faded with his solemnity and they nodded in agreement. Buckling the sword belt around his waist, he handed the blade he stole from Arys off to Makaidel, who was still examining the new weapon. The mage grasped the sword offered him awkwardly as Jacob began walking towards the castle doors.

"Wait a minute," Makaidel stated, looking closer at the sword he now held. "This is…" He glanced up in surprise at Jacob's scarred face. Jacob only looked meaningfully back at Makaidel before turning towards the doors again. Serina fell into step beside him and the others followed as he passed by. He squinted as he stepped out into the sunlight. Soldiers and castle staff wandering around the courtyard cheered and saluted him, but he paid them no mind.

"Where's the ship?"

"Parked west of town." Thayer pointed. As one, they all climbed the stairs down to the courtyard and strolled toward the castle gates. The others spoke as they left the castle grounds and rejoined the town, but Jacob remained silent with his thoughts, Lunas's words echoing in his mind.

"How long will it take to get there?" Thorn asked.

"I don't think we'll be able to land any closer than the outskirts of the forest," Thayer replied. "We should get there by morning if we fly in shifts again." As much as Jacob wished for this final trial to be over with, he was looking forward to a night's rest on his soft bed on the airship. The range of emotions he had felt over the past few hours had left him weary and he felt he still needed more time to think and to accept his duty.

My duty, he thought distractedly as they walked through the town. He had never even been able to decide what his major would be in college, even with his senior year in high school looming only a few months in the future when he had left, and now he had chosen to face someone of incredible power in battle for the fate of a world. *I've really changed a lot since I came here.*

"Come on, people, make room."

Jacob blinked as his attention returned to the world around him. Townspeople lined the streets as they continued toward the airship. Many of them tried to get closer to him, but his companions had surrounded him, and Makaidel pushed his way through the crowd to get them to the airship safely.

"I guess they really missed you."

Jacob turned to Serina, walking beside him, who shrugged with a smile. Raising his gaze, he glanced at Kalista, holding off the crowd of admirers a few paces apart from them. She smiled at him.

"She wouldn't shut up about finding you after you left."

Jacob turned to Thayer, walking on his near side with a grin and keeping the townspeople from getting closer on that side.

"Hey, you're the one who wanted to give up on the whole thing 'cause you said we could never do what Garrett did," Kalista retorted.

"*You* said that?" Jacob raised an eyebrow at Thayer.

Thayer shrugged. "Well, I mean, with the stuff Dharius put you through, I probably wouldn't have lasted as long as you did. The kid couldn't even stand to watch it."

"Hey, neither could you!" Makaidel called back as he shooed away more townspeople trying to get closer to Jacob. "And anyway, we're not a team without you, Garrett."

Jacob blinked, shocked by their words. "You guys really thought that much of me?"

"You came through a lot of things that would have killed a lesser man," Thorn remarked from behind them. "And you're the one who's led us this far. We wouldn't have made it this far without you. None of us were willing to give up on you." Jacob breathed slowly, absorbing their words.

"If nothing else, you're our leader," Thayer added. "Even I have to admit you're a much better person for the position than anyone else."

"We just couldn't go on without you," Kalista stated.

Makaidel turned to face him, walking backwards down the street. "You really knew what you were doing all this time. I'm glad I got to travel with you." The young mage yelped as he backed into a villager coming forward to offer a basket of pears. Turning, he pushed the townsperson back, continuing on through the streets.

Jacob turned as Serina took his arm. She smiled at him. He smiled back, warmed by their words.

"Thanks, everyone. I'm… I'm sorry for the way I treated you guys, and for leaving like I did."

A chorus of apologies and assurances rang around him. He chuckled as they all spoke at once, telling him that he need not apologize after what had happened to him. He glanced around at each of them in turn, truly feeling accepted within the group. Even Thayer smiled appreciatively as his gaze swung past the pilot.

Finally, they reached the edge of town and continued toward the airship.

"Man, those crowds were insane." Makaidel stretched as they crossed the grasses towards where the airship was parked.

"I could've used some of that food those people were offering, though," Kalista stated.

"It's a wonder you're in such good shape, the way you eat," Thorn commented with a grin. Kalista stuck her tongue out at him. Laughter spread around the group as Thayer lowered the gangplank and they climbed onto the ship and up to the upper deck.

"You're staying up here now?" Jacob asked Kalista as the propeller whirred to life.

"Yeah. It's still a little unsettling being on something so far from the ground, but I've gotten used to it." She yelped and clutched the gunwale as the airship lifted off the ground with a gentle lurch. Jacob snickered.

Thayer flipped some switches while the airship rose into the air. "So, are you ready for this?"

Jacob gazed out over the open plains stretching away below them.

"Yeah. Let's go to Dharius's castle."

Earth

31

AS PREDICTED, THEY arrived at the outskirts of the forest the next morning. The group stood silent as the airship lowered to the ground and the whirs of the machinery keeping it aloft faded.

Once the airship powered down, Thayer turned and faced the group, gathered above deck. "Are we ready?" Nods and murmurs traveled around the group.

As ready as I'm ever going to be, Jacob thought, which he wasn't convinced was going to be enough.

"It's now or never," Makaidel stated. "Today we end this."

"Just be careful," Thorn added. "Dharius has three of the element stones. All we have going for us is the Hero's pendant." Jacob shifted uncomfortably as gazes turned in his direction. He glanced at Serina, the only one who knew that his pendant was nothing more than a piece of amber set in metal. She frowned briefly. He grasped the hilt of the sword of Aurius hanging at his side reflexively, trying to find comfort in what it represented. A tingle spread up his arm.

"Let's go."

Jacob led the way out of the airship and across the grass towards the forest. He paused before the twisted trees, gazing uncertainly at them. The forest surrounding Dharius's castle was darker and more sinister than the Serpent Forest surrounding the Alorian ruins. He hadn't noticed it the last time he was here. A chill ran up his spine as he thought back to his escape. It seemed like a dream now, something that couldn't have been real. He was as disturbed by the memory of what had happened to him as he was by his own actions when he escaped Dharius's clutches.

Serina stepped forward. "Are you okay?"

Jacob shivered. "I… I killed people when I escaped."

"This is war," Makaidel replied with a dark look. "If you hadn't killed them, they would have killed you."

Jacob frowned. He had never thought much about the morals of war, but he felt uncomfortable with the realization that he had murdered people. He had taken the lives of people whose only crime had been that they were in his way. He fingered the hilt of his sword, uncertain if he could justify his actions.

"I killed Arys."

Makaidel glared into the forest. "He was a traitor who deserved to die. My only regret is that I didn't get to do it myself." Jacob glanced at him in surprise. "Come on, let's get moving." The others followed after Makaidel as the mage walked into the forest. Jacob hesitated, then continued after them, Serina by his side.

A lump formed in his throat as he thought more about what he had done. He knew, also, that they would be facing more human guards when they arrived at the castle. It had been easy enough to fight when all they had faced so far was mindless monsters. Arys had betrayed them all and Jacob had been ready to kill him at the earth stone altar so long ago, but to know now that he had truly done it, he felt guilty and ashamed. Was it, he wondered as he gazed forward at Makaidel, a difference from living in a more advanced time?

Or is it just another sign that I'm not really cut out to be a hero?

He shook his head, knowing such thoughts would only distract him.

The jagged tree branches wove closely together overhead, casting the forest into premature twilight. The darkness left a chill in the air that crept into their skin from the mist rolling over the ground. The undergrowth was thick between the trees, but the path to the castle was surprisingly clear.

Great, grotesque orlocs leaped out from the depths of the forest to confront them regularly, intelligent and dangerous enough to require them all to fight at once. Though they outnumbered the creatures and the Runic Seals most of them had learned cut their foes deeply, they escaped few battles without injury.

"Maybe he's trying to heal Aurius of the orlocs," Makaidel remarked after they dispatched a particularly strong beast, "but he sure keeps some bad ones close by."

The journey through the forest took several hours. Its length surprised Jacob, and he wondered how long he had stumbled in a daze through the castle and beyond when he escaped. They reluctantly stopped for lunch in the forest, eating a restless meal which was interrupted once by another orloc attack. Despite his best efforts, Jacob's anxiety rose as they continued through the forest. He was nervous and excited about the final confrontation with Dharius, eager and relieved to finally be close to returning home, afraid that he wouldn't be able to do so, and, despite everything, a little disappointed that his adventure would soon be coming to an end.

Finally, in the middle of the afternoon, they reached the end of the path. The trees thinned as they came out from under the canopy of leaves into an overcast sky. They stopped and gazed through the entrance in the outer wall at the immense, spectacular castle rising over the barren plains in the distance. A lump grew in Jacob's throat as a murder of crows flapped into the air from the nearest tower, cawing as they flew over the forest.

"Wow," Kalista uttered.

Thayer shaded his eyes as he gazed at the castle. "Jeez, it's even bigger than the king's castle." Jacob shivered as he thought back once more to his escape from this very place. He had no idea how he had managed to find his way through the castle.

Serina laid a hand on his shoulder. "Are you alright?" Closing his eyes, he inhaled deeply, pushing back the tide of emotions that threatened to overwhelm him. When he opened his eyes again, he saw that everyone was looking at him.

"Let's do this."

The others stood aside as he led the way towards the open gates in the castle walls. No guards could be seen on or around the outer wall, but Jacob knew what would happen. He drew his sword, the polished blade gleaming in the pale daylight.

"Get ready, everyone."

Without question, the others drew their weapons as they approached. Jacob flexed his fingers around the hilt of his sword as he strode forward in the lead. The forest and the castle grounds loomed silently around them, sinister and dark.

Suddenly, a roar split the air as the ground trembled under thunderous footfalls. They all crouched into ready positions, watching the castle gates closely. A huge troll bounded out, swinging a club as large as Jacob. He lunged to the side as the immense weapon slammed down behind him, spraying dirt in all directions and leaving a two-foot indentation in the ground. Spinning around, Jacob slashed at the beast's leg, the others already engaged in battle.

The troll was surprisingly agile for its towering height, turning to face all of them at once and swinging the club in precise movements. Glowing streaks of weapons and spells whirled around Jacob, but they were invisible to him. His gaze remained focused solely on the troll, and with practiced skill, he dodged the creature's attacks and charged in to slash with his sword. No fear, excitement, or concern colored his mind as he fought without hesitation. His movements were calculated and coordinated, never a step out of place.

The troll lasted long against the barrage of attacks it suffered, but eventually, it succumbed to its injuries and toppled over, quaking the ground as its massive body collapsed. A last wave of healing energy washed over the group as everyone relaxed and put away weapons. Jacob wiped the blood off his blade, pleased that the metal was not stained or chipped from the efforts.

Makaidel drew the back of his arm across his forehead with a grin. "That wasn't so bad."

Jacob glanced through the gates. "It's only just beginning." The young mage frowned. Turning, Jacob continued towards the castle, keeping his sword in hand. He knew he was going to need it.

More orlocs assaulted them as they crossed the castle grounds while the clouds overhead slowly darkened. Thunder rumbled across the sky and in the distance, they could see lightning sparking through dark clouds. Jacob's eyes narrowed, the coming storm enhancing the finality of this last challenge.

At last, they reached the castle. As they began to climb the stairs leading up to the main door, a roar rang through the air, paralyzing in its power. They all scattered as a dragon swept in, spewing flames over the wide granite stairs. The battle was even more furious than the encounter with the troll at the outer wall. Jacob darted across the ground, rarely getting the opportunity to attack as the dragon kept to the air, but always ready when an opening presented itself.

The wind picked up as the battle raged on, whipping Jacob's hair and clothes about him as he chased after the dragon. The sky overhead grew dark. The dragon's roars filled the air as the flames it spat lit up the castle grounds. For half an hour they battled the dragon, Makaidel's spells and Thayer's needles streaking through the air as Jacob, Thorn, and Kalista darted across the castle grounds and Serina's healing spells flowed regularly around them.

Finally, a calculated slash from Kalista's sidearm blades tore the dragon's webbed wings, grounding it, and Jacob drove his sword into its chest. He leaped backwards quickly, pulling his sword out as the dragon collapsed to the ground with a final roar. Panting, he wiped his brow while Serina sent another wave of healing energy washing over them. Only then as Jacob gazed down at the fallen creature did he realize what he had just faced. He stood gazing for a while at the body of the dragon, amazed to behold it.

"Garrett?"

Makaidel's curious voice brought Jacob out of his reverie. Shaking his head, he strode after the others into the castle.

As soon as Jacob stepped inside the huge front doors, he found the others already engaged in battle with guards. He raced forward to assist, though a lump grew in his throat at the thought of fighting real people. Soon, he found himself alone in a sword fight with a guard who grinned eagerly at him. Jacob fought as carefully as he had against the troll and dragon, but was reluctant to attack when an opening presented itself. He couldn't help wondering about the guard's past and possibly family, and the circumstances that must have brought the guard to Dharius's service.

"What's the matter?" the guard taunted as he lunged forward. "Afraid to fight back?"

A moment later, Jacob pushed the guard's sword out of the way and swung high. The flat of his blade smashed against the side of the guard's head. As the guard stumbled from the blow, Jacob slammed the hilt of his sword against his head. The guard's sword clattered to the floor as he collapsed, unmoving but still breathing.

Jacob turned to find the others finished with the guards they faced. He cringed at the sight of the guards sprawled across the floor, some with huge, bleeding wounds marking their bodies, eyes eternally open in horror. One lying near Makaidel had been scorched nearly beyond recognition.

"Is he dead?" Makaidel asked, gazing at Jacob.

Jacob swallowed hard, looking away from the bodies lying around them. "Close enough."

The mage's eyes narrowed. "We can't leave them alive or they'll just come back for us later. Finish him off!"

Jacob glared darkly at Makaidel. "He won't bother us anymore. Let's just go." Turning on his heel, he continued through the cavernous entrance hall of the castle, the others following behind.

It wasn't long before another group of guards raced forward to confront them. Jacob fought with the same caution as he had minutes earlier, eventually slamming the pommel of his sword down on the back of the guard's neck and knocking him out. He turned. Thorn had knocked his opponent unconscious and Kalista kicked at her foe's head, doing the same. Thayer shot a series of needles into a guard's chest, hesitating and then relaxing as the guard toppled over.

Behind him, Jacob saw Makaidel's hands glowing as he gazed down at an already unmoving guard. Jacob raced towards him, feeling simultaneously ashamed and angry at the young mage's actions.

"Fire…"

"Stop it!" Jacob cut in, grabbing Makaidel's shoulder. The mage yelped as he stumbled, the spell he had nearly cast fizzling out.

"What are you doing?" Makaidel snapped, wresting his shoulder free.

Annoyance grew to frustration as Jacob gazed at the angry look returned him. “You don’t need to kill them.”

“They’re our enemies! If we don’t…”

“They’re human beings, just like us!” Jacob retorted. “And they’re doing the exact same thing we’re doing, fighting for what they believe in.”

Makaidel’s eyes widened, taken aback by the statement. Shaking his head, his expression turned dark again. “How can you say that after what they did to you?”

“Dharius and Graxis were the ones who tortured me.” Jacob motioned at the guards lying around them. “These guys had nothing to do with that. We don’t have the right to kill them.”

“I’ve got to admit, the kid’s right,” Thayer remarked. “If we leave them alive, they’ll just come back for us later. They would’ve killed us.”

“That doesn’t matter. There’s always another choice. I won’t condone murder!” Turning, he strode furiously ahead.

“You okay?” Thorn asked as Jacob passed by him.

Jacob stopped with a sigh, staring at the floor in front of him. “Enough people have already died because of me. I just don’t want to see any more death.” The group fell silent behind him.

Kalista stepped forward. “I think he’s right. It’s the king’s job to punish lawbreakers.” Jacob turned to glance at her with a weak smile.

“I agree,” Serina added. “It’s not our place to judge them.”

Thayer scoffed. “Sure, the girls agree with you.”

“No, he’s right.” All eyes turned to Thorn. The large man, the most intimidating of them all, raised his head, his muscular arms folded. “If we kill them just because they’re in our way, then we’re no better than them.” He turned a steady gaze to Jacob, who smiled back at him in relief.

“Okay.” Jacob glanced at Makaidel, the mage’s expression now subdued. “I guess you’re right. I’m sorry.” Jacob smiled faintly, relieved that he had gotten through to Makaidel.

Thayer shrugged. “Whatever. Makes no difference to me.”

“We should keep moving,” Thorn stated. Nodding, Jacob turned and continued through the castle.

The castle was enormous, and it took them hours to navigate through it. They crossed rooms filled with elaborate series of switches and traps and faced orlocs more dangerous than any they had yet fought. Thunder occasionally boomed through the walls of the castle from a distance, but when they weren’t engaged in combat, the immense rooms and halls they passed through remained eerily silent.

Late that afternoon, their path led them into the dungeon. Jacob shivered as he stepped into the cool cellar, his back tingling from the memory of his time here. At his request, they searched the other cells, but none of them held any other prisoners. He was relieved to find each cell he opened empty.

"Hey, Garrett!" Kalista called out from a far corner of the dungeon. Jacob ran after her voice and paused as he turned a corner to find her holding a sword in scabbard out to him. His eyes widened. "Isn't this your sword?" Walking forward, he took it, clutching the weapon like a beacon of strength. He never thought he would see it again. As he slid it partially out of the scabbard, he saw that the blade was intact, and the cooled magma that had coated the metal was gone. Glancing around, he also found the Alorian dagger Cassandra Deacon had given him. His heart leapt when he saw his wallet lying beside the dagger. Quickly, he opened it up to check its contents. His student identification card, the one Dharius had been examining when he was first brought to the castle, was inside, in its rightful place. He breathed a sigh of relief.

"What's that?" Makaidel asked as Jacob shifted his sword belt to slip the wallet into his pocket.

"Nothing." Jacob rose and strapped his own sword over his shoulder, keeping the sword of Aurius in his hand. "Let's go." A swell of strength flowed over him at having retrieved his belongings. He felt whole again, the small plastic card like a confirmation of his own identity, something he had lost since he had come to Aurius. He glanced briefly at Serina, who smiled hopefully at him, before strolling back through the corridors of the dungeon.

The afternoon grew late and torches began to light the elegant halls of the castle, though who lit them, they couldn't say. Jacob found himself traveling familiar halls, each one invoking a painful memory in him. He pushed them out of his mind as he continued through the castle, knowing the end was drawing near. His arm felt warm as he grasped the hilt of the sword of Aurius.

Finally, they came to the final hall before the throne room, the golden double doors at the end now shut. A pair of enormous orlocs ran roaring forward to face them as they drew near. Jacob and Kalista spun and slashed, Thorn and Thayer charged and kicked, and Makaidel and Serina slung spells in all directions as the corridor resonated with the sounds of battle. In fifteen minutes' time, they had dispatched the two beasts, their huge, ungainly bodies eternally sprawled across the polished granite floor. Jacob stood straight, his gaze fixed on the doors to the throne room as a last healing spell washed over him.

Now, he knew, the final battle would begin.

32

WITHOUT A WORD, Jacob strode towards the double doors. He paused before them, inhaling deeply. In one motion, he threw them open, the beautiful doors crashing against the walls. The sound echoed through the throne room as he walked inside, followed by the others. His eyes narrowed as he came down the long red carpet leading towards the throne. Graxis sat sideways on the throne, grinning eagerly at them as they approached.

"I knew you'd come. Gluttons for punishment, you are, like moths to a flame."

Thayer made a face. "Oh, you did not just say that."

Graxis slid languidly out of the throne. "Laugh all you like. You're all going to die here." The scorpion-creature fixed his sadistic grin on Jacob as he approached. "Except I might let you live, to see you cry and beg for mercy again." Jacob didn't react to the taunts and stood still as Graxis drew near. "That was terribly *sss*atis*ss*fying." Graxis came within arm's reach of Jacob, flashing pointed teeth at him.

Suddenly, Jacob swung his sword. Graxis leaped backwards just out of range of the beautiful blade, then jumped high overhead into the center of the group. Dark purple sparks flashed over his barbed tail as they all raced forward. Before they could attack, Graxis slammed his tail into the ground, the barb chipping the granite floor and sending a shower of stone fragments into the air. Lightning surged across the floor from his tail. Everyone cried out as the sparks wrapped around their legs, the energy draining and paralyzing them. As one, they collapsed to the floor, lightning crackling over their bodies.

Graxis laughed. "You got lucky last time, *heroes*. I'm far more powerful now than I was last time I faced you. You don't *ss*tand a chance against me."

"You think?"

Graxis turned curiously as Jacob slashed, his sword slicing across the scorpion-creature's shoulder and chest. Graxis screeched, backing away.

Jacob held his sword out, blood sliding down the blade.

"How… how did you…" Graxis attempted, clutching his wound.

"You're too predictable." Jacob's feet tingled from jumping over the sparks of lightning that had shot across the floor. "And you're not the only one who's gotten better!" He charged, swinging his sword again, but Graxis leaped over and behind him. Jacob spun, catching Graxis's tail with his sword and flinging it away. The scorpion-creature lunged, swinging his clawed hands and tail with blinding speed. Jacob backed away as he tried to parry all the attacks, moving beyond instinct as if he could see each blow before it came.

"Too predictable, am I?" Graxis feinted, pushing the sword away, and before Jacob could react, the barbed tail drove into his shoulder. He cried out, the tip of his sword dropping to the floor with a clang as he grasped the wound tightly. Jacob moaned as Graxis stood straight, grinning maliciously at him. Jacob's arm pulsed, stinging and burning at once, and it went numb under the pain.

Graxis chuckled darkly. "My venom is e*ss*pecially dangerou*ss* with the enhancements Lord Dhariu*ss* has made." Reaching forward, he wrapped a hand around Jacob's neck. "I'm going to enjoy watching you writhe to your death." Jacob emitted a strangled sound under the grip. He felt feverish, his entire body burning up, and the sword began to slide out of his fingers.

Desperately, he grasped the sword in his left hand and swung. Graxis released him as he leaped out of range. Jacob staggered, feeling weak. His vision swam as he gazed at the scorpion-creature, who grinned in amusement at him.

Suddenly, Graxis let out a screech as a streak of glowing light shot through the air and into his back. As he spun, Jacob saw needles protruding from the dark flesh, and he struggled to turn. His vision focused as he glanced at Thayer, arm-mounted crossbow held out towards the scorpion-creature. The burning began to fade and he felt more alert. Before he could look around at Serina, Graxis spun, swinging his tail around and slapping Jacob bodily away.

"Magma Rain!"

Jacob rose to see the ground crack beneath Graxis, but the scorpion-creature leaped away before the lava that shot into the air could touch him.

"Fool me once." Graxis grinned darkly as sparks flashed over his tail.

"Jump!" Jacob yelled just as Graxis slammed his tail into the floor, sending lightning shooting over the floor again. Jacob jumped up, lifting his feet as high up as he could manage, just as the others did. Kalista and Makaidel reacted too late, and they yelped as they collapsed again. Thorn rushed in, swinging his arm around, though Graxis jumped free before the blow could land. Jacob raced after Graxis and slashed, but the blade only cut through open air. He could still feel the poison stinging through his arm and shoulder, though he had regained feeling in his sword arm. Putting the pain out of his mind, he continued to attack, struggling to keep up as he had the first time they had faced Graxis.

The scorpion-creature seemed even more careful about avoiding attacks than before, and frequently when he spread the paralyzing lightning spell across the ground, at least one of them was hit. They all darted around the elegant throne room after Graxis, struggling to dodge his attacks.

As the minutes wore on, they seemed to get more tired and their movements slowed before Graxis did. Jacob's arm ached fiercely, wearing down on his own attacks, and some of the others were struck by the barbed tail as well. Though Serina's healing ability was able to keep the venom from spreading, Jacob could tell that the pain hindered them. It annoyed Jacob. He had been in such extraordinary pain the last time he was in this castle and had fought better for it, but he couldn't make himself swing his sword faster or harder now for the way his arm throbbed in response. Graxis never allowed any attack to hit him, even when they seemed to move exactly where the scorpion-creature intended to go.

Jacob thought furiously as he darted across the floor. Nothing they did was working and they had to employ some new strategy if they hoped to defeat Graxis. Surrounding him wouldn't work, as the scorpion-creature could leap far over them in one bound. Attempting to use someone as a feint or decoy had failed to work, as Graxis had been able to dodge both the obvious attack and the subtle one. The only thing that was able to slow him down was to hit him, but they had failed to land a blow since Thayer's needles embedded in his flesh.

Jacob skidded to a stop as he came up beside Thayer, who was busily reloading his crossbow with needles.

"This isn't working, you know." Thayer watched Graxis carefully as he reloaded his weapon without looking at it.

"I noticed," Jacob replied flatly, panting from exertion. "Do you have any ideas?"

"I can cover a good area with a rapid-fire shot, but I'm just as likely to hit one of you guys as I am to hit him."

"Get ready to do that." Jacob turned and ran towards Thorn. "I'll try to get you a clear shot. And see if Makaidel can do the same thing!" Thayer cocked his crossbow as Jacob darted across the floor.

"Tell me you have an idea." Thorn wiped at his brow, sweat glistening over his body.

"I hope so." Jacob's voice betrayed his own uncertainty. "Thayer's going to try a wide-range shot. Try to get out of the way on my signal without letting Graxis know." Thorn nodded and raced towards the scorpion-creature as Jacob made his way over to Kalista.

"I can't keep this up much longer," Kalista stated breathily as Jacob drew near. Jacob repeated his plan to her, hoping it would work. His chest burned with every breath, he was so worn out from the battle. Nodding, she ran off around the other side of Graxis, glowing weapons held at the ready.

At a glance and a quick nod to Thorn, Jacob charged, swinging his sword around with the weight mostly in his left hand. Thorn barreled forward on Graxis's other side, the two of them converging on the scorpion-creature's location. As they drew near, Graxis leaped straight up into the air. Jacob stumbled as he tried not to slash Thorn and ended up slamming his shoulder into the large man. Before he could recover his balance, Graxis spun in his fall, slapping them both away with his huge tail.

As he fell, Jacob saw a line of glowing needles streak across the room above him. Graxis snarled as three of them embedded into his collarbone. In that moment, a tongue of flames shot out from Makaidel's hands with a flare of light from Serina's staff, both blasting Graxis just after the needles struck. Before the light from the spells had even faded, Kalista's grappling hook sailed through the air and wrapped around Graxis, pulling him off his feet. He grunted as he hit the floor hard on his side.

Graxis struggled against the rope holding him, hissing as Thorn leaned on his tail and pinned it to the ground. By the time Graxis opened his eyes, Jacob had his sword to the scorpion-creature's throat. Thayer and Kalista stood behind him, weapons held out, while Makaidel and Serina stood to Graxis's other side, spells glowing in their hands.

Graxis's eyes narrowed as he scoffed at them. "You don't have the guts to kill me. I *ss*aw what you did with the guard*ss*."

"The guards didn't do anything wrong," Jacob replied steadily. "Dharius duped them, making them believe they'd be spared. You've caused nothing but pain your entire life." He stepped forward, glaring down at the scorpion-creature through his scars. "Besides, even if this is a sin, no hell is worse than what you did to me." Drawing back, he ran his sword through Graxis until the blade clanged against the floor. The scorpion-creature let out a wheezing hiss, his eyes bulging. The sight was vindicating to Jacob, but he felt more relief simply that it was over. As he pulled his sword out, Graxis fell back, wide eyes staring unseeing at the ceiling.

A collective sigh spread around the group as they relaxed. Jacob's arm trembled and he felt dizzy. A healing spell washed over them. Jacob groaned, clutching his shoulder.

"The poison." Kalista, Thayer, and Makaidel echoed him. Serina strode quickly over to Jacob and put her hand to his shoulder. He cringed, moaning, as he felt the invasive fluid seep back through his body and out the wound where it had entered. Pins and needles shot up his arm, but before the sensation fully spread, he felt the flesh of his shoulder close up and the pain abated. He panted in relief as Serina drew the venom and healed the wounds of the others.

Makaidel gazed down at the body of Graxis. "We did it."

Kalista carefully unwound her rope and grappling hook and put it away. "Yeah."

Thorn flexed his fingers after Serina healed his wounds. "Now there's just one battle left."

Jacob gazed down to the far end of the throne room, where a small door led into a round chamber with a red marble floor. "Dharius."

THEIR FOOTSTEPS ECHOED around the throne room as Jacob led the way to the door at the back, centered beneath two pennants. None of them spoke a word as they crossed the elegant hall, flashes of lightning outside glowing through the stained glass windows lining the room. Jacob flexed his fingers around the sword of Aurius, pushing down the flood of emotions that threatened to drown him at the thought of facing Dharius in the final battle. He allowed himself no uncertainty or hesitation. In this moment, there was nothing but resolve.

Without slowing his pace, Jacob opened the door and stepped inside. The gilded pillars ringing the chamber reflected against the polished red marble floor, both shining from the occasional lightning bolt visible through the windows high above. Torches circled the pillars, sending flickering shadows dancing across the glossy floor. Jacob stepped forward with eyes for none of it.

In the center of the chamber, cloak streaming over the floor beneath long, dark hair, stood Dharius. His smooth laugh rippled across the air as the others stepped in and spread out beside Jacob.

"I must admit, I'm glad you defeated Graxis." Dharius turned, smiling darkly at Jacob as his hair and cloak swirled around him. "It would have been a shame to miss this final chance to face you myself." The talismans of water, fire, and earth hung around his neck, the teardrop-shaped stones glinting in a flash of lightning.

"Graxis is dead," Makaidel stated.

Dharius looked amused. "Of course he is, otherwise you wouldn't be here."

Serina shook her head. "Don't you care at all?"

Dharius chuckled. "Dear, sweet Serina, don't tell me you care about him now."

"I thought he was your most important servant!" Kalista exclaimed. "Doesn't it bother you at all that he's dead?"

The Alorian turned his amused gaze to her. "Graxis was useful. But it had to happen sooner or later."

Thorn shook his head as Thayer made a disgusted noise. "That's cold."

"You're despicable," Makaidel growled. "A real leader cares about everyone under his command. You have no right to rule over anyone."

Dharius laughed softly. "I don't care who rules, I just want to see this land healed from the poisonous influence of you humans and your filthy magic. Besides…" He turned his dark grin to Jacob, silently and stoically watching the exchange. "*Garrett* was right. Graxis simply fought for what he believed in. He was always prepared to die for our mission."

Dharius drew his elegant Alorian sword as a pall of darkness fell over his free hand. "Now it's your turn." The group scattered as Dharius flung his arm around and the shadowy spell shot across the room. The spell exploded silently against the far wall, the room trembling with its force as thunder cracked outside.

Soon, the chamber filled with the voices of Kalista, Thorn, and Thayer yelping in fear or effort as they raced toward Dharius, Makaidel shouting his spells as he slung them at the Alorian, and Serina calling warnings to everyone as she darted about casting healing spells. Unlike Graxis, Dharius stayed in the center of the room, swinging his sword around to face those who approached and fending off the spells and projectiles shot towards him with his own magic. The room swirled with energy, streaks of glowing weapons and spells spiraling around Dharius as his own dark spells cut through the frenzy surrounding him. The Alorian moved fluidly, a satisfied and perfectly calm smile on his face as he spun to face everyone as they approached.

Jacob raced toward Dharius's cloaked back, bringing his sword down with all his strength. Before the sword hit its target, however, the Alorian spun, bringing up his own sword to block the blow. Sparks flashed as the beautiful blades clashed, but Dharius's arm held. He paused just long enough to grin at Jacob before flinging him away with a quick swipe of his sword and turning to redirect Thorn's incoming punch.

No trace of concern or struggle appeared on Dharius's smooth and elegant face as he spun to face every attack, every movement practiced and deliberate, like a dance. The chamber roared with magic and movement as Jacob charged the Alorian over and over again, managing to avoid injury but failing to cause any. Once again, his companions were invisible to him as he focused solely on Dharius.

The battle was furious, yet seemed coordinated with the way they were unable to hurt the Alorian. Magic spells flashed across the air towards and away from the center of the room as glowing weapons swirled and circled, the spacious chamber seeming crowded with bodies. Jacob was so engrossed in his own movements and the fluid way Dharius moved that it took him a while to realize no blows were landing on their opponent. Dharius moved slower than Graxis had, but each action flowed into the next as if the entire battle was choreographed. He casually parried, blocked, or guided every attack away from him, his expression perfectly serene and unconcerned. Glares of rage, determination, or focus marked the faces of Jacob's companions as they pressed their attacks relentlessly. White flashes of healing spells glowed against the battlers frequently. Makaidel's voice rose in pitch from running around the room constantly.

Again and again Jacob charged the Alorian, subconsciously studying Dharius's moves and slowly changing the way his blows struck. Carefully, attack by parried attack, he guided Dharius's movements to expect a certain swing from him. He kept his expression neutral, and by the look of the same knowing grin Dharius gave him each time they caught each other's gaze, the Alorian didn't suspect anything sinister of Jacob's swings.

Thunder roared outside, the glow of lightning filling the chamber at regular intervals. Still the battle raged, bodies rushing in a circle around Dharius. Jacob consistently ached from a swipe of the Alorian sword or a dark spell slicing through his clothes and skin before Serina's healing spell reached him. He panted from exertion, but wouldn't allow weariness or pain to slow his movements. There was no turning back and no second chance for this confrontation. Months of travel, adventure, and hard-fought battles had brought him to this moment, and it was the only one he had to accomplish his mission and save Aurius. Nothing colored his mind except determination to win.

Turning, he charged Dharius again and swung just as he had at least a dozen times previous. Dharius, expecting the blow, raised his sword to parry without, it seemed, even thinking about it. Jacob was counting on that. He angled his sword just enough to glance off the Alorian's blade. Before Dharius could adjust his stance, Jacob turned his sword back around and slashed. His sword dipped just below Dharius's blade, tearing into the exposed cloth beneath his black enameled breastplate and slicing a quick, slender cut in the Alorian's side.

Dharius yelped as he stumbled back from the blow, struggling to fend off Kalista's attack coming in from his other side and the surge of needles that streaked across the air from Thayer's crossbow at once. Jacob charged forward to swing again as the attacks all drew in upon the Alorian at once. Abandoning the smile for the first time, Dharius pointed his sword downward and slammed it into the ground. As the attacks all began to converge on Dharius, a blast of magic roared out from where his sword tip struck the marble floor. The surge of energy disintegrated Thayer's needles and sent Jacob and Kalista flying.

By the time Jacob rose to his feet, he found Kalista already leaping towards Dharius again. The Alorian lunged uncertainly away from her attack as a green glow lit up before his outstretched free hand, blasting away the spells and needles that flew towards him. Jacob allowed himself an eager smile at the sight. As he had hoped, his minor wound had thrown off Dharius's rhythm, and now the Alorian struggled to fend off all the attacks that closed in on him.

Jacob raced forward and swung, now grinning at Dharius the same way the Alorian had looked at him earlier as their swords locked. Dharius swung furiously, his sword slashing across Jacob's collarbone and chest. Jacob yelped as he stumbled back.

Then, a streak of glowing white energy ripped across the air, blasting against Dharius. The Alorian cried out as he staggered back, turning a dark gaze to Serina. Ignoring his own pain, Jacob raced forward, swinging his sword again. Dharius managed to parry his blows and send him reeling backwards. Before Jacob could advance again, Dharius lifted his sword and slammed it down onto the floor again. The chamber lit up from the glow of the huge blast that emanated from his sword tip, flinging Jacob clear across the room to slam against the wall. His cry of pain echoed that of all the others.

As they dropped to the ground, they all crouched into ready positions, but hesitated. Dharius stood panting at the center of the room, shoulders hunched, but he grinned beneath the shadows of his long hair.

"Impressive," he remarked smoothly. "You are giving me the fight I was hoping for." He drew an armoured finger across his chest. "But the real fight has yet to begin." The talismans hanging around his neck emitted soft lights, their blue, green, and red glow reflecting off his armour. Out of the corner of his eye, Jacob saw his companions tense.

Dharius stood straight, lifting his sword off the floor. Leaning his head back, he thrust the blade into the air. In a flash of light, the chamber disappeared and they found themselves on the roof of the castle. Jacob felt his back twitch uncomfortably as he realized he was atop the very tower where he had been tortured before. He forced the thought out of his mind as the others gazed around and murmured uncertainly.

Dark clouds roiled overhead, wind buffeting them and snapping the pennants hanging high atop the castle. Lightning sparked between the clouds, lighting up the top of the castle at frequent, irregular intervals.

"The cleansing begins tonight."

Their eyes returned to Dharius. He stood calmly and confidently several paces away, sword tip lying against the floor in much the same way, Jacob realized, as the captain of the guard at Dekaal castle, where he had first learned to truly use a sword. The talismans around Dharius's neck glowed brilliantly, the blue, green, and red lights so bright they nearly hurt to look upon.

"We'll never let you do that!" Makaidel yelled back over the roar of wind and thunder around him.

A corner of Dharius's mouth moved up. "You think you can defeat me?"

"We did get the better of you downstairs," Thayer answered slyly.

Dharius lowered his head as his grin widened. "You fought fairly well, six against one. But are you so powerful alone?" Dharius raised his free hand to the sky, palm up. They all glanced upward as a roar rumbled with the thunder from a distance.

Suddenly, enormous shadows seemed to materialize out of the night sky directly above Dharius. Jacob dove to the side as he caught a glimpse of huge claws approaching not ten feet from him. He somersaulted and came up on one knee as screams sounded around him.

"Garrett!"

He glanced over his shoulder to see Serina being carried away in the claws of a dark-scaled dragon, reaching her hand out to him. His gaze lingered only a moment before he turned back to face Dharius. There was nothing he could do for his companions now. He stood, now the only one remaining on the roof of the castle with the Alorian.

"And now it's back to just us, Jacob Marshall." Dharius grinned in amusement at him. Jacob narrowed his eyes at the casual use of his real name. "Just like old times." Jacob began to circle the edge of the rooftop as Dharius did the same. "I'm so glad we got to meet again. You've been quite the thorn in my side these last months. It will be terribly satisfying to finally finish you off. And once I get the final element stone, the rest of those pathetic humans will fall in your wake."

Jacob betrayed his own surprise with a twitch and a slight enlarging of his eyes. "You haven't found the last element stone yet?"

"It's only a matter of time." Dharius sounded confident as he continued circling the rooftop in the same direction as Jacob.

Jacob grinned darkly. "No, it's not. The element stone of air is right here." Reaching into his shirt, he pulled out his own pendant and held it up. A flash of lightning illuminated the familiar talisman rendered crudely on its chain.

Dharius's eyes widened as he caught a glimpse of the amber teardrop. He stopped in his tracks. "You've had it all this time? How…"

Jacob laughed aloud, stopping across the platform. "It doesn't matter! The talisman came into Aurius with me. I made this!"

Dharius's head lowered, the smile gone from his face. He charged so quickly across the roof that Jacob barely had time to raise his sword to stop the Alorian's from falling on him.

He laughed again as his arms trembled to hold off Dharius's sword. "Go ahead, take it. There's nothing magical about it. Don't you get it? There *is* no fourth element stone!"

Dharius's eyes narrowed in a dark glare as he gazed across the locked swords at Jacob. He shoved Jacob away, their swords clanging as they struck together again. Jacob struggled as he took a step backwards from the force of Dharius's attack, the edge of the roof looming only a few paces away.

Dharius's expression calmed and the casual smile returned to his face. "I don't know how you came to Aurius or what it means, but your appearance can't have removed the real air talisman from the world. It's still here somewhere. And in any case, it'll be much easier to search for it once you're dead."

Jacob spun his sword, managing to break away from Dharius's blade and step to the side, the platform stretching away beside him. "You really think you're going to win?"

Dharius let out a deep, loud, sinister laugh. "You think you're going to defeat me? I have powers beyond your greatest imagination. You don't stand a chance against me!" Jacob threw himself aside as Dharius swung his free arm around, a dark spell shooting off into the night sky where he had just stood. By the time he recovered from his escape, Dharius was upon him. Jacob struggled to parry the blindingly fast swings of the Alorian sword. After several clashes he barely blocked, Dharius slapped Jacob's sword off to the side, causing him to stumble for balance. As he did so, Dharius slashed again, his sword tearing open Jacob's ribs. Jacob yelped and clutched the wound, then turned and ran as Dharius approached again.

Dark spells slammed the ground around Jacob as he fled, sending stone fragments flying into the air. A blast hit his shoulder, spinning him around. As he turned to face Dharius again, he found the talismans around the Alorian's neck lighting up the night, and a huge, spiraling streak of red, green, and blue rushed towards him. Unable to flee in time, he raised his sword in instinctive defense with a yelp.

He stepped back a pace as a force pressed in on him, a great light flaring before him. He opened his eyes curiously after the blow he had expected didn't come. As the light from the spell Dharius cast faded, Jacob gasped, and even the Alorian fell still in wonder.

Jacob's sword glowed brilliantly in his hands, spreading warmth and energy through him. His eyes widened as his gaze traveled down from the blade. Inside the hilt at the junction of grip and crossguard, visible through the metal like a gauzy curtain, he could make out a yellow teardrop centered in a triangular symbol.

"The talisman," Dharius uttered in wonder. "You do have it." He laughed as he charged across the roof towards Jacob. "You brought it right to me!" Jacob raised the sword of Aurius to parry Dharius's sword, but the attack was so sudden that a few swipes later, he stumbled and fell onto his back at the edge of the roof. Dharius bore down on him, slamming his sword against Jacob's blade inches above his chest. The Alorian crouched over him, pressing down on the locked swords with all of his weight.

Dharius chuckled as his face drew nearer to Jacob's, his silver eyes alight from the glow of Jacob's sword. "This is perfect. The four element stones are here, together, and as soon as I get rid of you, I can heal the world." Dharius laughed as Jacob gazed uneasily around to find eight stories of open air beneath his head. His arms trembled as the Alorian sword pressed ever closer to his throat, the weight too much for Jacob to hold back. Jacob's breath sped as he tried to think of a way to escape, hoping the sword of Aurius could save him even as it dropped to within an inch of his body.

Desperately, Jacob moved his leg and kicked up. Dharius's eyes bulged as Jacob's boot struck between his legs. The Alorian's grip slackened immediately as he doubled over the blow. Reaching up, Jacob shoved Dharius to the side, using the moment while the Alorian fell over to scramble to his feet. As he spun to face Dharius again, he found the Alorian still hunched over from the attack, though he gazed at Jacob as he clutched his thigh.

Dharius glared at him with the deepest, most unbridled hatred Jacob had ever seen. "That," he snarled, "was low." Jacob shifted, a little ashamed of having to resort to such a measure. He waited, holding his sword out as Dharius cringed and straightened.

"Fine." Dharius raised his sword to point it straight out at Jacob. "If that's the way you're going to fight, then no holding back." His eyes narrowed. "And no mercy." Swinging his sword around, he charged, Jacob mirroring him.

They met at the center of the platform with a clash that rang over the roar of wind and thunder around them. Dharius's sword flew in a blur and Jacob's glowing blade spun and swirled to meet it again and again. Sparks flashed as their swords crashed together, a small flicker of orange between the yellow-white glow of Jacob's sword and the light from the talismans around Dharius's neck.

Jacob felt nothing as he fought, his sword seeming to move of its own will. He stopped every swing of the sword with incredible speed and moved clear of every punch, kick, and magic spell Dharius slung at him. His perception was impeccable, acting in the split-second before every blow landed to avoid it. Guided by the sword, they were perfectly matched.

Jacob flinched but didn't slow his movements as a slash from Dharius's sword cut his cheek. Dharius reacted similarly when Jacob's sword broke through his defenses and struck his unprotected upper arm. Jacob twisted as he stumbled from a spell that blasted against his shoulder to meet Dharius's next sword swipe. Dharius somersaulted across the ground when Jacob kicked his foot out from beneath him and came up to parry Jacob's next swing.

On and on they fought as the storm raged around them, alone on the castle roof. Neither of them ever seemed to take the advantage over the other, and with all his concentration on Jacob, Dharius didn't allow him to guide his movements in a way that left him vulnerable. They each suffered more wounds, none of them deep enough to cause serious harm or slow them.

After a lengthy spar, they separated, panting as they gazed at each other with swords out. Jacob's long hair whipped around his head and Dharius's longer hair and cloak billowed in the wind.

"You wouldn't stand a chance against me if you didn't have that sword," Dharius remarked.

"Probably," Jacob replied, "but you still have to fight us both."

Dharius's expression softened. "You've seen the monstrosities borne of the humans' dirty magic. Why do you fight so hard to protect them?"

"Because…" Jacob stalled, suddenly unable to put into words why he was so intent on defeating Dharius. He shook his head. "Because there's always another choice. You don't have to kill people to make change happen."

Dharius's eyes narrowed. "You think the humans would change just because I told them to? They love their filthy magic. They've created an entire caste based on it. They would never give it up even if they believed that the orlocs were caused by them."

"I'm not saying what they're doing isn't wrong. But killing everyone isn't the answer, either. If you just tried to make them listen…"

"Listen!" Dharius snapped. "My people tried for years, for decades, to get them to change their ways, but the people in power wouldn't even give them the time of day. Humans are too set in their ways, no matter what the consequences of their actions are. Their magic is good for them, why should they care what harm it's causing anyone else?"

"If they knew they were the cause of the orlocs and suffering, they'd be willing to change! You just haven't given them a chance!" Jacob felt his heart pump strength through his body with his words. He had taken on the role of the hero because it was his duty, but now that he said it aloud, he truly felt that he was fighting for something he believed in. He clenched his fingers around the hilt of his sword.

Dharius lowered his head, glaring calmly out from the strands of hair blowing over his face. "They had their chance. They chose to do nothing. The rest of my people left, abandoned the home that the humans had ruined. Just because I refused to give up my home, I've been left alone here in the wasteland the humans have made of Aurius for nearly a century. I won't let them drive me out of my homeland and I won't let them destroy it any longer. And I'll let nothing get in my way!"

"And I won't let you kill people for any reason!" Raising their swords over their heads, they charged at each other again. Thunder crackled overhead as their swords crashed together. Jacob's wounds twinged at the movement and his muscles burned from weariness, but he set it out of his mind as he continued fighting Dharius.

Some minutes later, while Jacob and Dharius still fought fiercely, a flash of light flared at the far end of the platform from where they grappled.

"Garrett!" Thorn shouted across the rooftop.

"Stay back!" Jacob called back as he spun and slashed, more cuts bleeding all over his body. He knew in that moment that this battle was his, and it was his duty alone to defeat Dharius.

Moments later, Kalista's voice rang across the air as she reappeared. Jacob saw Thorn holding her back over Dharius's shoulder as he continued to fight. He only faintly noticed Makaidel return to the rooftop, followed by Thayer. Whether they were injured from their battles with the shadowy dragons, he couldn't spare enough attention to tell.

"Garrett! We can help you!" Kalista called out, sidearm blades held at the ready. Jacob didn't answer her, too focused on his battle with Dharius to respond.

"I must say," Dharius stated with a grin as their swords clashed together, "despite your earlier blow, I admire your honor, fighting me alone." With a fierce blow, he shoved Jacob backwards a few paces. "But I still have the upper hand." He raised his free hand into the air. Before Jacob could rush forward, he saw one of the shadowy dragons appear in the air beside Dharius, clutching a light-clad body. His eyes widened as gasps and exclamations sounded behind him.

"Serina!" Jacob cried. She let out a cry as the dragon squeezed its talons around her, her staff dropping to the rooftop.

Suddenly, Dharius charged. Jacob barely managed to block the blows that rained down on him. The Alorian pressed forward so hard that Jacob lost his balance and fell onto his back. He gasped as he looked up, his sword still in hand, though his arm had fallen to the side. Dharius held his sword to Jacob's neck, the blade hovering steadily just in front of his throat.

"Stay back!" Dharius yelled as Jacob heard footsteps begin to approach behind him. "Or I'll kill them both." The footsteps halted, still several paces away.

"She's your own daughter!" Makaidel yelled.

"And she chose her side in this battle." Dharius lowered his head to grin darkly at Jacob. "Now, give me the sword."

Jacob hesitated, gazing uncomfortably between Dharius, towering over him, and Serina, suspended ten feet above the rooftop by the shadow dragon. He had never felt more resolve to defeat Dharius, yet in that moment, he had never felt more uncertain about the consequences of doing so.

Holding his hand out towards the dragon, Dharius clenched his fingers into a fist. Serina cried out as the dragon squeezed her tighter.

"No!" Jacob pushed himself up on his elbows, but Dharius's blade against his neck shoved him back down. Still Serina shrieked, struggling weakly against the dragon's claws. "Alright! Here." Hand shaking, he lifted the sword off the ground with a slack grip, holding it towards Dharius. Leaning forward, Dharius snatched the sword out of his hand. He laughed as he drew back, holding the sword of Aurius up triumphantly. The dragon faded and disappeared, dropping Serina to the roof.

Stumbling to his feet, Jacob ran over to her. He gently lifted her head and shoulders as she coughed.

"Garrett," she uttered weakly. "I'm sorry…"

"Are you okay?" He brushed her hair out of her face. She nodded as she sat up.

"Yes!" Dharius shouted. Jacob and Serina turned to gaze at him. He held the sword out in front of him, the light it emitted illuminating the top of the castle. "Finally, I have the last element stone!"

"What?" Makaidel screamed from the other side of the platform.

"The sword!" Kalista shouted, pointing at the blade Dharius held out. In the blinding glow of the sword, Jacob could see the talisman hidden within its hilt, shining brilliantly. Thayer swore.

"Now, the cleansing can begin!" Clouds of glowing magic spiraled around Dharius, spreading out in a huge blast that covered the entire rooftop. Jacob yelped and threw his arms up in front of his face as the rest of the group screamed.

Jacob lowered his arms when he realized the blow didn't strike. The misty magic seemed repelled by a green-white bubble of energy before him. He snapped his gaze to Serina, who held an arm before her face protectively but gazed forward in concentration.

Jacob glanced at Dharius, now glowing with blinding light as flashes of blue, green, red, and yellow flared around him. His laughter rang across the rooftop over the roar of the magic he conjured.

"Congratulations, heroes. You get to watch the world healed by my hand. Not that you'll be alive to see the results." His laughter rose, seeming to ring across the castle and all of Aurius into the night sky.

Jacob glanced through the bubble of energy protecting him to the rest of the group. They crouched on the floor, clearly unable to move. He looked back at Serina, still sitting beside him.

"Serina!" he yelled over the roar of magic and thunder. "Can you get me through to him?"

Turning to face him, she nodded. "I think so."

Jacob stood, facing Dharius through the swirls of magic, glowing brighter now than before. The misty clouds spread out over the entire castle, whipping around Dharius like a tornado. Across the platform, Makaidel collapsed. Jacob stepped forward, struggling through the maelstrom. His clothes and hair whipped around him, but as he stepped toward the edge of the bubble of protection, it spread forward. He glanced back at Serina. She stood now, staff in hands as she gazed in deepest focus at him. The bubble closed in behind him as the one around her opened up. He nodded to her.

Facing Dharius again, he drew his own sword over his shoulder, the one he had brought as a prop into Aurius. Summoning every ounce of strength he had, he moved his feet forward into the heart of the storm. He stood only twenty feet from Dharius, but each step took greater strength than he had ever put into anything he had done. Slowly, he drew near. Dharius held up the sword of Aurius, eyes closed as he commanded the magic that swirled from the sword and the talismans around his neck, oblivious to Jacob's approach. The magic lit up the Alorian's form, his body seeming to glow from within and bathing him in white light.

Jacob brandished his sword as he came within a few paces of the magic that ripped at the bubble of energy surrounding him. Tendrils of energy broke through the protective barrier, slicing with scorching power against Jacob's skin. The bubble shrank as he drew closer to Dharius. He could almost feel Serina's desperate struggle to keep the protection around him. Still he pressed forward, even as more magic ripped at his body the closer he came. He groaned, barely able to remain standing and his feet feeling like he was sloshing through tar. Dharius became painful to look upon, lit as he was like an angel. Jacob swallowed, feeling his nose bleed as he came within arm's reach of the Alorian.

"Hey, Dharius!" he yelled.

Slowly, the Alorian opened his eyes and turned, clearly confused by

Jacob's approach.

"That's my sword!"

In a feat of strength he would never be able to understand, Jacob pushed forward and thrust his sword up under Dharius's breastplate. The Alorian's eyes widened as he bent over the sword buried in his flesh, his arms falling to shoulder height. Jacob struggled to keep on his feet in front of Dharius, holding his sword in the Alorian's body.

The magic swirling around them snapped and billowed, conflicting waves of energy crackling as they crashed against each other. The maelstrom grew even stronger and Jacob felt the bubble around him fading. Reaching out, he grasped the sword of Aurius still in Dharius's hand. A surge of energy like a lightning bolt crackled up his arm. His arm shook as he tried to keep his grip on both swords while magical energy ripped at his body in every direction. He yelled, overwhelmed by magic.

Without knowing what he was doing, he pulled the sword of Aurius out of Dharius's hand and swung it across the Alorian's chest, slashing through the chains around his neck. Dharius fell over backwards as the talismans sailed to the ground, clanging audibly over the deafening roar of magic. Jacob's own sword slid free of Dharius's body as the Alorian collapsed to the ground before him, eyes closed.

Jacob groaned as energy surged over him, seeming to bore through every inch of his body and tear him apart. The teardrops of emerald, sapphire, and ruby shattered in their talismans at his feet, sending sparks of green, blue, and red flying in every direction. Jacob leaned back and screamed, crossing his sword and the sword of Aurius above him as the rush of energy completely overtook him. He felt his very life force flow out of his body, through the sword of Aurius, and up into the air high overhead. As it did, a streak of light and warmth spiraled around him, a familiar sensation mixing with the incredible power surging over him.

A column of light shot up into the air above the roof. It gathered high up in the sky, an incredible flare of magic energy that lit up the castle and forest surrounding it like daylight. Monstrous shrieks rose up from the forest as the beasts that inhabited it evaporated under the light. The sphere of light that burned away the storm clouds around it trembled as it hovered, until finally, it burst in a wave of energy that shot over all of Aurius. Jacob collapsed on the rooftop, swords clattering to either side as he fell limply to the cool stone.

34

"GARRETT! GARRETT!"

Jacob opened his eyes slowly, his vision blurring as he gazed at the dark rooftop beside his head. Leather-clad feet raced by his head and crouched beside him. He struggled to turn his head as Kalista lifted his shoulders off the ground. On his other side, he felt the large hands of Thorn help push him to a sitting position. Thayer knelt before him.

"Are you alright?" Kalista exclaimed worriedly, digging through a pouch on her belt for a potion.

"Yeah." He laid a hand on hers to stop her. He blinked, regaining his senses. The magic on the rooftop was gone and all was dark and still, a stark and oppressing calmness after the chaos that had covered the scene moments before. Even the storm had abated, leaving the castle in silence. The energy that had consumed him was gone, and he felt only the wounds he had received in the swordfight with Dharius. He nodded as Kalista gazed at him worriedly. "Yeah, I'm okay."

Suddenly, the group around him drew in a collective gasp as the castle rumbled beneath them.

"Whoa!" Thayer exclaimed.

"The castle's going to collapse." Leaning forward, Jacob pushed himself to his feet with the help of the swords beside him. He glanced off to the side. Serina lay where she had fallen from the dragon's talons, propped up by her arms with her head hanging wearily between them. Makaidel crouched beside her.

"We have to get out of here!" Jacob raced toward Serina, ignoring the body of Dharius and the talismans lying at his feet, fragments of jewels crunching under his boots as he darted forward. Jacob sheathed his sword over his shoulder and the sword of Aurius at his side as he knelt beside Serina.

"Come on!" Thayer yelled behind him, and he, Thorn, and Kalista raced toward the trapdoor leading into the castle.

Jacob laid a hand on Serina's shoulder. "Are you okay?" She nodded weakly, though her arms trembled. Jacob glanced up at Makaidel. "Go on!" Nodding quickly, the mage turned and ran after the others. Jacob grasped Serina's shoulders and helped her to her feet. A large chunk of the castle broke off behind him, tumbling eight stories down to the ground. Taking Serina's hand, Jacob ran forward. She seemed weary, but she managed to stay on her feet and keep up with him.

The castle crackled and rumbled around them as they climbed down the winding staircase, the rest of the group already half a turn below them. As they came near the bottom of the staircase, Jacob saw Makaidel, Thorn, Kalista, and Thayer paused at the doorway, gazing uncertainly at the room outside.

"Which way do we go?" Thayer shouted over the crumbling of the castle.

"To the right!" Jacob yelled as he and Serina reached the last few stairs. Without question, the group turned and ran into the adjoining hall to the right. Jacob and Serina raced after them. Jacob recognized the hall they entered from the torture he suffered at the castle a few weeks ago, but that dark time was far from his mind as they fled. The guards still scattered through the halls ignored them as they struggled to escape as well. Great blocks of polished granite crashed into the floor ahead and behind them and pillars shattered and toppled over, making the journey treacherous.

They raced through many of the rooms they had crossed to come into the castle, the traps and puzzles they had overcome now solved and allowing them easy passage. They ran through various rooms without abandon, concerned only with escaping the castle before it collapsed on top of them.

Suddenly, Jacob skidded to a stop as he came into a room he had entirely forgotten about. To cross this room on their way in, they had to time their passage across a series of raised metal platforms above what seemed to be a bottomless pit. The platforms had lifted and dropped at regular intervals, allowing them little chance for mistake before they would plummet into the darkness below. The timing only just allowed them to cross one way, without being able to return.

This was the room where Kalista would meet her death.

Jacob snapped his gaze to the side, where the rogue struggled to hold down a lever at a console that was keeping the metal platforms straight up. The rest of the group had already crossed most of the room to the stable floor on the far side and shouted encouragements for Jacob and Serina to continue.

"Go on!" Kalista exclaimed. "I'll keep it up for you!" Jacob laid a hand on Serina's back, urging her ahead, but hung back rather than flee with her. He strode over to Kalista. A hint of fear touched her features that contorted as she struggled to keep the lever down. Jacob grabbed her upper arm. She turned to him with a gasp.

"What are you…"

"My ass you're staying behind to die." Reaching into his boot, he drew the ancient Alorian dagger Morrie Deacon had given him and shoved it into the groove behind the lever, wedging it into place. Sparks shot up around the dagger and the machinery groaned at the effort. Grabbing her hand, Jacob raced forward across the platforms.

Cables snapped with warbling sounds as they darted over the platforms. The whole room trembled. Jacob leapt from platform to platform as the metal plates began to fall around him. He felt no fear as the floor gave out in parts beneath him and simply continued pulling Kalista along over the pit. The rest of the group watched with bated breath as they bounded across the room, the floor falling away faster and faster as they continued.

The last square platform against the edge of solid floor on the far side of the room had already given out by the time they reached the platform just before that. As Jacob stepped onto the second platform, he felt it sink and begin to fall beneath his feet. He pushed out with all his strength, pulling Kalista along behind him. He stretched his arm out as far as he could reach, reminded of the cliff in the mountains where they had first met her.

His fingers touched solid stone. He clutched the edge as tightly as he could as he fell. Kalista's weight pulled down on his arm as he fell against the side of the stone platform. Kalista yelped as she slid down, almost slipping out of Jacob's grip. He tightened his fingers around her hand, even as she moaned from the painful grip.

"No… friggin'… way!" Arm trembling from effort, he struggled to pull Kalista up. He bent his leg and pushed her up with his knee as Kalista's hands touched the floor he hung onto. Thayer and Makaidel swiftly pulled her up onto the solid stone. Jacob felt his fingers begin to slip off the floor. Throwing up his now free arm, he grasped Thorn's outstretched hand and let the large man pull him up onto the floor.

By the time Jacob stood on the ledge leading out of the room, most of the group had already run ahead. Kalista gazed wide-eyed at him, wringing her hands.

"Um, Garrett, I…"

"Go on!" he cut in, pointing ahead. Clamping her mouth shut, she turned and ran ahead. With a quick glance over his shoulder at the immense pit they had just crossed, he raced after her.

As they returned to greater and simpler halls, the floor became littered with shattered blocks of stone. Huge sections of the walls began to cave in.

"There's the door!" Makaidel yelled from thirty feet ahead of Jacob.

"Hurry!" Looking up, Jacob saw cracks spreading over the distant ceiling above and large blocks sank downward. He darted around falling stones as large as cars crashing down as he ran through the final hall of the castle towards the doors they had entered that afternoon.

Finally, he raced out the front doors after all the others just as he heard the ceiling cave in and walls collapse behind him. He continued running forward out onto the castle grounds without looking back.

At last, he allowed his pace to slow, his lungs burning as he panted. He reached the others and halted, halfway across the castle grounds towards the outer wall. Turning, he gazed at the castle.

Towers toppled over and entire wings of the castle crumbled into rubble, dust kicking up over a hundred feet into the night sky. A few last guards skittered out of the castle. In a great shuddering roar that shook the ground, the castle completely caved in on itself. After a long moment, the great crashes and crumbling sounds faded and the ruins of the castle fell still.

Knees trembling from weariness such as he had never known, Jacob collapsed to a sitting position on the ground. Serina quickly kneeled down beside him, laying a hand on his shoulder. He felt a wave of energy flow over him, healing his wounds for the first time since the group was separated. He still felt exhausted.

"It's over," Makaidel stated softly. "It's finally over."

Jacob heard footsteps approach behind him. "Garrett, I, uh…"

"Hey, guys," Thayer cut in gently. "Why don't you help me bring the airship around?"

"Yeah," Makaidel replied.

"That's a good idea," Thorn added.

"O-okay," Kalista stated after a short pause. Jacob sat still as their footfalls turned and walked away. He didn't think the question had been directed at him, nor did he think he could get up even if he wanted. Serina remained by his side as the others headed towards the forest, legs folded beneath her as she gazed at the rubble of Dharius's castle.

"It is over," she stated softly as the sounds of the others faded into the night. "Isn't it?"

Jacob nodded, his head feeling like lead. "Yeah, it is."

She glanced at him. "Are you alright?"

He let out a heavy sigh. "Yeah. Just tired."

She smiled, the night seeming to grow brighter for it. "Go ahead and rest. I'll keep watch for you." Jacob smiled wearily at her, far too tired to argue, and lied down on his side. He was asleep almost as soon as his head touched the ground.

❧

Jacob slept deeply for many hours, awaking only long enough to climb onto the airship when Thayer flew it over to the rubble of the castle. No one bothered him as he slept, and by the time he awoke, they approached Vanimar. Cheers rang through the streets as they crossed the town towards the king's castle, but it affected Jacob little. He was still reeling from the battle atop Dharius's castle, and despite sleeping for so long, he still felt tired. Defeating Dharius had seemed to lift a weight off his shoulders, to release a stiffness that had kept him going when he wasn't certain he could any longer, and now all he wanted to do was lie down and sleep. From the way his companions looked, it seemed that some of them felt the same way.

Lunas rose with a proud smile as the group entered the throne room.

"Heroes!" He spread his arms. "I feared for you when I saw the light from Dharius's castle and the wave of energy washed over the land. It gives me great joy to see you all safe."

"Thank you, Your Majesty." Thorn lowered to one knee as they came near to the throne.

"Do not kneel. Today you are held in the kingdom's highest esteem. You've saved us all. I would like to hear everything about your journey, if you feel up to it."

Jacob was relieved that the others took charge of reliving their experiences up to and inside the castle. He stood silently, letting the others speak. He remained quiet when their narrative came to his fight with Dharius alone on the castle roof. The king looked directly at him with a knowing smile and the others continued their story.

"I see," Lunas stated after they finally finished their tale. "So, the sword of Aurius itself contained the element stone of air."

"Yeah." Makaidel turned to Jacob. "But then, what…" Jacob simply shook his head, silencing the mage.

"The mages of this town, and I imagine representatives from all over the kingdom, would like to speak with you about what happened." They all turned back to Lunas at his words. "They told me they experienced something very strange when that wave of energy struck and would like as much information about it as you can provide."

Makaidel stepped forward. "Please allow me to talk to them, Your Majesty."

Lunas's eyes widened as he gazed down at the young mage. "Why, you're Makaidel, Lord Kyutu's heir."

Makaidel shook his head. "I'm Lord Kyutu's son, but not his heir. I'm a mage." Lunas's eyes enlarged further. "And I think I understand what the mages felt when that wave of energy hit. It was natural magic, like Dharius cast. We have to get the mages to change the way they use magic if we want to prevent something like this from happening again. I can tell them about it, and maybe Serina…" He glanced over his shoulder. Lunas followed his eyes curiously.

Serina smiled and slid a lock of hair behind an ear. Lunas straightened in surprise.

"You're Alorian?"

"Half Alorian," she answered, hiding the details of her parentage. "But I cast magic naturally like an Alorian."

"We'll make the mages understand that this is the proper way to cast magic," Makaidel continued.

Lunas nodded. "I understand. I'll arrange a meeting for you two with our highest mages, and they can pass down the word from there. There will undoubtedly be dissent, but hopefully what transpired last night will help convince them that this is the only way.

"Now, it is a time for celebration. Our kingdom is saved due to the selfless actions of you brave heroes. I invite you all to a ball here at the castle tonight, and until that time, all the comforts of the castle and the town are yours."

"Thank you, Your Majesty." Makaidel bowed. They all turned to walk out, except Jacob. He stepped toward Lunas.

"Garrett?" Serina asked curiously, glancing over her shoulder. The others stopped and turned to him.

"Is something wrong, Garrett?" Lunas asked calmly. Jacob undid his sword belt and removed the sword of Aurius from around his waist.

He held the sheathed sword out to the king. "Here, Your Majesty. This should go back where it belongs."

Lunas looked strangely at the sword. "This sword is yours, Garrett."

Jacob shook his head, still holding the sword out. "No. It belongs here. It should be kept safe, for when it's needed again."

Lunas hesitated, then nodded and took the sword with a smile. "I will always remember this sword as belonging in your hands." His smile widened with a knowing look. "You are a true hero, Garrett."

Jacob smiled genuinely, an action that seemed strange and unfamiliar to him. "Thank you, sir." Bowing, he turned and walked out of the throne room with the others.

The group split up as they settled in for the day. Thayer went into town while Kalista and Thorn wandered the castle and Makaidel examined the king's library. Jacob remained in the castle, sometimes in Serina's company, but usually alone as she went off to meet with the city's mages with Makaidel. Jacob spent most of the day sleeping or sitting by a window, staring outside and thinking about the events that had transpired.

Neither relief nor disappointment touched his mind as he reflected on his adventures, though he knew that deep down, he felt both. Lunas's last words to him echoed through his mind with memories of the confrontation at the castle, and he realized that he had finally learned what it truly meant to be a hero. He had never stopped to think about dragging Kalista through the room she would willingly have died in, nor had he ever felt concern for his own life as he rescued her. He had simply known, instinctively, that he had to do it. And when he faced Dharius alone on top of the castle and had abandoned his own fears to fight for a cause for which he was willing to sacrifice himself, he at last had understood what the Garrett he had been playing had known all along.

Recalling the duty and danger from the safety of the king's castle, however, he wasn't certain he could have done it again. And the look on Dharius's face when Jacob ran his sword through the sorcerer remained burned uncomfortably into his mind. In the same moment that his quest had become more important to him than himself, he had come to understand and respect Dharius. For though their methods were different, they had both been fighting for the same cause. And the more Jacob considered it, the more ashamed he felt. Dharius could have done extraordinary things had he survived. Instead, Jacob had slain him, someone who cared deeply for Aurius and had been driven to desperation by the inaction and apathy of its inhabitants. Even chilling reminders of the torture he had suffered from the dark sorcerer could not allay the guilt at having killed someone who, in the end, had only wanted to do something good.

Makaidel chose to change into fancy clothes fit for the son of a lord for the ball that night, but the rest of them remained in their worn traveling clothes. The elegant ballroom, sparkling with crystal chandeliers over a polished granite floor, was filled with well-dressed men and women, but they, in their cleaned but wholly common clothes, were hailed and applauded as soon as they entered the room. An entire wall of the room was filled with tables covered in white cloth piled high with all manner of food and drink. The dishes were fancy and delicate for Aurius, yet not too unlike modern catered food, Jacob thought. A small orchestra sat at the far end of the ballroom, filling the room of chattering nobles and taciturn servants with music.

Jacob donned a convincing smile as he spoke with people, slowly making his way across the room. Nobles stood straight-backed in finely embroidered coats and ladies in voluminous gowns smiled shyly and waved their fans as they listened to him talk of his deeds as if he enjoyed the telling. He conducted himself casually, too wrapped up in all the things that had happened to feel uneasy at the elegant people and room surrounding him.

He let out a sigh as he stepped onto a quiet balcony outside the ballroom. Despite the size of the room, the ceiling rising three stories above them, it felt close and enclosed, and he relished the open night air outside. The full moon shone overhead, bathing the balcony and the castle grounds far below in pale blue light. He strolled over to the carved stone balustrade and leaned against it, gazing out. Over the castle walls, he could see the town, alight in celebration of its own. Despite himself, he smiled to gaze upon it. A soft night breeze rippled past him, tousling his freshly cut hair. It was still too long for his taste, but it was at least back to the length it had been when he started his journey.

"Oh, there you are."

Jacob glanced over his shoulder to find Serina standing at the glass-paned door into the ballroom. She smiled as she walked over to him. He looked out over the castle grounds and town again as she leaned against the railing beside him.

"Are you okay?"

"Yeah. It's just a bit too crowded in there for me."

Serina leaned forward with a murmur. "I know what you mean. I couldn't imagine going to balls like these regularly." He half smiled. She turned her head to gaze at him. "How are you feeling?"

He sighed, shaking his head. "I don't know." He leaned on his elbows on the balustrade. "I know I should feel glad that it's all over, but… it was a hard fight. A really hard fight."

"It was," Serina replied softly.

Jacob frowned. "I killed him." He hunched his shoulders. "It… it doesn't seem right."

She laid a hand on his shoulder. "You had to. We all saw it, there was nothing else you could've done."

"I know. It's just…" He sighed again. "I feel like a hypocrite, saying all those things to him about how there's always another choice, and then… I just killed him." His heart felt small and hollow as he spoke. "I took a man's life. Not just a man, but someone who could have lived for centuries longer. It's not right." Serina simply squeezed his shoulder.

He cleared his throat. "How about you? How are you feeling?"

She sighed, running her fingers along the stone railing. "I guess kind of the same way. I mean, I know he was a horrible person and he had to be stopped, but he was still my father. And in the end, he just wanted to do the same thing I did. We just wanted to heal the world." Jacob just gazed at her, uncertain what to say. "I guess I take after him more than I thought."

Jacob rose and laid a hand on her shoulder. "He did have redeeming qualities." He smiled faintly. "You got all of them, without any of the bad parts."

She smiled in amusement, looking away. "You're sweet to say that."

"It's true."

She gazed up at him with his words. Slowly, a real smile spread on her face. "I guess, in a way, he really did do what he wanted." Reaching forward, she took his hand. "We all did."

He paused, considering. "Yeah. I guess we did."

"Garrett, I'm… I'm sorry for messing everything up on top of the castle."

"You didn't," he answered quickly. "Everything worked out. Maybe even better than it would have if he hadn't taken the sword." He couldn't help blinking in surprise at his own assertion, realizing that it was true only after saying it. They might have defeated Dharius without him taking the sword of Aurius, but then the wave of magic that destroyed the orlocs would not have been released.

Serina's smile widened. "I guess it did." She rubbed his hand. "I just wanted to say thanks for rescuing me. It was really brave and sweet of you."

He smiled softly, stalling as he tried to come up with a good response. "I wasn't going to let anything happen to you. I never would." The memory of the battle drudged through his mind, hazy and distant, and he thought of the streak of light that grounded him when he thought his very life was going to flow out of the sword of Aurius. "And anyway, you saved my life up there. I should be thanking you."

She squeezed his hand. "I didn't want anything to happen to you, either. I'm just glad everything worked out in the end."

He nodded musingly. "Me, too."

She hunched her shoulders. "I know this victory is hard for you to accept, but… maybe we could just celebrate anyway. Just for tonight."

He smiled, warmed by her words. "Okay." Her smile widened. Taking his hand, they walked back inside the ballroom. The sounds of revelry filled the room as bodies swirled over the floor. He glanced at Serina as she backed into the throng, shrugging her shoulders as she pulled him into it. Smiling softly, he followed her onto the dance floor and began spinning around with her.

Nobles and ladies smiled at them as they danced together, Jacob spinning Serina around to the richest music he had heard since he had come to Aurius.

At length, he found himself bumping into Lunas. "Oops, I'm sorry."

The king held a hand out to Serina. "May I?"

"Ah, sure." He allowed the king to take Serina's hands and begin dancing with her. Jacob watched them for only a moment before a girl his age in a ruffled green gown took his hands imploringly. He began dancing with her uneasily, but soon relaxed and donned a smile as he followed the motions of the people around him. Every now and then, he traded partners as he made his way around the dance floor.

Several dance partners later, he found himself near where Thayer and Kalista danced together.

"Your turn," the pilot stated with a grin as he released Kalista in a spin. Jacob quickly grabbed her before she lost her balance. Thayer leaned in while she struggled to regain her footing and uttered, "She's got the hots for you, champ." Jacob raised an eyebrow at the pilot, then turned his gaze to Kalista. She smiled nervously as they began dancing together.

"Um, Garrett," she began, so softly that he could barely hear her over the chattering crowd and music. "I… I wanted to thank you for saving me in the castle."

He swallowed, wanting strangely not to have this conversation. His daring escape across the room of falling platforms with her had not been thought out, and it didn't seem to be a choice he had consciously made. "You'd've done the same for me." He stretched his arms out before pulling her back towards him.

"Of course. But, I… I was ready to die there. I felt like if I could save you guys, even if it meant sacrificing myself, I could be remembered for doing something right… for once."

Jacob allowed his empty smile to fade, reminded again of Renaldo, his childhood friend on the coast. "It's not the first thing you've done right. Besides, you could do a lot more great things if you survive. You don't have to die to be a hero."

"I guess." She glanced away uncertainly.

"Look," Jacob continued, drawing her attention back to him, "you saved my life when we first met. I wasn't ready to die then, but I didn't ask for your help, either. You were just there. So, I had to do the same thing." Her eyes widened as she absorbed his words.

Slowly, she smiled. "Okay. Yeah. I… thanks, Garrett. You're the first person who's really believed in me."

Jacob smiled softly. "Well, I'm glad I could help." He spun her around before drawing her close to him and pausing in his movement. "But what you really need is to believe in yourself." Her eyes closed faintly and he saw them glisten.

He grinned. "Now start having some fun, this is our celebration!" She yelped as he spun her around and pushed her away into the arms of a noble who had just traded his partner to someone else. Chuckling, Jacob made his way off the dance floor and over to the tables of food. Thorn and Makaidel stood nearby, each holding a crystal goblet of wine. Jacob sighed.

Thorn grinned sidelong at him. "Don't tell me you've had enough already. You know these things last halfway through the night."

Jacob half smiled, already growing tired from the charade he put on. "Right now, I just want to sleep." Thorn and Makaidel murmured in agreement. "And anyway, what about you two?"

Thorn snorted with a grin. "I've already had two partners complain of having to crane their necks to dance with me. And the people around me keep saying I'm stepping on their toes, but believe me, if I did that, they'd know." He jabbed his thumb in Makaidel's direction. "It's even harder to find a partner my size than his." Jacob chuckled faintly.

Makaidel stuck his tongue out at them. "I'll have you know, the princess asked me personally for a dance." Jacob raised an eyebrow, not realizing Lunas had a daughter. The young mage sighed as he gazed into the crowd. "I just can't get into this, not after the adventure we had. I wasn't meant for this kind of life." Jacob nodded slowly, watching the silk-clad bodies swirling across the floor.

Suddenly, Kalista appeared at the edge of the dance floor and waved to them. "Hey, Thorn! Come on!" She jogged forward and took his hand. "You've hardly danced at all tonight."

Thorn chuckled. "You sure you want me to come? I don't think the other people out there would like it."

"Ah, let them clear a space for you." She pulled him towards the dance floor. "We earned this!" Laughing, Thorn thrust his goblet into Jacob's hands as he followed Kalista into the crowd.

"I guess I should go, too." Makaidel gazed at a young courtesan smiling at him from the edge of the dance floor. "Got to keep up appearances and all." He glanced at Jacob. "You coming, too?"

Jacob shook his head. "You go ahead. I'll join in later." Makaidel shrugged and approached the dance floor, leaving Jacob alone by the tables. Jacob glanced down at the goblet in his hands, the one Thorn had been using. With a shrug, he downed the rest of the wine in it.

The dancing and revelry continued late into the night as the candles lighting the hall burned low. Every now and then, some noble would raise a goblet for a toast to the heroes and cheering filled the hall before the music started anew. Pair by pair, people left the dance hall as the hour grew late and the full moon traveled across the sky. Half the people remained on the dance floor when Serina made her way over to Jacob and offered to leave with him. Yawning, he accepted, and before long, he had fallen asleep in a plush canopy bed in an enormous guest room in the castle.

35

THE FIRST GOODBYE came the next day.

"You're staying here?" Makaidel stated, wide-eyed, as they stood at the entrance to the castle.

Kalista nodded. "The king said he could use someone with my skills. I won't be joining the regular army, I'll be more of a messenger to him."

"A king's lackey." Thayer grinned. "I wouldn't have figured."

Kalista narrowed her eyes at him. "I'll have you know, I'll have the power to assassinate, if necessary."

Thayer held up his hands defensively. "Okay, okay."

"I'll miss you." Serina stepped forward and the girls hugged. "Please feel free to come visit Shelas anytime."

"I will, thanks."

"I'm glad you found what you wanted to do." Thorn held out a large hand. Kalista smiled widely as she shook it.

"Thanks. I hope you find your path, too."

He shrugged. "Maybe I'll come down this way sometime, too."

Kalista grinned. "I'd like that."

Makaidel rubbed the back of his neck. "Well, thanks for your help. I'm sorry for the mean things I said when we first met. You really did help us out a lot."

Kalista smiled down at him. "Thanks, Makaidel. I appreciate that." Makaidel flushed as she spoke his name.

"Well, it's a shame we never got any real time alone." Thayer took Kalista's hand and raised it to his lips. "But I'll come back to see you."

"In that case," Kalista stated as she casually slipped her hand out of his, "there's no need to say goodbye." Snickers traveled the group as Thayer sent her a sly grin. "Anyway, I guess you were useful to have around, and you do dance pretty well, when you're not acting like an idiot."

Thayer laughed. "I'll take that as a compliment."

Kalista then turned to Jacob. "Garrett…"

Jacob held out his hand with a sad smile, knowing he wouldn't be able to come back and visit her like the others could.

"I..." Kalista began to reach her hand out to his, then threw herself forward and wrapped her arms around him. Jacob put his arms around her as well and hugged her tightly, not feeling uncomfortable with the action. She had given him much on their long journey together, and despite his initial thoughts about her, he had come to respect and admire her greatly. She had become one of his closest companions, a better friend than many he had made in years.

"Thank you so much," she uttered into his ear. "For everything."

"And thank you." He squeezed her shoulders.

"I hope we'll get to see each other again sometime."

"I wish we could," he uttered almost inaudibly.

"What?" she asked as she pulled back.

"Nothing."

She shook her head, smiling. "Take care, all of you."

"You, too," Serina stated. Turning, the group began to cross the castle grounds toward the outer wall and the raised portcullis leading into the town. Jacob glanced over his shoulder. Kalista waved at him. He waved back, though his heart felt heavy to leave her behind so soon. Thayer bumped him with his elbow as he faced forward again, but Jacob didn't have the heart to joke with the pilot about the exchange.

Cheers rang through the streets as they crossed the town towards the airship parked in the fields outside. Jacob glanced around, realizing this was the last chance he would have to see this town. He had hardly gotten to know it, even though he had come to it twice.

Before long, they left Vanimar behind and boarded the airship. Makaidel sighed as the machinery whirred to life, lifting the airship off the ground.

"I can't believe it's really over." He gazed over the edge at the ground dropping away. "It's been so long."

"It has," Thorn replied. "A lot has happened since we left." Jacob only nodded, watching the ground pass by beneath them.

"Cheer up, guys," Thayer stated as he manned the helm. "Next stop, Dekaal, and we're bound to have another party when we get there."

Makaidel chuckled. "Yeah, you're right. I can't wait to tell dad all that happened."

"How long will it take to get there?" Serina asked.

"Dekaal's pretty far." Thayer flipped a switch and turned away from the helm. "Depending on wind, could be a week."

Thorn shrugged. "Guess we'd better settle in, then."

Jacob found it difficult to occupy himself through the journey. As they had done before when traveling on the airship, they took turns cleaning, cooking, manning the helm, and sleeping, but it wasn't enough to keep him busy all day, and he awaited their arrival at Dekaal both eagerly and anxiously.

At Jacob's request, they made a stop halfway to Dekaal. None of them objected as Thayer steered the airship a little off course. The townspeople cheered as they landed and strolled through the cobblestone streets, but Jacob paid them little attention.

Finally, they came to the southwestern edge of town and upon a pleasant house with a white picket fence surrounding it. Jacob hesitated only a moment before opening the gate and walking up the path to the house.

The front door opened almost immediately after he knocked on it and Cassandra Deacon appeared. Her eyes widened briefly as she took in the sight of the scars marring Jacob's face, but she smiled at him after a moment.

"It's good to see you all again."

"I just wanted…" Jacob began.

"Please, come in," Cassandra interrupted, stepping aside and motioning them through the door. Jacob nodded in thanks as he stepped inside the house and the others greeted her as they followed him inside.

Once Cassandra closed the front door and turned to face them, Jacob stated, "I just wanted to tell you that we did it. The orlocs have been stopped and the Alorian is dead."

Cassandra smiled. "I'm glad to hear that. I thought of you all when the light passed over here. It felt… warm." She shook her head. "But, where is…"

Serina stepped forward. "Kalista decided to stay in Vanimar. She's working for the king now."

"I'm glad. She's a sweet girl." She glanced at Thayer, standing quietly at the back of the group. "Now, who is this?"

He stepped forward. "My name is Thayer, Mrs. Deacon. I operate the only working airship in Aurius. My companions told me about your husband. It's an honor to meet you." Makaidel gazed in surprise as Thayer bowed politely to Cassandra.

Cassandra's smile grew sad. "Come with me, I'd like to show you all something." Curiously, they all followed her across the main room and out the back door. She led them down the stairs off the back porch and around to the side of it. Jacob's eyes widened.

In the center of the garden now lay a tombstone inscribed with the name Morrie Deacon.

"I know you weren't able to recover the body," Cassandra stated, "but I needed to put something up as much for the boys' sake as for myself."

Thorn laid a hand on her shoulder. "I'm sure he appreciates it."

She chuckled sadly. "I'm not entirely sure about that. He always said not to mourn death, because it then begins a new life as history. But…"

Serina stepped forward as she trailed off. "I understand, it still hurts that he's gone." Cassandra nodded.

Jacob lowered himself to one knee before the headstone, hardly listening to the others speak.

"What are you going to do now?"

"Oh, don't worry about me. I've already had several people ask to see Morrie's notes. They want to make an expedition to the ruins, even if they're destroyed, and they've promised me a portion of any profits they make on it."

Jacob closed his eyes as he reached out and laid a hand on Morrie's headstone. "Thank you, Morrie. We wouldn't have been able to do it without you. I'll never forget what you did for us, and… I'm sorry. I'm sorry I failed you." His throat constricted. "Rest in peace, Morrie. It's over now."

The others fell silent as he rose with a sigh. As he turned, he found Cassandra gazing at him.

"You know, he told me the morning before you left that he was really glad he got to meet you, Garrett. He was so happy that his work was going to make a real difference in the world, no matter what happened." She glanced away with a sad smile. "It's almost as if he knew something was going to happen." Jacob's eyes widened briefly, then he nodded. He supposed Morrie's death was the only possible outcome of that situation.

Still… I managed to save Kalista.

Instead of making him feel guilty about Morrie, however, the thought lifted his spirits. He had made a positive change in this world. He smiled as sunlight poured out from behind the clouds and lit up the garden and backyard of the Deacons' house.

"Garrett!"

Jacob turned as Shane clomped down the wooden stairs and raced around everyone to him. Jacob took a step back as the young boy barreled into his legs, grabbing him tight.

"Can you stay and play?"

Jacob knelt before the boy with a sigh. "I'm sorry, but we have to go."

"No!" the boy shrieked, wrapping his arms around Jacob's neck.

"Won't you stay for lunch?" Cassandra asked.

Serina shook her head. "We don't want to be a bother."

"It's no bother at all, please…"

"No," Makaidel cut in, shaking his head. "We really should be going."

Cassandra hesitated before nodding with a smile. "I understand. Shane…"

Shane pulled back. "I wan' a piggy-back ride!"

Jacob couldn't help smiling at the young boy's determined expression. "Alright, come on." Shane cheered as Jacob turned around and allowed the boy to climb up on his back. Taking Shane's legs under his arms, he stood and carried the boy inside after the others.

"Well, I'm glad you all came, even if you didn't have much time. Would you like anything to eat or drink before you go?"

"We really shouldn't…" Makaidel began.

"Elias," Jacob stated suddenly, stopping in his tracks. The older boy stood at the end of the common room, gazing uncertainly at them. Jacob slowly lowered Shane back to the floor as Elias approached awkwardly. The conversation fell silent around him.

"Garrett…" Suddenly, he ran forward and wrapped his arms around Jacob, sniffling. Jacob gazed down at the boy in surprise. "I'm sorry I was so mean to you. Mommy said you tried to help daddy, and I…"

"No, it's okay," Jacob cut in, kneeling in front of the boy. He raised a hand and rubbed Elias's hair. "You were right to be mad."

Elias sniffled again. "I… I liked playing with you, Garrett." Jacob only smiled as Elias reached forward and hugged him again. Pulling back, he stood, and he was relieved to see the boy smile up at him.

"Thanks again for everything, Mrs. Deacon," Thorn stated, and the others echoed him.

"I'm glad to see you all again," she said. "Please feel free to come back anytime. You're all welcome here." They all began to make their way over to the door.

"Come back and play with us again, Garrett!" Shane and Elias called out, waving excitedly. Jacob couldn't bear to lie to them and simply smiled and waved back.

Cassandra, Elias, and Shane followed them all to the front door and continued waving and calling out their goodbyes as the group walked down the path and rejoined the town. Before long, they had returned to the airship and began to lift off the ground.

"Any other stops to make before we head to Dekaal?" Thayer asked as the ship began moving forward with a soft lurch.

"No, I can't think of anywhere else," Makaidel answered. "Garrett?" Jacob simply shook his head as he watched Quinlan stretch away behind them.

"Alright, then." Thayer flipped some switches. "Should only take us a few more days, then."

The journey passed quietly and uneventfully, and as predicted, they soon arrived in Dekaal. Their arrival was far quieter than it had been in Vanimar and Quinlan, Jacob supposed because word of their triumph over Dharius had not yet made it to the distant city. Heads turned as the motley group passed through the streets, but none of them paid the glances any mind. Except, perhaps, for Thayer, whom Jacob caught winking at women occasionally. Makaidel rolled his eyes with an exasperated sigh when he saw Thayer ogling a young woman.

Jacob glanced sidelong at some students who stared oddly at them as they passed by the Twin Oaks Academy, where Jacob had once felt intimidated by the rich and well-dressed students. He held his head high with a scoffing sound, knowing that none of those pampered students could do what he had done. Once they heard about his adventures, they would be celebrating him, and he couldn't help feeling satisfied by the thought.

"Lord Makaidel! Thorn!" Rollis smiled as the group passed through the outer wall of the castle. His mustached smile widened as his gaze fell on Jacob. "Garrett and Serina. Welcome back, all of you."

"Thanks, Captain." Makaidel smiled and offhandedly introduced Thayer as he continued toward the castle.

"I trust you were successful, then?" Rollis fell into step beside them.

"Yeah." Makaidel began running across the castle grounds. "I've got to tell my dad!" Thorn chuckled as he jogged after the young mage. Jacob decided to follow at a more sedate pace, Serina by his side.

Thayer made a noise. "Kids."

Jacob raised an eyebrow at the pilot. "Don't tell me you wouldn't do the same thing."

Thayer laughed. "Yeah, I probably would, if I had someone that close to talk to about it."

"You don't get lonely by yourself all the time?" Serina asked.

He grinned as he leaned in toward her. "Well, that's why I spend so much time in towns." Serina simply smiled, though Jacob frowned at the suggestive way Thayer looked at her.

Makaidel and Thorn already stood before Lord Kyutu by the time Jacob, Serina, and Thayer entered the throne room. Lord Kyutu rose from his throne as they began walking down the carpet leading towards them.

"Garrett and Serina." His gaze lingered briefly on Jacob's face, but Kyutu said nothing regarding the scars he had gained since he first came to Dekaal. "I'm glad to see you all again. And this is…"

"Thayer, My Lord." Thayer bowed as they came up beside Makaidel and Thorn.

"A pleasure." Kyutu nodded. "My son was just telling me about your travels. It sounds like you've had quite an adventure." Jacob simply nodded and allowed Makaidel to continue his story.

"So that's what that light was," Kyutu mused when Makaidel finally finished. "Our town's mages were concerned when it passed over us. Your help will be invaluable in explaining what happened." Kyutu smiled down at Makaidel. "I'm proud of you, son."

Makaidel beamed. "Thanks, Dad."

"Well, I need to spread word throughout the town about what happened, but I think that a celebration is in order. I hope you can all stay for a few days."

Serina exchanged a glance with Jacob. He nodded with a smile. "A few days, sir."

"In that case, please make yourselves at home. You are guests of honor at my castle. Please ask my staff for anything you need."

"Thank you, My Lord," Serina stated with a bow. Makaidel remained in the throne room to speak with Lord Kyutu as the rest of them left.

The following days passed in much the same way as their time in Vanimar had, though Serina stayed by Jacob's side more often. A ball was held at the castle that night, though by Makaidel's suggestion, they only remained there for a short while before joining the larger celebration in town. Jacob felt more at ease among the townspeople, the dancing and festivities less formal and more energetic than Lord Kyutu's ball. The citizens welcomed and cheered their arrival and he ate and drank heartily, eventually retreating to a room at a fine inn offered for the group free of charge.

Before long, Jacob, Serina, and Thayer prepared to say their goodbyes.

"I knew there was something special about you when I first saw you, Garrett," Lord Kyutu stated as they stood in the Dekaal throne room for the last time. "You've become a true hero, and I feel honored for having been a part of your journey to save the world."

Jacob smiled. "Thank you, sir."

"And Serina." Kyutu's sharp eyes crinkled with a smile as his gaze turned to her. "I hope you will return to help teach our mages the proper way to use magic."

She bowed. "I would be honored, My Lord."

"I want to thank you again for all you've done for me, for Dekaal, and for all of Aurius. Your name will be remembered throughout history, Garrett, and I hope this small token of my appreciation…"

"No."

Kyutu gazed sharply at Jacob. Jacob simply shook his head. "I didn't do this for any reward, sir, and it wouldn't be right for me to accept one now. What matters is that Aurius is safe. I don't need a reward for that."

Kyutu's eyes narrowed, but momentarily, he smiled. "You really are a hero, and a better man than most I've met. Go forth, then, with my blessing, and I hope you will come back to visit sometime." Jacob simply bowed, then turned to walk out of the throne room, Serina and Thayer behind him.

As they turned the corner into the hallway outside the throne room, Jacob smiled to glimpse a familiar face. "Thorn! You're stationed in the castle now?"

The large man, back in castle uniform as he had been when they first met, grinned as he caught sight of them. "Actually, Lord Kyutu's ordered me to be Makaidel's personal bodyguard."

"Hey, that's great."

"But," Serina asked curiously, "where is he?"

Laughter circled the group. Thorn pointed towards the entrance of the castle. "He asked for some time alone. I'll give it to him this time."

"So, is this what you really want?" Jacob asked.

Thorn shrugged, smiling. "I'm not entirely sure yet, but it's a good place to start. And anyway, I may not like the city so much, but I have to admit, it does feel like home."

Jacob smiled down the entrance hall, gazing out the doors towards the distant town. "I know what you mean."

"Hey." Jacob turned to find Thorn holding a large hand out to him. "Thanks for having me along. It was really good getting to be part of this."

Jacob smiled as he shook Thorn's hand. "Thanks for coming. You're a great guy." Jacob's eyes widened slightly as Thorn pulled him forward and put his free arm around Jacob's shoulders.

"They're right, you know. You are a hero."

Jacob's smile widened. "Thanks. You are, too."

They smiled at each other for a moment before Thorn nodded toward the entrance. "Go ahead. Makaidel will kill me if I keep you waiting, and Lord Kyutu will kill me if he finds out I'm not by his side." Grinning, Jacob strode down the entrance hall as Serina and Thayer said their goodbyes.

Jacob glanced to the side as he walked out the huge front doors to the castle. Makaidel jumped up from where he perched on the railing of the wide stairs.

"Oh, hey! So, um, you're leaving then." Jacob nodded. Makaidel rubbed the back of his neck, glancing away. "I, um, I just wanted to say, uh…"

Jacob blinked, surprised at the mage's awkwardness. "What is it?"

Makaidel sighed, then looked Jacob in the eye. "I know I teased you a lot while we were traveling, but I hope you didn't take it to heart. I'm… I'm glad you were in charge. You really are a hero, and you're the best person for the job. I couldn't have done what you did. And I wanted to say… I really respect you."

Jacob's eyes widened as Makaidel held his hand out formally. He shook it, dazed by Makaidel's words. "Th-thanks."

"Thanks for letting me come along. I had a lot of fun, and I enjoyed being with you."

Jacob glanced up with a smile, a lump in his throat from the mage's words. "Thanks. I'm glad you came with us." They exchanged a smile just before Serina and Thayer stepped out of the castle. Serina hugged Makaidel as they said their goodbyes.

"You guys come back here anytime," Makaidel stated as they descended the wide stone stairs to the castle grounds. "You'd better come visit!"

Serina laughed lightly as she waved back at him. "We will, I promise. Take care!"

"You, too! Goodbye!"

Jacob waved back as they crossed the castle grounds and walked out the front gate towards the town. He sighed.

"Well, I'll bet you guys are ready to get home after all this time," Thayer stated as they crossed the drawbridge over the moat.

"Yeah," Jacob answered quietly, staring at the ground ahead of him.

"Oh, yes," Serina replied. "I'm sure Adella's worried about me."

Once more, the town cheered as they passed through it towards where Thayer had parked the airship. As they traveled down the cobblestone streets, Jacob wondered briefly if Thayer parked it the farthest he could from the castle on purpose. The pilot certainly seemed to enjoy the attention they received as they crossed the town.

"Last stop, Shelas," Thayer stated as the airship whirred to life around them. "Any last stops you want to make before we head there?" Jacob and Serina shook their heads, the airship seeming empty with only the three of them left on it. Without another word, the airship rose into the air and began flying north.

It took only a day and a half for them to arrive at Shelas. Cheers rang up in the streets as they passed within the walls of the town. Jacob supposed Lord Kyutu had sent word of their exploits and their coming as soon as they had arrived at Dekaal. He forced himself to smile as people chattered excitedly to him, feeling tired of celebration and wanting only some peace and quiet.

Serina must have picked up on his feelings, or else felt the same, as she guided them through quiet streets away from the main crowds until they finally arrived at the house where Jacob's long journey had begun.

Serina climbed the stairs and opened the door. "Adella?"

As Jacob and Thayer stepped through the door, a voice called out, "Serina!" The elderly woman shuffled quickly over to Serina and embraced her. "Oh, I'm so glad you've arrived home safely! Word came from Dekaal, I've been waiting for you to come home."

Serina smiled. "It's good to be back, Adella."

"And Garrett, I must…" Adella cut herself off with a gasp as she turned to Jacob. He frowned slightly as her eyes widened at the sight of the scars on his face. "Oh, my…" She turned to Serina. "You weren't able to do anything for him?"

"She did wonders," Jacob replied quickly before Serina could say anything. "I probably wouldn't be able to see out of both eyes if it weren't for her." His back twinged at the memory of his long recovery from his torture at Dharius's hands. He pushed it out of his mind, knowing Adella couldn't know of the scars covering his back.

Adella smiled as she gazed back at Serina. "Well, if there was anything anyone could've done, it was Serina." Serina smiled at the praise, though a hint of sadness touched her eyes. "Please stay here as long as you'd like, all of you."

"Oh, no, thanks, ma'am," Thayer answered. "I'm itching to get back into the air again." All eyes turned to him.

Adella smiled. "So, you're Thayer, the airship owner. Well, I must thank you for bringing Serina home."

"It was my pleasure." The pilot grinned. "She was delightful company." Jacob rolled his eyes as Thayer winked at Serina.

"Oh, Thayer, are you really leaving?" Serina asked, stepping towards him.

He grinned slyly at her. "Why, do you want to come with me?"

Adella narrowed her eyes. "Serina…"

Serina laughed innocently. "Thanks, but I'd like some time to rest at home." Jacob couldn't help smiling at her.

"But yeah, I need to get moving again," Thayer continued. "I'm still not used to the idea of having people on my ship. I need some time alone for a while."

"Thank you again for letting us use your airship," Serina stated. "You were a great help to us."

He grinned. "My pleasure. I just hope you'll extend the hospitality when I come back this way." He winked at Adella before making a quick salute to Jacob. "Garrett, nice knowing you." With that, he turned and walked towards the door.

Taken aback by the abruptness of Thayer's departure, Jacob just managed to say before the pilot left, "'Bye, thanks for everything." The door shut and he was left alone with Serina and Adella.

"So, what are you going to do now?" Adella asked. "If you need a place to stay, you're welcome here."

Jacob's gaze dropped to the floor. "Thanks. I…" He glanced at Serina. "I need to go to Merakis." She nodded knowingly.

"Would you at least like to stay the night? I know Merakis isn't far, but I'm sure you must be tired from all your travel."

"Actually…" Jacob caught a hopeful smile from Serina. "Yeah, that sounds nice. Thanks." He did feel tired, even with the comfortable travel in the airship.

Adella cooked a pleasant dinner for them, one of the nicest and most comfortable meals he'd had since the dinner at Morrie Deacon's house so long ago, and after a few hours of regaling her with stories of their journey, he fell asleep in the same bed where he had once woken up the morning after he came to Aurius.

36

THE NEXT MORNING, Jacob and Serina left Shelas quietly. It only took them a few hours to travel by foot to Merakis, and by noon, they stood before the ruins of the town.

"How horrible." Serina gazed out at the blackened remains of buildings. Jacob's eyes traveled slowly over the rubble, trying to remember the night that orlocs had raided the village. The event was so far distant that it seemed like a dream. It had seemed as such when it occurred, too.

"Of all the towns that were hurt by the orlocs, I guess this is the only one that won't be rebuilt."

Serina laid a hand on his shoulder. "People will come back here someday."

Jacob glanced away. "I'm not sure I'd want them to. None of the people who actually lived here are going to return. It seems like if other people move in, they'd just be encroaching on their memories." He shook his head. "I don't know."

"No." Serina looked out at the town again. "I think you're right. I'd hate to see Merakis die like this… but even if people do move back, it won't be the same." Jacob sighed as his attention drifted to the forest spreading west of the town. A warm front had accompanied their journey to the ruined village. The forest, trees barren from the fall chill, looked much the same as it had when he first came to Aurius.

Catching his gaze, Serina asked, "Why don't we stop for lunch?" Jacob simply nodded and sat with her as they set up a picnic lunch. They ate quietly, both of them immersed in thought. A knot formed in Jacob's stomach as his departure drew closer.

Finally, they finished, and Jacob folded the blanket they ate on and put it back in the basket Serina had brought. Taking a deep breath, he walked to the edge of the forest.

"Are you sure you…" Serina began, then cut herself off with a shake of her head. "No, of course you have to go back."

He turned to face her. "I'm sorry. I wish I could stay. I really do."

She glanced into the forest. "Are you sure this is going to work?"

He sighed, gazing down the path. "Honestly, part of me is hoping it won't." His head sank. "But it will. I don't know how, but… it will."

Serina shifted. "I'm going to miss you."

He turned to her, a lump in his throat as he gazed at her. "I'll miss you, too." *More than you know.* She smiled sadly as he gazed at her innocent face, so perfect and… sisterly. *Yes, that's the word for it.* He had desired her greatly when he first came to Aurius, and had to admit that he still did, but it seemed the longer he stayed in this world without being able to see Tina, the worse he felt for feeling such things. He cared immensely for Serina and wanted only to protect and be with her, but now, all he wanted from her was to be her friend.

"I'm really glad I got to be with you throughout all this." Her eyes glistened wetly. "I'm sorry for the things you had to go through." She raised a hand and gently ran a finger down the scar tissue on his face. He smiled, closing his eyes at her touch.

"It's not your fault." He took her hand. "Thank you. Thank you so much. I never would've been able to deal with everything if it weren't for you… especially after I escaped Dharius's castle."

She rubbed his hand. "I hope you'll be able to come back and visit sometime."

"I will," he answered, lying, for the first time, to spare her feelings.

Tears rolled down her face as she leaned forward and embraced him. He held her tight, relishing the lavender scent of her hair and the feel of her body against him one last time. "Goodbye, Garrett. I'll never forget you."

"I'll never forget you, either." His voice was choked and tears gathered beneath his eyes. He rubbed at his eyes as he pulled away. "Thank you." Clearing his throat, he turned to face the forest.

"Garrett," she stated quickly. He paused and glanced back at her. She hesitated, gazing at his feet. After a moment, she looked up. "What's your name? Your real name."

His eyes widened slightly with the question, then he smiled. "It's Jacob. Jacob Marshall. But," he stated before she could say anything, "my friends just call me Jake."

"Jake," she repeated. His heart thudded faster to hear his real name spoken by her. She smiled. "I'll remember that." His smile widened as he gazed into her bright blue eyes. The lump in his throat grew as he raised his hand to her face. He knew he would never have another chance in his life to be with her.

Leaning forward, he hesitated, then quickly kissed her on the lips. His voice came out in a hoarse whisper as he stepped back. "Goodbye, Serina."

Afraid to look back in case he would never be able to leave, he turned and began walking through the forest. He wiped his eyes as he strode down the path, the lump in his throat now so large he could barely breathe.

Jacob glanced distractedly about the forest as he walked deeper into it. It looked so similar to the one he had left behind outside the convention, so long ago. He felt the weight of his wallet in his pocket, his sword belt creaking as he walked. Rubbing at his eyes again, he cursed his fate. He knew he couldn't stay in Aurius, much as he dearly wanted to do so.

The sun shone through the jagged branches of the trees as he walked further into the forest, wondering how he would be able to get back, if he could at all.

Suddenly, a wave of dizziness washed over him. He groaned as he staggered in place, trying to steady his vision. A buzzing noise filled his ears as the nausea passed. He blinked and glanced up, though nothing looked different. The buzzing remained, yet it seemed distant. He glanced around, wondering if something had happened. The forest looked the same as it had a moment earlier.

Then, his eyes widened as he realized what the buzzing sound he heard was. It had been so long since he had heard the noise, it sounded entirely foreign to him.

Traffic!

It was the sound of cars driving down the main road outside of the convention center. His face lit up with the realization that he was home, but as soon as it came, the elation disappeared. He glanced back into the forest the way he had come, though he could see nothing of Aurius deeper in. In fact, as he gazed between the trees, he could see the highway rising up above the forest a few hundred feet away.

He let out a sigh. He hadn't wanted to tell Serina as much, but somehow he knew that he would never be able to return to that world. As relieved as he was to finally be home, a part of his heart would always remain in a place he could never return to. And he would never again see the only companions he had for months, the dearest friends he ever had. He slammed a fist against a tree beside him.

Sighing again, he began walking forward, but stopped after one pace. He glanced down at himself strangely. His body felt awkward, and as he looked down at himself, his tunic no longer seemed to fit the same way. It took him a moment to realize that he looked the same as he had before he went to Aurius. He grimaced at the sight of the fleshy stomach his months of hard travel and battle had worn away.

As he stood straight, however, his eyes shot open. He hadn't felt the scar tissue on his face when he contorted his features. His breath sped as he realized he couldn't feel the marred flesh over his cheeks, nose, or mouth at all. He ran a gloved hand over his face, but his skin felt the same way it had all his life.

Noise ahead caught his attention. Between the trees, he could see the group of dark-clad people he had seen just before he went to Aurius. Jacob raced ahead to them, finding them chatting casually, the live-action role-playing game they had been playing apparently over.

"Excuse me," he stated urgently as he came upon them, panting from the unfamiliar strain on his out-of-shape body, "do any of you have a mirror?"

The group looked oddly at him, but one girl, eyes standing out starkly from the dark eyeliner she had applied, stated, "Yeah, here." Opening her purse, she handed him a compact makeup case. He snapped the case open quickly and looked in his reflection. His eyes widened and he inhaled sharply.

The disfiguring scars were gone, as if they had never been there. His skin was pale once more, freckles standing out sharply beneath his eyes. Yet, he thought as he gazed closer at the reflection, perhaps his skin was a little darker than it had been before he went into Aurius. *Am I as overweight as I was before I left?* He could no longer remember.

Dazed, he shut the compact and handed it back to the girl with a distracted, "Thanks." The role-players sent him another strange look before moving on, leaving him alone in the forest once more. He realized then that he couldn't feel the scar tissue that had so recently covered his back, as well.

As he reached his hand behind him, he felt one remaining scar pull at his flesh near the small of his back. It was the place where Dharius had drawn a sword as hot as a brand across his flesh, both slashing and flaying him alive. Before Jacob's fingers touched his back where the wound had been, he shivered from the memory and pulled his hand away.

Averting his gaze, he caught a glimpse of the sword hanging by his side. Slowly, he wrapped his fingers around the hilt and he began to draw it from its scabbard. A flash of the way he had run that sword through Dharius sparked in his mind and he slid the sword swiftly back with a cringe.

Inhaling deeply, he slid the sword partly out. The blade was a flat slab of steel an eighth of an inch thick. It was a prop sword, just as it had been when he first entered Aurius.

It's like it never happened, he thought distantly. He squeezed his eyes shut as flashes of memories flitted across his eyes, of the battles he had fought, the torture he had suffered, the incredible places he had been, the feeling of the element stones in his hand, the long nights, the months of being someone else, the food, the air, Serina. The scar remaining on his back pulled at his skin as he set his shoulders back.

No, it was real.

"Jake! Hey, Jake!"

Jacob looked up with a start. It had been so long since he had heard someone call him by his real name that it sounded foreign, a relic of a distant memory that reminded him of his childhood. He saw the woman who had given him a ride to the convention, the blonde girl a few years his senior dressed in frilly Gothic fashions, jogging towards him. He could hardly remember her name, it had been so long since he had seen her.

"Jake, what are you…" She stopped herself short and drew back as she gazed at him. "Are you okay?"

He shook his head. "Yeah. I must have fallen asleep."

She motioned towards the ravine where he had come for rest, so long ago. "Well, we'd better head back or we'll be late for the masquerade."

"Okay." He had no idea how he could focus on a costume contest after all that had happened, but knowing it was what he should do, he followed her up the hill and back toward the convention center. He glanced over his shoulder when he got to the top of the hill. There was nothing out of the ordinary about the forest stretching out below him. He shook his head and walked after the woman who had found him. He could hardly believe that after spending so long in Aurius, barely any time had passed here.

He put on a mask through the costume contest much as he had in Aurius, and the afternoon passed in a daze. After the contest ended, he excused himself to the hotel room he shared with the other people who had taken him to the convention. He didn't leave the room the rest of the day.

Sunday morning, Jacob changed into the T-shirt and jeans he had worn on the trip to the convention, packing up his costume in his duffel bag. He wasn't certain he ever wanted to see that outfit again. The day dragged on and the convention continued around him, but he remained in the hotel room, spending much of his time staring out the window, deep in thought. He felt alone at the convention, surrounded by people he barely knew, or didn't at all, and wanted only to go home. He still felt exhausted, as he had since the battle with Dharius had ended.

The day didn't end soon enough, and he was glad when the rest of the group finally returned to the hotel room and packed up to leave. They asked about him as they changed into normal clothes, and he told them he was better, but still feeling under the weather. He was glad he could still lie easily and convincingly.

He gazed out the window on the drive home, staring at nothing in particular while he thought. The car was more spacious on the ride home since Jasmine, the girl his age who had come with them to the convention, had gotten a ride from someone else earlier that day. As the world passed by at speeds that seemed impossible to him, he thought about the events of the past day, a span of months to him.

He was relieved to finally be home after so long in a foreign world away from everyone he knew, but it was a bittersweet return at best. He still had all the problems to face as he did before he went to Aurius, but none of them seemed important anymore. Realizing that he had forever lost some of the best friends he had ever had was the worst sting of all. As he thought of the various books and movies he had seen in which the hero was taken into a far away world and stayed behind at the end, he realized that they were misleading. Anyone could go to a world of magic and wonder and remain there for the rest of their days. The hard part was leaving that place and returning home.

Still, as he thought about Tina, his family, his other friends that he dearly missed, and the world around him that was undeniably his home, he knew he couldn't have remained in Aurius. Even knowing that he could never return there, he still felt torn between worlds as if he still had to make the decision, and the mere thought of the people he would never see again brought unbidden tears to his eyes.

He felt ashamed of his body after he had gotten it into such good shape during his adventures in Aurius and was determined to restore himself to that condition. He vowed that he would start jogging every day and weight lifting if he could. Perhaps he would also sign up for fencing lessons or take classes in *kendo*, the Japanese art of swordfighting. Even as he drove along the highway to return to a life of tedium and peace, his hand itched to hold a sword again.

The number of things he knew he had to do after he got home grew larger with each passing mile, but it didn't bother him anymore. He no longer wanted to spend his days sitting around at home, playing video games and making costumes. He was ready to be an adult and start a life of his own. He had to fill out college applications, look for a job for the remaining summer months, and take driver's education classes. And this year, he was determined to apply himself and do his best at school. Perhaps he would look into joining the theater club at school, since he had discovered that he was apparently good enough at performing to convince people who hadn't known he was acting that he was someone else.

The other people in the car talked about the convention as they drove along the highway. The things they had done, the people they had seen, the celebrities whose autographs they had paid to receive, the various toys and knickknacks they had bought. None of it mattered to Jacob anymore. He had bought two action figures before he had taken that fateful rest in the ravine on Saturday afternoon, but he hardly wanted to take them home now. It all seemed pointless.

"Jake, are you okay?"

Shaken out of his reverie, he nodded. "Yeah, I'm just tired."

Emily, the girl sitting in the front passenger seat, glanced over her shoulder at him. "Don't feel bad about the costume contest. It doesn't mean your costume wasn't good."

He shook his head. "It's just frustrating that I didn't win anything, after all the work I put into it." The words were empty and hollow to him, but they sounded convincing to the others.

"Don't worry," stated Karen, the woman who had found him in the ravine. "You can take it to some smaller conventions. With the amount of detail on it you're bound to win something."

He sent her a completely false smile, hardly wanting to visit another convention at all. "Thanks." With that, he turned and gazed out the window again. He didn't even bother trying to tell them anything else. He knew that he would never be able to tell anyone the truth about what happened that weekend.

Jacob fell silent as the others resumed their conversation. The car sped down the highway, trees and buildings blurring past.

Finally, as the sky was alight in pink and orange from the setting sun, the car pulled up to Jacob's house, stopping at the sidewalk cutting through the front yard. Jacob grabbed his duffel bag, lying on the seat beside him, and opened the door.

"Thanks for coming with us," Karen stated as he stepped out of the car.

"I hope you feel better soon," Emily added.

"Take it easy," stated Eric, the driver.

"Thanks for the ride." Jacob waved as he closed the door. Slinging his duffel bag over his shoulder, the black plastic tube holding his sword slapping against his legs, he strode up the front walk.

He gazed up at the house as he approached it, the magnolia tree rising to the right. It had been so long since he had seen this house, yet it had never felt more like home to him. He smiled faintly as his eyes passed over the familiar house. It had become home to him, as much as his old house on the coast had been.

Dropping his eyes, he climbed the stairs up to the front porch. He hesitated with his hand on the doorknob. It was like returning from a long vacation, or a semester studying abroad. As familiar as the house was to him, it had been a long time since he had last seen it. Inhaling deeply, he opened the door.

The front hall looked the same as it always had, the staircase leading to the second story rising at the far end beside the doorway into the living room. He closed the door, glancing into the dining room to his left. Nothing had changed.

"Jake?"

Jacob raised his head. "Mom?" His eyes widened as his mother stepped out into the entry hall, smiling at him.

"How was your weekend?"

Jacob walked forward quickly and wrapped his arms around her. She made a surprised noise.

"Well, it's good to see you, too. Something happen at the convention?"

He stepped back, smiling at her. "It`s good to be home."

She grinned. "I'm glad to hear it. I was just about to make dinner. How does enchiladas sound?"

"Sounds great." The word was like music to his ears, and his mouth watered merely to imagine the savory Mexican wraps after months of medieval fare. "Do you want me to help?"

She cocked her head to the side, surprised at the offer. "Sure."

"Okay." He shifted his duffel bag on his shoulder. "Let me just put my stuff away and I'll be right back down."

"Okay." Her voice betrayed her bemusement at his behavior. As he began climbing the stairs, she stated, "Hey… did you get a tan this weekend?"

He smiled enigmatically over his shoulder. "Something like that." Turning, he climbed the stairs up to his room, leaving his mother shaking her head with a smile in the living room.

Jacob paused as he came to the top of the stairs, glimpsing the poster of *Legend of Aurius* pinned to his door. His eyes passed across each of the character portraits, rendered so crudely, it seemed, after spending so much time with the real people. His gaze lingered on the image of Serina for a long moment. With a sigh, he walked into his bedroom.

It still amazed him that the room he entered looked exactly the same as the last time he had seen it. His bed had never looked so inviting, but he knew he couldn't sleep yet. He dropped his duffel bag onto the floor beside the bed. He wasn't certain what he was going to do with the costume of Garrett. Likely he would hang it up at the far corner of his closet and leave it there. The scar on his back stretched as he nudged the plastic tube with the sword in it out of the way.

Reaching into his shirt, he pulled out the talisman still hanging around his neck, his own rendition of the Hero's pendant. He gazed at the pendant for a while, stroking the imperfect amber teardrop. Finally, he walked over to his dresser and laid the pendant and chain at the bottom of his sock drawer. His heart ached for the friends he had left behind as he slid the drawer shut.

Sighing, he turned to face the room again. His head tilted to the side as he caught a glimpse of a folded-up piece of paper in the wire wastebasket beside his computer desk. Walking over, he picked up the paper and unfolded it. A phone number was written on it. His breath caught in his throat as he recognized the numbers. After a moment, he picked up the telephone on his desk and dialed. He listened to the phone ring, a foreign sound to him. Finally, there was a click on the other end.

"Hi, Tina. It's me."

The End

About the Author

A perpetual temp who has worked for a number of evil empires, Catherine pours her energy into entirely too many hobbies. She lives outside Toronto, Ontario with her husband and a black Himalayan with a penchant for sliding into walls. Visit her blog at http://thejinx.wordpress.com/ .

8611642R0

Made in the USA
Charleston, SC
27 June 2011